S0-DRE-117

Book Two of The Legends of Eorthe

By

Charles Beamer

Glimmothinscukin

THOMAS NELSON PUBLISHERS
NASHVILLE

Explanation of Eorthean notation and Earthean setting of the musical text by Mark Jaeger.

Published in Nashville, Tennessee, by Thomas Nelson, Inc., Publishers and distributed in Canada by Lawson Falle, Ltd., Cambridge, Ontario.

Text art by Phillip Francis
Maps by Bettye Beach
Book design by Steve Laughbaum

Library of Congress Cataloging in Publication Data

Beamer, Charles
Lightning in the bottle.

(The legends of Eorthe / by Charles Beamer; bk. 2)
Summary: Accompanied by their spoiled cousin and a mute orphan, Jodi, Martin, and Eric return to the Land of the King which is now threatened by the spreading Darkness.
[1. Fantasy] I. Title. II. Series: Beamer, Charles. Legends of Eorthe; bk. 2.
PZ7.B365Le 1980, bk. 2 [Fic] 81-1690
ISBN 0-8407-5233-4 AACR2

Contents

Part 1

Part 2

To

Bradley Stone
Geoffrey Stone
Eric Whitmore
Doug Wilson
Steve Simmons
Stan Simmons

Black winds that bite
in dark of night
shall go but when
Light comes again!

CB

Part 1

Chapter 1

The Kingsmen Are Called

Calls can be funny things. There are, of course, many kinds. There is the kind when the telephone rings, and you jump up running and scream, "I've got it!" There's the kind of call that is a knock on your door by someone you don't want to see, so you avoid answering it for as long as possible. But the kind of call that came to Earth one Friday afternoon in midsummer was not any of the kinds of calls one ordinarily expects to hear. It was a faint, yet clear call, and it was thrilling to those who recognized it.

When the distant but distinct call came, Jodi Kay Westphall was playing badminton with her brother, Martin, and their cousin Richard. Their parents all had gone on a shopping trip, and before they had left they had given Jodi and Martin one specific instruction: *Take care of Richard!* But taking care of Richard, who was ten, had been no easy task for Jodi, who was fourteen, and Martin, who was ten and a half. Jodi and Martin were, by nature, rather shy, especially in new situations. They liked quiet games (though they often argued about the rules and about who was "cheating"). And if no one offered them anything exciting to do, they were content to spend their days quietly. Jodi would listen to her records and read romantic novels about kingdoms and princes, and Martin would play with his codes and spaceship toys.

Richard, however, did not fit into any of Jodi's and Martin's favorite activities. "I don't want to!" seemed to be his most-used cry. After three-quarters of a day of frustration, Jodi finally suggested badminton. It was a game Richard quickly loved—not for the delicacies of deftly dropping the bird over the net or lofting it over one's opponents. No, he loved it for the pure, savage pleasure of smashing the shuttlecock with deadly slashes of his racket. After an hour of dodging whistling shuttlecocks, either Jodi or Martin gladly would have told you: "Richard is a brat!"

So, when the call of the Horn of Meet came ringing through the northern sky, Jodi and Martin looked at each other with relief as well as joy. "Let's go!" Martin said, heading toward the house.

"Wait," Jodi said, suddenly feeling reluctant to leave her home and everything she knew. "Let's make sure. After all, it's been a year since we heard it, and . . ."

Again the Horn of Meet sounded through the clear summer sky above the ordinary back yard of the ordinary house on the very ordinary Mulberry Street.

"What're you two standing there for?" Richard whined.

Jodi and Martin frowned at him.

"Come on!" he demanded, hitting his racket against one open hand. "I was winning!"

"Winning isn't everything," Jodi noted dryly. "Now be quiet . . . please."

"Hey! You can't tell me what to do!" Richard objected, rushing to the net. But the brother and sister were facing northward, ignoring Richard as they listened intently. When the third call sounded clearly above the noises of cars and air conditioners, they nodded to each other.

"No doubt," Jodi said.

"Let's go," Martin added, sprinting toward the house. Jodi ran after him.

"HEY! Where're you going?" Richard shouted.

The brother and sister stopped; Jodi squinched her mouth and looked questioningly at Martin.

"Let's leave him," Martin whispered.

Jodi shook her head. "We can't . . . and you know it. Besides, maybe he's *supposed* to go. After all, he's a lot like you used to be."

"He is *not!*" Martin snapped.

Jodi grinned teasingly. "Before you met the King, you sounded a lot like him."

Martin glared at her. "He and I may be cousins, but *I* don't live in a snobby suburb, and *I* haven't spent my life with baby-sitters!"

Richard swung under the badminton net, half pulling it down, and hurried toward Jodi and Martin. Glaring suspiciously at them, he demanded, "What's going on?"

"We . . . uh, we've got to go somewhere," Jodi answered, heading for the back door of the house.

"You're not leaving me here by myself!" Richard stated.

Jodi and Martin shrugged and went inside. Quickly they went to their rooms and placed clothes, blankets, and other necessities into their packs. Without explanation, they went into the kitchen and added such items as fruit, a loaf of bread, a jar of peanut butter, and a sack of cookies to their loads. They each also packed a large, plastic bottle of water. Richard saw, naturally, that something was up—something probably exciting and possibly against The Rules. He hurried off to stuff his belongings into his flight bag and almost missed hearing the front door close softly as Jodi and Martin left. He barely had time to read the note they had stuck on the mantel above the fireplace:

HAVE GONE ON ANOTHER
HUGE ADVENTURE
DON'T WORRY!
WE LOVE YOU. Jodi Westphall
Martin Westphall

A pencil was lying on top of the mantel, and Richard hurriedly scrawled his name at the bottom of the note:

Richard Brogan

He then raced out the front door, leaving it wide open. "Hey!" he shouted. "Wait up!"

But Jodi and Martin were hurrying along, almost a block ahead.

Richard finally caught up with them several blocks later. They had stopped at a corner and were staring up a cross street at a plain white house that stood in a neat yard.

"What're you looking at?" Richard panted. "And where're we going?"

Jodi gazed thoughtfully at Martin. He shrugged, grinned, and said, "Tell him."

Jodi stared seriously at Richard. "We're going on a mission."

Richard laughed—a short, coughing kind of laugh. "You mean, like spies or something?"

Jodi's gray-blue eyes narrowed as she frowned at him. "I mean, a mission as in *purpose*—something we have to do."

At that moment, a young man—fifteen or so—with

dark blond hair ran from the nearby white house. He had a pack on his back, and he jumped off his front porch like a fullback leaping a tackler. He was followed by a woman's concerned voice: "Be careful, darling; don't get your feet wet, and stay away from . . ."

The voice suddenly stopped, and a worried-looking woman came onto the porch. "Eric?" she called anxiously.

Eric returned dutifully to her. "Yes, ma'am?"

"When will you come back this time . . . from Eorthe?"

Jodi saw Eric's shoulders square and his body stiffen. When he did not answer, the woman left the porch and went to him. "Whatever happens," she said sorrowfully, "remember that we love you . . . and that we respect your responsibility." With a relieved, satisfied expression, he kissed her on one cheek, briefly embraced her, and went toward Jodi and her companions. When he reached them, he looked back and waved to his mother.

As the four young people hurried on up Mulberry Street, Eric Vanover's squarish face and yellow-flecked green eyes broke into a smile. "Hullo," he said to Jodi and Martin. "Who's your friend?"

"Our cousin," Jodi replied as though she had said, "Spinach."

Eric studied the dark-haired, dark-eyed boy and wondered if his sneer was supposed to be a greeting. "Is he coming?" Eric asked.

"We're *stuck* with him," Martin said disgustedly.

"Say, what's going on here?" Richard asked, hurrying into the lead.

Eric stared unblinkingly at the spoiled-looking boy. "We're a group of Kingsmen. We've heard three calls of the Horn of Meet, and we're going to answer it."

"Let it ring!" Richard sneered, hoping the others would laugh. When they did not, Richard dropped back and let the others stride past him. Down into a dry creekbed they ran and hastened northward.

When they passed the Mulberry Street gang's clubhouse in the huge oak tree, they became involved with another uninvited problem. A thin boy with limp black hair was swinging on the rope ladder. Martin yelled, "Get away from there!" and the boy dropped down.

But instead of going away, the boy—who seemed as young as Martin—came shyly to the edge of the creek. Jodi felt sorry for him, for she knew he was the boy who had been placed in old Mrs. Harkess's foster home. Jodi had heard that the boy and his parents had been in a horrible car wreck. The boy had lost a finger, the ability to speak, and his parents.

Richard, eager now to impress the Kingsmen, said, "I'll take care of him for you." He dropped his flight bag, doubled up his fists, and ran toward the boy.

"NO! Leave him alone!" Jodi commanded sharply. "He's just a waif," she added, remembering the word "waif" from a book by Charles Dickens.

Richard, who had stopped with a puzzled expression, looked at Eric. "Right," the older boy said. "Come on," he added, beckoning to Richard. "We need to reach the river by tonight."

The thin, T-shirt clad waif believed Eric's motion included him, so he slid down into the creekbed and trotted after the group.

From then on they made good time. Quickly Eric led them out of town, across a few miles of farmland, and into the wilder land. By the time the sun was setting, they were out of sight of even the most remote farmhouses. And still the waif followed them.

Richard, by then, was wishing he had not followed anyone. Switching his bag from one hand to the other as he stumbled along, he demanded, "Where *are* we going?"

Without slowing, Jodi answered, "To the Land of the King."

For a moment her cousin was silent as though deciding whether or not to take her seriously. Then he began to laugh. "You mean England?"

"England has a queen," Jodi replied dryly. "Where we're going, there's a king—*the* King, the Lord of Light."

Richard thoughtfully plodded over the rough ground. "Are you kidding me?" he finally asked.

Martin grinned back at him. "You'll see," he said brightly. Eric—who had been to the Land of the King several times—kept their course due north, and they crossed several miles of open and unfenced rangeland. Darkness came. First Venus, then the stars slowly appeared. The moon began to rise in the east, and it spread silvering light over the group of five figures steadily walking across the broad land.

Eric had looked back several times, and finally he commented to Jodi, "That waif is still following us."

Jodi glanced back at the boy. "Do you suppose he was called too?"

"I don't know. Let's let him catch up so we can ask his name."

"But haven't you heard . . ." Jodi began. Eric, however, held up one hand and went toward the waif. The thin boy stopped and tensed; to Jodi, he seemed like a young tree from which all leaves have been torn.

"What's your name?" Eric inquired, touching the boy on one arm.

The waif opened his mouth and made several soft sounds.

"He can't talk," Jodi explained quietly. She went on to tell what the neighborhood gossips knew about the youth. When she had finished, no one said anything for several moments. Then, for some reason, Richard became irritated.

Abruptly, he grabbed the boy's right hand and pointed at the knuckle of the boy's missing little finger. "Let's call him 'ol' nine fingers.' "

"Richard!" Jodi cried, looking with embarrassment at the waif, "he's not deaf!" Richard dropped the boy's hand. Jodi sighed, looking at Eric. "Let's just call him the waif . . . until maybe . . ."

Eric returned her smile. "The King will know his name," he said confidently. Turning to the waif, he asked, "Are you sure it's all right for you to go with us?"

The boy nodded.

"Your foster mother won't be upset?"

The waif frowned thoughtfully, then shook his head.

Eric nodded and set off; the waif and the others followed. Rapidly they went down into a broad, shallow valley. At the bottom was a meandering fog bank; mist swirled from the top into the pale moonlight. Barely visible within the fog was a wandering line of large, shadow-black trees.

Looking at the fog and dark trees, Jodi asked the waif, "Are you sure you want to come with us? We may face danger . . . and hardships."

The boy nodded firmly.

"What danger and hardships?" Richard hesitantly asked.

He was ignored as Jodi gently touched the waif. "Well, come on then," she said, turning to catch up with Eric and Martin.

Richard was left standing behind the group; he glared at them for a moment, then ran to catch his cousins. When he passed the waif, he said, "Yeah, and you'd better keep up."

"Stop it!" Eric commanded, turning for a moment to give Richard a hard look.

"Stop what?" he protested. "I was just trying to . . ." He broke off his sentence when Eric turned and began hiking toward the trees again. The others followed in a row.

The black, curving sweep of fog-bound trees seemed to grow taller as the young people neared it. And when they came still closer, they saw that dense thickets of willows bordered the larger trees.

"What're we going to do?" Richard whined, looking fearfully at the thickets.

"Ford the Great River," Jodi answered while trying not to stumble as they went down an eroded ravine toward the willows.

"Ford?" Richard snickered. "We're going to *drive* across?" He seemed so relieved to laugh that he forgot to watch where he was going. He tripped and would have fallen had not the waif quickly caught him. Richard straightened, gave the boy a peculiar look, and hurried on.

When they entered the willow thickets, they quickly lost their bearings. They were confused further by the fog, which now was drifting overhead, hiding the stars and moon. But Eric steered them toward the heavy, whispering sound of a river.

The group soon came to a riverbank and stopped around Eric. He pointed toward a barely visible band of noisy white water and said, "There's the ford."

Jodi took Eric's right hand and held it tightly as she whispered, "Remember last time?" He nodded happily.

Richard squirmed and nudged Martin. "Boy, *they're* mushy-gushy," he said.

Martin turned away from him and dug in his pack. He brought out his flashlight, switched it on, and began to shine the bright beam across the water. After a while, they saw a small light swing back and forth through the fog on the other side of the river, then move forward.

"Who's coming?" Richard asked tensely.

"Hopefully it's old Michael," Eric replied, looking toward the spark of light. "He's the ferryman at the junction of the Dain and Great rivers—which is where we are."

After a moment's silence, Richard quietly said, "I think where we are is *lost*—either that or you're all crazy."

No one responded; they all were looking across the dark water at the figure slowly emerging from the fog.

"I mean," Richard continued nervously, "first you hear some kind of call that I didn't hear. Then you start talking about kings and missions . . ." His voice faded as a large-bellied old man waded the final thirty feet toward them. He was knee-deep in swirling water, and he was carrying a long staff over one shoulder. In a notch on top of his staff was the handle of a lantern. Richard edged backward.

"Greetings," came a voice as deep and purling as the river's flow.

"Hello, Michael," Jodi replied cheerfully. "Remember us?"

Old Michael swung down his staff and shined the lantern's dim yellow light toward each of the young people. "You three Kingsmen, yes; the other two, no."

"We're answering the call," Martin said with a hint of pride.

"Have other Kingsmen crossed?" Eric inquired.

Michael slowly answered, "You are the first . . . at this crossing."

Jodi thought he sounded sad or concerned, so she asked, "What's wrong? Has the Land been invaded again?"

"No, well . . . you'll see," Michael said. He turned his back toward them, stooped, and looked around to see who would be first to ride across. Eric ushered Jodi forward and helped her climb onto Michael's back.

"You're going to let him *carry* you across?" Richard whispered to Martin.

"You don't have to go, you know," Martin retorted.

Perhaps it was the eagerness in Martin's voice that made Richard stifle any more questions he had and patiently wait his turn. But something soon happened that gave him an absolute rash of questions.

Richard was the last one ferried across the river. When Michael set him on the ground, the boy immediately began staring open-mouthed at the Kingsmen. "You . . . you've got on *armor!*" he stammered. Martin, Jodi, and Eric grinned at him. "And what're those round things on your backs? Shields?"

"We've got swords, too," Martin said nonchalantly, patting the short, shiny scabbard by his right side. "They're invisible until we cross the boundary into the King's Land."

The others, meanwhile, noticed that another startling change had happened. The air was numbingly cold. Jodi, Eric, and Martin looked to their left and saw pale light glinting from ice along the edge of the Dain River. To their right they saw that the branches of the mighty trees were white. The peacefulness of the scene told them that—despite their fears—no sorcerer or beasts had invaded the Land again. But the trunks of the huge trees should be dark brown, not white . . . with snow! "Winter's come to the Land," Eric concluded. "But how?"

"Ahh," Michael sighed, leading the group up a path, "come to my hut and sit by my fire, and I shall tell you what I can."

Chapter 2

Journey Into the Unknown

The five children and their host fitted snugly into the single, small room of the bark-covered hut. The children gathered closely around the pot-bellied stove in the center of the room and held their hands to the warmth of its fire. From a bulbous, copper teakettle, the ferryman poured each of them a cup of tea. None of the little clay cups matched, but no one noticed because the tea was so refreshing and warming. Jodi held her nose in the steam rising from her cup and was delighted by the tea's invigorating aroma.

"To begin with," the old man said slowly as he sat on the edge of a low, narrow bed, "you must understand that, other than the King, there is *nothing* in Eorthe more precious to us believers than Abba's great gift: His Lightning. As the magicians say, what faith in God is to you Eartheans, the Lightning of Abba is to us. But the Lightning is in grave danger. When you Kingsmen drove the sorcerer Obit from the Land, it was but one victory in a long history of defeats.

"Now, listen closely: There are two sorcerers, and either of them is far more powerful than Obit. One of these sorcerers is in the northern continent of Rud; the other is closer, in Gueroness.* Between them they have conquered much of Eorthe."

The Kingsmen were bursting with questions, and Martin spoke most quickly of them all. "So there *is* more to Eorthe than the Land of the King?"

"Oh, my, yes!" Michael replied. "The continent of Gueroness is closest to us across the southern part of the Alamantian Ocean. To the northwest of Gueroness lies the continent of Eoramia. Most of it is ruled by the fairest Queen of Light Eorthe has known: Queen Dorcas, Prince Morgan's mother. To the northeast of Eoramia stands the continent of Rud, which has been almost entirely conquered by . . . by the northern sorcerer. And to the south and east of Rud is the untamed continent of Oraibi.

"In the middle of the Alamantian Ocean, far from the four continents, lies the island kingdom of Alamantia. There, the Lightning in the Bottle is kept. To that island, which soon will be his realm, young Prince Morgan Evnstar has been sent to insure the bottle's protection."

The young people absorbed all the information they could and asked Michael to repeat several parts of it to make sure they got their geographical bearings. Then Jodi leaned forward and asked, "But who are these sorcerers who are so much more powerful than Obit?"

Michael drew back and wagged one finger before his lips. Next, with one fingertip on the dirt floor of the hut, he wrote four words:

SARX — Gueroness
JABEZ — Rud

"Can't the armies of the four continents defeat just two sorcerers?" Eric asked, adjusting his armor.

---

*For the pronunciation of Eorthean names, see the Glossary on page 296. For the location of the lands of Eorthe, see the section of maps starting on page 314.

Michael slowly shook his head, letting his face drop until his bearded chin was almost against his chest. "I don't know where to begin or what to tell you, for the history of Eorthe is long and complicated. Briefly, more than a thousand years ago there was a great Eorthean king: L'Ced. He and *the* King, the Lord of Light, began this age—Eorthe's Third Age—by leading the tribes out of the Days of Darkness into the Second Light, the Light of the King. But since then, corruption has spread far and wide. The kings who came after L'Ced were not as faithful as he was, nor were they as wise. The Lord of Light was, for the most part, forgotten; he now has few allies. As I said, even the Lightning—Mankind's protection against the Darkness—is in danger."

Jodi's face was the saddest Martin ever had seen it. She said, "I can't believe people won't follow the King."

Michael lifted his head and looked sternly at her. "Many people of Eorthe have turned away from the King. They have listened to these sorcerers. So many have listened that I fear . . . or hope . . . that this age is coming to an end."

"But who *are* these sorcerers?" Martin inquired impatiently.

Michael's stern look deepened. With one finger he wrote:

SONS OF INGLOAMIN

Even before the last letter of the name was written, a moaning sound and a black mist rushed into the hut. The mist dimmed the fire, and the wind blew out Michael's lantern. Michael, retreating from the mist, fell backward onto his bed. The three Kingsmen instantly drew their swords. The blades flickered with an eager blue light, and the Darkness began to withdraw with a hissing sigh.

"Murks?" Martin asked in a bare whisper.

Michael gasped for air and struggled to sit up. "W-w . . . worse," he rasped, clutching his throat and trying to breathe.

Jodi was first to realize what had happened. She scuffed out the names written on the dirt floor, and the mist faded entirely.

They waited . . . and waited. The waiting was hardest on Richard because he was *afraid.* Growing up, he either had been left entirely alone, put with baby-sitters who ignored him, or spoiled outrageously. His parents both were successful in careers—so "successful" that they had scant time for a child. As a result of his almost constant loneliness, he had nurtured deep fears—which seemed to him to have arisen from nowhere. To make the matter worse, no one had taught him (though they had *told* him) that there was One in whom he could believe who would keep him from being afraid. Now, he was absolutely terrified.

Gradually, flickering flames again arose from the embered sticks in the stove. With one stick Michael relit his lantern as well as several candles on wall sconces. The polished copper backs of the sconces reflected the candlelight so that the room became bright.

"Can you go on with your story now?" Eric asked the old man as he sheathed his sword. The metal made a ringing sigh as it slid into the scabbard, and the fading blue light was swallowed.

The ferryman continued to have difficulty breathing, but he resumed his story as though it were urgent that he do so. "The King has left the Land. With the going of his power and the spread of the Darkness, the Land has been overcome by winter. The Darkness, by the way, is the main weapon of the sorcerers. Those who are weak in spirit are drawn into sleep . . . and death . . . by it; their bodies gradually turn to ash.

"The magicians," he continued, "also have gone. North, they said. They told me to send all Kingsmen to the harbor at the mouth of the northern branch of the Great River. Ferryman Branchus is to convey all who come, however few, to Gueroness." He stopped and put his right hand to his chest as if he were in pain.

Jodi sheathed her sword and poured tea into his cup. She placed the cup into his large, rough left hand.

"Thank you," Michael said with a kind smile.

Martin slid his sword into its scabbard and began digging in his pack. "Let's have supper," he suggested cheerfully.

Michael shook his head. "No, this tea is enough to sustain me." But the others eagerly began eating.

Jodi refilled her teacup and again held her nose into the steam rising from it. "What kind of tea is this?" she asked, munching a red apple.

Michael smiled at her. "I brew it from the only green, living thing left in the Land: leaves from the King's throne in Reginald-Wharford Hall." Looking earnestly at them, he added, "As you hasten northward in the morning, I beg you to stop at the Hall to gather some of the leaves. They will comfort you . . . later."

Martin's eyes widened as he lowered the peanut butter sandwich he had been eating. "We're to go on by ourselves?"

Michael sighed and nodded. The Kingsmen looked at one another, and their expressions became so grim that Richard hardly recognized them.

In a while, the Kingsmen spread their blankets close to the strange stove and rolled up with only the tops of their heads showing. The waif, however, had no blanket. Old Michael saw his plight and handed him a huge, thick fur robe from the foot of his bed. The youth smiled his thanks, feeling the soft fur. He draped it around his thin body and lay down between Jodi and Eric. Michael nodded with satisfaction and eased himself back on his narrow bed, pulling another robe over his bulk. Within minutes, he went to sleep and began snoring.

Richard stood looking at the others as though waiting for one of them to tell him what to do. (If anyone did, he planned to tell them just what he thought of the entire situation!) At last, when he began to become very cold and still no one paid any attention to him, he whined, "If you think *I'm* going to sleep on this dirt floor, you're *crazy!*"

Jodi sleepily looked at him but said nothing.

Richard sobbed once and sat down, fumbling in his flight bag. He practically tore a blanket out of it, jerked out and put on two additional shirts, and flopped down on the smoothly swept floor.

"You'd be warmer over here," Jodi suggested.

"Leave me alone!" Richard snapped. "*You're* to blame for all this . . . this mess!" He sobbed again. "See what your stupid *mission* has gotten us? A cold, dirt floor to sleep on! If this king of yours is so great, how come he can't at least afford some *beds* for us!"

Nothing further was said. The fire popped. A cold wind sighed around the outside of the hut, and snow flakes whispered against the bark walls all night. And though Richard dreamed of his warm bed back home, he later would dream of the comfort of Michael's hut.

As dawn came to the Dain Valley, the overcast sky began to glow silver-white. The snow had stopped falling, but the air was cuttingly cold. When the five young people finished breakfast, they and the ferryman emerged from the hut. The Kingsmen had their packs slung over their armor. Richard stood holding his bag with his blanket draped over him; he looked almost like a miserable old man. The waif was wrapped in Michael's fur robe; only his frail white hands, tousled black hair, and large dark eyes were showing. He and the others stared in amazement at the white world around them. Windswept snow was roundly lipped over the banks of the rushing, silver-green river. The north wind gusted against the snow-drifts, rousing flights of sparkling crystals that stung the faces of the children and old Michael.

One by one, the youths shook hands with the ferryman and sadly left his company. But they had floundered only twenty or so yards upriver when he called to them: "Wait! I'll send help!"

He went into his hut and returned with a foot-long ram's horn. He set the horn to his lips and blew a shrill blast, causing snow to trickle from nearby drooping boughs.

When he had blown twice more and had waited ten or so minutes between calls, the children heard a plunging sound coming from the Forest. Soon, they saw a large, brownish shape with snow flying from its fur bounding toward Michael. When the great bear reached the ferryman, it shook snow off its head and nuzzled Michael's hand. The ferryman pointed to the young people and spoke to the bear. It raised its broad head and bounded toward the five. With a whuff-growl at Jodi and Eric, it went ahead of them to break trail.

"Thanks, Michael!" Jodi called back, waving. He waved in return and stood watching until the children had gone from sight.

Even with the path pounded deeply into the drifts by the bear, the going was difficult. Each step required effort because the snow stuck to their sneakers—which hardly were meant for such hiking. Richard bitterly envied the Kingsmen their armor, which he saw kept them warm. He trailed further and further behind, and soon he began to whine, "Can't you slow down? I'm not used to this, and my feet are *freezing!*"

Eric went back and helped Richard wrap a spare shirt around each foot and reddened ankle. When he almost had finished, Richard snatched the shirt sleeves and snapped, "I can do it!"

When they started out again, Jodi asked, "I wonder where the King has gone? And where's Waymond?"

"Who's Waymond?" Richard called, jogging to catch up.

Martin replied, "He's a King's magician."

"Magician!" Richard snorted, caught between disbelief and hope.

Hours passed as they continued to struggle forward. The sun rose higher, burning a vague white disk through the overcast. By noon, the Forest of Always had given way to snow-covered hills that came down close to the riverbank on the young people's left. They entered a narrow valley by a path close to the river.

Far ahead—beyond a strange cathedral of trees—they could see a tall, ice-rimmed waterfall cascading into the valley. The bear led them toward the tree-cathedral, which straddled the river. The waif could tell that the towering, overarching branches of the cathedral's walls once had been covered by ivy. Now, however, the hall was a skeleton of brown ivy stems, bare branches, and tall, closely spaced trunks. The waif also could tell that Jodi and Martin were becoming excited as they approached the place.

"Remember the Ceremony of the Upraised Swords?" Jodi asked Martin.

"I sure do!" Martin exclaimed, patting his sword. "Let's go inside."

They turned aside from the path. The bear stopped; its breath came out in twin, white curling plumes as it watched the children wade through drifts of snow to the hall. They went through the bare branch doors and down the riverbank past white-draped benches of dead grass. Richard watched closely as Jodi and Eric went onto a bridge of dry branches that spanned the river at the end of the hall. In the center of the bridge was the only alive looking thing in the entire valley: a green, leafy throne.

Jodi began picking pointed, oval leaves from the boughs of the throne. Eric helped her stuff them into one of her pack's side pouches, then zipped it closed. "It's like," Jodi whispered, "the throne *knows* the King will return."

Richard flinched; her words confirmed his feeling that some power was in the hall—a good power, a power to which he was attracted. He then envied the Kingsmen again, and he felt a strong urge to become like them. When Eric and Jodi passed him, going out of the cathedral, he hastened after them, calling, "Say, how could I become a Kingsman?"

Unfortunately, the Kingsmen ignored him, thinking he would laugh if they answered him. Richard shrank within his blanket. Feelings of resentment quickly arose from the dark corners of his imagination. *What right,* he gloomily thought, *do my smart aleck cousins and that bossy Eric have to treat me like what* I *think and feel aren't important?* Anger gushed from his well of emotions and cast a shadow over his vision. And his "other" voice, as it had many times in the past, grumbled, *No one loves you, and no one ever will!* He clenched his numbed lips and stumbled blindly after the waif, hating everyone.

The waif was dragging his heavy robe between the snowbanks beside the bear's trail. In his head swarmed thoughts he would have given anything to be able to say: *Look! Look at the bright white snow! Look how the river curls past those icy brown rocks! Look at the waterfall ahead! It's like . . . it's like . . .* But he lacked even thoughts to describe the ice cascades that rose before the group where the river roared and tumbled into the snowy valley.

The waif hugged his warm robe to himself and wished his parents were alive to see the waterfall—and just once more share with him their irreplaceable love. That thought brought a rush of memories: the skidding car, the tearing crash . . . and the feeling of his own voice forever sinking into his innermost being when he had been told that his parents were dead. Since then, he had feared any contact that might lead to love—until the urge to follow Eric and the others had overpowered his resolve. Now, watching the Kingsmen filled him with a longing to become like them—and to meet their King. That longing kept him going.

When the group of young people had managed to climb the steep, winding trail to the clifftop, the bear stopped. At first, Eric and the others thought it was allowing them to rest. Then, however, they saw the problem. Looking skyward, they saw traces of the same unnatural Darkness that had rushed into Michael's hut. Eric exchanged a concerned look with Jodi.

"Are we in danger?" Martin asked, grasping his sword hilt.

Frowning, Eric muttered, "I'm afraid so." Then he looked at Richard: The boy was standing near the edge of the cliff. He was wavering slightly, holding his cold-reddened hands to his eyes. "What's the matter, Richard?" Eric asked, going to the boy.

"I'm . . . *nothing*!" he answered.

Eric heard the anger in the boy's voice and put one hand on his left shoulder to steady him. Richard jerked away. "Leave me alone!" he exploded.

"I didn't want you to fall," Eric explained.

Richard sniffed, "I don't care if I *do* fall."

The bear snorted impatiently. Eric turned and saw it jerk its squarish, black muzzle toward the sky. Eric looked back at Richard. In an authoritative tone, he said, "Richard, this is no game. We're in a world you're going to have to get used to. There are powers here that do terrible things to weak, rebellious . . ."

"I'm not *weak*!" Richard flared. The ends of his black eyebrows stretched upward, and his temples throbbed with the pulse in his veins. "Don't *ever* call me that!" he added in a murderous tone.

Jodi quickly came between Eric and her cousin. Facing Richard, she asked, "Are you all right?" She stroked his red cheeks with one hand.

Recoiling from her touch, he asked, "How could I be all right? I can't feel my toes or fingers, I can't breathe, and this Darkness . . ."

"Is it making you afraid?" Jodi asked.

Richard blinked at her; slowly, head lowered, he nodded.

She put her arms around him and drew him close. He fought to keep his distance, then sagged against her armor and began rubbing his eyes with both fists.

Eric waited a while, then asked, "Do you think you can go on?" Glancing at the darkening sky, he added, "I'm afraid we'll have to hurry to the harbor; I think we've been found."

"Found?" Richard asked hopefully, pushing Jodi away.

Eric sighed, wondering whether or not to help Richard go on. The bear took charge of the situation. With an impatient snort, it ambled back and positioned itself in front of Richard.

Now Richard never had seen a large animal outside a zoo cage (in fact, he guiltily remembered having teased zoo bears by pretending to throw them peanuts). The boy forgot his other troubles and became scared stiff by the closeness of the huge bear.

"It's all right," Jodi said reassuringly. "He's gentle because he's been charmed by the King. He wants you to ride him."

Richard found himself faced with a dilemma: If he believed her, it would mean believing the King was real and had power enough to charm a bear. On the other hand, if he maintained his independence, he would have to struggle through the snow to wherever they had to go. Frowning, he nibbled the inside of his lips as he looked from the bear to Jodi and back.

Cautiously, Richard finally put his hands on the bear's rounded, thickly furred back and leaned forward.

"Get on," Eric urged, starting to give Richard a boost.

"I can do it!" the boy snapped. Reluctantly, he climbed on. At once the bear started northward. Whuff-snorting, it rapidly plunged into the wooded hills west of the Dain River. Richard clutched the bear's coarse but soft, long fur and tried to keep from falling either backward or to one side.

At a more rapid pace, the bear and four young people floundered up and down the hills until they came to the northern branch of the Dain. The bear—with Richard wobbling on its back—ran down a snow-hidden trail into the valley formed by the river. The children waded along in its footprints, wishing for snowshoes.

After they had crossed the Dain River on an ice bridge, they faced ridge after ridge of snow-blanketed hills. The young people's spirits drooped as they thought of the cold and deep snow they yet had to face. Steadily the sky blackened and, because of the blackness, the air took on a deadening quality that deepened the silence of the snow-bound wilderness. By the time the children could hear the distant roar of the Great River ahead, they were numb. And with the numbness came a powerful desire to sleep.

In the midst of a wide yawn, Martin fell forward. Sputtering, he got up and brushed snow from his face. Jodi laughed gently and commented, "You look like a snowman."

"Good thinking, Martin," Eric said playfully as he grabbed a handful of snow and rubbed it over his face. "Wakes you up!"

They noticed that when the fur-wrapped waif did as they did, the dirt on his face became streaked. Richard hooted, "You look like a goblin!"

Before he could finish laughing, the bear bucked him headlong into a snowdrift. Trying in vain to get unstuck, Richard flailed his arms and legs. Jodi and Eric, grinning, went to help him.

"I can do it!" he spluttered, slinging snow from his blanket as he glared hatefully at the bear. The animal rumbled in an impatient way, reminding Richard that it was no zoo bear.

Remounted, Richard lapsed into a grim silence. He did not speak even when the bear plunged into the Great River at a shallow ford and splashed toward a dark green, snow quilted forest. The forest proved to be only a half mile or so wide. When they emerged on the far side, they stared speechlessly: Before them was a seemingly endless expanse of whitecapped water. Unbroken by land or ship, the blue-gray ocean stretched in a slight curve from horizon to horizon under a thick overcast.

"The Alamantian Ocean," Eric muttered, very much out of breath. The others gathered behind him, deeply disheartened by the prospect of crossing an ocean after having exhausted themselves in the snow.

"We've got to cross *that?*" Martin asked, clapping his arms around himself to keep warm.

While they thought, a distant voice saluted them: " 'Looo. . . ."

They squinted into the fading light toward a point of land where a tiny figure standing on the beach seemed to be waving at them.

"Do you suppose that's the ferryman?" Eric asked, cupping his hands to his mouth and blowing frosty breath through them.

"One way to find out," Martin said, going down the ice-crusted beach.

Richard clung to the bear's long fur as it loped toward the figure. Rapidly, the sullen boy sank into sleep and blackness; he saw neither the man nor his bonfire on the icy, golden shore. When they reached the fire, Jodi poured a cup of tea from the ferryman's steaming teapot and forced Richard to sip it. Only then did he awaken fully and notice the sailboat tied at a jetty just inside the mouth of a large, natural harbor. Then, shivering both from fear of crossing the ocean in such a small craft and from coldness, Richard followed the others down to the jetty. They boarded the boat and silently watched the old but surprisingly nimble ferryman cast off.

As he hoisted the mainsail and jib, an angry wind laced with black mist came from the north. Shrinking from it, Richard crawled into a space under one bulwark. There, he fell into deep sleep, unaware that Jodi covered him with a quilt provided by Branchus, the ferryman of the Alamantian Crossing.

While the sailboat slowly left the harbor behind, the Kingsmen and the waif looked astern at the receding shore. The bear had gone, and they soon lost sight of even the bonfire's glimmer. Wondering where Waymond and the King were, wondering where their obedience to the King would lead them next, the Kingsmen turned and stared into the wind-filled darkness ahead.

Chapter 3

The Prince Returns

Meanwhile, many hundreds of miles across the Alamantian Ocean to the north, another part of the war against the sons of Ingloamin was unfolding. Morgan Evnstar, prince of Eoramia and Alamantia, let his slim but muscular body glide beside the great bulk of Unthoriumgai, Father of Whales. Morgan rested as he glided, for he and the Guardian had been swimming hard for hours. As he rested he looked around at the blue world in which they swam. It was refreshing, Morgan felt, after years of living in danger on the land, to be immersed in a safe world—a world as old as the first rain and as young as the most recent shower. Adjusting his gills—gifts from Queen Eliadenor of the Sea People—he looked down, past the whale's vast length, into the blue-green, clear water. Thousands of feet below he saw the rock ribs of Eorthe.

Following the whale deeper and deeper, Morgan began swimming strongly again. At last, in the depths, they joined powerful currents that swept the pair eastward toward a green land set far from the continents.

"You're sure," Morgan asked for the fifth or sixth

time, "that even the Lightning in the Bottle is in danger?"

The wavering voice of Unthoriumgai came slowly from deep inside him, bell-clear and haunting: "By Mankind's faith in the Lightning is Eorthe sustained; that faith has grown dim. The Darkness has come in the wake of faith's retreat, and danger threatens even Alamantia. Your father's death signaled the beginning of the end. A new king is needed *now* to protect the bottle!" His voice echoed into the shadowy canyons far below them.

Morgan frowned. "But why won't the King, Lord of Light, just kill Ingloa . . ."

"I would not call the danger to us by naming it," Unthoriumgai warned, rolling slightly to one side to squint at the young man. The whale's bright black eye seemed tiny on the huge, wrinkled side of his head.

"Shouldn't we at least have brought the Leohtians and my mother's army in the warships?"

With a powerful thrust of his flukes, Unthoriumgai levered himself forward in the jetflow, then began to reply. "There was not time for *you* to be brought by one of the *maralamans**—nor, in all likelihood, will there be time for you to be crowned. Furthermore, the army under your mother's leadership will be needed elsewhere."

"What could be more important than protecting the bottle?"

"All concerns of the King will become clear in time," Unthoriumgai said seriously. "Now, please talk less, Boy of Land and Sea. Talking your language tires me, and soon I will need all my strength. The bottom is shoaling up as we reach the kelp beds before the

---

*See the Glossary of Ancient Eorthean Words, page 299.

mouth of River Iverwain, and the current waxes strong."

Morgan looked ahead: Waving gently in the blue-green depths in misty shafts of sunlight were the outposts of the kelp beds. Thicker and thicker became the forest of rippling green blades as the swimming pair neared their destination—Morgan's birthplace, Alamantia.

The current gradually swung around until it was flowing toward them, slowing their progress with a broad outflow from the still distant river. Morgan was forced to swim to Unthoriumgai's back and cling tightly to the barnacles there as they entered the center of Iverwain's great outpouring. The whale, fanning his massive flukes, fought mightily against the streaming current. He swam toward a black-green, deep channel between high, underwater cliffs. As he and the prince entered the dark rift that cleaves Alamantia, the current became focused on them. Morgan clung to the barnacles and shut his eyes against the powerful flow.

As soon as his eyes were closed, his mind began to whirl with excitement. Morgan began recalling one of the history lessons his mother—Queen Dorcas Evnstar—had taught him. Her words rolled through his memory like the current rippling over his body. She had said:

Morgan, in the beginning was Abba, the Father of Light. Forever, He has created Light within Glimmrainath, the Void. One of the outposts of Light Abba made to shine forth was Eorthe. When Eorthe was formed, it was *Light. The Father then formed Humankind to glorify Him in the First Light of Perfection.*

But from Glimmrainath came Ingloamin, the Lord of Darkness. He was jealous of perfection and of the Light.

When he saw the Children of Light on Eorthe, he was filled with envy—for they, insignificant beyond reckoning in the vastness of Glimmrainath, had what he lacked and never could have: the spark, the bright beginning of life and a fearlessness therefrom. In wrath, Ingloamin set out to corrupt the Children of Light. Many, though not all, turned from Abba's Light to strength and power they imagined were their own—strength and power of the Darkness. Deluded by the illusion that the power was their own, pride took root in these men and women. In pride, they set out to make Eorthe their own. Then, their corruption became complete, for they came to love their world and themselves exclusively, forgetting Abba. Evil was born.

From Ingloamin and women of great evil, sorcerers were born. Using evil powers, the sorcerers raised armies and cruel beasts to strive with the ancient Guardians and the remaining Children of Light for mastery of Eorthe. The planet itself was wounded by the Volcanoes of Tava, and the Darkness spread even to Eorthe's core. Thus, the First Light of perfection was ruined. The Second Age began in corruption, and for centuries the Days of Darkness prevailed.

Finally, Abba heeded the prayers of those of His children who mourned the lost First Light. He sent His son, the King—whom some call the Second Light—to forgive and comfort the mourners with Love. The Second Age ended, but because much of Humankind willingly had turned from the First Light, Abba thereafter gave us a choice: We can dwell in the Darkness, or we can seek the Second Light. The Third Age thus has been a time of choosing and of separation. To aid Humankind in finding him, the King created the Jewels and anointed Sisters to carry the Jewels' light before the people. The King also empowered magicians and sent them to teach the tribes how to drive out the Darkness. Then, the tribes began to war against the le-

gions raised by the sorcerers. But the Darkness separated the people from the King by doubt and fear, divided them within themselves and from one another, and pitted them against the animals and other creatures of Eorthe.

At that time, Abba caused a king of great power to arise. His name was L'Ced, meaning "Shepherd" in the Allumerian language. To L'Ced was given Wisdom. It was he who wrote the Book of L'Ced, a record of life in the Light. Also to L'Ced was given the sword Suloy, one of many nathnor *swords made by Thorinsheld to recognize and destroy evil. The other swords were given to stalwart warriors among the Children of Light. Those warriors were named Lords of the Swords. The Lords became great leaders and heads of the noble Houses. Few of their swords, or their descendants, today are still in the King's service; their falling away gave rise to the need for the Kingsmen from afar.*

Morgan paused in his mental recitation to renew the vow he had made to the King several years earlier: Never would *he* fall away or break faith, not even for a moment! Morgan cringed whenever the memory of his father's weakness at a critical moment in history recurred to him. Never would *he* become so entangled in court politics and alliances that he would hesitate to do the right. And *never* would he marry one of the princesses whom well-meaning friends and relatives had urged upon him. He feared that if he married any such Eorthean girl, he would become so entangled in worldly politics that he would forget his pledge to the King. However, before he allowed himself to begin dreaming of what he *would* do as king, he resumed his mental recitation:

L'Ced—with the Lords of the Swords, the magicians, and the Sisters of the Jewels—rekindled the tribes' love for life in the Light. Fearlessly then, the tribes began to win their battles against the Darkness. And when Abba was satisfied that much of Humankind again truly desired to live in the Light, He sent His Lightning to cast Ingloamin into the Void. However, Leilamar—Shadow Guardian and child bearer for Ingloamin—and her sons Jabez and Sarx escaped the Lightning by hiding deep in the corrupted Caves of Rainath. Thus, though the Third Age began with bright promise, the seeds of further corruption already were planted.

The Lightning did much more than cast out Ingloamin. To replace the ruined First Light, the Lightning created Sul and Omiglimm, the sun and the moon. Furthermore, the Lightning created a split in time and space. A new world was formed within the old. The magicians tell us that the new world—Earth—was created free of evil. We are told that it shares Eorthe's alternation between hours of light and hours of darkness—perhaps reflecting the choice Abba gives both worlds. In Earth, as in Eorthe, Jewels of Light were formed. The two worlds, the magicians tell us, are joined only by the Great River at the southern boundary of the Land of the King. Each world to the other is but a legend to most.

Abba, knowing that on Eorthe there remained the seeds of corruption, decided to make His power available to the Children of Light to strengthen them and to be the ultimate protection of Eorthe against the Darkness. Thus, He contained a part of His Lightning in a small, simple thing—a bottle from Thorinsheld's workshop. The King gave the fragile, seemingly ordinary bottle to Acuerias, most wise of magicians. Acuerias entrusted L'Ced with the bottle and with the sword Gafailnath, a mighty sword that ever recognizes and hates evil. When L'Ced laid aside his sword Suloy and took up Gafailnath and the bottle, Acuerias gave him and the tribes a warning: If faith in Abba left their hearts, the Darkness would return and a king would be raised up to unleash the Lightning from the bottle. If, however, the people maintained their faith, the light from the Lightning would strengthen them. L'Ced and the tribes accepted the warning willingly, and they looked to the Lightning to keep their faith as strong as Gafailnath's blade.

When L'Ced thought to build a capital for his throne, he sought council of the tribal leaders. Queen Eliadenor and her Sea People successfully proposed that Alamantia be the seat of Eorthe's government. The green isle of Alamantia was built into a great kingdom. Imnatride was chosen to be the capital; there, at the fork of the River Iverwain, rose the town and castle. The King himself built a fountain in the square that joins the castle and town, saying, "Let all creatures forever drink from this, my water, and remember peace therefrom." That same day, the Lightning in the Bottle was placed high in the majestic tower, Glimmothtyrn, in the center of the Castle of Imnatride. From there, for centuries, Light radiated to all Eortheans—until your father, Mervintide Evnstar, allowed the Council of Lords to make its terrible decision.

Soon after the building of the new capital began, the seeds of corruption sprouted: Leilamar and her sons, Jabez and Sarx, emerged from hiding and began to prepare for the return of Ingloamin. Long did King L'Ced and the Lords of the Swords and their successors hunt her and her sorcerer sons, but as the splendor of Alamantia grew, the chase was abandoned and gradually forgotten—as was faith in the Light of Abba. And as faith waned, the power of Leilamar and her sons increased. When your father became king of Alamantia, he inherited rule of an undermined world . . . and died as a result.

Morgan shifted his position on the whale's back and peered into the murky depths of the rift. For a mile or so ahead, he could see nothing more than the vague, dark green kelp columns, rippling in the powerful current. Morgan shut his eyes and "listened" to another lesson:

Morgan, thirty years ago your father inherited two kingships. From his mother, Queen Gloralanin Oenor, Mervintide inherited the crown of the nation of Eoramia—which his mother's father, Gustan Oenor V, had formed of the lands of Eoramia, Corlis, Ispenth, and the Four Kingdoms. From his father, Glimmfinial Evnstar, Mervintide inherited the throne of Alamantia. Mervintide thus became the seventh ruler of the fifteenth Ruling House and stood at the end of a line of Alamantian kings stretching almost 1200 years back to L'Ced, the Shepherd.

During your father's reign, many creatures forsook life in the Light. Pilgrims no longer came to stand at the foot of Glimmothtyrn, the Tower of the Lightning, to sing praises to Abba. Fewer and fewer creatures came to drink from the King's fountain. Songs about the casting out of Ingloamin were forgotten, as were the legends recalling the horrors of the Days of Darkness. To complicate your father's problems as king, Alamantia had grown encrusted with wealth and with a system of rule by officials. Many of the lords and officials, as well as the common people, actually embraced the Darkness. Abroad, fewer and fewer armies remained loyal to the throne of Alamantia.

Thus, nearly ten years ago, rumors of evil began to come from families fleeing from the south and north. Six years ago, the continent of Gueroness was conquered by war lords who in turn were mastered by Sarx, the youngest son of Ingloamin. Next, the northern continent of Rud fell to the conqueror Go'drun. Jabez, the eldest son of Ingloamin, long and in deep secrecy had supported Go'drun. When the conqueror was at the height of his power, Jabez killed him and openly began the spread of the Darkness. In the remote mountain land of Tavares, Jabez established a kingdom whose center is the ancient wound of the Void—the

Volcanoes of Tava. Most recently, the sorcerer Obit, servant of Jabez, and his slave army almost destroyed the Forest of Always in the Land of the King.

During Mervintide's thirty year reign, he gradually was worn down by the opposition or apathy of the nobles and officials and by the steady decay of Eortheans' loyalty to the King. The "rebellion" of the Council of Lords was the final blow: Sixteen years ago they made their dreadful decision to take the Lightning in the Bottle down from Glimmothtyrn. The King, Lord of Light, then appeared to me in a dream. He told me to have a child by Mervintide so that the throne of Alamantia might have an heir. The King gave me to understand that if I agreed to do as he asked, I would in time give up the child to his service.

You, Morgan, are that child. When you were born I took you to live with my people in Espereim; I reared you to be a leader of men and a follower of the King. I've taught you the faith I have learned as a Sister of the Jewels. I know you hold love for Abba, for His Light, and for the King. It is only because of that knowledge that I can send you away from me into your own destiny. Into the King's hands I now commit your life.

Morgan smiled, remembering his meetings with the King in the garden of his mother's castle, Glimpalatyrn. He tried to open his eyes, but the black-green current was still too strong. Therefore, he let his mind go back to his final conversation with his mother:

"But what is my destiny?" he had asked.

"In part and for now it is to protect the bottle," Queen Dorcas had replied. "If you accept and fulfill this part of your destiny, the powers of Darkness will be banished from Eorthe. However, if you hesitate or fail, all Eorthe will suffer another age of darkness and terror!"

Morgan shuddered with a chill. He opened his sea-green eyes and saw that Unthoriumgai's back was breaking above the waves of the upper Iverwain. The whale spouted, raining Morgan with cold spray. He wiped strands of hair from his face and stood on the back of the slowly swimming whale.

From that moving stage Morgan beheld for the first time the land he had known only from the pictures drawn by his mother's words and by the singers' songs of Alamantia the Fair, Guardian of the Seas. Along the grassy riverbanks, yellow flowers bloomed. Flights of red butterflies wafted down to the flowers on a fresh breeze. Behind the flowers grew *weyidmintreos*—towering trees with gray, wrinkled trunks and needle leaves in clusters of ten. And behind those trees soared cliffs green clad with mosses and ferns. Higher, *scututreos* and *treotophs*—"shield pines" and "oaks"—formed forests that stepped down to the brink of the cliffs.

Further upriver, V-shaped cuts in the clifftops opened into valleys. By looking up those valleys, Morgan saw rolling pastures and farms. Flocks of sheep and geese and herds of cattle and horses grazed almost motionlessly in deep grass. Dark green *sulde*—corn—crowned by golden tassels grew in irregularly shaped fields. Workers in the fields shouted joyful greetings to the whale and youth as the pair came upriver. As they went farther, the cliffs diminished, Iverwain's banks became lower and closer together, and Morgan could see the breadth of the land. Then he saw children running from the fields to the riverbanks, waving bright caps and scarves. Unthoriumgai seemed unaware of them as he pressed against the flow, but Morgan's excitement grew. At last he was in Alamantia! And it seemed far more friendly and fair than he had imagined it—especially in a time when war had spread over much of Eorthe. Coming now into his kingdom, the prince felt as if he were coming home.

Yet, he knew his mother was right when she said it was better for him to wait until now to go to Alamantia. He knew he was better off not to have grown up softened by the rich court life in Imnatride. And he knew he was *much* better off not having grown up around noblemen anxious to have him marry their daughters for political reasons!

Morgan looked ahead and saw that the Iverwain was branching; one fork turned northward, and the other continued eastward. To his left and right, the land flattened out into broad plains. In the distance on either hand were mountains. He looked at the spearhead of land between the branches of the river. There rose the hills and mountain of the capital, Imnatride, and its castle.

Morgan's face lit with admiration as he gazed at the stone, tile-roofed houses near the river. The upper stories overhung the lower ones, and in many of the lower stories were shops with gaudy signs above their doors. The buildings resembled the people who were coming from them: sturdy and comfortable. Behind the waterfront house-shops rose the hills, covered with the red tile roofs of sizable homes and mansions. Then came the gently rising, thickly inhabited slopes of the mountain. Atop the mountain stood the shining white wall and towers of the Castle of Imnatride. Four main towers, tall and thin, pointed skyward above the circular wall. A fifth tower soared in the midst of the four; it, Morgan knew, was Glimmothtyrn. It had been the repository of Eorthe's treasured vial: the Lightning in the Bottle. Morgan's smile faded as he thought of his father's failure to protect the bottle.

"But where in all this beauty is the danger?" Morgan called to Unthoriumgai.

The whale turned toward the broad harbor in the

left-hand fork of Iverwain and blew a billowing jet of spray that swept over Morgan, chilling him. "Within the beauty, it lies," the whale's wavering voice warned.

Morgan's expression clouded . . . but soon he smiled again as he watched old women and sailors, merchants and children, farmers and shop workers rushing to the wharfside. In gay profusion of dress and color, the people cheered both the youth and Unthoriumgai.

"Hail, Father of Whales!" a burly sailor in a red-and-white striped stocking cap called. "Have you indeed brought us the prince?"

The whale blew spray high over Morgan as, by barely fanning his flukes, he crowded himself into the harbor. He nestled his head against the stone wharf as the crowd surged forward. All eyes were focused on the youth, who sat down on the whale's right side above his eye.

"Are you *he?*" shouted an old woman in a flour-dusted apron and dress.

"Behold!" a young man in the back of the crowd cried to latecomers from the castle above, "Unthoriumgai has brought him—as he promised he would!" The young man's words were swept away by the clatter of horses' hooves and carriage wheels rattling down the paving stones past him.

Conscious of the eyes upon him, Morgan removed the pink-red gills from the small hole below each ear and tossed them down for Unthoriumgai to catch in one corner of his great mouth. Then, the prince leaped ashore. He gladly accepted a robe from a fisherman's wife.

The clamor diminished to a murmur as the crowd cleared a pathway for Morgan. At the far end of the path he saw a great lord striding toward him with many attendants in tow. But before Morgan could greet the lord, he heard the whale turning with difficulty in the broad harbor. The youth again faced the river. "Until the King's need brings us together once more!" he cried, raising his right hand in salute.

Unthoriumgai swung his gray-black tail high above the green water; myriad droplets cascaded from his flukes as he held them poised for a moment, then slammed them down with great force. The explosion boomed and echoed against the houses and hills. Waves raced to rock the fishing boats tied near the jetties of the harbor. With that farewell, the whale slid beneath the surface of Iverwain. A rising swell marked his passage back toward the ocean.

"And *are* you the prince?" a deep voice demanded from behind Morgan.

The youth turned, holding out his right hand; on his third finger flashed the signet ring bequeathed him by Mervintide and brought by Unthoriumgai. "I am Morgan Evnstar, son of Mervintide, grandson of Glimmfinial," he replied, looking steadily at the richly dressed lord.

The man opened his purple and yellow outer gown—revealing a gilded chestplate, wide belt, and ornate scabbard—and set his fists on his waist. "I am Baldwin, Regent of Alamantia, Lord of Ispenth—your uncle! Welcome, my king!" the man said loudly enough for most of the crowd to hear. He stood beaming while the crowd began to chant, "Hail to the king . . . *hail to the king!*" Suddenly then, Lord Baldwin hastened to embrace Morgan.

Morgan was crushed against the man's chestplate in a bearlike hug. Next, he was shaken at arms' length. "Could be," the Lord of Ispenth said, nodding seriously, "could be you are he. But so slight and young!" His large, brown eyes twinkled mischievously.

Morgan had, of course, heard of Baldwin, Mervintide's youngest brother. The prince had listened by the hour to the songs of Baldwin's prowess in battle and of his loyalty. "You're like a legend to me," the youth said, ignoring the crowd and the carriages full of courtiers around them.

"And you, son of my brother and king, are to me but a song sung by Queen Dorcas!" Baldwin declared, throwing back his bushy brown bearded face to laugh heartily. "How fare the land of Eoramia and your mother?"

"Both are well, despite the refugees and the attacks from . . ."

"Come!" Baldwin said loudly—too loudly, Morgan thought. "Let's not stand here discussing distant difficulties!" He wrapped one heavy arm around the youth's shoulders and led him to a saddled and richly blanketed horse. As he swung onto his own heavy horse, Baldwin boomed, "After all, this is a time for celebration! Your welcome has been prepared!"

So it was that Morgan Evnstar came at last to Imnatride, to Alamantia, his kingdom. Unfortunately, despite the appearances to the contrary, Unthoriumgai had been right about the presence of danger within the beauty . . . as Morgan soon would learn.

Chapter 4

A Thief in the Depths

Lord Baldwin and his nephew led a procession upward along winding streets toward the castle crowning the mountain. Trumpets blew before them to announce their coming. The trumpets' call mingled with the cheers of the people who were gathered along the cobblestone streets. Women and children leaned from upper story windows and tossed red, yellow, pink, and blue flowers as they waved to Morgan. Smiling, he waved back, glancing at the flowers spiraling down between the banners and flags that crisscrossed above the streets.

Lining the higher streets were soldiers; they were standing rigidly at attention, armed with ceremonial pikes. Morgan noted that the soldiers were few in number and seemed heedless of any approaching danger. He pondered that fact as his procession crossed a square where five streets met and went around the large pool of the King's fountain. Morgan glanced up as he entered the shadowed archway leading to a massive, open gate and passed into the outer courtyard of Castle Imnatride. There, Morgan noted that there were none of the preparations for war that were everywhere in the land from which he had come. He saw that barracks had been converted to storehouses. He saw that stables for war horses had fallen into disuse. And he saw huge catapults and other machines of war rusting in out-of-the-way corners near silent armories.

"Where is the might of Alamantia?" Morgan asked Lord Baldwin as they walked their horses beneath a pointed archway into one of the inner courtyards.

"Disbanded," the lord laughed, throwing wide his arms. "Dispersed to distant lands, for only there have the rumors . . ."

"Rumors?" Morgan interrupted, frowning. "More than rumors, Uncle, have brought thousands of refugees into Espereim!"

In an irritated tone that bordered on being commanding, Baldwin said, "Hush! Do not ruin the fineness of the day!" They dismounted, and attendants led away their horses.

Morgan noted from Baldwin's tone that the warrior was used to command—and was most un-used to deferring to a youthful king; but Morgan also noted in the man's tone an anxiousness to cover something from discovery. Thoughtfully, the young prince followed the regent up broad stairs past facing rows of honorary guards and into the castle. Soon, they entered a hall whose ceiling soared far above them. Looking upward in awe, Morgan said, "Surely Alamantia still is Guardian of the Seas."

Their footsteps on the glistening stone floor echoed into the dim reaches of the hall as Baldwin grudgingly replied, "Aye, it is, and so it ever shall be. But, lad, the threats you mention do not lie nearby; the rumors of dark arisings come from afar, from lands in Rud, Oraibi, and Gueroness. It was in answer to those rumors that, soon after your father's death, the Council of Lords voted to disperse the armies in our warships. But those continents are far away. The powers of evil, if they indeed have arisen, cannot have grown so great as to threaten us here!" He strode on, bowing to groups of brightly dressed nobles and to gray-robed officials. Entering the throne room, Baldwin turned and faced the crowd that was streaming in. He beckoned to Morgan to climb the steps to the broad, benchlike throne beneath its gilded canopy, then shouted, "Behold! Your prince has come!"

The cheer that went up temporarily banished worry from Morgan's mind. He watched the celebration start, and he began to enjoy himself. He gladly listened to the minstrels' songs, and he clapped for the dancers from many lands. He especially enjoyed the Allumerian maids who whirled below the throne, holding blue and white scarves high above their heads to make a streaming flower. However, after the lavish banquet in the afternoon, Morgan again thought of the words of warning given him by his mother and Unthoriumgai.

"Uncle," he asked the warrior-regent standing beside him, "do you still wear the sword of which the minstrels sing in the 'Song of Eliadenor'?"

The Lord of Ispenth patted the sword at his left side. "Aye, the Flame of Ispenth is with me still. Why do you ask?"

"Does it not grow warm in the presence of evil?" Morgan inquired.

Baldwin nodded gravely, annoyed that the youth persisted in bringing up disturbing matters.

"As a favor to me," Morgan whispered, "unsheath it now."

"Nay, I will not draw it in the presence of a company such as this," Lord Baldwin stated, dismissing the request with a wave of one ringed hand.

"Please," Morgan insisted, "as a gesture to satisfy my doubts."

Baldwin obviously was displeased, but he stood and beckoned for Morgan to follow him. They left the throne room and entered a small, stone-walled chamber. Narrow windows set high in the gray walls admitted a hazy light. Music and bright laughter pursued them until Baldwin shut the heavy door. The room was empty, except for a large, knee-high stone slab in the center and a tomb beside it. Morgan asked, "What room is this?"

Baldwin went to the elaborately carved, white stone tomb. "Your father lies buried here." He glanced at Morgan to see the youth's reaction, then added solemnly. "And beneath yonder slab is the burial place of the Lightning in the Bottle."

Morgan went to stand by the grave. As the youth silently looked at it for several minutes, Baldwin read a mixture of emotions on his face: sadness and regret . . . anger and disappointment. Morgan glanced at Baldwin, who averted his eyes with a slight frown.

The prince's voice came clearly but softly: "My father ignored the age-old warning and forgot the Light. I must not do the same—and add further disgrace to House Evnstar. Now, please, draw your sword!"

"Very well," Baldwin said with sudden seriousness. "You shall see that Sulnspen, the Flame of Ispenth, sleeps still."

With the singing of *nathnor* against steel, he drew the ancient blade from its scabbard. Immediately, the room's gray light seemed to flow into the sword, and gradually it began to glow. Brighter and brighter grew the blade until it was a white flame scattering the gloom of the chamber. Baldwin frowned as he squinted at his sword. "It lives," he whispered. "But whence comes the evil it senses?"

Morgan went to the low, stone platform. "You said the bottle is kept here?" he asked.

"Yes, below," his uncle replied absently, lowering his sword.

Morgan looked at the thick surface of the eight foot square platform. "I must see it," he stated.

"You may, but the descent is long and hazardous, for in the roots of the castle—nay, in the very roots of the mountain itself—lies the bottle."

" 'Ever doth the Darkness seek to absorb the Light,' " Morgan muttered to himself, quoting from the Book of L'Ced. The words reminded him of one of the old songs, and impulsively he began to sing aloud:

Lightning ever bright
from blue sky you shone;
banishing Man's night,
we cling to you alone.

Come into our lives,
help us make our mark,
though our ears hear lies
and all the world be dark. . .

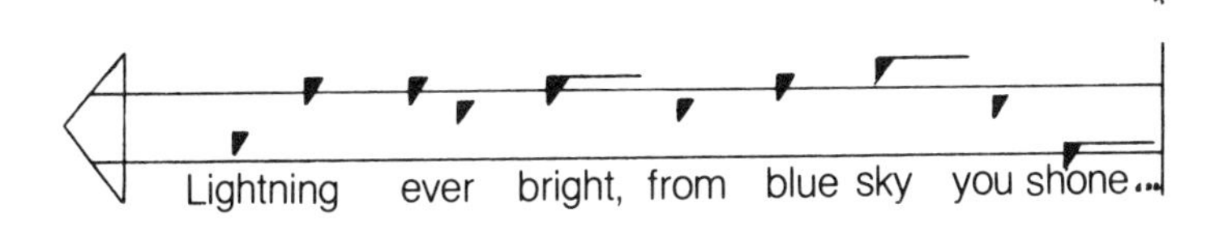
*
Lightning ever bright, from blue sky you shone...

While Baldwin stared, Morgan's words fell like bright raindrops and echoed slightly in the chamber. "How do you know *'Efil Espere'?*" the regent asked in a hushed voice.

"I learned 'To Fill with Hope' as a child—when my

---

*See the appendix on Eorthean music for explanation of Eorthean notation and its translation into Earthean setting, p. 305.

mother sang me to sleep," Morgan replied almost impatiently. "Quickly now, take me . . ."

Baldwin sheathed his sword and stepped onto the slab. He lifted an iron ring from a recess. "Come, help me," he grunted, leaning backward with both hands gripping the ring. Morgan added his strength, and, with a grating of stone against stone, he and Baldwin lifted a trapdoor cut into the center of the slab.

Instantly, air rushed into a square, black shaft. Morgan leaned over the brink and listened to a hollow, sighing sound coming from far, far below. Then, slowly, there came from the shaft an outflow of whispering shadow. Morgan hastily drew back as the shadow spread and darkened the chamber. Its whisper, Morgan thought, was like the exhalation of some vast, sleeping thing that had been awakened. The foul breath stung Morgan's and Baldwin's eyes, and they caught their breath as they pushed the trapdoor forward; it fell with a loud *thud*.

"That shadow and those stinging fumes are not of this castle," Baldwin stated. With a jerk, he left the slab and strode toward the door.

"How long since the shaft has been opened?" Morgan called, following him.

"Years," Baldwin replied, coughing as he entered the throne room.

"Could some evil have crept in from below?" Morgan asked.

"Not unless it could gnaw its way through the rock ribs of Eorthe!" Baldwin replied, crossing the throne room to a closed, wooden door.

As the black fumes flowed out of the chamber into the throne room, cries of consternation arose as though from a flock of frightened birds. Music and laughter ceased abruptly. Courtiers and officials, entertainers and servants fled, heeding neither Baldwin nor Morgan. The young king heard Baldwin, from beyond the wooden door through which he had gone, shout, "Warriors of Alamantia! Find your weapons and follow me! Danger besets us below, where the bottle was placed!" Baldwin then ran back across the throne room and beckoned for Morgan to follow him back into the chamber.

Soon, twenty or so grim-faced veterans hastened into the chamber, some carrying torches. The incoming warriors were broad of shoulder and tall of form; they appeared to have the sturdiness of aged oak wood. As they gathered around Baldwin, Morgan surveyed them, wondering why he had not seen them earlier. He noted their ugly scars, their horny hands clenching sword hilts, and their eyes flashing with violent fire. These men wore armor—worn and old—instead of fine clothing like the courtiers wore, and their muscles looked as knotted as lumps of iron.

The shaft was reopened, and torches were thrust into it. The flames sputtered and tried to die, but they revealed a narrow stairway. It ran down one wall for twenty or so feet, turned at a right angle, and ran down the next wall to another right-angle turn twenty more feet below. After two turns, the stairway no longer was visible in the flickering torch light.

"Why was the Lightning stored down there?" Morgan demanded. "Why was it ever taken from Glimmothtyrn?"

Baldwin glanced at the veterans, who had grumbled in agreement with Morgan. "Some bitterly regret that it was," the regent replied, "and some even now would replace it in Glimmothtyrn's crown. But most who came to the court in latter days spoke against it, saying it was too bright for their comfort. The Council of Lords therefore decided that for 'safekeeping' the bottle should be put in a place where its light would not disturb the . . . our peace and prosperity."

Morgan sighed, looking toward the hole. "Surely,

that shaft is the opposite of what the Lord of Light intended for the Lightning!"

Baldwin slowly winced. "So I said—and so said the men around you now. But I fell silent, and they were banned from the court. Those who found the Light troublesome whispered sweet words into your father's ears—until, finally, Mervintide began to agree that the Light no longer was needed. He was convinced that Alamantia's strength lay in its isolation from the continents rather than in any power contained in such a simple thing as a crystal vial." Baldwin sighed, clenching the hilt of his sword.

"Now, as we feared," one of the veterans grumbled, "evil has crept into the castle roots. Aye?"

"So it would seem, Asaph," Baldwin replied absently.

Asaph jerked his narrow, black-bearded chin toward his companions. "Well, who'll go with me to fetch the bottle?"

"I will," Morgan replied first.

Asaph laughed, then choked on the bitter air. "You? You're but a stripling. What do you know of fighting evil things?"

Baldwin squared himself. "A lad he may be, but *king* he'll soon be crowned. Remember that as you wag your tongue so loosely!"

Asaph hesitated, then bowed. "Your pardon, Prince Morgan."

Another of the veterans—a man with intense hazel eyes above high, broad cheekbones—stepped forward. "If he's to follow us, shouldn't he be armed?"

"Yes, Lucian, he should be," Baldwin agreed. He turned to the tallest warrior in the group. "You, Petard, go to the Warden of the Treasury. Tell him your lord requires Gafailnath."

Petard bowed slightly and left. While he was gone,

Baldwin and the others peered into the shaft, holding torches into the darkness. The smoke from the torches rippled in the black, uprising air.

"What manner of evil do you suppose it is?" Lucian asked.

Asaph answered in the measured syllables of the ancient language, *"Garainath na-pere ma conseroth!"*

" 'That which kills hope and strength,' " Lucian translated in a low voice. He gave Morgan a questioning look. "Boy, are you sure you want to follow us?"

Morgan looked steadily at him. "I do not want to follow, but to lead you, for to me was given the charge of protecting the bottle."

"Aye, if it's yet below," Baldwin growled, staring into the shaft.

After a while, the men heard Petard returning. Baldwin straightened and whispered, "Gafailnath comes."

The warriors drew back respectfully as the Warden of the Treasury followed Petard into the chamber. The squat and squarish warden was carrying a well-wrapped bundle on his outstretched arms.

Lord Baldwin stepped forward and took the bundle; the warden bowed stiffly, then left the room. The regent began unwinding the wrappings. Under a plain cloth was a cotton one on which were three figures: a great whale, an enormous green-yellow serpent, and a silver and black archer mounted on a stallion. Beneath the second covering was a third, richer in weave and design. Under it was a cloth woven of threads of gold and *nathnor*. Because of the silver-clear *nathnor*, the cloth seemed to have a light of its own.

As Baldwin unwound the final covering, Asaph stepped to him and bowed, "My lord, I mean no offense, nor do I mean to challenge you, but what if this lad is . . . is not the one to receive the sword?"

Baldwin looked from Asaph to Morgan, then in disbelief back to the warrior. "He came riding on Unthoriumgai, wearing the signet!"

Asaph bowed again but did not withdraw. "M'lord, you know as well as I the warning Acuerias, the King's magician, gave us ere he departed Mervintide's coronation. If this lad is not the true heir . . . if he was sent from the sorcerers . . . we all will be destroyed."

Morgan stated, "Sir, Acuerias has been my teacher. He treats with no impostor. The sword 'That which fails not,' will not reject me."

After a moment of silence, Baldwin announced, "We will take the risk." He unwound the final turn of the gold and *nathnor* cloth and bared a scabbard rich in jewels, metals, and workmanship. On the scabbard's sides were embossed letters in the ancient alphabet of Eorthe:

GAFAILNATH

Baldwin presented the sword to Morgan. The youth placed his right hand around the sword's long handle and cradled the scabbard with his left hand. Silently, he went to stand at the foot of his father's tomb.

Morgan instantly felt the ruling presence of the Lord of Light. Words came to him, and he repeated them aloud: "I will bear this sword . . . as Lightning ever bright . . . and with it will lead . . . our steps ever toward the Light!" He took a deep breath . . . and drew the blade.

Instantly a radiance as blue-green as an ocean pool yet as bright as sunlight flashed over the group. The warriors and even Lord Baldwin shaded their eyes, for the sword shone stunningly. Morgan, however, looked into the outrushing glow and smiled.

"Our king!" Asaph instinctively exclaimed, dropping to his knees. The others did likewise, then touched their foreheads to the stone floor. Gafailnath's flame glowed on the crowns of their dark heads.

As the sword shimmered in the air, the whispering shadows in the chamber sighed as though in pain and flowed back into the shaft. When the veterans arose, they felt refreshed. Looking at the shining sword, their spirits soared; it seemed that the majesty of the days of L'Ced suddenly had returned.

Morgan strode to the shaft, stood for a moment on the brink, then descended with quick, sure steps. The hissing shadows fled downward before him. The veterans and Baldwin were quick to follow.

Ever lower led the stairs, making a corner turn after each twenty-foot drop. The shaft echoed with the thunder of the warriors' bootsteps, and constantly the shadow retreated before the light of Gafailnath.

A part of Morgan's mind was counting the steps, and when his count passed two thousand he saw that the chamber at the bottom of the shaft was near. There, the darkness was thick, and heat rose from it with a pulsing, gurgling sound. As Morgan slowly went down the final steps, Gafailnath's flame grew.

Baldwin, seeing the thickening of the shadow, drew Sulnspen. It blazed brightly, adding to Gafailnath's light. The combined light of the swords shone upward over the veterans, who had stopped along three flights of steps to stare down at the shadow. When Morgan and Baldwin cautiously went into the dark chamber, the veterans silently followed.

Baldwin immediately went toward a shattered stone crypt. "The bottle," he announced, "is gone."

The men gathered around him, looking at the scattered fragments of the crypt. Petard, though, began sniffing the air and squinting toward the dark recess of the chamber to their right. "The pulsing sound and heat grow stronger," he observed.

Toward the dark alcove Morgan led the men. As he and Baldwin entered it, both swords shone with a strong, vibrant light—yet the light could not pierce the darkness that was cornered in front of them.

"There lies the thief," Lucian commented, "at bay, it seems."

As though the shadow heard him, it began to sigh deeply. With the exhalation came a strong, bitter smell. As the cesspool wind passed the swords, long sparks angrily streamed from them. Morgan squinted into the alcove. "It would appear that the shadow before us is blocking the passage through which it came," Morgan said, anxiously switching Gafailnath back and forth as he wondered how they could recover the bottle from the thief.

"Judging by the heat and pulsing," Baldwin said, laying his left hand on Morgan's shoulder to restrain him, "I'd say the passage leads to one of the rivers of fire in Eorthe's ribs. Perhaps we should . . ."

"Nothing can be gained by holding back now!" Morgan stated. Boldly, he stepped forward and thrust his sword into the thick gloom.

When the light pierced the darkness, a deafening hiss blasted from the alcove. Numbed, the veterans drew back . . . and back, but Morgan went forward. Again he thrust Gafailnath into the miasmic foe. The shadow roared more loudly and began to flow swiftly into the rear of the alcove. And from there, Morgan saw a red fire glimmer, then burst forth.

As the shadow being disappeared with a great sigh—its victory exhalation—the calamity began. From the alcove spewed a geyser of molten lava. Morgan and the others scrambled away, gained the stairway, and began racing upward for their lives. The liquid flames licked at the feet of the slowest two warriors and dragged them down. The horrible smell of burning flesh made the others spring up the steps two or three at a time. Behind them, gurgling and splashing, the lava filled the dark shaft. It caught a third warrior . . . then a fourth and a fifth. While those men were consumed, the lava paused as though taking a deep breath, then pulsed upward again—a sloshing, orange-red square of fire. It was then that the last man on the stairway slipped and was overtaken by the lava. Petard's scream was the worst and echoed long into the chamber above.

When Morgan and Baldwin reached the head of the stairs, they stopped only long enough to help the other men scramble out—and to see the lava come to a halt at ground level. Then, led by the young king, the men began making their way outside to see what effect the theft of the Lightning had had. Quickly they went into the throne room. There, no light shone, not even from the tall windows. A few guards and courtiers lay crumpled on the floor. And, to the horror of the passing warriors, the stiff corpses all seemed to be growing coats of gray ash! Asaph and Lucian began to pray, but the other veterans simply ran.

Warily, they hurried outside the castle, crossed the courtyards, and sprinted through the outer gate into the square. The King's fountain, in the center of the square, was completely dry. The day had turned to dusk, and the sun was hidden by long, stringy black clouds advancing from the north. The clouds flowed sternly southward as though marching to war. Below the clouds, a thin blanket of black mist reached deadly fingers into the city. And in doorways and gutters along each of the five streets leading downhill from the square were bodies. All appeared stiff; all were twisted; and all were becoming ash-coated. The only visible movement in the city was one dog, writhing in agony on the cobblestones.

"What has befallen?" Asaph asked, yawning as he came beside Baldwin.

"The Darkness has come," Baldwin replied. Tears sprang unheeded into his eyes. "All those good men, all these good people . . ." he murmured. Slowly, he turned to Morgan. "I have failed, my king, in my duty as regent." The great lord stiffly lowered himself to the paving stones of the square. "And before our fates overtake us, I ask your forgiveness."

"If anyone failed, it was my father," Morgan said sadly. "Stand and pray the Darkness does not likewise come within us, for I will have need of your strength in the days to come."

"I will pray, as you must," Baldwin promised, anxiously looking toward the marching clouds, "though naught but sleep and death will come of *this!*"

"How can the magicians be warned of the Lightning's theft?" Morgan demanded, frowning.

Baldwin fought to keep his eyes open, blinking at the veterans around him who one by one were sinking into slumber and beginning to stiffen. "In Glimmothtyrn's crown," Baldwin struggled to say, "is a sea conch. Blow it," he ended, collapsing in a heap upon the gray glistening stones.

Morgan looked upward. With its top half hidden in the ominous, black-gray clouds, Glimmothtyrn rose in the center of the four lesser towers. As Morgan lurched back toward the castle, praying hard, he wondered—could he climb to the top of the tower before sleep overcame him? And if he made the climb, would he have strength left with which to blow the conch? A sooty nighttime fell quickly as he began his climb, and he fought numbness each step of the way.

Chapter 5

The Demons of Gueroness

The sailboat pitched and drove into the north wind —first on an eastward tack, then on a westward tack. The ferryman Branchus sat by the long-handled tiller, telling Eric how to set the mainsail lines when the tack changed. Martin had been given the job of changing the set of the half-reefed jib. That assignment meant he had to go scrambling to the sharply upturned bow each half hour or so. Between changes of the tack, the young people huddled aft under the warmth of the waif's robe. There, they sat watching Branchus, who had lit a stubby pipe.

"Have any other Kingsmen crossed?" Jodi asked him.

"Only one other young'un's crossed here," Branchus replied, snatching the pipe from his thin lips with a merry look at Jodi.

Eric, puzzled by the news, asked, "But where are the others?"

"Don't know," the ferryman chirped above the slicing of the wind.

"This dark wind," Eric began, "How long has . . ."

"Been comin' since the King went," Branchus interrupted. "Ho, now! Change'a tack!"

Eric and Martin groaned and reluctantly left the warmth of the fur robe to go to their stations. When the shift of course had been made, they hastened back under the robe.

On sailed the boat, northward for four more days, apparently alone on the ocean. Constantly the cold wind blew against the reddened faces of the young people and Branchus. Constantly the boat rose and fell, jarred each time high, swelling waves thumped under the bow. Eric and Martin's hands were so cold-deadened that they could no longer feel the soreness and blisters that pulling on the lines caused. Their faces had been cold for so long that the boys no longer felt the spray stinging them each time they went forward. They ate mechanically; they slept gratefully. And the only change during those days was when stringy black clouds scudded low from the north in a mass, obscuring the sun and sky. By then, the children—including Richard—had become so hardened and grim that they watched the clouds without comment.

The dawn of the sixth day was dismal. The children were huddled in deep sleep when Branchus's sharp voice startled them from dreams of the warm world they had left. "Land ho!" he cried. With numb excitement, the children opened their bleary eyes.

The first thing they noticed was that the sky above the stringy clouds was yellow—the color of sulphur, Jodi thought. She blinked at Eric and Martin, then stared at the ferryman.

"Yep!" he said, snatching the stubby pipe from his mouth. "Sky here's yeller!"

"Here?" Martin sleepily inquired. "Where is *here?*"

"We're almost to Gueroness."

The children couldn't decide whether to be glad or afraid.

When they finished eating breakfast from their dwindling supplies, the young people went forward and expectantly stared ahead. By squinting into the wind that ruffled their tangled hair, they saw the land the ferryman had announced. It spread across the horizon in a thin, pale brown curve.

As the boat drew nearer the shore, the wind grew both stronger and warmer. The ferryman, Eric saw, was now using great skill to work the boat close enough for a landing. He gave curt commands to Eric and Martin and seemed impatient for each change to be made. The boys barely had time to notice that far in the distance across the land rose a jagged line of mountains. The tips of the mountains were fired a pale yellow by the partially visible sun. On the broad land before the mountains, not a plant, an animal, or a person could be seen. Only the peaks and what appeared to be ruins of a large city broke the bleak vista. The Kingsmen's spirits sank: The idea of being deposited on such a forbidding land was dismaying, and the thought of being *left* there was almost terrifying.

As the boat worked nearer the shore, the children sighted a landing. Branchus turned the sailboat and made a final tack into the wind. Eric scrambled to the bow and stood upright. Turning, he shouted above the whistling of the wind, "A cave's near the landing . . . a shallow one covered by a huge rock slab!"

Nearer the boat plunged until it entered calmer water in the lee of the land. It coasted to a stone wharf, and Eric jumped ashore with the bowline. He held the boat reasonably steady until the others had jumped out. Richard came last, looking around suspiciously. The moment he was ashore, the wind seized the boat. It tore the line from Eric's hands, wheeled, and scudded southward. Branchus waved over one shoulder.

As he and the sailboat rapidly diminished in size, the young people faintly heard him call, *"A-Abba conseroth seu!"**

They were left with the sound of wind streaking over the flat land and the stinging of sand upon the backs of their necks. Reluctantly they turned into the wind and made their way toward the cave.

"Look!" Eric cried, running ahead.

Martin squinted into the flying dust and saw a human form in the cave. "It must be the Kingsman Branchus brought," he called, helping the waif control the flapping of his great robe.

"It's a girl!" Eric yelled back. "And something's wrong!"

Jodi hurried to join him, and together they stooped to enter the cave. The girl, who appeared to be near Jodi's age, was clad in a white cotton dress under the bright armor of the King. She was huddled in the middle of the sandy floor. Her long, glossy black hair was in disarray; her legs were drawn up to her chest, and she was holding her sword straight up before her.

"What's the matter with her?" Richard asked. "Is she crazy?"

Jodi ignored him as she pulled back the girl's hair and looked at her pleasant, rather broad features. Stiffening with surprise, Jodi softly asked, "Rachael? Rachael!" she repeated, naming the Kingsman from Mexico she had met in the Land of the King the year before.

The girl responded by clenching her sword and murmuring, "I love you, my King . . . I love you."

"What's she muttering about?" Richard grumbled.

---

*For definitions and pronunciations of Eorthean words and phrases, see page 304.

He kicked around the cave, looking at the floor. "And what're these tracks from?"

Eric looked at the sandy floor while Jodi took Rachael in her arms and rocked her back and forth. Eric knelt, touching claw and hoof prints of several shapes and sizes trampled into the sand. Standing, Eric saw that a two-yard wide path of tracks came in from the desert, encircled the girl, then went back out into the desert and scattered. "Demons," he concluded.

Martin shuddered, staring at the many tracks. Jodi looked from him to Rachael's face. "Oh, what you must have gone through," she whispered to her friend. "But it's all right now."

"Throw some water on her," Richard suggested.

Eric sighed tiredly and knelt by Jodi. "Try the throne leaves."

Jodi unslung her pack, unzipped one side pouch, and took out three of the leaves from the King's throne. She smelled their fragrance and smiled as she held them under Rachael's nose. The effect was almost instantaneous: Rachael awoke, laid down her sword, and leaned forward to hug Jodi.

"Thank goodness she's stopped carrying on," Richard said disgustedly.

"The demons," Rachael murmured, holding Jodi's shoulders. "I . . . I was okay . . . until last night, when *they* came," she said, coughing dryly. Jodi took a jar Eric offered her and gave Rachael some water. They took no notice of Richard, who sat on a nearby rock, sneering.

"Demons," he muttered. "I knew she was crazy!"

"Has Waymond or any other magician been here?" Eric asked, taking the water jar back from Jodi and capping it.

"No, and if it hadn't been for the armor, shield, and

sword . . . *they* would have taken me!'' she trembled, closing her large, long-lashed eyes.

Jodi hugged her. ''I think you were awfully brave to have answered the call by yourself,'' she said firmly. ''And how you lasted out the . . .''

''I wasn't alone,'' Rachael said with sudden eagerness. ''The King was with me . . . or at least his light, his warmth was. I cried out to him when *they* . . . those demons . . . came yelling and screaming, running around like crazy and . . .'' She put her hands to the sides of her head and shut her eyes. Then she grabbed her sword. ''But I got some of them! They pranced too close, and I got them!''

''Good for you!'' Eric laughed.

Rachael smiled weakly. ''At least I didn't fail the King. I never doubted he would help me—and he did!''

Richard sullenly stood. ''How can nightmares hurt you anyhow?'' When the others stared at him, he flustered. ''Well, that's *obviously* all that's wrong with her! I mean, *everyone* has nightmares. They're no reason to go *loony!*''

''I don't have nightmares,'' Martin said mildly. ''Not any more.''

''Me neither,'' Eric sniffed.

Richard glared at them. ''Well, everybody *I* know wakes up with . . . with *things* dancing in the darkness.'' He made wiggly motions with his fingers. ''All you have to do is turn on the light,'' he added.

Martin chuckled. ''Seen any light switches around here?''

Richard turned away to kick a rock.

Rachael shakily stood and noticed the waif for the first time. She saw that a tear was poised on one of his cheeks and concluded that he was concerned about her. She went to him and knelt. Taking his hands and looking into his eyes, she assured him, ''I'm all right now." Turning to Jodi, she asked, "Who is he? An apprentice?"

Jodi thought briefly, then nodded. "Yes, I suppose he is. But we can't even ask him his name; he can't talk."

"Can he write?" Rachael asked.

Martin immediately dug in his pack. "Ha!" he grunted, going to the waif with a pencil stub and a scrap of paper. "Thought we might need to leave another note for someone," he explained.

The waif put the pencil tip to his dirt-smeared lips and went to a fairly flat rock. He wrote a message on the paper and handed it to Eric. Eric read the note aloud:

"When will I meet your King?"

Rachael looked intently at the boy. Frowning, she asked Jodi, "Why does he have such a . . . a hurt look?"

Jodi sighed and told her quietly about the wreck and the death of his parents. Even before she had finished, Rachael helped the boy stand and wrapped both arms around him. Impulsively, first Jodi, then Martin and Eric joined Rachael and the waif in a tight circle, drawing their arms around the boy. At first he squirmed, but gradually he relaxed.

"So, what do we do now?" came Richard's cutting voice.

Rachael cleared her throat and went outside the cave. One by one, the others joined her. Squinting into the dusty wind, Rachael said, "When I called on the King, he sent his warmth and light . . . and a voice."

"A voice!" Richard whooped. "Now it's *voices* she hears!"

"It said," Rachael persisted, " 'Northward until met.' "

Eric shaded his eyes and stared into the barren distance. On the horizon, perhaps a hundred miles away, stood the naked mountain spires. Halfway there, the hazy ruins of a large city rose from the barren land. Much nearer, perhaps fifteen miles away, stood the barely visible ruins of a village. Not a speck of green could be seen.

"It appears that Gueroness once was inhabited," Eric commented.

"It sure looks dead now," Jodi observed.

Quietly, Rachael stated, "If the people are dead, I think I know what killed them."

"Yeah," Martin muttered, "that southern sorcerer's demons."

"Probably," Eric said, looking toward the ruined village. "Northward it is," he added, starting off. The others trailed behind him.

"Can't we even rest for a while?" Richard whined.

"You 'rested' all the way across the ocean," Martin snapped.

Richard glared bitterly at Martin and kicked a rock—half hoping it would hit the other boy. But he only hurt his foot. With a pained and angry expression, he came along last. If only he had known then what lay ahead, he surely would have run into the ocean and tried to swim home.

Walking slowly, the line of young people trailed a dust plume that rose from the bone dry land and streamed away in the wind. By late afternoon they were tired, but they had come only to within a mile or so of the deserted village. Eric watched the yellow disk of the sun sink to their left, then he looked ahead at the distant mountains. He guessed that at least four more days of travel would be needed to reach the spired range, and he began to doubt that he and his companions could reach the peaks, much less cross them.

As nightfall came, Eric climbed to the top of a low hill and sank down. He unslung his pack and took out his water jar. Nearby, Martin plopped onto the hard, pebbly ground and began rummaging in his pack for food. The others did likewise, and slowly a camp took form.

"At least in the darkness," Jodi said as she unrolled her blanket, "we can't see that spooky city we have to pass."

"Or those mountains we have to climb," Martin added.

It all was simply too much for Richard. "Wait'll we get home," he mumbled. "Boy, are you going to get into trouble!"

"Have some cheese and bread," Rachael offered, sitting near him.

Richard refused . . . until his stomach overrode his resentment. Then, he snatched the food and muttered, "Thanks."

By the time he had finished eating, the others were asleep, having cleared a space of pebbles and moved their blankets close together. Richard looked scornfully at the others and went down from the hilltop. Shivering in the chill night air, he spread his blanket on the sand. Perhaps it was because he had gone away from the group that he was the first to hear the sounds.

They began in the middle of the night when the darkness was most complete. From the direction of the ruined village came noises unlike anything Richard ever had heard. Then, as the sounds rose louder, a red glow burst up and began to rush toward the camp. Richard, by this time, was sitting up, pinching both arms to make sure he was awake.

The red glow approached like a low-flying comet. Ball-shaped in front with a long tail of red-orange sparks behind, the glow rushed toward Richard and began to separate into the distinct shapes of many strange bodies. Richard blinked, listening to the pitter-patter of claws, the thudding of hooves, and the snickering, shrieking, wailing of many strange voices. Richard put both hands to his ears; thus, he did not hear Eric shouting for him to join the others.

They, of course, had awakened. Leaping up, the Kingsmen had slung their shields on their left arms and had drawn their swords. When Eric saw that the demons were heading for Richard, he sprinted downhill, brandishing his blue blazing sword. He grabbed Richard and dragged him uphill while the boy stammered, "Th-th-they're *real!*"

Howling and screeching, the demons of Gueroness began racing around the hilltop camp. The flaming feet of the demons kicked up hot flying sand, and their red bodies trailed wisps of flame and smoke. All were shrieking with complete abandon, and their fangs and flickering tongues drooled red fire.

Staring through the bright, pure blue radiance cast by their upheld swords, the Kingsmen realized that only the blades kept the demons at a safe distance. But then the creatures began hurling flame darts toward the group. The darts arched high and fell sizzling to melt the sand where they struck.

Eric yelled, "Kingsmen, form a square and hold up your shields! Richard, Waif—get inside the square!" Thus, even when the demons hurled a whole volley of fire darts, the missiles glanced harmlessly from the roof of shields and sputtered onto the sand.

Hair in flames, tails whipping, claws churning the sand, the demons raced around and around. The waif cowered, and Richard stared at the scene as though his worst nightmare had come triply true. Eric and Rachael, meanwhile, slashed at reddish legs that danced too close, sending more than one demon howling away. Martin whacked at a foot or two, but he was too frightened to lean very far out, even though his blue flaming sword seemed eager for battle.

The heat from the whirling beasts grew intense, and their stench became unbearable. The young people's ears rang from the constant screeching. They were sweating heavily, blocking flame darts with their shields, turning from side to side to chop at thrusting arms and kicking red legs. Richard at last could stand it no longer.

"Mmoooootthhh-eerrr!" he screamed, shoving his way between Eric and Jodi and running down the hill. The circle of beasts parted to let him go through.

"Richard!" Jodi yelled. She would have gone after him had not Eric held her back. "Rich-ard!!" she yelled again.

The waif instantly saw the measure of her concern. Suddenly, he sprang out of the square and raced in pursuit of Richard. The demons roared and waved their arms before him, but he dodged between two huge brutes and ran into the darkness, whirling his fur robe over his back. The Kingsmen watched in horror as a dozen or more flame darts struck the waif's back, setting his robe afire.

"Let's go, Martin!" Eric commanded. "Remember what I taught you!"

Together they leaped down the hill to attack the ring of demons. It parted with a scramble of claws and hooves; half of the demon pack hurried after the two boys who had fled, and the other half barred the Kingsmen's way.

"For the King!" Eric shouted, attacking the largest demon. Martin took a deep breath and lunged at another one. Slash! Slash! whistled Martin's pulsing blade in the "crossing-hands" stroke Eric had taught him. An arm fell from the demon, and a gash across its belly spurted sizzling black blood. Back fell the remaining demons, stumbling in confusion. Rachael joined the fray, hacking and slashing, hacking and slashing. And when one tall, knife-thin demon sprang over Eric to attack him from behind, Jodi's courage welled up. She ran down the hill and hewed the demon cleanly in half. That began the rout!

Soon, the surviving beasts scattered across the black desert, shrieking threateningly but powerless to withstand the blue flaming swords. Martin was in hot pursuit of a lumbering, triple-horned monster when Eric called him back. "Richard and the waif went that way!" Eric cried, pointing east. The four Kingsmen silently began running in a widely spaced line. In the dark, they stumbled over the body of the waif. He was face down; black, foot-long darts protruded from his smouldering robe.

"Ohhh!" Jodi cried, sheathing her sword and laying down her shield as she and Rachael knelt by the boy. When Eric and Martin saw they could do nothing, they raced after the fast departing glow of the other demons.

Side by side, Eric and Martin ran without speaking, steadily gaining on the demons. When the boys came close, five of the flaming creatures stopped and faced the Kingsmen. Eric and Martin, sure of the power that was with them, never slowed. They cut their way through the rearguard and attacked the others.

Left and right they slashed, keeping their shields before them. Flame darts hissed time and time again off their shields and armor and blazed within inches of their faces. But finally the last demon lay smoking and fizzling. Eric and Martin then bent over the quivering human who lay crumpled where the demons had dropped him. "Richard?" Martin asked, kneeling by the boy's face. His eyes were open and his mouth was moving, but no sound came out.

Eric and Martin rested, then picked Richard up between them and began walking toward where the girls were. "By the way," Martin sighed, "I'm sure glad you taught Jodi and me how to use our swords and shields properly." He shifted his part of Richard's weight and added, "Last spring, I thought you were just playing."

"You can thank Waymond for the techniques," Eric said, stumbling and quickly catching himself, "if we ever see him again."

"Over here," came Rachael's strong voice from near the melting, sputtering body of a large demon. Eric and Martin changed direction and soon rejoined the girls, who were carrying the waif between them. Slowly the group made its way back toward camp.

Atop their lonely hill, Jodi bent over the waif and put one cheek before his nose to see if he was breathing. Martin, meanwhile, let go of Richard and got his flashlight from his pack. He turned it on in time to illuminate his sister's tear-stained face as she looked up and said, "I think the waif is dead."

"Maybe the leaves from the King's throne will help him," Eric said.

She pulled her pack to her and got a handful of the bright green, oval leaves. She held them under the waif's nose, but he did not stir. With a sad sigh, she laid down the leaves and turned the boy onto his stomach; carefully, she removed the waif's robe and scorched, pierced shirt. "His back is burned and punctured by small black holes," she told the others. "I think the flame darts poisoned him." Crying but trying not to, she took her water bottle and a cloth from her pack and gingerly began washing his wounds. Rachael got a small bottle of antiseptic from her pack and knelt to help.

"Wish we had some wood to make a fire," Eric

mused, frowning. "Then you could brew tea from the leaves."

"I've got matches," the ever-ready Martin said, "if we can find something to burn."

"How about this?" Rachael asked, dragging over the waif's partially burned robe. "And these?" she added, getting a handful of waxed paper food wrappings from her pack.

They started a fire with the waxed paper, shredded the robe, and laid strips of it on the tiny blaze. Soon, they were able to heat water in a cup. Jodi slipped eight leaves into the steaming water and waited for the tea to give off its invigorating aroma. When it did, she took the cup from the flames, let it cool, and motioned for Eric to lift the waif's head. She poured sips of the tea into his half-open mouth. He gagged, frowned briefly, then smiled and gradually awoke. When he sat up, they washed his scorched back with the remaining lukewarm tea. While Rachael dressed his black wounds, Jodi went to Richard and held several leaves under his nose.

Richard evidently had not been injured, for he soon began to look at his companions and at the black pools of melted sand over which Martin was shining his light. Richard shivered, knowing that each black spot had been a demon—one of those horrible, *real* creatures through whom the Voice had spoken while he was alone with them. Then he felt the Kingsmen looking at him. He whirled on them. "Why're you staring at me? It wasn't *my* fault that kid got hurt!"

After his outburst, they settled down to keep watch until the dawn came. But by the time the sky grew yellow above them, they were deeply asleep.

Chapter 6

City of the Dead

When Eric awoke, his right hand was still on his sword hilt, as was Martin's on his. Jodi and Rachael were sleeping by the waif. Richard was curled in a ball, twitching from bad dreams. Eric wakened the others, and in thirty minutes they were on their way—northward. Eric and Martin walked on either side of the waif to help him, though he was surprisingly strong. Richard trailed behind the girls, staring sullenly at the ground.

As the day steadily grew hotter, they came to the deserted village. Curious but wary, they walked down the main street between rows of ruined adobe houses that looked charred on the inside.

"It's like flames suddenly burst inside each home," Eric observed.

Rachael pointed to a blackened corpse curled against a doorway. "That one almost made it outside."

"What a horrible way to die!" Jodi shuddered, looking away.

"And look," Martin said with morbid interest, "the body isn't rotting."

Eric drew his sword and went with Martin to look at

the corpse. Then the older boy slipped inside the house through the charred, splintered doorway. He looked around at blackened furniture and other corpses, then saw a large, sealed stone jar in one corner. With his sword Eric pried off the leather lid and cautiously tasted the liquid inside the jar. "Water," he pronounced as Martin joined him. "Bring in the bottles," he told the younger boy.

"You're going to fill them with *that?*" Martin asked, wide-eyed.

"Our bottles are almost empty," Eric stated. "We've seen no other water, so let's look on this as a blessing from the people who died here."

Martin did as he was told, and soon the water bottles were refilled. The water indeed turned out to be a blessing because, as they went on, they passed the village well and found it dry. Leaving the village, they crossed a riverbed—also dry. And all the miles of bleak desert before them looked thoroughly parched.

They camped that night beside a creekbed; along it, Eric and Martin scrounged enough firewood to cook their first hot meal in seven days. In the morning, they walked steadily along an eroded road that led due north, and by the end of the day the ruined city ahead had grown large against the mountain-studded horizon.

The next day, as they approached the ruins, their conversation turned—as it more and more frequently seemed to—to the subject of water.

"At home each day," Rachael told Jodi, "I walk six miles to the well we use; then I carry two five-gallon *latas* on a wooden yoke back home."

"Big deal," Richard sneered, wiping his dusty mouth.

Jodi ignored him and asked Rachael, "Don't you have running water in your house?"

Rachael smiled and shook her head. "And if the dry season lasts too long, our well goes dry. Then we have to walk far back into the mountains to get water from a spring."

"No wonder you could make the trip here alone," Jodi murmured.

Rachael simply smiled. "I love the King."

Water continued to dominate their thoughts and sparse conversations. Frequently, one or another of them would mention a river or a fountain they had known. And—as they bypassed the ruined, mud-walled city in the late afternoon—they speculated about what it would be like to die of thirst. When the sun set, they stopped, feeling perhaps more thirsty than they really were.

Jodi went to examine the waif's wounds, which by now were festering from infection. Jodi trembled as she used the last of her water to bathe them. Only with an effort did she manage to re-wrap the boy's back. Then, they slowly ate supper, sitting in a loose circle and gazing at the still distant mountains. When the night chill crept over the children, they rolled up in their blankets, shivering and weak and very thirsty.

In the morning they had to force themselves to begin walking. Sore muscles, blistered feet, and the need to conserve their diminishing water made each of them suffer all that day and all the next. Mile after mile crept by. They passed within sight of more ruined villages, and they saw several cemeteries whose graves were broken open. The eleventh day of their trek ended as the rays of the sunset slanted across the broad land and fired the mountains purple-red with gilded tips. In a moment, though, the light faded. The desert sank into blackness. The silence was complete, crystalline pure.

By late afternoon of the next day, they had crossed a

wind- and sand-scoured valley crisscrossed by the faint remains of irrigation ditches. The hardpan valley ended at long slopes that led upward to foothills; above the hills hung a haze. Above the haze shot the ramparts of the mountains blocking the young people's path. The peaks of the mountains rose so high that their tips seemed to merge with the yellow sky. From horizon west to horizon east stretched the jagged, hostile-looking peaks. The mountain range seemed absolutely impenetrable.

Eric stopped, panting as he felt nausea roll through him. He dug in his pack for salt, poured some onto his palm and licked it, then passed it to the others—who were watching their leader with concern. He also found some smushed sticks of gum in the bottom of his pack. He and his companions slowly chewed the gum as they looked toward the forbidding mountains.

" 'Northward until met,' " Eric said grimly. "Hope it's soon."

Richard snorted, "Met! We'll be met all right—by more nightmares!"

"No," Rachael said firmly, "help will come."

Richard would have spit if he could have. "The only help we'll get," he choked, "is to die quickly."

They all turned to stare at him. For the first time, the possibility of dying became extremely real. And, as though Richard's words finally had pierced their resolve, they made camp where they were. They slept fitfully, their overtired minds swarming with dreams of climbing and falling . . . climbing and falling.

In the morning, even Eric was too dejected to go on—until Jodi remembered the leaves from the King's throne. She quickly handed out the fresh, unwilted leaves, wondering why she hadn't thought of them before. Smelling the leaves, the young people began to walk northward.

As noon came and went, the pace of the group slowed. The ground steadily was climbing toward purplish foothills that rose to the base of the mountain ramparts. Following a faint road, the children wound upward into the foothills, half blind from the sun's glare and numb with exhaustion. By sunset they reached the top of the highest foothill and collapsed at the base of a pinnacle just below the soaring peaks.

The wind sweeping down upon them was chill, and they turned their backs to it to look at the way they had come. From their vantage point perhaps a thousand feet above the desert floor, the distance they had traveled seemed incredible! "If it hadn't been for the leaves . . ." Eric began, twirling a leaf under his nose. "Let's go a little farther," he suggested, stretching to ease his muscles.

Rachael picked up her cactus-fiber pack and looked north toward the darkened ramparts rising before them like nighttime itself. "Does the road go on?" she wondered aloud, helping the waif stand.

"Let's just stay here," Richard whined. "If we keep going we'll fall or meet something awful."

"Look," Eric said patiently, "the moon will rise soon. When it does, there'll be enough light for us to see where we're going. We're out of water, and we *must* find some . . . before tomorrow's heat."

Rachael and the waif, while the others were talking, climbed around the base of the pinnacle below which they had rested. "Hey!" she called back, "The road seems to go on over the mountains!"

The note of surprise in Rachael's voice cheered the others, and they hurried to catch up with her and the waif. They then could see the faint line of the road winding up to a pass that actually seemed reachable. All day, they now realized, the pass had been hidden from their view by the pinnacle!

"It's probably the road the demons use," Richard gloomily commented.

Jodi felt that again his words had pierced their resolve. "He's probably right," she sighed, coming to a stop.

"If this is the road they follow," Eric reasoned, taking one of Jodi's hands and leading her onward, "that means their home—and their master—are somewhere ahead of us."

"Oh, thanks a lot!" Martin complained, looking upward as he walked.

Stopping frequently to rest and to listen for demons, the young people continued to climb the road. The cold wind whipping down from over the mountains whistled into an increasingly deep chasm below them. At one point, Richard tossed a stone over the road's edge and counted twelve seconds before it clattered against rocks at the bottom.

Like a polished brass shield, the moon—larger and closer than the children ever had seen it—crept into the sky. Its light gilded the road and made golden reflections gleam from the Kingsmen's armor. And, when the young travelers finally gained the crest of the pass, they saw the bronze light flooding onto a strange scene far below.

Stretching out of sight to the east and west, a valley lay at the base of the mountains. Revealed by the eerie moonlight, the road the young people had been following led to the center of the valley. There, sprawled over the low hills of what appeared to be a glacier's moraine, was a silent city. Beyond it rose the dark foothills and soaring, black ramparts of another mountain range, but it was the city that held the young people's attention.

Pale towers, tilted walls, roofs slanting askew all gleamed in the moonlight. Narrow streets ran between what appeared to be blocks of small, stone houses with strange spires at the ends of the roof ridges. At the near edge of the city, slabs of stone in scattered groups shone like dull gold bars. Some slabs had fallen, some were tilted, and others stood upright with statues atop them.

"Un cuidad de los muertos," Rachael whispered in Spanish. For the first time since the others had found her in the cave, she seemed terrified.

"A graveyard?" Eric inquired.

"No . . . a city of the dead!" the girl replied, trembling.

"A necropolis," Jodi murmured.

"We're going to *that?*" Richard demanded shakily.

Fingering his sword hilt, Eric did not answer. He began tightening the straps that held his armor to his body, and the other Kingsmen followed his example—preparing for a battle that seemed inevitable. Eric and Martin then led the way downward along the steep, winding road. The waif stumbled along between them, trying to whistle.

Stealthily, flinching at the sound of each pebble they kicked, they entered the valley. An hour passed. The shadows from the far mountains lengthened as the moon began to set. And finally, they entered the city.

Cautiously, swords drawn, the young adventurers walked up a broad, broken avenue—expecting to see the red glow of demons rise at any moment from the graves and mausoleums that now surrounded them. Staring at the decaying crypts, Rachael gripped Jodi's free hand so tightly that Jodi thought her bones would crack. Ahead of them, Eric and Martin kept close together, constantly prepared to slash at upspringing demons. But, despite the deepening cloak of darkness, nothing happened. They could *feel* evil beings around them, and they imagined that creatures were waiting just below the surface of each grave and time-eaten tomb—yet none appeared.

Gradually, the children began to relax and look more closely at the sides of nearby crypts. Eight or so feet higher than their heads, the stone walls leaned this way and that. Each was bordered by a wide band of carvings: serpents coiling, strange birds eating flesh from humans, men struggling to kill one another with barbaric weapons. In the center of each wall were deeply carved scenes. Conquerors, presumably buried inside the crypts, stood arrogantly over mounds of slain creatures. Warriors forever frozen in stone brandished spiked clubs over cowering slaves. Tribute was shown piled before war lords on squarish thrones.

"I wonder who built this place?" Eric whispered, looking down silent side streets.

"Whoever it was is dead now," Martin muttered, looking at his sword. It flickered with blue light. "I hope," he added, holding up his blade.

"It senses evil nearby," Eric commented, becoming more cautious. He, too, held up his sword and watched it flame into life.

Suddenly, six sparkling rings of fire whirled from the sky toward the young people. They tried to duck and run, but a spinning hoop settled over each of them. Eric, like the other Kingsmen, hacked at the weird ring imprisoning him. Sparks flew as the sword struck the spark hoop. Eric's arm was jolted, and his blade violently was repelled. He took a deep breath, then said, "Looks like we'll soon meet the demons' master."

"Greetings!" a deep voice immediately rasped with a triple echo. "Welcome to Byzarnium, capital of Gueroness." Holding their arms away from the fire-rings, the young people turned to look for the one who had spoken. "Do not be afraid, my little ones," the deep voice resumed soothingly. "The *sulomens* around you will do no harm—if you obey me exactly."

Eric looked up, expecting some giant form to be standing over them.

"No, I am some distance ahead of you," the voice grated with restrained power. "Go on as you were and you will come to my . . . our . . . home."

"Who are you?" Eric asked loudly. His voice echoed among the crypts.

"I am the ruler here. I am your King."

Rachael threw off her fear of the place and tightened her grip on her blue pulsing sword. "We have only one King," she shouted, "and he doesn't live in a graveyard!"

Heavy laughter boomed before them, and the fire-rings shimmered in response. "Come to me and you shall see your King," the voice ordered.

Infuriated, Rachael told the others, "Don't listen to him!" Then, compelled by the forward surging hoops, she went with the others. As she went, her main comfort was that the power controlling the fire-rings could not make the Kingsmen release their swords. The blades glowed threateningly as the group of children went slowly over a slight hill. They then saw a huge building at the junction of four broad streets.

The building was, Jodi decided, an ancient temple. From a raised mound, steps rose to open, columned walls. A flat-pitched, stone roof covered the temple, and in front were two statues of the most awful creatures she ever had imagined. Appearing huge and powerful, their hideous faces leered in frozen hatred. While the young people were led closer by the *sulomens,* they saw that in the center of the open-walled temple burned a fire that cast little light.

"Welcome to the fore court of my palace," the grinding voice said. "May you dwell long and prosperously herein, living without shame or restraint!"

Richard was the only member of the group not angered by the offer. As he and his companions were drawn up the steps into the place, Richard actually began relaxing. In fact, he went ahead of the group and walked straight to the fire. When the others came up beside him, they saw that he was holding his hands up to the feeble flames burning from the top of a pyramidal altar. Behind the altar, the steps leading to a throne rose from deep shadow.

"Here will you drink deeply of eternal forgetfulness," the voice boomed, "and here will you serve the greatest power on Eorthe!"

"Who are you?" Eric asked again, squinting to see into the gloom.

Gradually, the fire on the altar rose higher, illuminating a figure seated upon the throne. To the children's surprise, it was a man—a tall, deathly looking man who in no way seemed to match the power of the voice. Eric frowned, sensing that the appearance of the man was but a disguise. Richard, however, sighed with relief. He hurried forward and knelt at the foot of the throne. The man smiled, revealing a dark, empty mouth. He flicked one hand, and Richard's fire-ring disappeared with a wisp of black smoke.

"At least one of you recognizes my power," the voice rumbled. "But soon, all of you gladly will kneel before me." The self-assurance in the voice irritated the Kingsmen, especially Eric. He, though, knew it would be foolish to goad the creature.

The flames continued to dance on the top of the altar, casting a flickering glow over the throne and part of the temple floor. The young people then saw that on each side of the throne was the statute of a huge, wolf-like beast. Obviously, if the beasts had been alive, they would have been fierce hunters and, judging by their bulging stone muscles, tireless in pursuit.

"Now," the voice resumed ominously, "since you still choose not to kneel, it is time you learned who your King is!" The figure rose and descended; strangely, his steps shook the building. "In me, as in my brother and my father, is the shape of the as yet unrevealed new world . . . a world you will see only in death if you do not bow before me!" The creature slashed a fleshless arm from his silky black robe and thrust a finger of bone toward them. "Bow down *now!!*" he thundered.

The fire-rings around the Kingsmen whirled faster, tightening inch by inch. When the rings began to whir against their shields and armor, sparks were cast off in bright showers. Their sword arms and blue flashing swords shook like willow wands in a gale. Then, the Kingsmen and the waif were enveloped in a down-rushing black cloud. They trembled, fell, and sank into unconsciousness.

Sarx, second son of Ingloamin, stepped toward them. He passed the cowering form of Richard, whom his voice already had conquered, and strode to take possession of the Kingsmen and their companion.

Chapter 7

Acuerias Comes

The sorcerer found, however, that though the *sulomens* bound the young people and his dark power had felled them, the Kingsmen and the waif were well protected. In anger, the dark figure returned to his throne.

Eric regained consciousness slowly. He felt cold stones beneath him. Without moving his head, he looked around. He saw that the fire-rings had been taken away. He looked at the unconscious bodies of his friends and noted that all the Kingsmen, including himself, still had hold of their swords. That fact told him the limit of the sorcerer's power. Hearing dim voices, Eric listened.

One voice was deep and trembled with a triple echo. The other voice was Richard's—small and hesitant but eager. Eric cautiously turned his head and saw that the pair was seated on the throne steps.

Richard slowly was shaking his head. "I don't know where this King they believe in is, I tell you."

"My power will become yours . . . but only if you help me."

After a moment, Richard mumbled, "But I don't even believe there *is* a King, much less know where he is."

The dark figure rose impatiently and lurched up the black steps. At the top, he twisted and sat with a whirl of his flowing black robe. "Watch this, then decide whom you will serve!" Fingers of bone stabbed from his loose black sleeves. Twin ribbons of flame shot into the statues of the gigantic wolves. The statues began to glow hotly . . . and a growl came from each massive beast. Their eyes flickered red and they crouched, then sprang from their pedestals. Their soaring leaps took them to the prone Kingsmen. With hot, foul breaths, the demon beasts snuffled the backs of the children—but they blinked and shied away from the blue glimmering swords.

At a silent command from their ruler, the wolves returned to the throne. Richard had scooted up five steps, but the wolves had only to lean forward to sniff at his face. Each of their mouths, Richard saw, easily could swallow his head, which he covered with both arms. The wolves reacted with growls, and Richard saw liquid fire drool from their partly opened mouths.

"All right . . . all right!" he screeched thinly. "But I still don't know anything. I've never even seen the King!" Dimly, he began to wonder: *If the sorcerer is as powerful as he claims, why is he so concerned about the King?*

The wolves sat on their haunches as the ruler sank lower on his skull-topped throne chair, apparently deep in thought. Richard's heart began beating more slowly, and he stared at the wolves. *Boy!* he thought, *what I could do with them! With them beside me, no one* ever *would make me afraid again or not pay me the attention I deserve!* If only he knew, or could learn, where the King was and tell the sorcerer. Above him, withdrawn into the shadows, the figure of darkness smiled an empty-mouthed smile.

As Eric listened, he heard the waif and the other

Kingsmen stir. Before the sorcerer could attack them again, Eric leaped up and yelled, "Stand, Kingsmen!"

Instantly, the ruler was upright on his throne. The wolves leaped forward, and a black cloud hissed toward the children. Eric fearlessly shouted, "In the name of the King, Lord of Light, STOP!"

The wolves hesitated, looking at Eric's sword, and the black cloud vanished. But the sorcerer swiftly came downward. Jodi, Rachael, Martin, and the waif roused themselves in time to see him striding down the steps with his robe flaring like great wings. As he came, an incredible change took place: The sorcerer began to grow!

At the base of his throne, he already was fifteen feet tall; in two paces more, he had grown to twenty. With each step, he shot upward and outward, losing his human face as he cast off his disguise and assumed his true form. Nebulas of sparks appeared where his eyes had been, and his face disappeared behind whirling tongues of fire. Flame came down as his breath as the evil being, now fifty or more feet tall, crowded the ceiling. Then, from under his billowing black robe, his arms became rivers of fire, and he drove fiery fists at the young people.

With sudden inspiration, Eric shouted, "The swords! Touch the tips together!"

The Kingsmen quickly united their swords; instantly, from the point where the blue flaming tips met, a solid, sizzling bolt of silver-white lightning shot upward. Shadows flew. The sorcerer leaped back, but the lightning struck him. Smoke fumed from his fiery face as backward he fell, shriveling.

"Runnn!!" Eric yelled. He sprinted from the building, followed by the waif, Martin, and the girls. Down the steps they ran as an explosion cracked the enormous stone roof and toppled many of the heavy columns. The sorcerer collapsed into a rising tower of sparks that blasted through the roof. From the wreckage dashed a frantic figure: Richard fleeing for his life. Behind him came two other forms: the hideous wolves.

When the roof fell with a tremendous groan, an explosion greater than the first blew the temple apart. Stone fragments thunderously rained down. Meanwhile, the children reached the main avenue and raced toward the northern mountains. Behind them bounded the fiery-eyed wolves, slinging glowing saliva from their mouths. And up from graves and crypts all around leaped demons and half-rotted ghouls with tattered clothing flapping, raving at their master's death.

Seeing the demons and ghouls leaping from each side, Eric and his companions ran faster than they would have dreamed they could! And when demons dashed into their path, Eric and Martin slashed them down with hardly a pause. The young people kept close together, guarding one another—until Martin suddenly stopped and looked back. With the "crossing-hands" stroke, he killed a ghoul leaping toward him . . . then thrust his sword through a spidery demon and stepped aside as the blackening body fell. Next, he surprised even himself: He went back to help Richard.

The wolves were snapping at Richard's head as he ran pell-mell in screaming terror. Martin stepped outside the path of the wolf on Richard's left side and neatly slashed its throat as it galloped past. It fell, tripping Richard. That event probably saved Richard's life, for the other wolf was about to tear off his head. By the time the remaining beast whirled and raced back, Martin had taken a stance over his cowering cousin. When the animal leaped, Martin did the only thing he could: He held his sword out before himself in both hands. The wolf fell upon the blade, which sank deeply into its chest. Martin was driven on top of Richard, but he did not hesitate. He leaped up, put one foot on the beast's body—which quickly was turning back to stone—and jerked his sword free. "Run, Richard!" he shouted above the din of screeching demons and ghouls. Richard did not need to be told twice. He ran after the Kingsmen, looking neither left nor right.

The entire necropolis now was awake, reddened with a fiery glow and canopied by gray smoke boiling up from the demolished temple. As the children slogged up the slopes toward the foothills, demons and ghouls shrieked after them. But as the fire within the temple died, so did the strength of the evil creatures. Fading glows marked the places where the demons returned into the dead soil, and dust blew from mounds where the ghouls crumbled. Soon, the entire valley settled into darkness and an eerie silence.

"So, you would have had the sorcerer's power?" Eric, breathing hard, asked Richard. Staring at the boy, Eric sheathed his sword.

"No . . . *no!*" Richard protested, shaking his head. "I only listened to him to stall for time, to try to save our lives!"

"Like Martin saved yours?" Eric asked.

Sullenly, Richard lowered his head and shuffled his feet.

"Speak up!" Eric commanded sternly.

Richard's lower lip came out a bit, then he whined, "Don't make me say it."

"Say it!" Eric ordered.

Richard, scuffling the road, muttered, "Thanks. And I'm sorry." He took a deep breath and added more freely, "I'm sorry for listening to that . . . that *thing's* voice . . . and for not believing in this King of yours."

"He's not just ours," Eric corrected. "Now, are you all right?"

"Yes," Richard said meekly, standing a bit straighter.

Eric looked questioningly at the waif, who nodded. "Good," Eric nodded. "Let's get away from this valley."

Martin and the girls sheathed their swords, and they all began walking up the dark road. Up through the foothills of the mountains north of Byzarnium they climbed in silence. Then, following switchback curves faintly silvered by starlight, they trudged up steep mountainsides into ever colder air. There, they were forced to stop each hundred feet or so to rest. It was during one of those rests that Rachael heard the most delicious sound she had heard in days. "Flowing water!" she announced, working her way along the almost vertical stone wall beyond the curve where they had stopped.

"Be careful!" Jodi called after her. As Jodi's voice echoed away, she glanced down the sheer cliff to the vague darkness below.

Rachael's footsteps scraped against rocks and grew fainter and fainter. The others dimly heard her clink a jar against rock. When she returned, she was smiling. In one hand she held a jar full of precious fluid—water! The Kingsmen and the waif restrained themselves—but Richard did not. He grabbed the jar and poured half of the water down his throat. Much of it sloshed onto his stained and ripped shirt. "Ahh," he sighed, lowering the jar. When he saw the others staring at him, he whined, "*Now* what's the matter?" Almost immediately, because he had drunk the cold water so quickly, his stomach began cramping, and he doubled over in pain.

"I'll go fill the other bottles," Eric said in a low voice.

"No, let me," Rachael said, unslinging her woven pack. "I can see well in the dark, and my feet know the way."

In three trips she filled all their bottles, even the ones they drained quenching their thirst. Then, exhausted and cold but satisfied, the young travelers huddled under their blankets and plummeted into sleep.

Hours later, hazy yellow light flooded over the six young people as they trudged down the far side of the mountains. Occasionally they stopped to rest and survey the boundless land before them.

Desert broken only by dry creekbeds and purple outcroppings of sharply shelving rock stretched for miles. Off in the distance to the north-northwest stood the ruins of a great, walled city. Far to the east were lines of red hills. Where the hills ended to the east-northeast began a range of dark mountains that marched northward out of sight. Halfway between those peaks and the youths was a large mesa. And above the northern horizon, beyond what seemed to be hundreds of miles of desert, hovered a shimmering band of blue and a faint line of green.

"Green!" Martin exulted, shading his eyes. "I don't believe it!"

"Is it an oasis?" Jodi wondered aloud.

"It's a mirage," Eric stated definitely, "but that person coming toward us is for real." He pointed.

They strained to see what his keen sight had detected. Finally, Martin cried, "Someone alone! I can see a dust trail."

Indeed, a thin plume of dust was rising from the desert twelve or so miles northward. Ahead of the dust, a lonely figure was moving very slowly.

"Come on; let's hurry and see who it is," Eric suggested, beckoning.

An hour of shuffling down the dusty road passed. Then—leaving the road when it veered westward—the young people spent another hour slipping and sliding down the talus slopes below the foothills. By noon, they were dragging along across the desert floor. Squinting into the bright, hot sunlight, they watched for the oncoming figure. It was nowhere to be seen—until they rounded a purple outcropping of rock.

"It's a fat old man," Martin cried, "wearing a brown, hooded robe!"

"He's on a burro," Rachael added, laughing, "one that's about half big enough for him."

"And he looks like he's asleep," Jodi observed, watching the dumpling of a man rocking slightly in time with the steps of his donkey.

The children hurried forward and surrounded the sleeping man and his gray and carmine-red burro. The animal came to a stop and waggled its tall ears at them. Then it bucked.

"Huh . . . um . . . what?" the man mumbled, opening his large, heavy-lidded eyes. The tip of his broad, white beard curled upward as he yawned. Then he stretched, and his pointed hood fell back, revealing a bush of hair so white that it almost glowed in the sunlight. "UmmmM!" he smiled, smoothing down the wrinkles of his loose brown robe. "Got it done?" he inquired, gazing at the young travelers.

"Do you mean, did we kill the sorcerer?" Eric asked.

The man drew back a bit. "Of course," he said casually.

"Well, yes, we did," Eric replied. "Or rather the King's power did."

The old man let his eyelids drift shut. "Good. I'm glad *that's* done." He blinked widely at the young people, and they noticed he had blue eyes beneath arched, brushy white brows. "I wasn't looking forward to dealing with *that* one, let me tell you! Did you find the spring all right?"

Puzzled, Rachael looked at Jodi, then went to the old man. "Yes," she said hesitantly, "but how did you . . ."

The old man winked slowly, shook back the loose sleeves of his robe, and reached behind himself to a saddlebag. The burro turned to watch as the man withdrew first a large old book, then a gemstone as big as his fist. The stone was milky blue and flashed with flecks of orange, yellow, and pale green. The thick book's worn leather cover had strange writing on it and was so large that when he opened it, it covered his ample lap. "Now let's see," he muttered, "which was it?"

The burro waggled his tall, furry left ear.

"Oh yes, you're right," the old man said happily, patting the donkey's thin neck. He held the gemstone into the sunlight and muttered a phrase of a strange language. While the young people watched open-mouthed, the colors within the stone began to swirl. Quickly, it became clear, and rays of sunlight caromed into it and refracted out, casting rainbows onto the sand. Then, in the stone, a rounded picture of Byzarnium formed. The old man peered closely at the center of the scene—where the blackened rubble of the temple lay—and nodded. "Yes, just as we hoped," he murmured.

"Who is *we?*" Martin inquired, patting the burro on the rump. The animal turned to glare at him. "You and the King?" Martin added hopefully, withdrawing his hand from the offended burro.

"*We* is *we . . . us,*" the old man repeated impatiently . . . then drew back. "Oh! You don't even known who *I* am!" He laughed gently and tipped himself forward politely. "I am Acuerias, a King's magician."

horses before smoothly swinging onto its saddle; she settled herself with obvious delight. Richard, with a suspicious look, awkwardly climbed onto another horse. Jodi and Eric helped the waif mount, then got onto the two remaining horses.

"That's better," Acuerias nodded, nudging the sides of Terserius. "On now to Espereim—capital of Eoramia and home of Queen Dorcas!" In a voice that jiggled with the steps of his trotting burro, he turned and added, "I hope your stay there—however brief—is enjoyable."

Eric loosed the reins of his horse and caught up with the burro. "Sir?" he asked, "Is it far? I mean, we've come a long way."

The magician, shaking with the donkey's steps, gently slapped himself on his broad, high forehead. "Of course!" he declared as though chiding himself. "How unthoughtful of me! I was to bring you *at once,* Queen Dorcas said." He stopped, reopened his book, then turned and smiled widely at the young travelers. "After all, you're to be accorded a heroes' welcome, for you've done what three armies in three years could not do . . . but you didn't know that, did you?"

Martin glanced at his astonished friends, then back at Acuerias. "Is that *all* we were called to do?" he inquired.

"Oh, no-no-no," Acuerias said quickly. "You've only proven that you can be of further service."

"You mean we've been through a test?" Jodi asked, stopping her horse.

The magician turned to look seriously at her. "Well, yes . . . and no. In any case, now that you've helped clear the southern skies of the Darkness, I can do as the queen commanded: bring you with all haste!" He found the proper incantation in his book and skyward called, *"A-Abba, y-oth Eoramia speth!"*

When Acuerias and Terserius vanished first, the children experienced a sinking feeling that they would be left after all to finish the trek alone. But then, the desert vanished from around them. They and their mounts began to soar through a dazzling whirl of red, green, and blue dots in a depthless white background.

When the whirl ceased, they found themselves galloping with Acuerias down a wide, grassy trail through a dark forest. They soon rounded a bend in the trail and saw an arch-like opening formed by two great trees. Through that opening, they could see a river valley, hills, and—in the distance and above the hilltops—a city that seemed filled with white towers. The riders emerged from the forest and began crossing the valley. To the left, between arms of forested hills, they saw fields untended and houses abandoned. To their right, the valley wandered a number of miles to a broad cliff. A rushing green river ran through the valley and disappeared over the cliff. There, a low, faint roar and a cloud of spray with a rainbow in it arose. Far beyond the cliff, the young people saw the Alamantian Ocean—*blue* . . . like the sky!

The blue startled them because they had become accustomed to the dusty yellow sky of Gueroness. Eric smiled at Jodi, and she grinned back. But had they been able to see the northern sky beyond the hills and city, they would not have been so happy; there, long fingers of thin, black clouds probed southward.

As the young travelers' horses trotted behind the fast-stepping Terserius, they approached a double-arched, white stone bridge spanning the river. With shouts of joy—as though they almost were home—Eric and Jodi urged their horses into a gallop.

"Wait!" Acuerias shouted. "The Leohtian guards don't know you!"

But Jodi and Eric were beyond hearing as they clattered across the bridge over the thundering water of River Limmwain.

Chapter 8

Heroes' Welcome

"Stop!" the old magician called, waving one hand vainly at the rapidly departing teen-agers.

In the excitement of their race, Eric and Jodi heard him not. Then suddenly, as they reached the edge of the hills, a wall of shimmering blue-white light perhaps fifty feet high shot up before them! Their horses shied, reared, and almost threw their riders. The wall appeared to be made of thousands of rod-shaped pieces of blue and white light; each rod seemed no more than a foot tall. As Martin and the others rode closer, they saw that the rods actually were small, armored creatures. The creatures were hovering stiffly, holding their arms and legs straight as they fitted tightly together to form a solid barrier.

By the time the magician reached the startled Eric and Jodi, the rods in the wall had begun to separate. Squads of tiny warriors flashed toward the humans. In rapid succession, the squads swirled around Eric and Jodi, then Martin and Rachael, and finally the waif and Richard. Richard ducked flat on his saddle and covered his head with both arms. The Leohtian squad nearest him dove with the obvious intention of attacking him.

"Alton! Oth-nath! Ya-se alanin!" Acuerias called, holding up his staff.

Slowly, suspiciously, the squad of creatures that had been about to plunge into Richard took up hovering positions. The children stared up at the creatures, noting that their bodies, swords, and armor were like sculptured blue crystal.

"What are *they?"* Eric inquired, trying to steady his horse.

"Leohtians, Guardians of Espereim," the magician replied, smiling gently at the small warriors. "They are the Light People . . . and you should be thankful you passed their test. Only in Richard did they find Darkness."

"What did you tell them about Richard?" Jodi asked.

"I said, 'Stop! Go not! He is a friend,' " Acuerias explained, "even though I, like the Leohtians, have my doubts about your cousin's loyalty." With a wave to the squad hovering over his head, Acuerias continued, "The captain of the Guard and his soldiers will escort us to Glimpalatyrn, the Castle of Espereim." Like a glittering blue cloud, the squad of Leohtians sped under the re-forming wall toward the hills ahead.

"Is everything here as mean as they are?" Richard asked as he kicked his horse to make it trot with the rest.

"Mean?" the magician repeated, turning to frown at the boy. "They are never *mean;* they are dangerous, however, to creatures who harbor the Darkness. When they meet even a bit of that force, they penetrate it. Our enemies cannot tolerate the entrance of light, so they die—as do the Leohtians who attack."

Richard almost sneered, but he thought better of it when he looked overhead and saw that the Leohtians still were eager to attack him. But, when he felt sure they were restrained by the magician's words, he said, "They don't *look* dangerous. Those wolves of Sarx . . ."

At the mention of the sorcerer's name, one of the Leohtians shot down and jabbed Richard in the rear with its sword. "OwwW!" the boy howled, lunging forward on his saddle. "Make him quit!" he wailed.

"Speak no more of evil!" Acuerias warned, clucking to Terserius.

Past thick woods, past flower-sprinkled meadows, and upward toward the magnificent city the group rode. As they drew nearer, they saw that Espereim's wall was built of polished white stones that curved outward at the top and flared outward at the bottom to join the brow of the hills. Inside the wall, the upper stories and steeply pitched, red-tiled roofs of houses and castles—also built of polished white stone—were visible. From the castles rose tapered towers with conical roofs high, high in the sky where pigeons wheeled in the sunlight. Jodi thought that the castles—especially the largest, grandest one in the center of the city—looked serene . . . and vulnerable. But if they were, the outer wall certainly was not.

It was thick, enormously tall, and pierced by one large gate. As Jodi looked at the gate, it ponderously opened. A company of soldiers—garbed in various kinds of uniforms and armor—galloped forth and swiftly raced down the road. Acuerias went ahead of the young people and waited for the leader of the soldiers to come to him.

"Greetings, victorious magician!" the leader called, lifting his open right hand in salute as his horse clattered to a stop beside Acuerias. He removed his worn, blue-and-white enameled helmet and glanced at the children.

"Greetings, Allumerian," Acuerias said, bowing slightly. "How goes the war?"

The man's expression clouded. "Not well, m'lord. However," he added with a faint smile, "the queen and all Espereim eagerly await your return! Famine, plague, and warfare will be forgotten for a time since already the celebration of your victory in Gueroness has begun!"

"Wait!" Acuerias quickly said as the soldiers began turning back toward the city. "It was not *I* who snatched victory from the closed jaws of defeat," he told the company. He turned and pointed to the Kingsmen. "*They* are the heroes." The soldiers stared silently, puzzled, as Acuerias casually asked their auburn-haired leader, "Fine lot, aren't they?"

"I suppose so," the officer agreed uncertainly. He urged his horse closer to the burro and leaned toward the magician. "But they are merely *children* . . . aren't they?" he whispered.

"Ah," Acuerias said loudly, "but see their armor!"

The officer nudged his horse and made it walk slowly around the Kingsmen. He returned to Acuerias amazed. "*Nathnor,*" he said reverently. "And from the workmanship, I'd say armor, shields, and swords were wrought by Thorinsheld!"

"They were presented their armor and weapons by the King himself," the magician explained so all the soldiers could hear, "so I would not question their value."

"Value!" the soldier exclaimed. "Why, that armor could buy . . ."

"No-no-no," Acuerias laughed, shaking his snowy head. "Not the metal, but *their* value—as warriors in the service of the King!"

The officer peered doubtfully at the young people.

"They slew Sarx," Acuerias added with a bemused smile.

"*They* killed the sorcerer who raised the demons?" the man repeated, dumbfounded. "Him who thrice defeated our armies?"

Acuerias nodded patiently, his eyes closed.

The leader drew back, openly happy. "Welcome then, bringers of hope and relief to Eoramia!"

To several soldiers, Acuerias said, "Go, spread the news that more Kingsmen have arrived—and that these are heroes!"

While the heralds raced ahead, the officer led the rest of the company at a processional pace toward the capital. The Kingsmen gathered around the magician, bubbling with questions.

"What's *nathnor?*" Martin asked. "And are we really heroes?"

"What did you mean by 'more' Kingsmen?" Eric wondered.

Rachael inquired, "What's an Allumerian?"

"And what did he mean by famine, plague, and warfare?" Jodi asked, looking around at the seemingly peaceful landscape.

"Wait! *Please* wait!" Acuerias laughed, holding up both hands. "All your questions will be answered in good time." He clucked to Terserius and looked toward the gate. Already, waving citizens were streaming out of the city. Acuerias resumed, "First, I can tell that the King has told you little about your armor. It, like your shields and swords, is forged of *nathnor,* an *extremely* rare metal in Eorthe. Small nodules of it are recovered by the Sea People from deep canyons in the Alamantian Ocean. Second . . . ah, what was your second question?"

"What's an Allumerian?" Rachael inquired.

"Oh, yes; well, Allumeria is a nation in northern

Rud. It was conquered by Go'drun, who in turn was killed by the northern sorcerer—causing many Allumerian soldiers to flee here. Here, they joined the remnants of the other armies of the once mighty Lords of the Swords—except those who fight on in Oraibi. Now," he sighed, "third? . . ."

"Are other Kingsmen in Espereim?" Eric asked.

"Yes," the magician replied, reaching for his great book. He turned to the Order of Call and read, "Lieutenant Andros and company of five from Greece." He nodded with satisfaction, put the book into his saddlebag, and added, "They arrived last week."

"And the famine, plague, and warfare?" Jodi inquired, frowning.

Acuerias sighed, looking toward the cheering crowds lining the city wall and thronging out the gateway. "As faith in the Light has faded, the Darkness has filled the vacuum. Crops wither; livestock are dying; people attacked by the Darkness sink into a sleep that leaves their bodies ashy. And either from choice or from fear, many of the tribes and war lords joined the sorcerers in spreading warfare from the north and the south. Your coming has freed Gueroness, but attacks from the north will continue —and probably increase now that the Lightning in the Bottle has been stolen."

Eric exchanged a puzzled look with Jodi, then said, "But we were told that someone named Prince Morgan had been sent to protect it."

They rode up the final slope, entered the shadow of the wall, and followed the soldiers and the darting Leohtians through the gateway into the city. As the young people and Acuerias rode their horses up the house- and shop-lined main avenue, the cheers of the crowd grew louder . . . but Acuerias's words became sadder. "Prince Morgan's fate is not known, but we fear he died after sounding the warning call from Alamantia. In any case, it was necessary that you Kingsmen be brought with all speed. Frankly, we need your faith."

It dawned on Eric then what the rest of their mission must be. "Are we . . . are the Kingsmen going to help rescue the Lightning in the Bottle?"

Acuerias leveled a sad, hard look at him. "Nothing in this world . . . nay, nothing in this *Age,* could be more important. You see, if we—the remaining believers—do not regain possession of the Lightning, there is no hope for Eorthe; neither the King nor Abba will interfere if we do not maintain our promise to keep faith. And if Prince Morgan is dead, so also has died our hope, for he and he alone was given the responsibility of releasing the Lightning from its bottle to drive out the Darkness and prevent the return of Inglo . . . of the Lord of Darkness."

Eric suddenly understood the great responsibility that the King was offering him and his companions. He looked at Jodi and saw that she, too, understood. Rachael was smiling, her rather broad shoulders squared, and Martin simply looked awed. Richard was grinning at the cheering crowd, and the waif was doing all he could just to hang onto his mount.

Eric straightened; he felt better now, knowing what the main objective of their mission was to be. He had had difficulty, as he was sure the others had had, simply forging ahead in the strange, hostile environment of Gueroness. But now that he knew their ultimate goal, and knew it to be a vital one, he felt much better. He and the others began to take note of the people lining the avenue. Arms reached toward them, and the Kingsmen reached back to shake hands. An electric feeling was in the handshakes, for both sides realized the importance of the Kingsmen's arrival.

The soldiers leading the group turned from the

main avenue and began leading the way up narrow streets to the castle that crowned the city. The Kingsmen soon noticed that despite joyful shouts, many of the adults and children along the streets were hungry-looking and hollow-eyed. Many wore tattered clothing. Many were wounded. The worst were soldiers whose bodies were partially blackened by a dreadful looking disease.

The Kingsmen forced themselves to smile and wave at the wretched people, whom they assumed to be mainly refugees. But their hearts sank at the thought of what had made the people of Espereim the way they were. For the Earth children, it was a staggering experience to look into the refugees' eyes, especially the children's. Never before had they *seen* the effects of war.

First one woman, then others broke from the throng and ran alongside Jodi's and Rachael's horses, crying, *"Orodon! Orodon ne-gloral Gueroness!"*

"What're they saying?" Jodi asked Acuerias, staring in amazement at a crying woman who took her right hand and kissed it reverently.

"They say, 'Thank you! Thank you for healing Gueroness,' which is their land," the magician explained above the crowd's noise.

"Tell them . . ." Jodi began.

"A-Abba conseroth seu!" he told the women and the crowd, speaking as a respected teacher would. The people murmured, bowing to the Kingsmen.

The young people and their group soon reached the magnificent castle that rose from the tallest hill of the city. By then they were above the level of the surrounding castles and could see the black clouds probing down from the north. But the sky behind the main castle was open and blue, implying a hope as soaring as the grand towers of Castle Glimpalatyrn.

The young people followed their guides through a

gateway into the first courtyard of the castle. There, they were flanked by rows of colorfully dressed knights; the tops of the walls around the courtyard were lined with soldiers who were saluting with their weapons. Filling the center of the courtyard were waving ladies and gentlemen.

The magician and his group entered another courtyard; it was even more crowded than the first. Looking up, the Kingsmen had a clear view of the seven, fine, white towers arising from the queen's castle. From one of the towers burst a fanfare of trumpets. A hush spread. A door opened high above flights of broad, white steps. Courtiers hastened out and took positions along either side of the stairs. Then, like a yellow flame in a slender white cloud, a lady appeared, and Eric's heart began beating faster.

"The queen . . . the queen!" people shouted. "Queen Dorcas is coming!"

"*She'll* send back the Darkness," someone called confidently.

From atop the stairs, the queen held her scepter toward the citizens in recognition. They cheered as the regal figure descended. Footmen helped the young people dismount. It was then that Jodi and Rachael saw how weakened the waif had become, for he sagged from his horse and would have fallen had not a footman caught him. The girls looked at each other, suddenly realizing what an ordeal the journey must have been for the wounded boy, though he had not once complained. Jodi was so concerned about him that she almost didn't see the others bowing to the queen as she stopped before them.

"Welcome, Children of the Light," Queen Dorcas said graciously.

"Thank you, your Majesty," Eric managed to say, bowing again.

"Come and be refreshed," the lady said, holding

out one arm so Eric could take it and walk with her up the stairs. "When you have bathed and changed clothes, you may join the victory banquet in the Hall of the Throne—though I fear our fare may seem poor in your eyes."

As he took her arm, Eric blushed, glancing at Jodi and Martin. Smelling the queen's delicate fragrance and sensing her warmth, Eric felt as if he were ten feet tall. Behind him, Martin and Jodi, then Rachael and Richard came slowly. Two footmen began to carry the waif toward another part of the castle, and the girls turned to watch them with concerned looks. Queen Dorcas, seeing their expressions, said, "Please do not worry about your companion; he will be well cared for."

After the other young people and their royal escort had gone far into the castle and had been greeted by hundreds of courtiers and attendants, the queen left them in the care of the castle butler. He led them to a long, narrow room lined with twelve beds; there, he watched attendants provide each youth with new, dark green clothes and sleeping gowns, soft leather boots, and cotton towels. Then, the butler took the young people to the baths—broad, stone pools of steaming, fragrant water—and asked them to be prepared for the banquet in "one-half turning of the glass," which Eric interpreted to mean one hour. With that, they were left to soak in the hot water.

Anxious to eat, they were ready before the hour was up and followed servants into a huge hall in the central part of the castle. Its ceiling rose into shadows above rows of columns carved with stone leaves and topped with stone flowers. Rows of down-tilted flags filled the spaces between the columns. The broad, stone floor was lined with tables; each table was lined with chatting guests.

Richard was taken to a table on the hall floor while

the Kingsmen were led to the low platform across the front of the hall; on the platform, a number of people were seated behind a long table. Behind the center of the table sat Queen Dorcas on a pale gold throne. Its tall back was covered with a tracery of leaf and flower designs, and it was canopied with white cloth. From her throne, Queen Dorcas overlooked the hall like sunlight come to rest.

Jodi followed the other Kingsmen onto the platform, where they were seated to the right of the queen. Looking out over the crowd, Jodi saw that Richard already had begun to stuff himself. Jodi then turned her attention to the queen . . . and noticed the tall, ruggedly handsome lord with thick, dark blond hair seated to her left. Dorcas saw Jodi's admiring gaze and leaned over to quietly say, "He is my brother, the Duke of Corlis, Mark Mansbridge."

In a while, as Jodi took several thin slices of meat from a platter being offered her, she heard the duke ask his sister, "Will you announce the Foregathering now?"

The queen nodded, even as Jodi impetuously asked, "Will the King join us for the . . . whatever it was?"

Dorcas smiled at Jodi, who regretted her rashness but saw no reproach in the lady's eyes. The queen said, "We shall hope to see the King soon, for never have we needed his presence more."

Martin leaned onto the table and nodded to his left. "Your Majesty, who are the others down there?"

She turned slowly and looked, then spoke softly but distinctly, "The armored youth is Lieutenant Andros. The young men beyond him also are Kingsmen. All of you from now on will be under the command either of my brother, the Duke of Corlis, or of General Talaman, who is seated just beyond that man dressed in brown with the brown beard."

"Waymond!" Jodi cried, pushing back her chair. She ran to the man in brown, threw open her arms, and hugged him as he, standing to take her in his arms, smiled hugely.

"Oh, Waymond!" she said. "We were afraid we'd never see you again!"

The magician solemnly shook hands with Martin, Eric, and Rachael as they came in turn to greet him. "I'm *awfully* glad to see the lot of you," Waymond told them, sitting. "I asked to come south this time, but I was sent to bring Lieutenant Andros and his company." He nodded toward the armored boy, who had black, curly hair, olive-tanned skin, and a forthright look. Waymond then smiled at Jodi. "I understand that not only did you arrive in good order, but that you've successfully performed the first part of your mission." He winked one brown eye and stamped one tall, brown boot. "I'm proud of you!"

They nodded, embarrassed because many of the nearby banqueters were staring at them. Eric then went to the Kingsman called Andros. He stuck out his sword arm to shake hands. "Eric Vanover," he said.

The youth, instead of shaking hands, snapped to attention and riveted his black eyes upon Eric's. "Lieutenant Constantine Andros, at the King's service!" Then, as Eric blinked twice, the youth relaxed, stuck out his hand, and shook Eric's hand warmly. He laughed, flashing rows of bright white teeth from his rather thin, angular face.

Andros proceeded to introduce his Kingsmen. "The tall one is Zorfu," he said, smiling more or less toward Jodi, "and the twins are Lykstros and Dastros; the big one is Angonimus, and the little one is Mykos."

Eric shook hands with each of the other Kingsmen, talked briefly with them, then went back to Waymond. "Will we be going with you from now on?" Eric asked, delighted to see his old friend and teacher.

"No . . . I'm afraid not. Tomorrow, there will be a Foregathering of War. As you may know, Prince Morgan has not been heard from since his warning came out of Alamantia. Therefore, we must plan a divided attack—one which . . . well, you shall hear it all in the morning." He beamed at the young people, his eyes twinkling merrily. "Lark lessons and mice musings, it's good to see you again!" he stated. "I'm *glad* you answered the call."

"Did you blow the Horn of Meet?" Martin asked, leaning against him.

"Not this time. Another magician—Master Slyne of the North—did."

After talking with Waymond a while longer, Eric and his companions returned to their seats. They hardly had finished eating when they were startled by a flourish of trumpets. Silence fell.

The queen stood, hands folded before herself, and announced, "Will those of you called to the Foregathering please come to the Chamber of Al-Calahcazad at the third turning of the glass in the morn watch. I thank all of you for coming to this celebration of the King's victory in Gueroness." Smiling, she bowed slightly to Eric and his companions as applause rippled across the hall. "Go now," the queen resumed to the crowd, "and share the good news among our people, for they will have need of hope tonight . . . and in the time to come."

Chapter 9

Foregathering of War

Servants carrying lighted candles showed the young people back to their long, narrow room. Two of the twelve beds had been partitioned off for Jodi and Rachael by a colorful folding screen. The servants remained, lighting the room with their candles, until the children had put on their new gowns and climbed into bed.

While moonlight from tall, narrow windows behind them poured silver shafts over their blankets, the young people lay listening to the sounds of celebration within the castle and from the city beyond. As they drifted into sleep, Jodi and the others felt good to have had a part in making the citizens and refugees happy—if even for a short while. Then, remembering the one empty bed in the room, Jodi wondered about the waif; she prayed he soon would be healed.

In the morning, a trumpet's clear song penetrated the room and woke the children. They hurried across cold stone floors to the steamy baths. After they had bathed, dressed, and eaten, an attendant in yellow livery led Richard away, saying that "the lady" wished to talk with him later. Another attendant led the Kingsmen to the main hall where they joined a colorful stream of people moving through a large, arched doorway. The doors, opened wide, looked to Jodi like matching wings . . . and she caught her breath when she entered the Chamber of Al-Calahcazad.

The pale walls—decorated with a band of colored stone petals—soared to a pointed dome ceiling. In the center of the windowless chamber was a large, highly polished table, and around it were perhaps two hundred chairs with high, rectangular backs. Except for the table, chairs, and a dozen or so candle stands, the chamber was unfurnished. It echoed with footsteps, people talking, chairs scraping on the rose-colored floor, and the clank of scabbards as men sat down.

Martin slowly entered the chamber, staring at tall, silent warriors, elaborately uniformed officers, and grim-faced lords; he assumed from the colorful variety of their clothes that they were of many nationalities. He also saw the three magicians, each with a staff; all of them were dressed in plain brown robes belted with golden chains. Martin of course knew Acuerias and Waymond, so he assumed the third magician was Master Slyne of the North.

To Martin, Slyne looked like a brown stone tower with rounded shoulders; his almost neckless, bald head seemed both tanned and oiled. Martin watched Slyne gaze over the crowd, and he saw that the magician's eyes were cold gray and piercing. Altogether, he gave the appearance of a man of great power who would be unmoved by anything. His staff—which he held upright in his right hand—was tall, thick, and black. Martin whispered to Eric, "I'd hate for him to turn his staff on me!"

As though he had heard, Slyne glanced at Martin, and his gray eyes flashed briefly with a blue sparkle.

Jodi, like her brother, had been staring at the crowd; she saw that not all the members of the Foregathering were men—nor did they all appear human. As an attendant led her and the other Kingsmen to chairs, she noticed four creatures who were about as tall as she was. They had broad-fingered, partially webbed hands; just below their peculiar ears were pink-red gills that quivered as the creatures breathed. They wore flowing, emerald green robes over which hung glossy, golden capes. When one of the creatures felt Jodi's gaze, she turned, blinked yellow eyes, and smiled. Embarrassed, Jodi smiled in return as she took her seat.

Eric and Lieutenant Andros were seated beside Rachael and Martin. Across the table from them was an old woman dressed in a loose black robe. A black cowl half hid her short, gray hair and her weathered face. Rachael noted that around her neck she wore a golden chain on which hung a large, blue jewel. From the jewel glistened a strong, blue light.

Rachael beckoned to an attendant, and he leaned close. "Who is that woman in black?" Rachael asked him.

"Queen Sybra Walun," the attendant answered, "the widow of King Tyzar; until recently she was a captive of Go'drun, the conqueror of Rud."

Martin leaned over to ask, "And who is this General Talaman?"

The attendant looked toward the side of the table farthest from the doors and briefly pointed to a large, swarthy man seated beside Queen Dorcas. The man's uniform was dark purple, gold trimmed, with high blades at the shoulders; his bristly beard was as black as his hard, bright eyes. "He is not a Lord of the Swords," the attendant said, sniffing. "He is a war lord who adopted the Faith of the Light. His home was Gueroness, but he came to rule Ispenth in Lord Baldwin's absence. And now he is Supreme Commander of the Armies of Eoramia."

The noise faded when Queen Dorcas stood between

the Duke of Corlis and General Talaman and announced, "As a prelude to the Foregathering, please listen to a delegation of refugees." She motioned, and a group of tattered, gaunt people came hesitantly into the chamber.

Their eyes, Martin saw, said more about their plight than did the pitiable tales they told. While they took turns speaking, Martin noticed a shadowy shape lurking near the rear of the refugee group. The shape appeared to be an old woman dressed in black, but Martin got the feeling that she was decidedly unhuman. When the delegation of refugees finished its appeal and bowed out of the chamber, Martin saw that the shadowy shape remained.

"If I could have your attention," General Talaman called in a deep voice, "I wish to express our sympathy for the unhappy people who have pled their needs before us—but I remind you: They cannot be helped unless the northern sorcerer is defeated! Let the Foregathering of War continue! Leohtians, advance!"

Through the arched doorway flashed a number of the blue light creatures. Most approached the general, but several swerved to his left—toward the shadowy creature, whom no one else but Martin seemed to have noticed. However, when the queen and the magicians saw that the Leohtians' intention was to attack the "woman," the queen cried a warning and the magicians leveled their staffs. But before the Light People or magicians could act, the shadow shape rose up and thundered, "Make not a move, you flies of light, else your queen be struck dead!"

Council members fell back as a black mist began to stream from the shadowy creature. "I have come," she hissed, "to offer you the terms of your surrender: You are to give yourselves body and soul to Jabez, son of Ingloamin, whose power is nigh unto completion. Soon, our Lord Ingloamin himself will return! What say you, you last sad lovers of a dead past and a powerless King? Will you willingly bow now or submit later . . . in agony?"

No words were spoken in answer. The shadow creature took the silence as a refusal of her terms, and abruptly the black mist gathered and shot toward Queen Dorcas. Instantly, the magicians sent lightning streaming—first to intercept the shadow being's attack, then to flash toward the attacker. But with a sinister laugh, she disappeared in an implosion of gray smoke. Soot drifted from the air where she had been standing.

Nearby Foregathering members climbed up from the floor, brushing themselves, as a general commotion broke out. The Duke of Corlis and several others stepped from in front of Dorcas Evnstar as the Leohtians swarmed around the room. The magicians calmly sat down.

When the council members were more or less quiet, Queen Dorcas shakily said, "That, my friends, was Leilamar, Shadow Guardian and child bearer for Ingloamin." Having named the danger, Dorcas made her way out of the chamber. As the queen walked, she held one hand over a large, yellow-glowing jewel that hung around her neck on a golden chain. She seemed to be absorbing light from it, for her slim, white hands and wrists were taking on the glow even as the chamber doors closed.

General Talaman thumped on the table with his heavy scabbard. Voices faded to whispers, then fell silent. "Having seen how crafty the Enemy can be, and having made certain no other Darkness is with us," he said, looking at the peacefully hovering Leohtians, "we can proceed. Captain Thrumingold, please report!"

One of the blue forms darted to Acuerias and hovered beside the old man's snowy-maned head. The magician cocked his head and cupped a hand behind one ear as he listened to the Leohtian's faint, humming voice. Then Acuerias began to translate: "Captain Thrumingold tells me good news: Leohtian scouts at last have located the Lightning in the Bottle!"

When applause and cheering burst out, Acuerias raised his hands and dampened the clamor with a frown. "But of the two thousand Leohtians sent north, only four so far have returned—and that fact possibly gives us an estimate of the Enemy's power. However, the bottle *has* been located." He bent to one side to listen to the light-rod warrior, then translated: "It is in a cave, in Tavares . . . under the Volcanoes of Tava."

"That's in the middle of the Mother of the Sky Mountains!" groaned an older man.

"We never can reach it there," a warrior stood to declare. He braced his legs and fidgeted with his iron breastplate. "Not in a hundred years!"

An Allumerian in an elegant blue and white uniform stood. "Are we sure the bottle is worth risking our remaining soldiers, much less the expense involved?"

He was overridden by a chorus of voices shouting, "Yes!"

A lord in a red robe embroidered in black slowly rose and waited for silence. The members of the Foregathering turned to listen to him, for he was To'bol, a lord of Smy'ra, and recently had come from the northern war. "We dare not openly set foot on Rud," he stated. "The ancient beasts, the southern Trogs, the renegade Kidronites, the Fearsors, the Obnars of Torang, and other unlikable creatures now roam freely under the pall of the Darkness that spews from the volcanoes. All who resist are blackened with the disease and fall to ashes."

"What about the Caves of Rainath?" someone asked. "Couldn't we attack through those ancient ways?"

To'bol shook his black-ringleted head. "They, too, are guarded—by servants of the sorcerer who actually travel through the rivers of fire."

Stillness followed his words, and despair was evident.

"We *must*, however," stated Queen Sybra Walun, "retake the bottle, or your land—nay, *all* lands—will become as enthralled and barren as mine!"

"Rubbish!" an aging general from Ispenth growled, rising to twist the ends of his silvery-brown mustache. "All you Walunlanders are alike. You simply were too weak!"

"I would ask you," a deep voice soothingly began, "who is certain that the Darkness must be fought?" All eyes turned to the speaker, a slender man dressed in a brown, black-striped robe. The council members knew by looking at his robe that he and his followers were from Tsur, a land west of Armazil, and they had heard him called Lord Ghazi. Silence came as the lord spoke again. "We of the desert tribes have not been harmed by the Darkness. It is, we have learned, even comfortable, being a great relief from Tschuma, which you call the Sun. Surely, Queen Sybra, you who once honored darkness would acknowledge that the Darkness is cruel only to those who fear or resist it." Ghazi ignored the Leohtians who began gathering over his head and continued, "Furthermore, we have not found the Master of Tavares unkind. He has left us our horses, our tents, our springs. Our women no longer are afraid to enter Omcrac, the Great Desert, by day to find the patches of quick-fleeting grass for our herds. Thus, I argue that the Ruler of Tavares is the only power present on Eorthe with the ability to rule all other powers . . . and bring peace to our world!"

"Enough!" shouted Queen Sybra, rising to cast a powerful gaze around the chamber. She touched her look upon each of the members, then spoke again. "My people lie as dead because of that Shadow Guardian's son! As lords Ghazi and To'bol say, the Darkness *comes,* though you who have remained comfortably here in Espereim may not yet feel it. But those who still remain free of it would do well indeed to prevent its coming to you next . . . *even,*" she shouted to quench a swelling clamor, "if it means sacrificing your families and all your precious wealth!" As she sat down, voices erupted like water from a burst dam.

The debate raged for hours. Could Tavares be attacked? Should it be? Was Jabez the new ruler of Eorthe, or did the victory in Gueroness mean that the Lord of Light was still all-powerful? These and countless smaller questions were flung back and forth, and the answers were few. The debate went on so long that the bewildered young Eartheans began to nod off to sleep. They awoke only when General Talaman began banging on the table with his scabbard.

"This is what will be done!" the general shouted. "We *will* go north to reclaim the Lightning in the Bottle. Those of you who will join us, do so; those who do not wish to fight for the Light, go now and forever more from these courts!" Voices murmured, but no one left. "Magician Slyne will lead the Kingsmen under Lieutenant Andros, and half the Allumerians, Tsur tribesmen, Smy'ranites, and other northlanders. They will cross Rud from the east and attack Tavares from the north.

"Queen Dorcas has expressed a desire to accompany her brother and magician Acuerias to break the siege of Darkness we assume has befallen Alamantia. Some of the Kingsmen, part of the Leohtians, the

Eoramians, the Gueroness and Oraibi refugee warriors, and Sea People pilots will go with Queen Dorcas, as will lords To'bol and Ghazi and their retainers."

A murmur of agreement answered him, and he went on quickly. "I myself will lead the third arm of our attack directly to Armazil. Magician Waymond and I will take the balance of the Kingsmen, Leohtians, Allumerians, and other northlanders with Queen Sybra and her warriors. Queen Eliadenor and some of her Sea People have agreed to guide us to the Lakes of Yore, where we shall establish an outpost. There, we will await the arrival of Queen Dorcas and, hopefully, Prince Morgan. United, we will drive north to join Master Slyne in a pincer attack against the sorcerer. AGREED?"

"YES!" thundered the reply.

But To'bol and Ghazi looked at each other and at others who remained silent. "A very commendable plan," To'bol said with a hint of irony. "Very bold and daring—and totally obvious to the northern sorcerer."

Solemnly, General Talaman ignored the criticism, saying only, "I deeply regret that so many of our forces and allies already have fallen. What troops are left are, I admit, woefully few to accomplish all we must do. Therefore, we each must constantly bear in mind for whom we fight. Let the Light reign in each of you!"

A cheer arose as weapons were thrust high. The cheer then faded. In the calm came a clear voice, that of Queen Dorcas, who had returned to stand in the doorway: "May the power of the King go with us!"

The members of the Foregathering filed respectfully past the queen to receive her blessing. Jodi and Eric saw quite plainly that not all had been strengthened by the general's words or comforted by the queen's.

On faces fair and dark, young and old, were frowns of doubt—though most bore expressions of resolve and confidence. Jodi saw that each person who passed the queen listened to gentle words and took from her the gift of a single green leaf. When Jodi took her leaf and bowed to the queen, she saw that it was a grapevine leaf and smelled like those from the King's throne.

Eric, Jodi, Martin, and Rachael wandered slowly through the splendid castle. They ignored the tall, oval windows of colored glass and the fine columns and tapestries adorning the walls, for they were absorbed in a discussion. They especially were concerned with how the Kingsmen would be divided. Talking quietly, they began to climb the stairway of a tower.

"Well, if we have to split up," Jodi said, "I want to go with Waymond. I know him, and I'd feel safe with him."

"Me, too," Rachael agreed.

Martin seemed undecided; he sighed, looking from Jodi to Eric.

Eric was frowning. "I'd rather go with Acuerias."

"Why?" Jodi asked sharply, "So you can be near Queen Dorcas?"

"Partly," Eric allowed. "But I'd also like to try to rescue this Prince Morgan everyone keeps mentioning. And I feel drawn to Acuerias."

"I figured you'd go with Waymond," Rachael said, stopping on the steeply spiraling stairs, "since you two are old friends."

"We are," Eric nodded, "but . . ."

"But he'd rather go try to rescue a prince than be with us girls," Jodi said with a teasing smile. "Ever since I've known him, the only things he's been interested in are camping, adventures, and history!"

"If you're through explaining me," Eric retorted,

"I'll ask you a question: Are you jealous because I want to help Queen Dorcas, or are you hurt because I don't want to go with you?" He gazed steadily at her.

"Maybe both," she said with a shy smile.

They turned and looked down the tower's stairwell as footsteps hurriedly approached them. Breathing hard, an attendant stopped on a step just below Martin. "The queen . . . requests all of you to attend her . . . in the garden." He pointed out a thin window in the tower side.

The Kingsmen went to the narrow slit and looked down. Below, covering perhaps five acres, was the most peaceful, lovely garden they ever had seen. The young people hardly noticed, at first, that the afternoon light was dim.

Beds of layered, colorful flowers curved among sweeping lawns, clusters of trees, and winding gravel paths, all enclosed by a high wall. The paths converged on a broad, circular white fountain. The fountain was not flowing, and water lay calmly in the pool at the base. At one side of the pool was a lipped outlet above a dry, white stone streambed. On the side of the fountain opposite the streambed was an arbor covered with a vigorously growing grapevine. Two of the queen's servants were carrying the waif into the shade of the grapevine. Richard trailed behind the attendants, followed by Queen Dorcas, the Duke of Corlis, and the three magicians.

The four Kingsmen, knowing that something important must be about to take place, rushed down the tower steps past the attendant who had come for them.

Chapter 10

Prayer of the Jeweled Queens

Jodi and her companions joined Lieutenant Andros and his Kingsmen—who were being led by a foot soldier in blue—as they all turned to go down a corridor. Jodi nodded absently to Andros, then looked ahead at the double doors barring the hall. The doors were made of red wood carved with a tracery of vines and flowers and the phrase, *A-ABBA CONSEROTH SEU.* The foot soldier pushed open the doors, revealing the garden. To Jodi, the place smelled and looked ancient, yet freshly new. She took Eric's hand as they went outside.

But while Jodi was looking at the garden, Rachael was looking upward. "What's happened to the sky?" she wondered aloud.

The young people stopped and stared where Rachael was pointing. Grayness was filling the lower atmosphere. High above the grayness, long rows of black clouds drifted from the northeast. The clouds were similar to the northers Eric and Jodi were familiar with back home, but this black cold front was more ominous.

"So," the foot soldier behind them muttered, "the spoutings of Tava reach even to Eoramia." With a solemn bow, he closed the doors.

The Kingsmen hurried toward the center of the garden, feeling chilled and anxious. Seeing Jodi hand in hand with Eric, Lieutenant Andros dropped back to walk beside Rachael, whose large dark eyes he admired. "Wonder what's happening?" he asked with a gallant smile.

She admired his smile, but before she could hazard an answer they entered the arbor. There, under the profusion of dark green leaves, they were met by Queen Dorcas. She showed them to a semicircle of benches carved in the shape of whales. The waif was lying on one bench, on his stomach, covered by a blanket. Jodi went directly to him; she knelt, wet a finger, and held it before his ashy, parted lips. "He's still breathing," she told the others as she stood.

Richard was sitting nearby, swinging his heels against the underside of his bench. His arms were folded, and he seemed to be pouting.

"What's wrong with *him?*" Andros whispered to Rachael.

Richard overheard him and muttered, "While the rest of you have been having all the fun, *I've* been stuck with that old teacher, learning 'manners.' " He jutted his rather sharp chin toward Queen Dorcas.

Dorcas smiled and said, "We'll begin something special as soon as the others arrive." She looked at Rachael and Jodi with tranquil, sea-green eyes, then turned and gazed toward the castle.

Before long, the red wood doors opened and the "others"—Queen Sybra Walun and a lady of the Sea People—came into the garden. Jodi could not keep from staring at the latter's large yellow eyes, peculiar ears, and trembling gills. Otherwise, Jodi noted, she was humanlike—even beautiful, with delicate lips, rosy-golden skin, and short silvery-blond hair. Her strikingly feminine figure was robed in a shimmering green gown. On a gold chain around her neck she wore a large jewel that flashed with rays of rich green light.

Queen Dorcas went to greet the others, saying, "Thank you, Queen Sybra and Queen Eliadenor, for coming so quickly. I would have waited until the appointed time, but . . ." She glanced skyward to call attention to the encroaching gray haze and the high-flying rows of black clouds. "Please join me, all of you, around the fountain."

Holding out her hands she led everyone except the waif and his attendants to stand in a circle around the lower basin of the fountain. The pool was perhaps twenty feet in diameter, and from its center rose seven smaller basins.

"Now, queens of Eorthe, Sisters of the Jewels of Powers Begatting," Dorcas murmured when all hands were linked, "pray as we were taught." The Jewels flamed: the blue of Sybra, the green of Eliadenor, and the yellow of Dorcas. Quickly and completely a hush fell over the garden as light spread from the Jewels. In a soft, clear voice, Dorcas began to sing *"Efil Espere"*:

Lightning ever bright
from blue sky you shone;
banishing Man's night,
we cling to you alone.

Come into our lives,
help us make our mark,
though our ears hear lies
and all the world be dark.

Clear light shining bright,
help us now be brave;
help us do the right,
for it's your love we crave. . .

Her words faded into a cool breeze that sprang up, rustling the leaves of the grapevine. Dorcas seemed asleep as the other queens sang the song in their own languages. Jodi, meanwhile, watched the pool . . . and she became puzzled when it darkened. When the water began to swirl with shadows, she became frightened. Tightly, she gripped Eric's hand on her right and Martin's on her left.

Barely breathing, the queens, magicians, and Kingsmen stared into the swirling pool—which soon began to show a clear scene of giant thunderstorms billowing upward. The Kingsmen looked at the sky, thinking that what they had seen in the pool was merely a reflection; but the sky was gray, streaked black from the northeast. The young people then realized that the scene in the pool was some kind of vision or prediction.

Jodi looked again at the pool and jumped back slightly when a mighty bolt of lightning split the billowing thunderclouds. The lightning crackled again and remained as a silver glow. Next, a white, flame-wrapped figure came from the brightest part of the lightning's glow. The figure slowly grew in size, holding his shimmering hands wide apart.

"It's the King!" Jodi cried. "He *is* coming!"

"A-Abba seimt!" Queen Eliadenor whispered excitedly, speaking for the first time. The other queens echoed her words.

Eric squeezed Jodi's hand and nodded at Richard. Her cousin was staring open-mouthed, and Eric figured he was fighting an inner battle: Was this a dream-image, or was it real? But Richard gradually lost his confused expression and began to look hopeful—as though he were praying that the King's coming was real.

Quite suddenly, the fountain pool became wind-ruffled and gray. At the same time, in the sky overhead, black thunderclouds rushed across Eoramia as the cold front from the northeast struck. Dark fingers of fog sank in among the towers of the castles, and the garden looked as though night had come upon it. The sixteen watchers gasped and held hands tightly as a chilling wind swept over them, fluttering their hair and garments and thrashing the garden trees.

Then, lightning flashed, splitting many miles of the blackened sky. Jodi winced, expecting a deafening clap of thunder. Instead, the lightning's glow remained as an aura directly above the watchers. Closer came the glow, sliding downward and increasing in size and intensity. Jodi felt a powerful sensation that the light was coming down to somehow rescue her from darkness. She began to smile . . . and her smile widened when she saw a figure emerge from the center of the approaching glow. The figure was a man—as in the fountain's vision—and he was holding out his arms. When Jodi saw plainly that the warmly shining figure indeed was the King, she felt pure, soaring joy.

"A-Abba seimt," murmured the queens. *"A-Abba seimt!"*

As the King's radiance spread over the group, light spread throughout the sky from one focal point directly overhead. The Darkness above the garden, the city, and indeed above all Eoramia faded into nothingness.

Watching the Darkness fade, Jodi looked at the focal point of the light—even as the others lowered their eyes. Suddenly, the point opened, and Jodi was dazzled by a brilliance of white light far brighter than the sun. In that glimpse into brilliance, she saw something which filled her body with stillness and her mind with silence. She sagged, supported by Eric and Martin.

Meanwhile, the King, clothed in white flame, had

come to rest upon the ground. He entered the circle of watchers between Dorcas and Sybra, smiling gently at them. Slowly, his glow diminished. Above him, the light in the sky faded from white to pale blue, then to deep blue. Birds began to sing in the garden, and a warm, southerly breeze sprang up—as Jodi repeatedly blinked, trying to look at the King.

He held his right hand toward the top of the fountain, and from the uppermost basin a silver-clear liquid began to flow. The liquid filled and overflowed each lower basin, splashing finally from the outlet in the bottom pool and running down the white stone streambed.

The King then turned to Dorcas and the other two queens. He seemed to communicate with them through his look, for they each soon nodded and bowed to him. The King next looked at each of the other people in the circle, and his gaze remained the longest upon Richard, who was staring with his mouth open. Smiling because the King's warmth had filled them, the people in the ring unclasped hands. When Richard's hands were released, he gave a slight cry and dropped to the gravel.

The King went and helped him stand, but the boy hung his head, shamed by the boundless love he had seen in the King's eyes. In Richard's head, his "other" voice quickly began to defend itself, trying to convince him that the King surely would punish him severely for having talked with the demons and Sarx. The King, however, drew the boy close against his side and led him toward the arbor. The others gathered nearby.

Gently, the King removed the blanket covering the waif's back and exposed his black, putrefying dart wounds. Firmly, the King took Richard's dirty hands and wiped them on his spotless white robe. The dirt,

Richard saw with amazement, left not one stain. Then the King held Richard's trembling hands upon the back of the unmoving waif.

Transfixing Richard with a steady, open gaze, the King softly said, "Love is the only way you must deal with others. Let me show you."

Richard's hands began to glow, and the light therefrom shone over the waif's back. The open, stinking holes gradually vanished, and the boy's skin became healthy once more. Awakening, rid of the pain and poison, he looked rapturously at Richard, then at the King. Tears began to flow down his cheeks. He made no move, seeming content to look into the King's eyes.

To Richard, the King whispered, "Ask him to speak."

Richard moved his mouth, but no sound came out until the King touched him. Then Richard murmured, "Please . . . say something."

The waif looked from the King to Richard and back. His lips formed the shapes of sounds . . . and he smiled broadly. Softly as a flower opening, he said, "I love you."

Eric, like the others, was greatly pleased that the boy had been healed, but he saw a shadow of grief lingering in the boy's dark eyes. When the waif stood, the King laid his right hand on the boy's head. Eric sighed with relief, for he saw the look of grief leave the boy like a shadow fleeing.

To the group, the King said, "Tonight we will hold a Ceremony of the Upraised Swords. These two young men then will be armed and armored as befits Kingsmen who, despite differing obstacles, have chosen to serve Abba." He smiled at the waif. "And tonight you may choose a name to signify your new life." Eric grinned to himself, glad that they finally would learn the boy's name!

The King turned to Jodi and held her head between his hands to clear her vision. "Daughter," he said tenderly, "not even the magicians have seen what you were given to see. Soon you will discover that you possess a power that not even they yet have been given."

Turning to Eric, the King resumed: "Lieutenant Eric, for the maturity and steadfastness you showed during the Gueroness Crossing you—in the near future—will be offered a reward. However, when it is offered, you may think it more task than reward." Eric would have asked what he meant, but the King laid one hand on Eric's head, then caressed each of the other Kingsmen before going to take the waif by one hand. He led him to the stream pouring from the lower fountain pool and beckoned to the other young people. "Come. Drink and be refreshed. Wash yourselves. But know that never again will the waters of Eorthe or Earth satisfy you as my waters do."

One by one, shyly at first, the children drank the sparkling liquid. Truly, it was refreshing. Quickly they removed their armor and rolled up their sleeves so they could wash themselves. When they had finished, they put their armor back on and gathered around the King.

"Know this," he began: "There are two masters Humankind may choose to serve. One leads his servants eventually into darkness and pain, but I lead those who trust and obey Abba into light and love. By coming here, despite all obstacles, you have proven your choice; you have shown your obedience. Because you have proven yourselves worthy, more will be given . . . and more will be asked."

"Are we to help fight the Darkness?" Martin asked.

The King smiled and stroked Martin's brown hair. "The Battle against the Darkness was fought and won long ago. Except for those who willingly listen and turn to him, the Lord of Darkness has been defeated. What you hereafter will be asked to do will be for three reasons. The first reason is the glorification of Abba. The second is your brothers and sisters of Humankind who seek the Light but are being attacked. The third reason is your own growth, so later you may be given greater power."

He stood and gazed at the young people for a moment, then began to walk toward the castle. Queen Dorcas went beside him, and the others slowly followed, talking among themselves about what he had said.

"Do those children," the queen softly asked him, "know how very special they are?" Wistfully, she looked back at the young people, thinking of her own son, Morgan.

"Everyone is special to me, my sister. And what those children have found, anyone may find. I always will come to those who seek me."

Part 2

Chapter 1

Departure of the Maralamans

Dawn sent long yellow rays through the windows of the Kingsmen's chamber. All of the young people were Kingsmen now, for Richard and the waif had received swords, shields, and armor during the Ceremony of the Upraised Swords held the night before. The waif sat on the edge of his bed, turning his chestplate back and forth so the sunlight lanced brightly off it. On the *nathnor's* silvery sheen glittered long, looping lines of a delicate design: the living throne of the King. The waif leaned close to look at the words engraved under the design: *Ne-A-Abba*.

"It's beautiful," he murmured, still startled each time he found himself able to speak . . . and still reluctant to do so.

"By the way," Eric said, sitting on the waif's bed, "I like your name—Jon."

Jon turned, grinning. "Thank you again for letting me come with you," he said quietly. "And thank you most of all for leading me to the King. I never dreamed . . ."

"Why don't you shout just once?" Richard interrupted.

Jon shook his head, smiling faintly, and began to buckle on his armor. Jodi and Eric knelt on his thin mattress to help him, then turned toward the door when it suddenly opened.

"*Idsule!* Good morning!" an auburn-haired man in a blue and white uniform cheerfully said. Eric and his friends recognized him as the leader of soldiers who had greeted them when they had arrived at Espereim. "I am Colonel Xan," he said, hooking his thumbs behind his sword belt, "and I bring your orders of the day. You are to pack quickly. The united army sails tomorrow afternoon, and we have a long ride to the harbor before then."

Bursting with questions, the Kingsmen hastened to carry out their orders. In ten minutes, packs over their shoulders, they followed Colonel Xan down through busy corridors and outside the castle.

In the innermost courtyard, Xan led the Kingsmen to a dozen saddled horses. When the young people had mounted, they saw trumpeters come from the castle and sound a flourish. Queen Dorcas came out, followed by General Talaman, the other two queens, the magicians, and various lords. A space in the courtyard cleared; horses were brought, and the leaders were helped to mount. The trumpets then blew again, and Queen Dorcas led the army from Castle Glimpalatyrn, cheered by a large crowd.

The Kingsmen rode with Colonel Xan's company—one of many forming a wide column that lengthened as it moved through the outer courtyards and down into the city. When they were well away from the castle, Eric stood on his stirrups, looked back, and guessed that a thousand mounted lords and warriors and four thousand foot soldiers were behind him.

The army slowly wound its way toward the city gate through throngs of well-wishing citizens and refugees. Many of the citizens ran to warriors and soldiers and gave them spare whetstones, small clay jars, and scarves on which hung medals. When a woman handed Rachael one of the jars, the girl unstopped it, sniffed, and said to Jodi, "I think it's medicine."

Jodi looked at the medal on a red scarf another woman handed her and saw an engraved picture of a tower. One of the nearby veterans, seeing Jodi's puzzled look, said, "It's Glimmothtyrn—the Tower of the Lightning, a source of hope."

Jodi hung the scarf around her neck and put the medal down inside her chestplate, looking along the sides of the streets at the refugees praying aloud for the success of the expedition. "What a glorious beginning," she said quietly, feeling a thrill.

Excited, Martin looked at his sister and said, "I hope this is as exciting as whipping Obit and his slaves last year!"

Rachael rode close, her expression serious. "I just wish," she told her friends, "that our hosts weren't divided among themselves. And I *sure* wish more had been said about relying on the King's power. General Talaman, for one, seems to think warriors and weapons are the only way we'll win."

"Maybe that's why," Eric said thoughtfully, "the King didn't show himself to Talaman and the lords."

"Who cares?" Richard exclaimed as he surveyed the army. "This should be more than enough to blow that sorcerer clean off the map!"

An old veteran riding near the Kingsmen spat to one side under his raised iron visor and glared at Richard. "*Nart,* this here's but a handful matched against what we're to face." He shifted his glare so it touched each of the Kingsmen. Slowly, he grinned. "I been ten campaigns in this war, so I warn you: We lack one chance in a thousand of coming back with skins, much less souls!" He winked, wrinkling a long scar on his face. "M'name's Tyrn, meaning 'stone.' Stones don't lie."

Richard laughed uneasily. "But we killed that other sorcerer."

Tyrn spat. "That what you killed was kin with demons and *obnars;* thems got nothing like *real* power." He leaned over to squint at Richard. "And it's said the Lord of Darkness himself soon will come sailing in from the Void. *He* could shrivel that fine armor you're wearing like paper in a volcano!" He laughed suddenly, scaring the youths, then dropped back.

The army soon passed under the archway of the city gate and wound down from the hills of Espereim into the beautiful Eoramian countryside. At a branch in the road, the leaders turned eastward—away from the road by which Acuerias had led Eric and his friends to the capital—and set a fast pace until nightfall. Then, in a valley to which the carts of the baggage train had been brought earlier, they camped for the night. The Kingsmen were so excited they hardly slept, and they were only half awake when the army started out again before dawn.

But by noon they were fully awake and had begun to hear a distant roar. When, still following Colonel Xan and the other leaders, they topped a ridge, they saw the Alamantian Ocean before them—vast and glittering blue. To their right was the River Limmwain, rushing over the rocky cliff at the land's end. The roar they had heard came, they soon saw, from the river as it rushed over the cliff, sending up a cloud of silvery spray through which a rainbow arched. Near the waterfall, the road wound a thousand or more feet down the cliff, and the Kingsmen lurched along it, thrilled by the scene.

Below and to their right they could see the broad,

blue-green basin into which the waterfall was thundering. North of the basin was a large harbor. In the dark green water of the harbor, three great galleys rode at anchor. The warships were long, with ram-tipped prows barely visible below the waterline. Along the ships's sides were three tiers of oars. Wide, square sails hung limply from the masts, and sailors were perched on the yards, sewing last minute repairs on the yellow and blue cloth. Eric thought that surely the masts had been trees in the Forest of Always, so tall and thick were they.

The bow of each ship, Eric saw, was shaped like a dragon's head with teeth bared and nostrils flaring redly. The sterns were upcurving, scaled tails. Eric smiled, caught by the fanciful idea that he was merely dreaming about the ships. But then he smelled tar fumes rising from vats as sailors re-caulked the ships' seams. He heard cannons rumble into place over wooden decks and the creak of winches as sacks of grain and kegs of water were hoisted on board from rocking longboats. The smell and sounds assured him he was not dreaming . . . and yet, the call of adventure that often had sounded in his dreams now seemed stronger than ever!

As the army column left the road and began to spread out on the harbor's shore, Martin pointed at the dragon-bowed ships. "I wonder if real dragons are ahead?" he asked Eric.

"No dragons," a nearby soldier answered, "but there're Trogs and Fearsors, Wraths and Wolvors aplenty . . . as well as one beast I've heard tales about called the Scourge of Scorius." He leered at the boys.

With the edge taken from their excitement, Eric and Martin looked toward the stone quay. There, rows of longboats were beached; by each boat stood a crew of Eoramian sailors. The sailors were clad in blue shirts and yellow breechcloths, from the waist of which bronze daggers protruded. They were looking at the leaders, who were assembling in the center of the quay. Above the leaders—rising and falling in the salty, damp breeze—was a cluster of Leohtians; more of their kind darted around each of the ships, helping sailors check and repair rigging.

At a signal from Queen Dorcas, several of the Leohtians above her flashed toward the warships. Within moments, a cannon boomed from each of the ships, startling the horses and young people. The warriors began to swim their horses into the harbor. Ramps were lowered with splashes, and the swimming horses soon began to clatter into the cavernous holds of the galleys. Along the shore, the longboats were dragged into the water; foot soldiers began boarding them, calling to their friends, *"A-Abba conseroth seu!"* as they were rowed to the warships. While the emptied longboats returned to shore for more soldiers, men appeared at the rails of the warships' top decks and silently began looking toward the land. Only then did the thought of being separated from one another sink into the Kingsmen. When they had dismounted, Jodi went to Eric and took his hands.

"Please," she said quietly, "can't we all stay together?"

"Jodi, I'm sorry, but . . ." He stopped when Waymond came to them, looking as though he had many things to do and little time.

"Kingsmen of Lieutenant Andros's group, go to the far *maralaman,*" he said, pointing toward Master Slyne, who was waiting by a longboat.

With a bow, Andros kissed Rachael's right hand, waved farewell to the others, and led his Kingsmen up the quay.

"Jon, Martin, and Eric," Waymond resumed, "go

with Acuerias. Rachael, Richard, and Jodi—come with me." He then noticed Jodi's tearful look. "That *is* what we decided, isn't it!" he asked, becoming concerned.

The young people glumly nodded.

"Don't worry," the magician said, stroking his thick brown beard. "You'll probably be together again." He smiled patiently.

"Martin? . . ." Jodi asked, her lower lip trembling. "You, too?"

Martin anxiously looked from his sister to Eric and back. "Jodi, I love you, but I've . . . well . . ."

"I know," she said sadly, "you've grown up enough to be away from your big sister."

They embraced one another and began to separate. Jon waved with his four-fingered hand, and with a sob Jodi ran back to him. She enfolded his maimed sword hand between her hands and murmured, "I love you."

He flinched with surprise as warmth rushed into his hand. In a moment, Jodi took her hands away. When Jon held up his hand in astonishment, they all saw that his missing finger had been restored! Staring at it, he flexed it again and again.

Rachael, her dark eyes wide, whispered to Jodi, "*That's* the power you got: the power to heal." She acted as though she wanted to touch Jodi but was afraid to.

Waymond smiled broadly and said, "By love are we healed." He then spread his arms to include them all. One by one, each hugged him. "Don't be afraid," he told them. "The King's light *is* with you."

After he had laid his right hand on the crown of each of their heads, they parted. Martin, Eric, and Jon followed Acuerias, Queen Dorcas, the Duke of Corlis and his officers, and several Sea People to two longboats. The oarsmen quickly took them to the warship at the south end of the harbor. Two other boats took lords To'bol, Ghazi, and Basmoth Bonasorte of Oraibi and their retainers to the same ship. Waymond, General Talaman and his officers, Queen Sybra and several black-suited warriors, Queen Eliadenor and some of her Sea People, Jodi, Rachael, and Richard were rowed to the galley in the center of the harbor. Meanwhile, the longboats that had unloaded the last of the foot soldiers returned to shore to pick up the baggage and a number of servants from Glimpalatyrn. Soon, the ramps were raised; they thudded shut.

Once on board, the young people rushed up four flights of wooden stairs to the topside rail and leaned on it, facing each other's ships. "Good-bye!" Martin shouted across to Jodi, Rachael, and Richard. Richard looked very excited—especially now that he was the only boy with the two girls and was away from the domination of Eric.

"We love you!" Jodi called to the other boys as Waymond came to stand behind her. Jon and Martin shouted back the same farewell, but Eric was silent. Turning from the rail, he began studying the ship.

He saw that the center of the galley was a long, railed opening, allowing a view of the lower decks. The great, stepped mast—braced by huge timbers—rose through the center of the opening. Rowers were stationed on benches along the sides of the middle three decks, the lowest one being filled with horses and foot soldiers and the top one being taken up by lords and their warriors. In the bow on the second deck Eric saw a red wood drum; it was mounted on a stand that was chest-high to a bearish man who stood ready with mallets. Eric flinched when a cannon was fired and the bearish man struck the drum.

Quickly, long oars were unshipped as Eric went back to the rail. He saw that the oars from the lowest level were some thirty feet long. The oars from the middle level were about forty feet long, and the oars from the highest tier stretched beyond the other two rows. Each oar was manned by four rowers, and they began to pull in unison as the drum throbbed with a doom . . . doom beat. Loudly boomed the rowing rhythm as the banks of oar blades dipped and pulled. Toward the harbor mouth went the three warships, their prows cleanly cleaving the blue-green water.

On Eric's ship, Queen Dorcas went into a cabin in the stern, as did the lords To'bol and Ghazi. Acuerias, meanwhile, joined Martin, Jon, and Eric on the top deck. The boys saw that the magician was carrying a shoulder bag, from the top of which protruded one end of his great book. Eric thought Acuerias looked a bit seasick, though only now was the open ocean appearing beyond the harbor mouth. As Eric glanced at the twin lighthouses on either side of the harbor entrance—each in the shape of a graceful, upward-reaching gazelle—then looked back at Acuerias, he asked, "Is the 'deck' of your donkey Terserius more to your liking?"

The magician tucked in his chin, causing his snowy beard to curl up at the edges. "Most definitely; my friend's gait is like that of a mother's rocking—but this ship has the roll of winds near the Void!"

Eric laughed. "Surely, it's not as bad as that; why, we've only now begun to meet the ocean swells. What if a storm comes?"

Acuerias groaned, turning away from the rail.

"Look!" Martin cried, pointing. "We've beaten the others out of the harbor!" He looked astern and down three decks at the Duke of Corlis, who was standing with several Sea People near the sailors manning the giant steering sweeps. "That Duke really knows what he's doing!"

"Good," mumbled Acuerias, moving away from the sight of the ocean swells stretching sunstruck to the horizon. "Maybe he can put a speedy end to this voyage."

"These are huge galleys," Eric observed for lack of anything else to say to take the magician's mind off his queasy stomach.

"Um-humph . . . well, actually," Acuerias replied, pulling his heavy book from his bag, "they are properly termed *maralamans.*" He opened his book as Eric and Jon moved to look over his shoulders. He pointed to the word at the top of the first of the following two pages.

He said, "*Maralaman*—literally meaning 'sea fortress' or 'warship.' "

"In ancient times on Earth," Eric said, "there were ships like these, but they were rowed by slaves and prisoners in chains."

The magician put one thick forefinger to his lips between his snowy beard and stained mustache. "Slaves? Oh, yes, um . . . now I remember: Evil finally came to Earth, too, didn't it?"

Eric nodded. "I'm afraid so. As a result, many of my people are like the ones in the 'Lament of the Children Who Lost the Light,' which Waymond once taught me:

All children born to choose
think not what they can lose;
our fear to temptation an open door,
we see only ourselves and cry for more.
Now wandering, we mourn what we have lost
and ever through the night we count the cost. . .

"Ohhh . . ." Acuerias murmured sympathetically. "Perhaps you understand more than I thought."

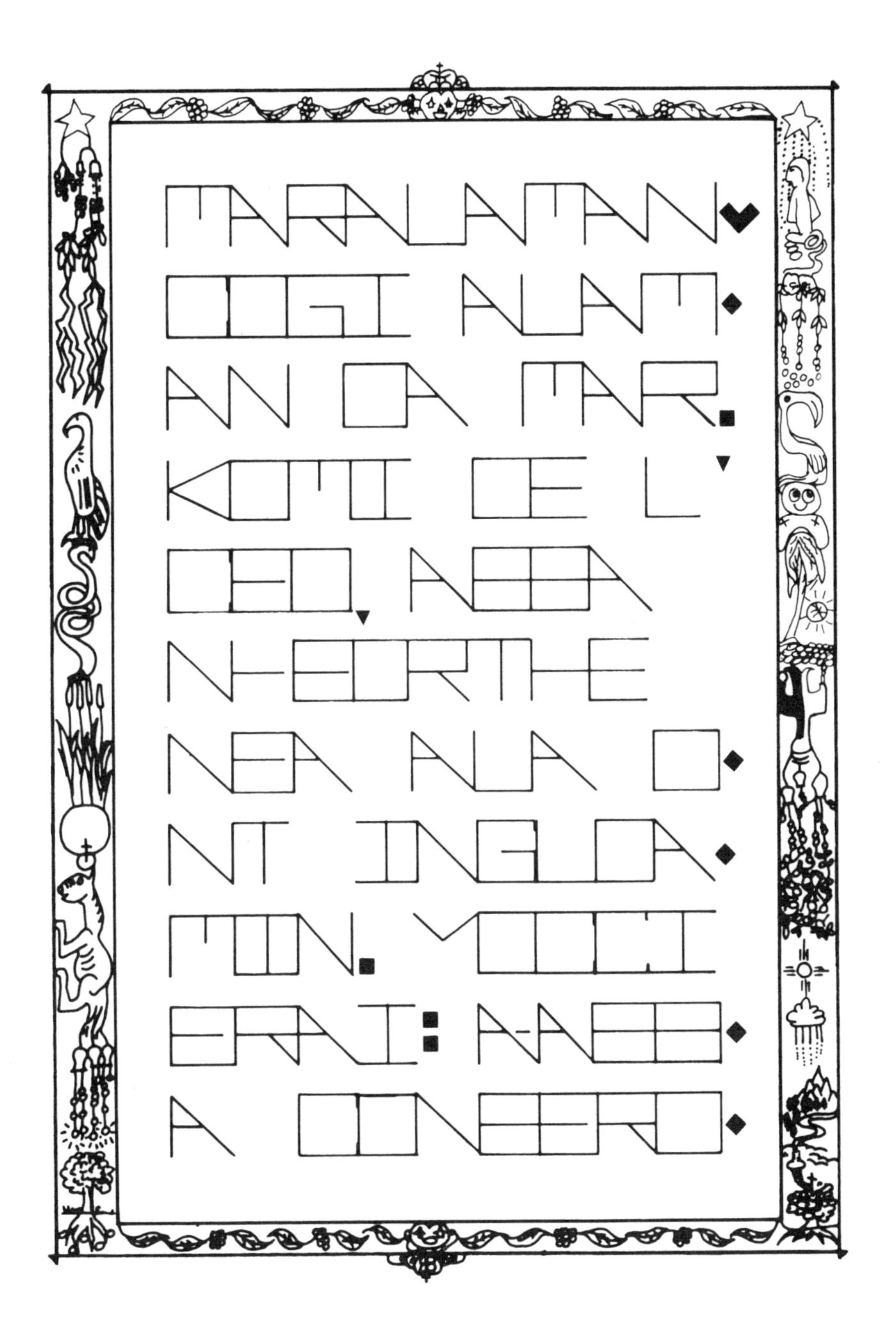

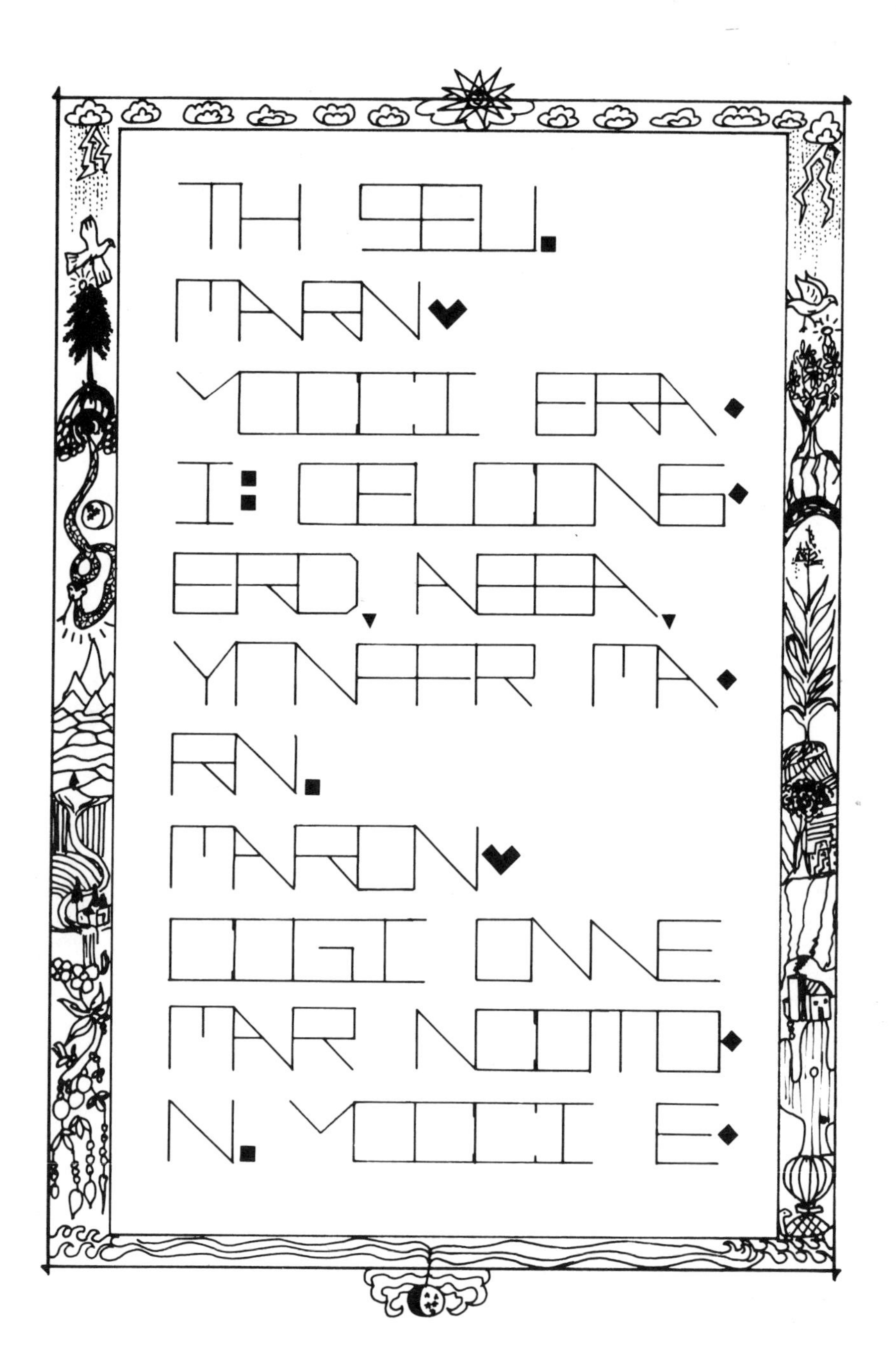

"Now we're really getting a lead on the other ships!" Martin shouted, turning for a moment to grin at Eric and Jon.

Eric scarcely glanced at Martin; he was more interested in the way the magician was smiling at him. It seemed that some barrier between him and the Eorthean had given way. "The writing in your book, Sir," Eric began with restrained eagerness, "it looks sort of like our writing."

Acuerias brightened and held the book open wide for Eric to study. "You see, it's printed in the ancient language of Eorthe. All the letters of the language are contained in this design." With one fingernail, he drew a pattern on the thick, soft paper:

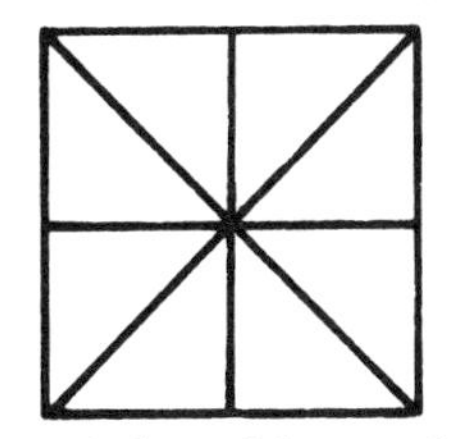

"Teach us some of the old words," Eric suggested . . . then asked, "Or is that against a magician's oath or something?"

"No-no," Acuerias laughed, bright-eyed. "The King charged us to share our knowledge openly with anyone ready to receive it." He smiled sorrowfully as he leaned toward Eric. "But youths willing to learn have become scarce. You, however, seem ready, so I gladly will teach you the old words and more—anything I feel you're prepared to understand." His smile became encouraging.

"Hey, they're hoisting our sail!" Martin turned to shout. Eric glanced at him, then back at the magician.

"This phrase here," the old man resumed, pointing to the page, "is one you heard me use a few days ago:"

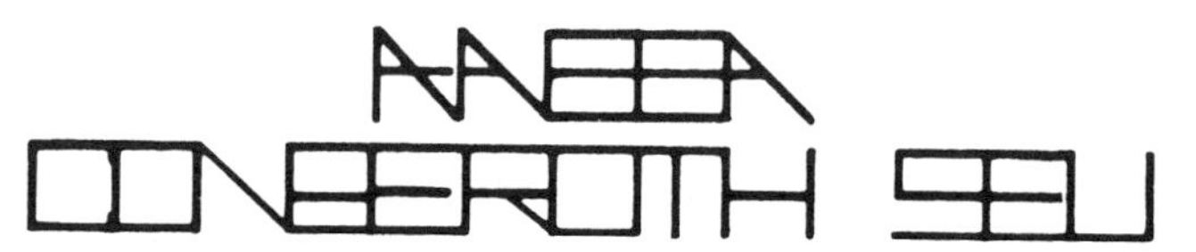

"It says, '*A-Abba conseroth seu,*' or, to separate it: 'A' is a prefix meaning 'the' in the common tongue; 'Abba' means 'Father' or refers to the King; 'conseroth' means strength; 'se' means 'is', and 'u' means 'yours'. Thus, we have, 'The King's strength is yours.' There is the implied meaning that his strength is a free gift and that 'yours' means anyone. Furthermore, we only . . . but perhaps I bore you?"

"No!" Eric said quickly, excited by the fact that Acuerias was willing to explain so much to him. "Please go on."

He patiently did so. At last, Jon, who also had been listening, asked, "Sir, isn't your language hard to write?" Acuerias smiled, looking at the boy's gentle dark eyes.

"No," he answered. "In the old days, before everyone began to scribble, the stonemasons and engravers used three flat *scuks,* chisels: one the width of any side of the design; one the length of the diagonal line; and the third a half, mid-stroke. The stonemasons held all three *scuks* in one hand, each between a different pair of fingers. They struck the appropriate chisel with a mallet. Smaller chisels were used for punctuation and finishing touches. With practice, one could write surprisingly fast, but when one uses the letters in books I suppose they are a bit awkward." He chuckled self-consciously. "I maintain the practice because of my respect for tradition." With a piercing look at Eric, he added, "One's traditions are very important, for they tie the present to the past and make the future more stable." Drawing back his snowy-maned head, he abruptly asked Eric, "Could you adopt Eorthean traditions?"

Eric's answer was quick and frank. "If I could learn those traditions well enough for them to become part of me . . . yes."

A cannon blast startled them. It was answered by two faint booms. Eric and Jon looked over the rail and saw that the other two *maralamans* were turning onto diverging courses. While their own ship bore east, the center ship—with the girls and Richard—veered northeast, toward its distant landing at the edge of the Swamps of Armazil. The third ship was steering almost straight north, toward the east coast of Rud . . . and toward black clouds lying along the northern horizon.

Eric looked ahead—toward Alamantia. Beyond the dragon bow, he saw an unbroken expanse of gently swelling ocean. He settled back, feeling the vibrating throb of the west wind against the blossoming sail. Gradually, though, the wind shifted and rose from the north. The sail's yards groaned to one side. Eric felt a chilling touch and, looking northward, he saw that the dark clouds were advancing steadily. They now seemed to tower from the horizon toward which the other two warships were heading. As Acuerias resumed teaching, Eric uneasily glanced at the fast-approaching clouds and did his best not to worry.

Chapter 2

Into the Swamps of Armazil

Jodi and Rachael shivered in the chill touch of the north wind, watching the other ships diminish to mere specks on the wind-swept vastness of the ocean. Waymond then put one arm around Richard's shoulders and led him forward, talking quietly to him. Soon, the long oars were shipped, the sail was hoisted, and the wind alone sent the warship tacking northeastward over the rising swells. Staring at the black clouds along the northern horizon, the girls became uneasy . . . and felt a sudden, sharp sense of loneliness. Jodi realized she missed Martin and Eric more than she had expected she would, and Rachael realized she missed the companionship of gallant Constantine Andros. Both girls were glad when a servant came and asked if they were ready to go to their cabin.

The servant led Rachael and Jodi through groups of warriors to a wood-paneled cabin in the upcurving stern. Almost immediately, another servant brought the girls fruit, bread, and several kinds of cheese; she also brought a sealed pitcher of water and two, white-glazed mugs adorned with suns. Impulsively, Rachael gave the first servant the little jar of medicine she had been given in Espereim, and Jodi gave the other servant her medal—much to the servants' surprise. The girls then sat on cushions piled against the back wall of the cabin and placed the food between them. Sunlight from large, open windows warmed their backs, though the cool, salty wind gusted in while they ate.

"I wish we weren't heading toward those black clouds," Jodi said quietly.

Rachael shrugged. "So many hurricanes pass over my home in Guerrero each rainy season that clouds don't worry me . . . nor even wind."

Lying back against the cushions, Jodi sighed. "I guess I should just be thankful that drumbeat stopped. It was giving me a headache!"

"Me too," Rachael agreed. "It was like my pulse pounding in my ears." She laughed slightly and added, "You know, I'd rather be on horseback."

"I wonder how far we have to go?" Jodi asked. "It seems like the farther we go in Eorthe, the farther there is to go. I was relieved when we reached Eoramia, and I guess I thought that was the end. But now . . ."

"The best place so far has been Espereim," Rachael said, eyes wide. "I thought Queen Dorcas was the most beautiful woman I've *ever* seen!"

Jodi frowned. "You and Eric . . ."

"Does he . . . like you?"

Jodi glanced at her. "He hasn't told me, exactly. He likes adventures more than girls."

"He'll change," Rachael said knowingly.

"No . . ." Jodi said thoughtfully, "I don't think so. In fact, I think I've lost him completely."

They were silent for a while, listening to the lap of waves against the hull, the wind sighing over the long ship, and the whir of warriors' whetstones against blades. Jodi turned over and picked at a purple tassel on one pillow. "I wish the King had come with us."

"So do I!" Rachael said. "I wonder where he went."

"There's no telling. Didn't he look grand?"

Rachael nodded. "He called Queen Dorcas 'sister' and you 'daughter.' Didn't that make you feel good?"

"Sure!" Jodi beamed. "But I was really scared when I looked at that light hole in the sky. I've never *imagined* anything like that!"

"What'd you see?" Rachael asked quickly.

"Well, it was sort of an eye . . . like a white cloud with an eye's pupil. Inside was . . . space, with lots of white flames."

"Was it powerful?"

"Gosh, *yes!* I thought I had melted. I couldn't see anything but spinning dots until the King held my head between his hands."

Rachael, awed, was smiling broadly. "How'd you feel this morning when you made Jon's finger grow back?"

Jodi looked down, frowning as she plucked at the tassel. "I . . . it sort of scares me, you know, to have that kind of power. I wonder if I'll get to keep it when . . . or if . . . we go back to Earth?"

After a moment's silence, Rachael said, "If my family didn't need me, I'd love to stay here—near Queen Dorcas and the King's fountain. I could spend a long time just riding horses over the hills of Eoramia." Thoughtfully, she added, "I wonder how the queens got to be Sisters of the Jewels?"

"I guess the King picked them," Jodi replied.

Rachael rolled onto her back and stared at the polished wood ceiling. "I wish he'd pick us next. I think my greatest wish in the whole world is to become a Sister and be allowed to wear a Jewel."

"I've been wishing that, too . . . but all the talk about sorcerers, war, and strange beasts really bothers me. Don't you feel strange here?"

Rachael laughed. "Yes; it's the same feeling I got when my family visited relatives in your country. I felt alone; I didn't understand much of the language, and I couldn't get used to how *fast* everything was."

Jodi sighed, then smiled at Rachael. "Thanks. I was beginning to think I was the only one who felt . . . weird."

Rachael reached over and took one of Jodi's hands. "Just remember: The King's Light *is* with us."

Jodi smiled and nodded as tears came into her eyes. "I'll still be glad when we can go home. I miss my parents . . . and my room."

"You have a room by yourself?" Rachael asked with mild surprise.

Jodi nodded, wiping her eyes. "And I go . . . I went to a school only six blocks from home and to a church only three blocks away."

Rachael sighed. "Nobody goes to the church in the town we live near, except a few old people and parents who want children christened." She was about to say something else, but a cannon blast startled them.

They heard the deep voice of General Talaman shouting commands and felt the ship change course. Pounding footsteps raced over the decks. Horses neighed as several more booming sounds shook the ship. Rachael and Jodi jumped to the open windows and leaned out.

First, they saw that the black clouds from the north were streaking overhead. Beneath the threatening blackness came a miles' wide wall of fog. And with the clouds and fog had come a number of what Jodi recalled from a book were . . . "Corsairs!" she cried. "Pirates!"

No sooner had she said the words than a cannon shot screamed toward the *maralaman* and struck it just below the waterline. The girls instinctively dropped to the floor . . . then cautiously looked out again. They saw that the warship's oars had been put out so she could fight her way into the wind. They also saw the triangular sails of the pirate ships flash pale gray as they swooped out of the fog to make firing runs, staying well clear of the *maralaman's* sharp ram prow.

When the girls saw yellow lightning flash from the warship, they knew Waymond had joined the fray. But, because of the thickening fog, he had few targets at which to aim. He did, however, sink two of the pirate vessels before they could dart back into the fog. Thereafter, the remaining corsairs stayed out of sight . . . though the noise of the cannon battle rose in volume as both sides fired blindly. The big ship was struck several times, but it continued to bore onward and managed to ram two of the pirate craft. The smaller ships sank quickly, and their long-gowned crews leaped screaming into the ocean. The running battle slackened only when the wind died somewhat and the fog completely quenched the afternoon light.

Excited and curious, Rachael led Jodi up onto the top deck. Looking for Waymond, they made their way through ranks of crouching warriors. When cannons boomed—flashing orange-red spurts into the sooty darkness—Jodi flinched. The smell of burned gunpowder was sharp in the sea air, and both girls wrinkled their noses as smoke shrouded them. When the breeze blew the smoke away, they noticed wounded men being carried below. Jodi went to the railing at the edge of the opening in the ship's center and looked down. In the bow on the second deck she saw Queen Sybra, Waymond—with Richard huddled near him, and some of the Sea People working in a makeshift hospital. "I've got to go below!" Jodi called to Rachael above the din.

But before she went down the nearest stairway, she paused to watch Queen Eliadenor climb onto the dragon's head at the *maralaman's* bow. As the light from cannon fire and sputtering torches flared over the queen's golden cape and glimmering green robes, she held up a large, pink conch shell. Setting the conch to her lips, she sent an enormously loud call shivering across the waves. As Queen Eliadenor dashed from her perch, Jodi went below.

Rachael went to the seaward rail among a group of warriors and looked over the battle scene. She set her jaw, wishing the raiders would try to board rather than standing off to trade cannon shots with the warship.

"Look at the maiden," a warrior jokingly said to a crouching companion. "She looks impatient to prick one of those Falrn dogs!"

"I am!" Rachael flared at the man. "And what are Falrn dogs?"

"Those pirates that beset us," the warrior replied, then asked, "You're one of the Kingsmen who slew the southern sorcerer?"

"Yes," Rachael replied, glaring down at a fast-moving corsair as it swooped close to the ends of the *maralaman's* oar tips.

"Look," a second warrior pointed, "they're trying to smash our oars an' cripple us! Go call the magician!"

"Huh!" the first warrior snorted, resettling his horned helmet on his thick brown hair. "Something better than a magician soon will come. Not even you could be so deaf you didn't hear the Sea Queen send her call!"

Rachael and the crouching men watched. Perhaps thirty minutes passed, broken frequently by red-flashing cannon fire, the sound of wood exploding, and the cries of wounded men. The tension grew steadily.

"There!" a man down the railing suddenly half

stood and shouted. They all looked where he pointed.

Rachael and the others saw a bow-shaped wave crested with white froth speeding across the ocean not a hundred yards from the warship. As the wave came on, the fog lifted above it. Slowly then, a black-gray form arose, an enormous mouth gaped high, and one of the pirate ships was seized. The hull burst into splinters as the onrushing jaws closed. Only bits of wreckage were left to swirl in the monster's passing.

The sea creature swam on, straight toward a trio of raiders. It dove beneath and around them, fanning its flukes to form a whirlpool. The three ships spun around and around close together. As Rachael caught her breath, the giant flukes rose up and crashed down on the three corsairs. The three pirate ships and their crews disappeared.

"Unthoriumgai has come!" a mariner shouted from the rigging.

"Un . . . what?" Rachael asked the delighted man next to her.

"Unthoriumgai—Father of Whales and ocean Guardian. You'll see that he's bigger than this ship—if he shows all of himself," the man gleefully replied, then set his square jaw. "Watch those Falrn dogs run for it now!"

Indeed, the remaining pirate ships wheeled and began fleeing northward. But the same evil wind that had brought them now held them back. At a leisurely pace, Unthoriumgai hunted down and destroyed them one by one. Then, with a final RA-*BOOM!* as his great tail spanked the ocean, the Father of Whales slid into the depths, traveling northeastward. The *maralaman's* crew was left with only the increasingly cold wind to worry them—and the sense of dread the Darkness brought. Rachael went below to find Jodi.

Jodi greeted her with excitement. "It still works!"

she exulted, grasping her friend's arms with bloodied hands. She bent down and, with a slight shudder, placed her hands on the torn side of a warrior. Her hands and the wound glowed briefly. The man, leaning up to watch, smiled broadly and began to cry, for he was healed.

Rachael felt ashamed of her earlier bloodthirsty thoughts. "And I wanted to do just the opposite to those pirates," she murmured.

Jodi looked gently at her. "We need both warriors *and* healers."

Rachael seemed satisfied and began to take water to the recuperating sailors and warriors. She even drank a dipperful herself, then grimaced. Looking up, she saw Queen Sybra watching her.

Quietly, the queen said, "Deeply I wish I could have brought the King's water to these wounded, as well as to those who lie enthralled ahead." She glanced toward the sky, then pushed up the long sleeves of her black robe and returned to work.

Thereafter, the voyage became heavily monotonous. Hour after hour, the warship rose and fell with the swells. Day by day, the passengers worked, ate, and slept with the ever present, ever throbbing drumbeat. Unfortunately, Jodi and Rachael had no work to do; they spent their time trying to stay warm and unafraid of the Darkness, which never departed no matter what the hour. It obscured even the nearest ocean waves and the tips of the long oars pulling the ship into the north wind. For nine more dreary days, the shipmates' nerves wore away like sandstone under a bitter wind. And Jodi became more and more depressed.

One night, Jodi awoke Rachael by crying and tossing in her sleep. Rachael laid her hands on Jodi's side and whispered, "What's the matter?"

Jodi stirred, mumbling, "The dark . . . the dark tunnel . . . I'm. . ."

Rachael gently shook her friend. "Wake up. You're having a nightmare."

Jodi sighed, relaxing, and drifted into deep sleep. Rachael lay beside her, praying that the Darkness soon would lift.

But it did not. Thus, when the cry "Land ho!" came from the bowman it aroused little more than grumbling among the sailors and soldiers. Jodi and Rachael, Waymond and Richard, and Queen Sybra went to the forward rail and looked ahead. What they saw did nothing to cheer them: a low-lying, gray shore draped in sooty fog. Jodi leaned against Waymond and shivered.

He wrapped one arm around her shoulders. Quietly, he asked, "This adventure isn't what you expected?"

"No," Jodi admitted dismally. "And this fog . . ."

"I *hate* this dingy fog," Richard complained.

Waymond turned to him with twinkling eyes. "Now, Private Richard, you're forgetting what I've taught you."

Richard let his head droop as he began to scratch inside his armor.

Waymond turned to Jodi. "And you, Miss Jodi! Frog flutes and toad trumpets! No one promised that we always would be comfortable. The King has promised us many things, but he never said following him would be easy." He arched his brushy eyebrows at her until she smiled and relaxed.

The ship slipped through the mouth of a broad harbor past gray sand bars. The shallow water around the shoreline was beslimed with great mats of bubbling green algae. Dead tree trunks poked up along the low land, which lay half hidden under the fog. The extent of the harbor was cloaked by fog, but the Sea

People guided the ship carefully. As it ghosted forward with barely stroking oars, the children could hear loud screeches of unseen birds and splashes of fog-hidden bodies diving into the water. The sound of the anchor being dropped scared the youths. Almost immediately they noticed swarms of gray snakes swimming toward them.

"Forget it!" Richard declared. "You're not gettin' *me* off this ship!"

While General Talaman bellowed commands from the stern, Colonel Xan led the first longboat toward shore. Other boats were put out, but the foot soldiers were reluctant to board them because the men on the ramps already were fighting an onslaught of gray, rippling snakes. General Talaman, livid and with his bushy beard twitching, shouted, "Cowards! Smite the serpents and do not fear! We've yet to meet the Enemy!"

"This fog is enemy enough," one young soldier muttered, hanging back.

"This is but a taste," said a doughty veteran in the uniform of Smy'ra. He shoved the youth before him down the ramp and into a longboat.

The foot soldiers and their gear crossed in the longboats, but the lords and warriors were forced to swim their horses ashore. The poor beasts were terrified and had to be pushed into the water. Once afloat, with their riders struggling with reins and swords at once, the horses struck out in a thick line for the shore.

Complaints could be heard from the departing soldiers. They griped about the cold water and about the fact that they hardly could see to kill the snakes. They also repeated tales about the Scourge of Scorius and other creatures rumored to be in Armazil.

"Well, shall we go?" Waymond cheerfully asked as he hoisted his staff.

"Across that water?" Richard whined, scratching

behind his chestplate. "It stinks! And I *hate* snakes!"

Indeed, the harbor smelled awful. And as the longboat bearing Waymond and the Kingsmen cut across the scummy water toward a cove, snakes and other slimy creatures thrashed out of the way. In the shallow water, the keel of the longboat grounded on mud. The oarsmen grudgingly got out and pushed the boat to shore, using their bronze daggers to kill as many serpents as they could.

Jodi was squeamishly terrified, but Rachael drew her sword; she slashed repeatedly into the water to help protect the straining oarsmen. Waymond joined her, shriveling snakes by the dozen with spurts of lightning from his staff. Despite their efforts, though, the snakes bit several sailors by leaping at them with wide-open, white-glistening mouths, their silvery fangs extended.

Colonel Xan greeted Waymond and his group when finally they stepped onto the slimy shore. Putting his winged helmet under one arm, Xan beckoned to nearby soldiers and told them, "Take the bitten men to camp; it's being set up on a low hill a hundred yards north."

"No, wait," Jodi said shyly. When Xan and the soldiers hesitated, frowning at her, she silently went to the oarsmen and closed her eyes as she grasped their bitten arms and legs. One by one, their faces registered their amazement. Gratefully, they knelt before Jodi—but Waymond sternly said, *"Vocciglorimm e-Abba!"*

With a strange look, Xan watched the sailors push the longboat back into the water, glanced at Jodi, then helped her and Rachael cross the slippery shore to less muddy ground. As he went, he told Waymond, "I've sent scouts to find the road that once went to Torang; men not otherwise occupied are killing snakes."

"Where *are* we anyhow?" Richard asked, flinging a mess of algae from his wet legs and stamping mud from his boots.

"This," Waymond said cheerfully, "is the shore of one of the Lakes of Yore; we're in the south of the Kingdom of Armazil." He continued to stride forward as he turned to look at Xan. "When General Talaman lands with the queens, we'll hold a council, but tell me now what *you* think."

Colonel Xan settled his helmet onto his head. "I think we should strike north quickly, without waiting for Acuerias and his group to join us."

Silently, the children followed the thoughtful magician and the quick-striding colonel through shreds of fog toward the camp. Each step they took squished, and when they looked back they saw that their footprints quickly filled with black water. Crossing low places that had been churned by the hooves of passing horses was even more difficult; the children frequently slipped in the mud. When they fell, they scrambled up quickly—afraid of being bitten by one of the snakes that seemed to be everywhere.

"How far do we have to go through this mess?" Richard asked.

"To the camp?" Xan inquired, helping Jodi and Rachael leap a ditch.

"No; to get out of this . . . swamp!"

"Oh, only about fifty miles," the blue-armored Allumerian replied. "You'd much prefer my country, I assure you." With a smile, he led the way to the center of a large, fairly dry island. It was surrounded by stark, black tree skeletons; their gnarled limbs were festooned with shaggy gray moss and writhing gray snakes. Knots of soldiers were scattered here and there, barely visible in the fog as they tried to pitch tents, light fires, and kill snakes. Waymond saw the frustration of the men who were trying to coax wet tinder and wood to burn; he left the Kingsmen and went among the warriors, igniting fires with lightning from his staff.

When Queen Sybra arrived, she told the leaders and Kingsmen that the *maralaman* had put out to sea and that Unthoriumgai had come for Queen Eliadenor. The Sea Queen, Sybra said, had heard the distant summons of a sea conch and knew that the eastward bound *maralaman* was in trouble. That news worried the Kingsmen, but the sight of the undaunted Leohtians flashing inland was comforting. The council members then went into a large tent.

The girls and Richard soon grew tired of waiting for the council to adjourn. They began to wander around the camp. They listened to the gossip among Tyrn and the other veterans, patted the warhorses, and counted the kinds of uniforms. Nearer and nearer to the edge of the camp, they groped their way.

Richard soon became tired. "Hey, let's rest a while," he whined. He slogged to a jungle-draped, long mound beyond the last group of soldiers. Disgustedly, he slapped mosquitoes away from his eyes and leaned against the side of the mound. At that point, it was about fifteen feet high.

"Look at that weird thing behind Richard," Rachael said, going to the mound. Vines had crept over it, and dead leaves were sprinkled along its rounded top. "It's *long!*" she breathed, trying to see either end of the thing. But the fog let them see no more of the winding shape than fifty or so feet in either direction.

"I wonder what it is?" Jodi asked, feeling creepy. She noted that underneath the vegetation the mound was dull green with yellowish veins. "It seems like a wall or maybe an ancient water pipe . . . but it's soft."

"Soft?" Rachael asked, unsheathing her sword. She

went to the mound and drew back her blade—even as Jodi gasped. Sharply, Rachael punched the green-yellow mound with the sword's point.

The tip sank in a few inches, and a black fluid began seeping out. Eyes widening, the children backed away. Then, stumbling, they ran for their lives: The mound had begun to move! As they fled, it moved faster—drawing itself into a coil. The ground trembled and dead trees crashed into nearby bayous as the enormous body awakened. Panic quickly spread among the troops as a ghastly head and weaving neck rose . . . and rose above the skeleton treetops.

Chapter 3

Darkness Over Alamantia

On the eastward bound *maralaman,* Eric continued to glance at the darkening sky. High, shelving black clouds had begun to soar overhead from the north. The red eye of the sun winked out in the west under the leading edge of the front, and the ocean swells were cast into gloom. By nightfall, the front stretched from horizon to horizon, trailing a concave wall of black. Staring at the sky, sailors nervously muttered, "The Darkness returns."

As torches were being lighted and placed here and there along the decks, the Duke of Corlis left the men at the steering sweeps and came onto the top deck. Stalking back and forth near Acuerias and the Kingsmen, he studied the sky. The boys admired the duke's engraved, polished armor and his lean, tall form (Eric guessed him to be at least six and a half feet tall). The boys also noted his hawk-like amber eyes and his proud bearing. The duke, however, seemed not to notice the boys, and he even ignored the dried meat, bread, and cheese being served by a steward. Occasionally, he glanced back down at the Sea People pilots.

"My dear Mark," Acuerias groaned, holding his

head, "*please* stop striding to and fro. You're causing me more dizziness than the rolling of the ship!"

The duke stopped, laughed, and sat down by the magician. "You're right, old teacher. I should be setting a better example."

With some hesitation, Eric moved over and sat near the duke. "Sir?" he began. When the man looked at him, Eric asked, "Should we call you Duke Corlis or Mark Mansbridge or . . . or what?"

The duke smiled as he swung his scabbard away from his long legs and leaned his back against the railing around the central opening. "Since you're new here, let me tell you something of both names; then you can decide which to call me." When Eric nodded, he went on. "My title—Duke of Corlis—is because I inherited a fiefdom south of Espereim on the Plains of Eoramia; thence come the finest horses known. My name, however, was given me by my father. Once, long ago during the war against the Lord of Darkness, an ancestor of mine was a lord in King L'Ced's army. During the Battle of Corlis Wood, the Lord of Darkness opened a chasm of deep fire between the king and safety atop a mountain. Holding attacking demons at bay, my ancestor led his cavalry to drag trees together and throw a bridge across the chasm—giving rise to our House name. Now, which name would you prefer to call me?"

Eric grinned. "Mark Mansbridge," he said quietly.

Having overheard bits of history among the warriors, Jon asked, "Did your ancestor become one of the Lords of the Swords?"

"Yes," said the duke with quiet pride. A murmur of admiration trickled among the listening warriors. Mark patted the scabbard at his side. "This sword is Corbansul," he said as though introducing a cherished friend. "And your names?" he inquired, looking at the boys.

When they had introduced themselves, Mark looked at Eric—and seemed to like what he saw. "You're from Earth?" he asked as though doubting it.

Eric nodded.

"What's life like there, Kingsman?" Mark leaned forward to ask.

"Well . . ." Eric stalled, not knowing where to begin. After all, he wondered, how could he explain such things as airplanes and computers? Or even electricity and heated running water?

"Go on, lad," the duke urged. He and the warriors listening nearby edged closer.

Eric, feeling skepticism in their habitually fierce looks, took a deep breath and began. When—after an hour or so of listening in mounting disbelief—the duke could stand it no longer, he demanded of Acuerias, "Is all this *true?* Surely it is but the spinning of a youthful imagination!"

Acuerias nodded slowly with a bemused smile.

By then a whole crowd of warriors, lords, sailors, and even stewards had gathered around. When they saw the magician confirm Eric's truthfulness, a ripple of excited voices spread. The Darkness was forgotten, almost, as more and more men clustered together to listen to the Kingsman.

Another hour passed, and Eric was saying, "Then, some scientists made a very tall thing called a rocket: Titan II. In the top end of it, three men flew to the moon. They walked around for a while, picking up rocks . . ."

"Rocks? Not *nathnor?*" demanded the astonished duke.

Eric started to laugh, but he stopped himself. "No, Sir—rocks, and dirt. Then they came back."

"She *let* them?"

"She?"

"*Omiglimm,* who reminds us of the First Light."

"He means the moon," Acuerias explained.

Again, Eric was tempted to laugh but didn't. "Yes, Sir; she let them."

"How did this rock-et fly?" the duke asked, glancing at the ring of intent listeners.

"The rocket flew by shooting fire from its tail," Eric replied.

The listeners murmured, glancing at one another. "It would seem," Mark said as though voicing the thoughts of the crowd, "that the Eartheans are masterful magicians indeed!"

Martin sat down on the other side of Mark, looking at the warriors. He thought they looked exceedingly grim in their horned helmets, embossed armor, bound leggings, furred cloaks, and long swords—but he was amused by the child-like look in their eyes. "If you think that's something," he said secretively, "you should see my pocket calculator. It can add, subtract, multiply, and divide numbers as big as 99,999,999!"

"Divide?" the duke asked.

"Yeah, you know: Two divided by two is one," Martin answered.

The duke drew a leather pouch from behind his belt and poured a handful of bright jewels into the palm of one hand. "Show me what you mean," he said, counting out a few stones that looked like rubies and emeralds.

Martin, surprised, looked at Eric for help. Together, they began to teach the great warriors and lords about subjects that, to the boys, were elementary. And that seemingly insignificant event opened up area after area. During the next five days all three boys were kept busy as teachers.

And the words the boys spoke were repeated from warrior to warrior, sailor to sailor, throughout the ship. The Darkness, therefore, had little effect on the men in the Duke of Corlis's command, for their minds were occupied with the outburst of strange knowledge: telephones, piped sewage, ready-made clothes and boots! The Eortheans listened in amazement.

Acuerias, however, was not entirely happy with the turn of events. Eric observed the magician's glum mood and, one evening at supper, asked him, "Has the Darkness begun to bother you, Sir?"

Acuerias looked long and hard at him. "Lad, do you think it wise to fill these simple people's heads with knowledge of such things as automobiles, telephones, and credit cards?"

Eric blinked. "I don't know, Sir. What do you think?"

Acuerias dug in his shoulder bag and produced the opal-like stone. Murmuring as he passed one hand over it, he called up an image. Eric looked at the image: a slowly moving picture of a large city on Earth. Smoke rose to join smog choking the sky; rivers were shiny with oil slicks and clotted with trash; traffic along the many freeways seemed fierce as it raced over long bridges above decaying slums.

"But Earth's not *all* that way," Eric protested.

Acuerias carefully wrapped his image stone and put it away, sighing.

So, the lessons about Earth went on as the Darkness deepened. Then, after one of Eric's explanations, the Duke of Corlis suddenly stood and gave Eric a startling look. "I'll do it!" he declared. "I'll ask the King to let me cross the Great River after we've won this war!" He looked excitedly toward the south as Eric stared at him, not knowing what to say. "Time, steersman?" the Duke called to the crew at the steering sweeps.

"Morn watch, end third turning of the glass!" came the shout.

"Noon," the duke translated, having recently

learned Earth time from Martin, "and yet the Darkness thickens." Watching him, Eric wondered if his resolve to go to Earth had been a momentary impulse, or . . .

"Land . . . arising!" came an uncertain call from the bow watchman.

Triamedes, chief pilot of the Sea People, came onto the top deck and hurried forward with the duke, Acuerias, and the Kingsmen. The duke looked questioningly at the bow watchman, who reported, "We hear waves against rocks, m'lord. And the wind, like the current, has shifted."

Mark listened, as they all did, to a distant, rhythmical pounding. It was louder than the drumbeat, which had begun to throb for the warship's oarsmen. "What think you, Magician?" the duke asked Acuerias. "And you, Triamedes?" he added, glancing behind the pilot as the now useless sail was lowered and tied.

While Triamedes sniffed the air, Acuerias gazed into his imaging stone. This time—because Acuerias had continued to teach him from the great book—Eric understood the Eorthean words the magician murmured as he passed one hand over the stone: "Corban of Abba, see for me." A scene appeared in the stone that frightened them: the crashing of waves against a semicircle of sharp rocks . . . rock teeth that were moving.

"That's not Alamantia ahead, but some foul trick!" the duke stated. To Triamedes he urged, "Call Queen Eliadenor at once!"

"What about Queen Dorcas?" Eric timidly asked. "Can't she . . ."

"My sister has no power over the ocean," Mark snapped, watching the pilot. From between his golden cape and emerald green robe, Triamedes pulled a large conch shell tied on a strap slung around his chest. His yellow eyes flashed as he set the pointed end of the conch—cut off and hollowed out as a mouthpiece—to his lips and sounded a deafeningly loud call. The blast he blew shrieked into the cold, wet wind.

"Back oars!" the duke shouted down to the oar-master.

The drumbeat boomed loudly as the rowers quickly turned around on their benches. Digging their oar blades into the waves, they slowly reversed the ship's progress. But the wave-crashed patches of rock—clearly visible now to those on the fore deck—moved even more quickly. Soon, the warship was encircled in a rising, closing reef.

"Back oars and hold her steady!" the duke shouted between cupped hands.

The warriors and sailors then began to grow restless, disturbed by the sound of surf booming beyond the wooden hull. It was a sound that to seafarers foretold almost certain death. Their uneasiness grew by the minute, for most of them could swim no better than a stone.

"Is it an illusion, magician," Duke Mansbridge asked, looking toward the reef, "or, if not, can you blast us a passage?"

Acuerias sat on the deck and opened his book as he put the Corban Stone into one pocket. *"Toph . . . treo . . . tyrns,"* he murmured.

"Hurry!" Mark urged.

The magician's expression lightened as he stood and moved toward a torch. Loudly then he read, *"Tyrns oth! Othre e-mar, vocci A-Abba!"* Lowering the book, he watched the reef—as did the other men topside.

A struggle began within the ocean. The water around the ring of rocks fumed and boiled. The reef ground to a halt . . . but did not go away.

"At least you stopped it," the duke sighed.

"Alone," Acuerias admitted sadly, "I lack sufficient power to break the force besetting us." He closed his heavy book.

In a voice so low that only Eric and Jon heard him, Mark muttered, "Then the northern sorcerer is powerful indeed, for he yet is far away."

"My lords!" shouted the bow watchman. "The wind . . ." His final words were swept away by an explosion of spray soaring over the bow. Before anyone could reach him, he vanished into the sea.

The others hastened below as the force of the east wind doubled. Even as they fought their way down the stairway, the gale tore at them. It drenched torches and forced the great warship again toward the teeth of the reef. Warriors and soldiers joined the rowers in frantically working to hold the ship steady . . . but it slipped ever nearer the ring of jagged rocks.

The hurricane soon was howling. Rigging snapped with sharp *cracks!* Horses helplessly thrashed in their stalls, wild with terror. The towering mast groaned and finally split up the middle; the huge iron bands binding the mast shattered into pieces that went flying like shrapnel. Then, Eric and the others began to feel a sickening sensation. The ship was spinning, gradually turning faster and faster.

"A whirlpool is forming beneath us!" Triamedes called, clinging to a deck support column. Desperately, he blew his conch again and again.

The Duke shouted to him, "We're done for; save yourself if you . . ."

His words were snatched away by a shrieking onslaught of wind and spray. Even though they were huddled under the stairway, the Kingsmen were drenched by the driving sea water. The long ship was lifted and slammed, wrecking oars by the dozens. Rowers were flung against one another as water spouted through their oar ports. Then came a prolonged shattering sound louder than the violent wind.

Eric, Jon, and Martin managed to grip hands, certain that the ship had struck the reef and was about to be sucked into the whirlpool. But as they swabbed salty water from their eyes, they glimpsed eerie green light flashing from astern. As the rending furor grew deafening, the ship rushed backward, out of the whirlpool and into calmer water. The Kingsmen looked at one another in disbelief and slowly stood. Then they joined the duke and a number of others who were scrambling up the slippery stairs to the top deck. There, the boys slid to the rail. When they looked toward the ocean, they were astounded!

A great, deeply wrinkled whale had come. It was, Eric quickly surmised, longer than the ship. It had rammed a hole in the reef, and the warship had been swept through the hole. With its tall forehead, the whale now was battering down the remainder of the reef. And, as Jon pointed wildly, Eric saw that the whale was being directed by Queen Eliadenor! Her golden cape and emerald green robes streamed in the wind's breath; green fire flashed from her Jewel as she held it toward the vanishing reef.

"*Oth,* Unthoriumgai!" the boys heard her scream as she clung to the whale's blowhole with her left hand. "Teach the rocks to rise no more!"

Meanwhile, the rowers untangled themselves. Even the wounded ones helped put out spare oars. In minutes, the ship was underway. The green fire flickering wildly over the ocean seemed to give them courage, and many of the rowers cheered as they glanced out their oar ports to watch the whale finish battering down the reef. Then they saw the Sea Queen stand and shout into the wind.

Slowly it died. In the growing calm Unthoriumgai turned broadside to the *maralaman.* On his back,

Queen Eliadenor held her Jewel toward the warship. Glittering, the green fire withdrew into the stone. "Where is Acuerias?" she called.

The magician came to the railing, dizzy with seasickness, his hood blown behind his sopping wet hair.

The Sea Queen called to him, "If the Power comes again, say to it, *'Othre-nath, vocci A-Abba ne-Imnatride!'* "

As her words rang into the night, the moaning wind faded until it could do no more than ruffle the receding ocean swells. Soon, the swells again were only the pulsebeats of the deep. Queen Eliadenor waved once as Unthoriumgai slid beneath the dark surface.

"What a whale!" Martin laughed with nervous relief. "He must have *flown* here to bring the queen from wherever Jodi's ship is!"

"I wonder," Jon asked no one in particular, "how Queen Eliadenor feels, alone with that whale in the depths of the ocean?"

As repairs to the ship hastily were started, Duke Mansbridge shouted, "Forward oars!" The drumbeat began. Oars splashed in unison. Men began treating one another's wounds and repairing the mast. Handlers sorted out the trembling horses and cleared away broken stalls. Triamedes set the course, and the Kingsmen, though wet and tired, did what they could to help with the repair work.

By the end of the eleventh day from Espereim, the bow watchman shouted, "*Land* arising!" There was no uncertainty about this call. As the Kingsmen, warriors, and the Duke of Corlis hastened forward, they could see tall cliffs rising ahead from the grayness of thick mist. The headlands were split by a dark, yawning rift, and the duke observed, "There lies the mouth of Iverwain the Great."

Under the guidance of Triamedes, the warship

negotiated the outlying rock islands and entered the deep channel flowing swiftly with the river's current. The rowers struggled for miles up the broad river, glancing anxiously at the desolate landscape on either side.

When the *maralaman* coasted into the harbor of Imnatride, Eric whispered, "The city looks deserted and the trees and pastures as dead . . . as in winter." The duke simply nodded sadly in answer.

"What's that place," Martin inquired, "on top of that black mountain?"

"That is Castle Imnatride," Acuerias replied. "From it rises Glimmothtyrn, Tower of the Lightning, where the bottle was kept."

The ship bumped sideways against the stone wharf. Sailors—glancing nervously at the gray forms lying along the dock—cautiously leaped ashore to tie up the ship.

Jon asked, "What did this place look like before the Darkness came?"

No one answered because all were looking at the gray corpses curled stiffly dockside. When Jon looked at Queen Dorcas, he saw that she was crying silently. Without a word, she followed the others from the ship.

The tramp of boots and clatter of horses' hooves grew loud as companies formed on the dock. The warriors tried to ignore the ash corpses—but could not. Nor could their horses, which trembled frequently. Queen Dorcas and the Kingsmen soon were mounted, and Acuerias climbed aboard Terserius. The duke then led the troops at a slow pace up cobblestone streets past silent, dark houses coated with what seemed to be soot. Those in the procession frequently glanced toward the gloomy castle, and they tried to avoid looking at the twisted, petrified-looking bodies that littered the streets.

"You'd never know that once Imnatride was white—dazzling—and that its people were content and productive," the duke commented to Jon.

The lord the boys had heard called Basmoth Bonasorte rode up beside the duke. "My men, Sir, are growing sleepy!" he reported.

"Mine too!" Lord To'bol shouted from nearby. "We'd best go back."

"Aye," Lord Ghazi echoed, "lest vainglorious leaders lead us to our doom."

The duke ignored the voices of dissent as he turned, making his saddle creak. "Acuerias, what can you do about this evil gloom?"

The magician consulted his book, lifted his staff, and loudly called, *"Othre, Epraimeth na-espere ma conseroth!"* For Eric's ears alone he added, "That means, 'Go back, evil thing that kills hope and strength.' " In a solemn voice, he then called, *"Vocci A-Abba!* Thus says the Father!"

They watched the sky shudder as though stirring in its sleep. Gradually, a pale, gray light brightened the sky over the island. Relieved, the column resumed its march.

Riding beside Eric up the mountainside streets, Acuerias shook his head and muttered, "I'm afraid I'm getting old. The Darkness didn't go, nor did the people awaken."

"No, Sir," Eric said absently, then asked, "What's that ahead where the street opens?"

The column came to a halt, and those in back stood on their stirrups to try to see what lay before them. Mark, the queen, Acuerias, and the Kingsmen slowly rode forward and stopped in a square into which five streets opened. Across the square was the gray-streaked outer wall of Castle Imnatride, pierced by a large gate; the gate—like a black, shadowy mouth—was open. In the center of the square stood an empty, cracked fountain; on the near side of the fountain a group of ashy warriors lay like toppled, ancient statues. And between the fountain and the shadowy mouth of the gate stood a slab of black stone, six or so feet tall with letters carved on it. Beside the slab stood a figure hooded and robed in black. Where the face should have been was empty, dark space. And where the black robe trailed onto the mist-slickened cobblestones, a wooden mallet and three flat chisels lay near a small pile of stone chips.

"It's as though the thing just finished carving a message," Eric whispered, feeling goosebumps prickle his arms and neck.

"Is it alive?" Martin, in a tiny voice, asked Mark Mansbridge.

The duke rode to the silent figure, which was a foot shorter than the black slab. Drawing his sword, Mark leaned over and touched the eerie watcher with his sword point. In an instant, the robe collapsed with a whisper, causing the duke's great stallion to shy away.

"Nothing," Mark mused as Acuerias joined him. Martin and Jon rode up to stare at the heap of black cloth. Behind them, soldiers and lords filtered cautiously into the square, carefully avoiding the group of ashy warriors on the paving stones.

Eric nudged his skitterish mount until it stood before the black slab. Remembering Acuerias's lessons in the ancient language, Eric read the first words of the carved warning: *"Oth-nath* . . . Go not." He looked toward the yawning gate in the castle wall . . . and shivered. Suddenly, their goal of recovering the Lightning in the Bottle seemed far, far away.

Chapter 4

General Talaman's Defeat

As the serpent reared its head above the army camp in the Swamps of Armazil, terror swept among the soldiers and horses. Even grizzled veterans bolted and scrambled toward the harbor. Some sprang upon the backs of wild-eyed horses and clung to them as the animals dashed into the swamp. Others fled on foot, mistakenly shouting, "The Scourge! The Scourge is upon us!" Their goal—battling the Darkness—was forgotten.

General Talaman rushed from his tent and stared up at the green-yellow head wavering over the scene from atop a mound of coils perhaps three hundred feet high. Then, seeing that his men were fleeing, Talaman drew his sword and bellowed, "Hold and fight! *Hold and fight!!*" But the men heeded nothing except their thoughts of escape.

Those who reached the harbor found, however, that there was no escape: The *maralaman* had departed. The men therefore could do nothing but seek hiding places. The confusion in the swamp became total as the serpent's head moved more quickly above its mountain of coils; almost majestically it chose its targets . . . as it had been instructed to do.

With a rushing HISSSS! the monster lunged among decaying tree skeletons for floundering men. Waymond reflexively unleashed yellow lightning from his staff as the monstrous head darted toward him. The snake withdrew from the smoking light, momentarily blinded. The pause gave General Talaman and Colonel Xan time to lead a band of hardened warriors to the attack. Brandishing swords and battle-axes, they ran to the nearest writhing coils.

Leaping up, they stabbed and hacked the creature's side. It recoiled, hissing a foul breath that scoured the men. Then down dove the fanged head. Colonel Xan and half a dozen warriors were snatched to their doom. Screaming, they fell from the snake's mouth one by one as it quickly recoiled. Waymond, slipping across the mud to a new position, held up his staff. Lightning sizzled skyward, causing smoke to erupt around the beast's eyes. It writhed, and its coils crushed fleeing men and horses, splintered trees, and flushed waves of black water from bayous. Again, the dauntless general and his men leaped to the attack, drawing black sap from the beast with each thrust of their weapons. A mad light now was blazing in General Talaman's eyes.

With a rushing roar of wind, the head struck. Some of the warriors were destroyed outright. The snake's tusk-like fangs ripped others, and they shriveled as poison consumed them. Waymond saw Jodi, Rachael, and Richard near Queen Sybra. He raced to them, leaping a deep ditch and ducking a coil as it slithered over his head. Beside the children, he again aimed his staff at the wavering head. ZZZCCRRAAACCKKK!!! sang the yellow lightning. The serpent's nostrils filled with boiling flames, and the creature rolled to one side, shutting its cold eyes. As it twisted in pain, it mangled the camp.

There now were but a few hundred men left alive, and most of them were thrashing through the black water and fog. Only General Talaman and twenty or so men steadfastly continued to shift and attack, thrusting their blades into the seemingly endless serpent. Once again down swooped the charred, yellow-green head. With screams Jodi never forgot, the veteran Tyrn and most of his fellow attackers were devoured. Quickly, the serpent recoiled and struck again, even as Waymond sent a blast of lightning to ward off the blow. The light bolt collided with the snake's gaping mouth just as the fangs ripped into General Talaman—who died thrusting his sword into the throat of his slayer. As the lightning charred the snake's mouth, a red explosion of poison burst up. The snake sagged—but its duty to its new master—the northern sorcerer—had been fulfilled. General Talaman and one third of the force that had sailed from Eoramia had been slain.

Wearily, the vast serpent drew back, sinking as it glared balefully at the magician and his cowering band. Waymond gave it no time to rest; holding his staff in both hands, he shouted, *"Es-A-Abba conseroth!"* as again he unleashed the lightning.

The enormous head was struck squarely between its eyes. Blinking, it was forced backward. The towering neck wavered unsteadily as the thick coils slithered across the swamp. Tall tree skeletons were shattered. Hiding soldiers and the remaining horses were obliterated.

"Run!" Waymond cried to Queen Sybra, who alone seemed unafraid. "My power does more harm than good," he added dejectedly.

Queen Sybra took Jodi's left hand and Rachael's right hand and led them quickly northward. Jodi was amazed by the strength in the old woman's hand and by her quick, unerring steps. Richard was snatched up by the magician. Within minutes, the five figures vanished into the misty fog.

Far away—across the vast swamps, beyond the long Slopes of Tava, hidden within the maze of peaks called the Mother of the Sky Mountains—sat the power who had aroused Tuwachu'a, Serpent Guardian of the South. On a contorted throne under Castle Hidlothnath, Jabez, the eldest son of Ingloamin, stared toward a chasm of brightly flowing lava. Fumes wreathed his head as he sighed with satisfaction. To two other powers standing nearby he murmured, "So easy . . . so very easy." Then, pressing his fingertips to his sunken temples, he thought, *"Pursue them, my poison-slave, and consume them!"* In response, the lava in the chasm boiled furiously, flinging red-orange droplets upward. The droplets splashed over the base of the throne, startling a pair of cave bears chained there. The larger of the two powers near the throne—who was called the Scourge of Scorius in honor of its defeat of that land—began to laugh. Laughter soon filled the cavern.

"The serpent is chasing us," Jodi gasped as Queen Sybra pulled her up the muddy bank of a bayou they had just crossed.

"Be still, child," the queen said.

Crashing, grinding noises came from behind them, and Richard glanced back with a terrified expression. "The Scourge is gaining!" he cried, leaping a ditch, then wading into a stand of cane stalks.

Waymond emerged from the rattling brown stalks close behind him. "That's not the Scourge; it's one of the ancient Guardians of Eorthe."

Ahead, Rachael forced aside downhanging veils of gray moss; a gray snake swung down, and she drew her sword and slashed it in half. "Then what . . ."

"Don't talk about the Scourge," Queen Sybra commanded, ducking under the scratchy moss behind Rachael and avoiding a shower of angry ants.

Silently, they looked back toward the oncoming snake. Through gaunt, black branches, they saw the green-yellow form winding after them.

Now, the snake, Tuwachu'a—being a Guardian—was not by nature evil. Before being mastered by Jabez, the snake had guarded the tribes of Rud against creatures like Bogloams that crept into the Caves of Rainath. It also felt great pride in being the patriarch of snakes*, and thus, deep inside its cold brain, it fought against its enslavement to the sorcerer.

The girls and Richard, however, knew nothing of the inner struggles of the vast beast pursuing them—and Waymond understood but little of the ancient creature. Thus, the terrified young people swam a deep channel and climbed onto an island, helped by the increasingly frustrated magician. Richard collapsed on the island, and Waymond stopped beside him, muttering, "Lightning won't kill it, and the Jewel of Tava . . ." He turned to Sybra with a puzzled expression. "Why can't you help us?" he asked her.

"Listen to me, Edessan," Sybra snapped in a low tone, "my power will work *only* if *nothing* threatens the serpent."

He drew back, frowning . . . then backed away, lowering his staff.

Queen Sybra quickly went to Jodi, placed her hands on the girl's shoulders, and turned her around to face the Guardian. Quietly, Sybra whispered in Jodi's ear, "We must return to the beginnings! I want you to say

---

*All Eorthe's snakes descended from Tuwachu'a, including Grag and other monster-serpents made by sorcerers from eggs stolen from the Guardian.

to that creature, *'Yo-cor glorimm, vocci A-Abba.'* It means, 'In the name of the King, I love you.' Repeat the words!"

"I *can't!*" Jodi cried, squirming to turn away from the awful sight.

"For the King you can do anything," Sybra stated, straightening, "and if we are to live, you must. Now, repeat the words!"

"But why *me?*" Jodi cried.

"Because you are innocent; the Guardian will listen to you."

Jodi hung her head, and the queen told her the words again. When she dutifully had repeated the words exactly, Sybra nodded. She stepped back, leaving Jodi to face the snake alone. Richard, realizing that he was as exposed as Jodi was, scrambled behind Waymond, who frowned at him.

Tuwachu'a's broad head, weaving atop the mighty body that stretched out of sight into the swamp, had come to the channel across from the island where Jodi and the others stood watching. With a *hisss!*, the head—far larger than the trembling girl—darted to within feet of her ashen face. Frozen in terror, she stared into the clear, pale yellow depths of the monster's scorched eyes and barely managed to say, *"Yo-cor glorimm, vocci A-Abba.* In the name of the King, I . . . love you."

The snake became motionless and blinked. It flicked out its thick, branching red tongue and twined the tips around Jodi's body without touching her. Jodi then realized that the King's invisible power DID protect her, and she saw that her words had kindled a response in the great beast. Therefore, and gladly now, Jodi called loudly, *"Yo-cor glorimm, vocci A-Abba!"*

Back and back the girl's words took the memory of the serpent. It recoiled slowly, remembering Him who had been its Maker. But instantly it felt pain as its new master transmitted the thought, *"Strike, my poison-slave! Strike!"* The words screamed in the Guardian's brain . . . but with monumental effort it continued to recoil. *"Strike . . . str-i-k . . . e"* echoed the fast-fading thought. But Tuwachu'a refused to obey anyone but its Maker any longer.

It paid a terrible price for resisting the sorcerer's power. Gradually, as the astonished humans watched, the serpent's great length faded from green-yellow to gray. Its coils stiffened and grew still. Its eyes closed as at last even the great head turned to stone.

Jodi breathed deeply and ran into Waymond's open arms. Richard cautiously climbed to his feet and went to the edge of the island. He picked up a slimy rock and flung it at the petrified serpent. "Take that, you worm!" Richard called. Then, seemingly satisfied, he returned to the others, scratching himself behind his mud-stained armor.

On the island they spent a wet and miserable night, huddled around a smouldering fire. Waymond made food appear for them, but it tasted damp. Later, as hours of darkness passed, Jodi and the others uneasily slept. Jodi, for one, was bothered by a recurring dream: She kept wandering from safety in the light into strange places filled with darkness.

Among the black peaks of Tavares, the Volcanoes of Tava continually argue with the sky and earth and fume in rage. Beneath Castle Hidlothnath, in a cavern-hall among the roots of the volcanoes, the sorcerer sat deep in thought as cold as the stone-cracking air of his land. In response, a surge of ashes and smoke flowed from the splintered cones into the sky. "Release the Wolvors," he commanded the other powers standing nearby. "Send forth the Obnars of Torang! The King's servants *must not* here be joined!" As the powers burst from Castle Hidlothnath, black lightning slashed from the clouds above Tavares into the tortured mountains.

In the gray, cheerless dawn, Waymond arose and began going south.

"Wait!" came Jodi's alarmed voice before he had gone far. "Aren't you taking us with you?"

"No," he laughed, surprised by her question. "I'm only going back to the army's campsite to see if I can recover your packs and my carpetbag."

Jodi's expression fell, and her shoulders slumped. But slowly she brightened. "*Then* are we going home?" she asked weakly.

Waymond finally understood what she had in mind. Firmly but gently he said, "We'll not go 'home' until we've done what we came to do: recover and release the Lightning in the Bottle."

"But the army! . . ." Jodi cried, staring southward.

Waymond smiled and held her close. Quietly, he said, "Were you alone left of all the King's servants, the task—the goal—would still be the same." He kissed the crown of her head and left her. She stared after him until he was swallowed from sight.

By noon, he had returned with the Kingsmen's packs and his leather-handled bag. From the bag he produced—much to the girls' delight and Queen Sybra's satisfaction—warm, wet towels. Richard, however, was actually reluctant to clean up, having found that the mud coating on his face and arms protected him somewhat from the droves of mosquitoes.

Refreshed for the time being, Jodi and Rachael followed Waymond, Sybra, and Richard as rapidly as possible northward. After floundering across a bog, they wended their way into a forest of gray, moss-festooned trees. Snakes writhed out of their path, but biting insects of all kinds swarmed to greet them. Thus began the next of the many remaining miles of swamp.

Through three days they traveled in that way, and by the end of the fourth day they hardly were recognizable as humans—nor did they feel they were. As the fourth night crept over the land of Armazil, Waymond halted. He fed the group, then announced, "We must go on. We're being watched, and we must reach a place of safety—a place to which only Queen Sybra can guide us . . . if she will." He looked at the queen, and for the first time the girls wondered why she wore black.

"I will guide you to Tophinole," Sybra replied sharply. "Saving my son Tzarn and his son Malac and awakening our land means more to me than preserving ancient secrets!" With a faintly sarcastic smile, she added, "And I'm glad you've become aware of the Watchers. I'd begun to doubt your powers." Her smile was both amused and critical.

Waymond lit fire from the tip of his staff; the yellow glow radiated over the five people sitting uncomfortably in mud on wet weeds, surrounded by looming darkness. When the girls looked at Waymond, they saw his wood-brown eyes flash as he stared at Queen Sybra. "You failed to warn us of the serpent," he said coldly.

"In the Foregathering, To'bol warned you that the ancient beasts had been awakened. But did you ask the King how such creatures are handled? No, you assumed *your* power would be sufficient, just as did General Talaman," she hissed, leaning forward as she squinted at him. "You risk Eorthe on the point of your pride—Magician!"

Waymond frowned but bridled his tongue and bowed slightly. "I will henceforth listen more closely to my master," he said calmly.

She nodded stiffly. "Lead on, Magician of *our* Lord. Two points east of north."

Waymond closed his eyes, turned his head slightly to the right, then led off in that direction. His upheld staff shed glittering reflections over the bayou before them. Into the black water they waded. Thick with slime, the water soon came up to their chests. Ripples ran from their struggling bodies and faded off beyond the light's reach . . . down, down the dark channel. In silence at the edge of the light, the Watchers patiently sat.

Illuminated by the yellow umbrella of light, the group trudged on, mile after mile. And frequently from the darkness around them shone eyes—eyes red and close together . . . eyes yellow and flickering . . . eyes silver and flamelike. In the magician's light, the ember eyes vanished. But, when Waymond went on ahead, the children looked aside to see the glowing eyes gradually reappear, each pair separated by heights and depths and widths of black night.

Sounds soon arose from unseen distances of water and boggy forest . . . sounds that seemed to mean the Watchers were becoming impatient. Scrapings rasped; groans rumbled; growls heavy and long made the air tremble . . . and grated on the children's nerves. And Richard, much to his terror, heard a voice seemingly intended for him alone. First from the left, then the right—as though searching—the voice whispered, *"Boy? Boy who talked with demons? Speak to me, boy."* Richard hurried on, afraid for his sanity.

One particularly loud sound startled Rachael, and she drew her sword. When it flickered blue, she commented, "Evil's nearby."

"Well, of course it is," Richard groused. "But this

armor's worse. It's making me itch something awful, and this shield is weighing me down!" He stopped, ankle deep in sluggish water. "I'm gonna take this stuff off!"

"Not if you want to live," Waymond warned. "Where are the leaves Queen Dorcas gave you?"

Rachael and Jodi dug in their packs and pulled out their grapevine leaves. Richard apparently had lost his, so Jodi gave him one of hers. Smelling the leaves cheered the children; the scent awakened memories of green hills and wildflowers, of rain falling gently and sun shining brightly.

"Onward now," Waymond urged quietly.

"Couldn't you just zap us there?" Richard whined, plodding heavily.

"Here, the dark power is all around us. *I* might get through, but you . . ."

Jodi shuddered, strongly remembering her nightmare of falling through a tunnel of darkness. She hastened after Waymond and Queen Sybra.

Gradually the day grew gray with a weak dawn. "This way," Sybra said, pointing through wispy fog toward an embankment. Up they climbed and, to their great relief, found themselves in a jungle on dry ground. "Yonder lies Torang, capital of Armazil," the queen said, aiming one finger north-northeast.

"Acuerias will also make for Torang," Waymond commented, "if he can."

"Then we must leave him some sign there, telling him of . . . of the haven, for I doubt he knows its location," Sybra said, striding forward.

"How can we leave any form of message?" Waymond asked, keeping pace with her. "The Watchers surely know all our languages and codes . . . or at least can transmit them."

Queen Sybra pondered the problem as the young people caught up.

"I know a code they don't," Jodi said, breathing hard from exertion. "Martin taught it to me last year from a library book."

"You assume," Waymond said gently, "that Martin will live to come to Torang with Acuerias." His words struck Jodi with the force of a slap.

Tears filled her eyes as she stared at him. Then, trembling, she put her mud-slimed hands to her once beautiful hair and sank to the ground. "No . . . oh, please, no," she murmured. "I couldn't take *that*."

Rachael moved quickly toward her, but Waymond waved her away and knelt by the sobbing girl. "Jodi, don't give up now. Come; you will find that—even if the worst happens—it is not your strength upon which you must depend. You also may learn that from a broken heart and exhausted spirit emerges a servant willing to rely totally on Abba." He lifted her with Rachael's help, then added, "As you have seen, I, too, have been led to lay aside my will and trust Abba!"

After a while, Jodi nodded, sighed, and gradually lifted her shoulders and head. Waymond then hugged her as he would have hugged the children he never could have, and they went on, through the dead jungle. Tediously, they walked until darkness came over them, then slept in a deadfall of trees while Waymond kept watch.

In the early dawn of the sixth day, they walked through low lying fog into thinning jungle. Emerging from it, they saw the capital city of Armazil, Torang, nestled against a land of bare, gently rising slopes. Cautiously, Queen Sybra led the group toward the city.

Reaching toward the clouds were the ornamented tops of hundreds of stone buildings. Each building had many rectangular, painted layers that decreased in size toward the top. No wall surrounded the city, but a river had been diverted into broad channels bridged by defensible archways. Nowhere in or around the city was there a single sign of life, although the travelers passed many ash corpses. It took Waymond and his group until the middle of the afternoon to walk around the city, and by then they were infected by the dark mood of it.

Up a miles' wide slope to a ridge they made their way, leaning into a strong wind from the north. On the ridgetop, Waymond said, "Surely Acuerias will come here to survey the land beyond. Let's leave the way marker here. Jodi, show me how to write Tophinole." He turned to Queen Sybra and asked, "What are the bearings by Mayic, the pole star?"

The queen closed her deeply wrinkled eyes. "Two degrees east of north, fifteen miles," she replied.

Waymond held out one palm, and Jodi wrote the code on it. Then, he aimed his staff at the ridge crest and said, *"Tyrn n-glim, kaomimt!"*

From a cloud of yellow light emerged an upright slab of white stone. The stone seemed stuck quite deeply in the earth. Waymond said, "There! Let them try to uproot *that!*" With the still glowing tip of his staff, he carved this message in Martin's code:

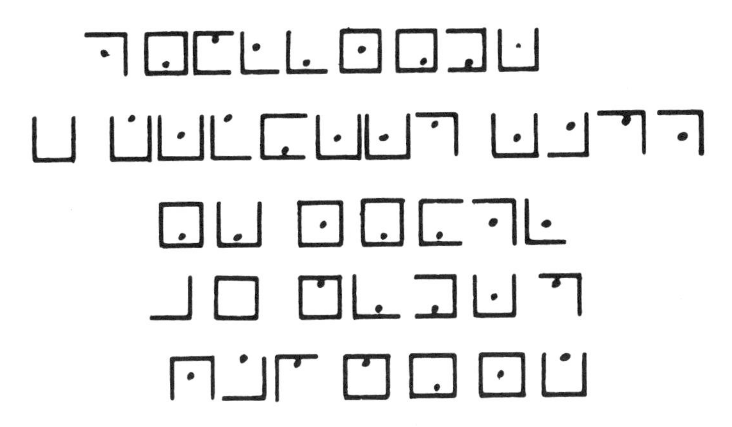

Before the white dust from the engraved stone had settled, they were on their way again—down from the ridge to a trough-shaped valley, then up to the next slope. Freed from the swamp and jungle, out of sight of the ash corpses, the children began to feel happy once more—until from behind them came a distant, deep, wavering sound. It was the baying of animals.

"Run!" Waymond commanded. Silently, they obeyed and began racing down the ridge toward the next one. With long strides under her flashing dark robe, Queen Sybra kept their pace. The baying became sharp and disharmonious, and the voices grew more widespread as the afternoon darkened to a gloomy evening.

"What do you suppose is chasing us?" Jodi called to Queen Sybra.

"Wolvors," the queen shouted back, running faster.

The beasts, led by an especially huge demon-wolf with saber-like fangs, stopped to sniff the white slab scored with Martin's code. Through the leader's red smouldering eyes, the distant sorcerer studied the strange markings. But he could make nothing of the message, and his rage made the chasm fires before him leap high. *"After them!"* his thought sped to the Wolvor pack. *"After them! Kill them . . . and* eat them!" Howling, the bristling beasts streamed over the Slopes of Tava.

A mile . . . then another went past under the steadily jogging feet of Waymond and his band. They climbed slope after slope, each one slightly higher than the one before. They ran faster whenever the baying became louder behind them. When Jodi paused atop one of the seemingly endless ridges, she glanced back—and promptly wished she had not. "The wolves are like the ones that other sorcerer had as statues!" she cried to Rachael. Together, they ran after Waymond.

"Why aren't they gaining faster?" Rachael called, looking back. As the light faded, the wolves' bodies were becoming less visible . . . but the glow of their eyes was becoming brighter and brighter.

Waymond, too, looked at the wavering tide of eyes. "They have no need to gain on us," he said, breathing hard, "because others come before us and from the east and west."

"We're trapped!" Richard wailed, stumbling.

"How far . . . is the haven?" Jodi asked weakly.

"Silence, child!" Queen Sybra snapped, gripping Jodi's hand tightly.

Another mile passed underfoot, and the band reached the top of a long slope. This ridge was the highest yet and seemed to be a breaking point in the land. Beyond a valley rose foothills some six miles away, dark gray in the early night. Beyond the foothills lay a shadowy mountain range. From it came a cold wind . . . and the sound of more baying voices.

"The haven is within the foothills," Queen Sybra said. Lurching, they all began to run into the valley below them. The four waves of Wolvors, meanwhile, relentlessly closed their trap. As blackness cloaked the land, the burning eyes of thousands of beasts cast a crimson glow over the valley . . . and the humans.

The Wolvor leader, Warfang, felt his fire drooling past his long teeth and listened to the voice drumming in his head: *"Kill . . . **kill** . . . KILL!"* The same command reached the other beasts, and soon their baying became frenzied, deafening, as they closed in upon their prey. Their long jaws snapped repeatedly in anticipation.

Chapter 5

Gafailnath Arising

Acuerias came to stand beside Eric outside the wall of Castle Imnatride. He read the remainder of the warning carved on the black slab. *"Oth-nath imt-o. Imt abbans Garainath na-pere ma conseroth!"* He sighed and translated, "Go not herein. Here reigns 'That evil that kills hope and strength.' "

The lords and warriors looked from the magician to the dark yawning gateway. Queen Dorcas broke the silence. She held up her yellow flashing Jewel, tilted her head so her long blond hair swung back, and loudly prayed, *"Abba, othi-y Gafailnath!"*

"Father, send us 'That which fails not'?" Eric guessed.

The magician smiled wanly and nodded to his pupil.

Suddenly Dorcas dismounted and strode toward the gateway. As she went into the deep shadows, her Jewel flared. When she held it up, shadows and gray fog shrank hissing from her path. The men followed in her wake. Looking left and right, weapons ready, they hastened across a courtyard to keep the Queen of Eoramia in sight.

Straight through inner courtyards, past scattered ash corpses, up the main stairway to the castle doors

Dorcas went—head high, eyes intent, jeweled necklace flaming brightly. She threw wide the huge double doors and went quickly to the chamber at the base of the central tower—Glimmothtyrn.

There, she knelt beside a form outstretched head down over the last three steps. In one hand the ash corpse held a sword; in the other hand was a pink sea conch. The Kingsmen and warriors hurried to gather around the body and the queen, who was murmuring, "My son . . . my beautiful son."

She held the yellow light from her necklace over Morgan's ashy gray head and the sword. In seconds, Eric and the others saw the sword flicker with blue fire. As the light from the Jewel of Corlis continued to flood over the corpse, the blue flame from Gafailnath grew stronger. The mingling yellow and blue lights resulted in a green glow that gradually spread up the arm of the enthralled prince. "Bring heated water," the queen commanded without raising her head. Several men started off at once while Dorcas bent over her son, whispering, *"A-Abba conseroth seu"* over and over.

When at last a steaming vat was carried into the room, Acuerias took a handful of grapevine leaves from his shoulder bag and dropped them into the water. Queen Dorcas then said to her brother Mark, "Help me—carefully." Together they lifted the stiff gray corpse and settled it into the vat. The ash coating became dark as the water crept over it. Dorcas bent and gently bathed the ash coating away. The sword, still clutched in the youth's right hand, pulsed with a sky blue light, but the conch clattered sharply to the floor as the youth's fingers straightened. Acuerias put the conch into his bag and leaned over to watch the youth's color turn from brown-black to pale brown. Finally, the prince breathed.

"Praise Abba!" Acuerias said thankfully. Smiling,

he watched Queen Dorcas continue to lave the fragrant water over Morgan until his eyelids fluttered open. The youth began to stir, then slowly sat upright.

"Mother," he whispered, leaning into her enfolding arms. The light from her Jewel enveloped them. "I was afraid . . . I had failed," he sighed.

"No, Morgan. You did not fail," his mother said reassuringly.

When the youth was well enough to walk, he asked that Lord Baldwin Evnstar, the warriors Asaph and Lucian, and the other veterans be awakened. Only the first three, however, responded. The others simply dissolved, muddying the vat's water.

Quickly then, the entire group returned to the *maralaman*. On the way, Lord Baldwin—whose voice sounded gruff and sleepy—asked, "The Lightning in the Bottle . . . has it been recovered?"

"No, my Lord Ispenth," Acuerias sadly reported, pointing toward the sooty sky.

"Then we must go north at once," the bear-like lord stated. With difficulty, he unsheathed the Flame of Ispenth from its tarnished scabbard . . . then smiled and bowed to Morgan. "Lead us, my king," he said.

Night was darkening the dingy sky as the companies reboarded the warship. Morgan, Baldwin, Asaph, and Lucian were fitted with new clothes, boots, and armor—while a number of warriors talked with them about how it felt to be overcome by the Darkness. Morgan then went to talk privately with his mother, Acuerias, and the Duke of Corlis. Frequently, they glanced toward the Kingsmen, especially Eric. Meanwhile, the ship was rowed out of the harbor and began to glide with the outflow of Iverwain.

Morgan took a seat on the dragon's head bow, and Queen Dorcas stood beside him. As the pair gazed back toward the Alamantian capital, Eric watched them. He noted that their profiles were the same and that both had a naturally proud bearing, the same sunlight-blond hair, and startlingly green eyes. When Imnatride had been left behind, Queen Dorcas tenderly kissed Morgan on one cheek and went below. The young king turned on his perch and almost broodingly looked ahead.

In a few hours the ocean was sighted, and waves could be heard breaking against the headlands and outlying islands. Into the wind the *maralaman* turned; the drumbeat throbbed loudly, the rowers pulled hard, and slowly headway was forced—northward. Supper was served by torchlight, and the voyage quickly settled into monotony . . . though for the Kingsmen, the boredom was short-lived.

King Morgan called the boys to him, and when they stood on the steps below the dragon's head, he said, "I am told that you three are blooded warriors and magicians." His look was searching and somewhat skeptical.

Eric glanced at Martin and Jon, then shrugged. "We're just Kingsmen," he said quietly.

"Just?" Morgan asked, shifting position on the gilded neck of the dragon's head. "In any case, Eric Vanover, I am to ask you if you now are ready to receive the reward our King promised you in his garden in Castle Glimpalatyrn."

"The reward I might feel was a task?" Eric asked, liking the young king but troubled by a shadow he saw in Morgan's eyes.

Morgan looked away. "Yes," he replied . . . then slowly looked at Eric with a gaze that became piercing. "Will you sign a covenant of apprenticeship with magician Acuerias? If you do, you will be bound by it. If you do not, you still can be of service in our quest to regain the Lightning."

Eric blinked, startled by the offer. He looked around until he saw Acuerias standing nearby. "Me?" he asked the magician.

Acuerias stepped forward, head bowed, hands clasped. "The King," he began, "has been well pleased with your skill and faith during the six years you've been a Kingsman. And you are needed," he added in a husky voice, looking at Eric, "because, if you agree, you will replace me."

Eric stared, feeling saddened, yet thrilled. He looked at Jon and Martin, who were staring wonderingly at him. "Gosh," Martin muttered, "I'd jump at the chance!"

Eric bowed his head, then looked at Acuerias. "Yes," he said simply.

The magician nodded with a smile, settled his hood over his snowy hair, and stepped backward.

"Good," Morgan stated. "Scribe!" he called toward the decks below.

In minutes a small man with nervous eyes and long fingers appeared. Humbly he stood below the dragon's head. "M'lord?" he inquired.

"In your best handwriting, draw up a covenant of apprenticeship," Morgan said in a regal manner, "to be signed by Kingsman Lieutenant Eric Vanover and Master Solemnus Acuerias Trg, King's Magician."

"And the length of service, m'lord?" the scribe asked.

Morgan looked at Acuerias, who sighed, "Unspecified."

Eric heard deep tiredness in the old man's voice. The scribe said, "Yes, my lords," and went below deck at a trot.

Morgan then turned to face the chilling wind, and Eric, watching him, thought that again the young king's look became brooding. Slowly, Morgan unsheathed Gafailnath and held the blue-glowing sword into the wind. "Thus shall we sunder the Darkness!" he spoke as though it were a vow. The lords and warriors on the fore deck looked at him, some hopefully, some dubiously.

Suddenly, Morgan gave them a self-conscious look. "Come, companions, this should be a time for rejoicing! Let me sing you a hunting song to celebrate our release and to remind us of green woods and fields where rabbits run beneath the sun's light!" In time with the throbbing rowers' drum, Morgan began to chant in a strong, clear voice:

(1) *Away, away*
with breath of day.
Soon comes sun,
down dark runs.
Feet feed hunger,
ever, ever.

(2) *Away, away*
with moon's full sway.
Soon comes sun,
down dark runs.
Hands feed hunger,
ever, ever.

(3) *Away, away*
with rain's light play.
Soon comes sun,
down dark runs.
Eyes feed hunger,
ever, ever.

(4) *Away, away*
when fogs delay.
Soon comes sun,
down dark runs.
Wits feed hunger,
ever, ever . . .
ever . . . ever!

The young king looked from Gafailnath to the Kingsmen, then to the other men standing nearby. "Now, that's a cheerful enough song to send you sleeping through this long night," he said, lying back. The Kingsmen bowed and went below to their cabins . . . glancing upward, as many of the warriors and lords did, at the figure reclining on the thick neck of the dragon's head. Eric was not alone in feeling uncomfortable about the king's behavior; instead of cheering him, Morgan's actions and song had made Eric wonder what the Darkness had done to the young king. But Eric shrugged, leaving the matter up to the King and Abba; after all, becoming an apprentice magician was quite enough to think about!

Two days blackly passed. Fog unrelentingly lay above the gray ocean swells that rose to meet the ship in unending ridges. During those days, Morgan, Baldwin, Asaph, and Lucian regained their strength. And Eric signed his Covenant of Apprenticeship. At the bottom of it, in dried red wax, was the impression of King Morgan's signet ring:

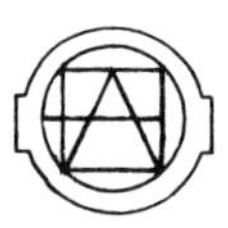

Eric had been sobered to read the terms of the agreement, but it did not seriously unsettle him to sign the curling, stiff piece of paper—and commit his life. Thereafter, he remained in Acuerias's cabin. Bent over his great book, the magician poured out deeper and deeper levels of his knowledge to the absorbent youth.

While the ship slowly beat its way northward for four more days, Eric expanded his knowledge of the ancient language of Eorthe. He then began to read Acuerias's book by himself. Patiently, the magician also taught his pupil to understand the limits of the "magic" revealed therein. And while Acuerias softly spoke, he whittled upon three, four-foot pieces of wood he had gotten from the ship's carpenter. "Ordinary wood," he had explained to Eric with a wink. "One piece of *scutotreo* from the mountains; one piece of *treotoph* from a valley; and one piece from the sea—*alcaneroth*." With an ever-sharp *nathnor* knife, the old man shaped the pieces of wood into twisting, turning lengths oddly formed.

On the afternoon of the sixth day from Alamantia, a watchman shouted, "Land . . . land ahead!" The call was repeated throughout the ship as bare feet and bootsteps pounded upward. Acuerias nodded and gave the three carved rods to Eric. "Now," he said to the tired but pleased young man, "fit the staff together as I've taught you."

Like three pieces of a puzzle, Eric worked the wands together, saying, *"Orcon, con-o A-Abba conseroth!"* With a vibration that made Eric's arms tremble, the woods glowed briefly with green light and snapped together, bonded in such a way that the joints were invisible. At that moment, in the green glow, Eric's armor sank into him. In its place slowly appeared a brown robe, belted and hooded. Smiling, Eric fingered the belt, noting that it was a supple chain of small, gold grapevine leaves. "I'm *really* a servant of the King now," he said, restraining the excitement he felt.

"Yes," Acuerias said softly. "But remember: Your new position merely gives you more responsibility."

"I know," Eric said soberly, looking at his staff. Feeling his thick, brown cotton hood rub the back of his neck, he tapped his staff on the plank floor. "You'd never guess from the appearance of this . . ."

". . . the power it can bring?" the magician supplied. When Eric nodded, the old man added, "Your initial training has been most abbreviated; therefore, I hope that you . . ."

"I will," Eric assured him. "The King must know I will use his power wisely, or he'd not have lent it." He caught a slightly sad look in the wise old man's eyes and went to embrace him.

"I'm coming full circle—at last," the aged magician whispered. Holding the young man at arms' length, he gazed into Eric's eyes; Eric looked back and felt he was looking into lighted wells: deep and blue and peaceful, despite the silver tears rimming them. "Will you carry my bag?" Acuerias asked as a tear fell onto his snowy beard. "In fact, you may keep it from now on."

Eric slung the bag over one shoulder and trailed behind the magician, who leaned heavily on his darkly polished staff. As they slowly climbed the stairs, Eric lightly tapped each step with the tip of his own staff. The slightly knobbed end of it felt strange in his hand—yet it also felt like the fulfillment of a childhood dream.

On the second deck, Jon and Martin ran toward Eric . . . then slowed to stare at his staff and brown robe as though trying to decide whether their friend's change was for real or for fun.

"I'm no longer a Kingsman," Eric explained, "nor exactly an Earthean."

After a speechless moment, Martin timidly asked, "Can I have your pack, if you won't be needing it? Mine's got a tear, and . . ."

"Yes," Eric said, suddenly feeling very different—and separated—from his younger friends. He stared at them until they became uncomfortable under his gaze. "Come on," Eric said suddenly, "I want to see this land that's been sighted!" He gathered up the edge of his robe and raced them up the stairs to the top deck as though giving boyhood one final fling. Acuerias said no word of reproach because he knew the time for laughing and playing all too soon would be over.

The coast of Armazil appeared even more dismal than Alamantia had been. The warriors and oarsmen stared at the coastline, and only the creaking of oars and the lapping of gray waves broke the silence. Although no snakes or other visible dangers greeted them, the deathly silence was less manageable than visible dangers would have been.

A half mile inland, at the edge of seemingly endless swamps, a rude camp was set up. Morgan, Queen Dorcas, and the other leaders gathered in an open tent out of the dripping fog. The Leohtians flashed in all directions on scouting missions. Within an hour, Captain Thrumingold and his squad returned with the news of General Talaman's defeat. The news spread quickly and greatly disheartened the troops. "What chance of success does the quest have now?" many grumbled as they tried to light fires.

Captain Thrumingold also informed Acuerias that five people had escaped the slaughter and had gone toward Torang. "Furthermore," the Leohtian sang into the old magician's ear, "we sensed that a number of our people originally sent to Rud were not killed, as we had feared. We feel that Light People linger still in Armazil, though we could not contact them because of the Darkness."

Morgan told the Leohtian, "In the morning, you will attempt to find the five people who escaped. We will go as quickly as we can toward Torang and hope to rejoin you—and the survivors—there." To Triamedes, Morgan said, "Take the *maralaman* out to sea and await our call." And to the watching warriors, the young king called, "Tomorrow, we will go onward—with the strength of the King *ever* in our hearts!" Unfortunately, the encouragement of his words was eaten up during the night by sounds and faint vibrations running through the marshy ground.

As a weak light came from the eastern sky in the morning, the horsemen and foot soldiers formed lines and floundered into the swamps. Each line sought the driest, least dangerous route . . . but all ways led into darkness. To make matters worse, the beautiful horses of the Plains of Eoramia—which the lords and warriors had thought would be a blessing—proved worse than useless. The animals had to be coaxed and pulled through the bogs and mire. As a result, the army began to disintegrate. And then, as frustration ate away the men's resolve, they began to hear voices.

At first, the soldiers thought the jeers and insults were from their comrades. However, the voices—speaking each man's language—began to assail them from all sides. *"Stupid!"* a hiss came. *"Can't you do better?"* rasped another voice. To some, voices croaked, *"You can't do it, and you should know it!"* Other warriors heard, *"What's it all for? Some powerless light in a bottle? How foolish!"* followed by sneering laughter. With sinking spirits, the men struggled on, trying to keep the leaders in view.

A few of the warriors, led by the members of House Evnstar, kept moving steadily ahead, singing ancient songs—one of which Queen Dorcas taught the Kingsmen:

Abba suesy, Abba séesy, unimt ma idglimm.
Suy alo-glorimm, alo-alaman, unimt ma idglimm . . .

But behind the leaders, warriors and lords wandered like homeless ants, shouting and cursing. At last Basmoth Bonasorte called out to Morgan, "It's no good, m'lord! We can't go on!"

Morgan took the sea conch from Acuerias and urged his horse to the top of a low hill. He blew the conch loudly. When the soldiers had gathered, they listened to the young king tell again the importance of regaining the Lightning and releasing it. For a time, his words of encouragement helped them. But, as more hours of exhausting travel passed, their situation became worse than ever—especially as strange voices whispered such things as, *"Fool! Where's your King* ***now?*** *Why isn't* ***he*** *here getting his precious white robe dirty?"* The men listened, growing more frustrated, filthy, and angry by the minute. *"Miles lie ahead,"* the grating voices came, *"**miles** of swamp and darkness. Just think how warm and dry you'd be back on the* maralaman! *It's waiting, you know. All you have to do is turn around and ride a few miles and you'll be **safe!"*** The men listened, and doubt gnawed at their resolve. The weaker ones turned and began sneaking back toward the coast.

"It won't do, m'lords," Basmoth panted, struggling for the thirtieth or so time to get his horse out of a boggy place. The dispirited animal stuck out its neck, rolled its eyes wildly, and refused to rise.

"Aye, 'tis foolish, as I warned," Lord Ghazi shouted, waving swarming mosquitoes away from his face.

The leaders held a council. The discussion was brief and furious, and it was decided that those who wanted to return to the ship should do so. King Morgan finished the announcement by saying, "Acuerias, you must lead them back, else the dark power lure them into eternal sleep."

Acuerias and many of the listening warriors were surprised by the decision, but inside they felt relieved. Only a few, like Basmoth of Oraibi, felt guilty about abandoning the quest.

"But, nephew," Baldwin Evnstar said, frowning, "if the army and Acuerias leave, with what shall we fight the sorcerer and his forces?"

Morgan smiled faintly, and again Eric noticed a slight shadow in the young king's eyes. "Magician apprentice," Morgan asked Eric, "are you empowered?"

Eric nodded, feeling the King's presence more than ever.

"My mother," Morgan turned to ask, "what help can you add?"

Queen Dorcas quietly said, "If the Three Jewels and the lights of the others empowered by the King can be united, we will have enough strength. But Queen

Eliadenor returned to the sea, and the fates of Queen Sybra and magician Waymond are unknown. Therefore, alone I can only continue to protect us from the Darkness."

Responding to an inner urge, Eric blurted, "There's another strength no one yet has named, and that is faith. The King told us to go. So we must go. He would not send us on a fool's errand."

"Well said, my student," Acuerias murmured.

King Morgan shot a look at the magician and quickly said, "Return now, faithful Acuerias, with those who wish to go." A hoarse cheer went up.

Within fifteen minutes, the dispirited lords and their warriors had splashed and slipped away, led by gloomy Acuerias and the now content To'bol and Ghazi. Only Morgan, Dorcas, Mark, and the two Kingsmen, as well as Eric, Baldwin, Asaph, and Lucian were left—nine against the Darkness. It was then that Morgan said something that gave Eric more understanding about the shadow he saw in the young king's eyes.

"Now," Morgan said with an odd tone of contentment, "now we can proceed to make right the duty in which my father failed, and in failure brought disgrace to House Evnstar!" He gripped Gafailnath's hilt, drew the blade, and pointed northwest. "By the strength of House Evnstar, let the power of Darkness be pierced!" He urged his horse into the swamp.

Worried, Eric shook his head slightly and followed the others.

Asaph and Lucian came last, glancing at the fleeing army. The pair of veterans shifted their wolf-hide packs, adjusted their weapon belts and armor, then spat onto the mire. Asaph said to Lucian, "Can't say as I blame 'em—the cowards." He jutted out his narrow, black-bearded chin. "But what bothers me," he added in a whisper, "is that young Morgan seemed glad to see 'em go."

Lucian grinned and slapped the grim-faced Asaph on his back. "Don't you remember when you was keen to be blooded—and claim the glory for yourself alone?"

Asaph slowly shook his head. "Aye, but who's to pay?"

The journey thereafter became less difficult only because there were fewer people with whom to deal. The hidden voices returned, but now they had less effect. The swamps, however, had a greater effect. The maze of fog-shrouded pools, mires, and channels simply were not meant to be crossed by horses. To make the matter worse, the mosquitoes were so abundant that Mark jokingly asked Eric to turn the black swarms into allies. Then, a worse predator appeared, tiny ones that bit with the fury of wasps.

"What *are* you?" Martin cried, slapping at the bugs around his eyes.

Morgan laughed. "In the ancient language, they are called *omensesminoths*—which means 'jaws with wings.' "

Martin flinched and scratched. "I wish this wind would blow them . . . whoa!" he yelled as his horse plunged through a mat of rotting weeds into a pool of quicksand. Baldwin was near enough to pull Martin free, but the boy's horse—struggling and screaming—quickly sank. That was the first of the accidents that befell their hapless beasts in the following three days.

Jon's horse drowned in a bayou, and Baldwin's large bay gelding broke a leg climbing a muddy creek bank. It had to be killed. Eric's horse, perhaps the weakest of the lot, simply lay down and refused to rise. Next, Queen Dorcas's dapple gray mare fell headlong into a broad, leaf-covered pit filled with water. The queen swam ashore, but her mare was so exhausted that she drowned. The duke gave his sister his own horse—a magnificent chestnut stallion. He carried the queen well as the group plodded from the deeper swamp and splashed their way toward the shore of a shallow, reed-lined lake. Morgan, still leading the group, suddenly shouted, "Clear land ahead!" With a yell, he released the reins of his horse and urged it into a gallop. Splashing wildly across the shallow water, the horse seemed exuberant to be within sight of freedom.

However, the animal abruptly slipped, twisted sideways onto its neck, and splashed into a hole; waves rippled outward as the beast struggled. Morgan swam to knee-deep water and pulled in vain on the reins. When the others caught up with him, he was sadly looking at the bubbles bursting from the brown water. As if chastized for his rashness, the young king walked head down behind the others toward the dismal shore.

"That leaves only you, valiant Warinmount," the Duke of Corlis said, patting the great stallion as the animal clambered up the final embankment beside his master. The queen smiled encouragingly at her brother.

Gradually, the ground rose. The nine travelers left the pools and scummy bayous behind. They crossed a dead forest of burned, tilted tree trunks and withered vines and saw before them the broadly swelling Slopes of Tava. And no sooner had they set foot onto the dry grass covered Slopes than a cold wind shrieked at them from the north, carrying with it black misty fingers of the Darkness.

Perhaps it was the bitter wind that aroused another of the ancient Guardians. In any case, while Morgan led his followers northwestward, they heard a sizzling sound approaching them fast overhead. They ducked as a bright glow roared from the east, passed over them, and burst flaming into the skeletons of trees downhill to their left. A rushing wind followed the fireball, slicing a path through the dingy fingers of mist.

The nine looked to their right and saw—a hundred or so yards away—a giant mounted on a huge, galloping gray stallion. The being astride the horse was notching a long arrow to his bowstring as his steed, thrice as large as the rearing Warinmount, raced into the lead of a herd of gray, roan, white, and yellow-tan stallions.

Eric, trembling, aimed his staff at the giant and shouted, *"Alton, vocci A-Abba!"* But larger and larger loomed the being and his herd.

The archer and his mount came to a gravel-scattering stop not six feet from the young magician. With eyes flaming like the sun, the archer looked down at Eric and his companions as he lowered his great bow and slid his arrow back into the quiver on his back. His steed arched his neck, flared his nostrils, and snorted gusts of wind that set Eric's robe flapping. The other stallions, perhaps forty in number, encircled the humans, sniffing at them and Warinmount—who seemed but a colt by comparison.

"Who are you, children from darkness?" the archer's voice billowed.

Morgan stepped forward, his right hand on Gafailnath's hilt. "I am Morgan Evnstar, King of Alamantia. We come on a purpose set for us by the Lord of Light!"

The archer drew back, puffing out his cheeks with an incredulous expression. "Even demons can name names," he declared.

Morgan unsheathed Gafailnath. In the gray, misty light, the sword blazed blue, startling the horses. "If you know this blade's light—as the myth-lore I learned at my mother's knee tells me you will—then you will know it would not endure a demon's hands upon it!"

The archer laid his bow across his lap and rested his right hand on the hilt of the great broadsword by his side, smiling. "So, Son of Olden Kings," he said in a gently rolling voice, "you know me?"

Morgan advanced until the chin of the archer's steed was almost above his head. "In song and painting you are known as Win-dor, Wind Lord of the West. But perhaps I am dreaming," he added with a smile.

The archer threw back his head and laughed a mighty laugh. "No, young Evnstar," he said, looking down again, "it is no dream you see. Now tell me, who are your companions?"

Morgan introduced them, the Lady Dorcas last. When named, she drew the Jewel of Corlis from inside her cape. From the stone came a yellow radiance like sunlight, which drove the black fingers of mist shrieking away. The archer held both arms out to the queen, palms upward. "By your light are you known!" he said reverently, then added, "And by your light was I drawn to aid you against this . . . this puny probing," he thundered, jutting his chin toward the black misty clouds, "by Jabez, son of Ingloamin!"

In response to the naming of Jabez, the black clouds rushed thickly from the north, and from the clouds a snaking, searching funnel appeared.

"Nay, you foul breath of night, harm us you shall not!" Win-dor bellowed as angry wind streamed through his black and silver hair. He signed to the horses, and they tossed their heads and began racing in a circle. A whirlwind arose, sealing out the searching black wind. "Now," the archer laughed, flexing his broad muscles as he slung his bow onto his back, "now we can talk in peace. This King's command you follow—what is it?"

Morgan quickly said, "We must recapture the Lightning in the Bottle and return it to Alamantia."

"And if you return the bottle, what will you do with the Lightning?"

"Release it to drive the Darkness from Eorthe!"

Win-dor leaned forward, arching one silver eyebrow. "Now *that* is much to my liking!" he rumbled. "For many years I have watched the poor kings and lords of Eorthe stay the Alamantian king's hand from releasing the Lightning—for fear they would lose their positions and wealth—until it was too late. How can we help you?"

"First, we have five friends whom we must find," Morgan answered. "They are several days ahead, fleeing toward Torang."

"Ahh . . . two nights ago one of my patrolling stallions saw five people beset by Wolvors in a valley near Torang, but by the time he brought the rest of us, the people were gone. Do you want to see if we can find sign of them—knowing, of course, that they may have been devoured?"

"We must search," Morgan replied, glancing toward the alarmed Kingsmen and Eric.

"And then?"

"Then we must somehow rescue the bottle, which my mother tells me Leohtians located in the Cave of Tava."

The archer stiffened and frowned. "Getting you to Castle Hidlothnath, which stands above the cave, will be little problem. But into either the castle or the cave I cannot go. They are outside my domain."

"And where is your . . . your domain?" Martin ventured to ask.

The archer's windy laugh almost knocked Martin flat. "Climb up behind me, tiny warrior, and I, *Win-dor*, will show you the halls and reaches of my domain!" The giant reached down one broad hand and hoisted the boy behind him with one smooth motion. The wind horses pranced eagerly, but Warinmount flattened his ears, rearing. Frowning, the archer added, "Your pony, though, will have to stay behind."

Proudly, Mark said, "Disparage not the descendants of your own herd!"

Win-dor laughed, throwing back his head so his breath burst skyward and swirled the low overcast. He called to his herd, "Finstar, Valaven, Fairwin, and others of you—take upon your backs these followers of our King!" Eight stallions knelt, and the humans—with some difficulty—mounted.

The Duke of Corlis uncomfortably asked, "But, Lord Win-dor, what about stirrups and bridles? How can we control . . ."

"Control?" Win-dor roared. "If you've the Light in you, you need no other control!" He laughed, nudging his steed. "On, Westwin! To Torang!" he called heartily.

At first the thunder of the herd galloping up the Slopes of Tava was loud. Then, the sound of hoofbeats faded as the stallions swiftly rose from the ground. Only then did Mark stop looking back and down at Warinmount. The boys, meanwhile, felt very small on the horses' broad backs, and they held on for dear life. Suddenly they burst up through the black clouds. Blinking as rushing wind tore tears from their eyes, the boys leaned over to watch the thick clouds covering Eorthe rapidly grow smaller below their horses' racing feet. Ahead, on the horizon and to the right of the setting sun, was the only sign of land—black, jagged peaks by the thousands, some belching vast plumes of smoke and ash.

"There stands Mount Tava," Win-dor thundered from the lead. "But this," he added with a sweep of his arms, "is *my* domain—mine and the King's!"

Chapter 6

To Thorinsheld's Workshop

Loping across the night-shrouded Slopes of Tava, the Wolvors closed in upon Waymond's group; Queen Sybra was in the lead with Jodi and Rachael, and the magician came behind, practically dragging Richard. Although Waymond repeatedly had unleashed lightning from his staff, the wolves were now near enough for the runners to feel the heat from the beasts' eyes and slavering mouths. Again and again, blazing yellow shafts tore apart the forward ranks of demon-wolves, but dozens more stormed over the charred bodies. It was obvious that the sheer numbers of beasts soon would overwhelm the exhausted little band.

Then, from the south, a spark of blue light appeared. Swiftly the spark flew toward the flaring of the magician's lightning, leading a shimmering blue cloud of the Leohtians from Acuerias's ship and from the earlier scouting expedition. Jodi and Rachael looked up and cried with relief when they saw Captain Thrumingold hover above Waymond's head and begin directing the attack of the hundreds of brilliant blue light rods flickering above the valley. Down dove the Leohtians, piercing the demon-wolves with blue light that ripped apart the beasts; nearby Wolvors also were killed by the explosions . . . but so were the attacking Leohtians. Rapidly the number of beasts diminished until only a few white-blue explosions flashed over the base of the dark foothills. Finally, the only surviving Wolvor was Warfang. He leaped straight toward Jodi and Rachael!

Captain Thrumingold, the only remaining Leohtian, instantly plunged upon the Wolvor, holding his sword above his head with both hands. Striking the beast's chest, the fearless captain disappeared into the soaring body. Blue light flickered briefly from the wound, then a white flaring explosion destroyed both creatures. White ashes rained over the crouching girls.

Queen Sybra gave them no time to mourn Thrumingold's death. "We must hurry," she urged them, "before others more terrible come."

Running as fast as they could, they climbed the base of the hills. As they entered a dry streambed between two hills, they became aware of the light, swift sound of many bare feet sprinting behind and to either side of them. But when the humans looked, they saw only shadowed rocks.

The streambed became more boulder-strewn the higher Sybra and her group went. They came to low, rocky cliffs—once waterfalls—and it was when they were climbing around the boulders in one of those falls that they first saw their pursuers: deathly gray figures emerging from the darkness on the hillsides above them. The silent, featureless figures seemed to be robed in yellow from their waists down, and each brandished a long, hooked knife as they slunk down the hillsides and into the streambed behind the humans.

"Obnars of Torang," Queen Sybra muttered, hastening up the streambed into a narrow canyon.

The others quickly followed her, glancing back at the gray tide of warriors following them into the ever-deepening shadows. Jodi and Rachael—seeing the patient way in which the Obnars were pursuing them—became afraid that there was no escape from the canyon. And their fear was heightened when Sybra led them to the canyon's end—the stone face of a cliff perhaps a thousand feet below the hilltops. Behind, they heard bare feet crunching on gravel and the swish! of knives. Waymond turned to blast the leading warriors while Queen Sybra looked at the wall of stone barring their way.

Holding out her Jewel of Tava, she murmured words in a consonant-filled language. In response came a deep, grinding noise that startled even Waymond. With a shower of pebbles and dust, the black rocks at the base of the cliff opened slowly. "Hurry!" Queen Sybra commanded. Into the haven's entrance they went. The rock door ground shut behind them. From the other side came thudding sounds and weak, angry cries.

From the absolute darkness came Richard's whine, "Can't we stop now? I'm *tired* and this armor *itches* me!"

Waymond tried to light his staff, but he found—to his dismay—that it hardly would glow.

"Ahh, you've discovered that your power is less here," Queen Sybra's voice came huskily from the darkness.

Rachael sensed betrayal and unsheathed her sword. It flickered blue and dimly lit the crouching figure of the dark queen.

"No, child," Sybra murmured. "Though the ancient power of Glimmrainath—the Void—is great here, the King's power is greater still."

Jodi felt a withered, strong hand take hers and begin

leading her and Rachael on—winding downward. Rachael sheathed her sword and took Waymond's hand. He took Richard's, thus they formed a chain snaking down the steep slope of a large tunnel. Their footsteps echoed slightly, seeming small and insignificant in the yawning silence of the passages and vast halls they passed.

The darkness bothered Jodi more, perhaps, than it bothered the others. It aroused her worst fear. She began to feel as though her nightmare of the dark tunnel had become real. She stumbled. "I'm spinning," she warned Queen Sybra. "I feel . . . I feel like . . ."

"Like you're going to die?" Sybra asked.

Jodi sank to her knees; her head sagged forward, and she groaned.

"It's a dream many people have," the queen said, pulling Jodi upright. "But you're a Kingsman, so hurry to the end of the dream and tell me what happens!"

Jodi stammered, "Eventually . . . a light . . . a bright light comes for me."

"And so it shall here," Queen Sybra stated, leading them on.

At the time, not even Waymond noticed that Richard had left the group. It was not until about ten minutes later that the magician grew worried. "Is Richard up there?" he asked, stopping.

"No," Queen Sybra said, alarmed. "I thought he was with you!"

"Richard!" Jodi cried, then screamed with all her might, *"Richard!!"*

Waymond forced a yellow glow from the tip of his staff. Its slight light flickered over nearby black crystal ceilings and walls, then faded away into dark emptiness. "Richard-d-d!" they called in unison. Their voices echoed far into the caverns . . . but there was no answer.

Calling frequently, they went back up the trail. No sign of Richard did they find until Waymond glimpsed a reflection and ran ahead. When the others joined him, they saw that he was holding Richard's shield and armor. As they stared at the armor, they felt a cold wind blowing from the left side of the tunnel. Waymond held his staff into the damp flow of air, and they saw the merest edge of an unfathomably deep space. "What a place for him to stop," Waymond muttered, listening to the sighing wind.

"Look there," Queen Sybra said, pointing to the ground behind a large boulder. They knelt to look at tracks pressed deeply into the dirt.

"A Bogloam was hiding in the mouth of the side tunnel," the queen concluded. "Let's hope it was only hungry."

"Only hungry!" Jodi cried, going toward the side tunnel.

"There are fates worse than death in the Caves of Rainath," the queen said, walking on down the tunnel. Waymond picked up his bag and followed, but Jodi and Rachael stood rooted before the side passage. Sybra returned and took their hands. "There's no use searching! These caverns are like the fine grain of your Kingsmen's swords: endless!"

"But it's my fault!" Jodi pleaded. "If I hadn't panicked . . ."

The magician came to her, holding out Richard's discarded armor and shield. "Like each of us, Richard must learn his own lessons," he stated.

"You're not going to give up on him, are you?" Rachael demanded.

"Rachael," Waymond said sternly, "neither the King nor I *ever* give up on anyone unless that person willingly embraces the Darkness." His upheld staff lighted the path as silently they walked on.

Jodi glanced back at the sighing side tunnel and shuddered. "What's a Bo-whatever it was?" she asked.

"Jodi," Queen Sybra said firmly, "let the King take care of Richard. Look," she added in a brighter tone, holding out the Jewel of Tava. Jodi looked at the stone's clear, blue light, and quickly her feeling of guilt lifted. "Now listen," Sybra said, clearing her throat. In a low, gutteral voice, the queen began to sing:

Lights downward streaming—
blue, green, yellow—gleaming
from the Father's brow,
Him who said, "Be thou!"

Light at first flooding
through Void unloving,
it founded Eorthe in living green,
flowing blue, and yellow keen.

Yellow became south, sun, youth;
green came into east, land, truth;
blue spread west, to sky and death.
(Black north quick forgot Light's breath.)

Then, by the hand of him who came,
these Jewels were wrought and by him named:
Corlis, yellow as sun's fire;
Tava, blue as sky's desire; and
Imnatride, green as sea's fame.

The conquering Father passed on,
leaving Eorthe its bright new dawn;
His Light he left 'gainst Darkness attacking
in the Jewels of Powers Begatting.

When the song's echoes had faded, Rachael asked in an excited whisper, "*Those* are the Jewels you, Dorcas, and Queen Eliadenor wear?"

"Yes, child," the queen said. "Now, we must hurry on. There is an ancient temple ahead where we can sleep undisturbed."

"A temple?" Jodi asked. "To what?"

Huskily, Sybra replied, "To the darkness that was comforting ere the Lord of Darkness corrupted it—and us."

They walked probably three miles through passages that constantly were changing: Now wide and roofless they soared, then shrank to shoulder-width with a low ceiling. Jodi felt the floor going ever lower, and with each step she fought the claustrophobia rising to control her. Just as she was about to panic again, the group came into an unimaginably vast chamber. Waymond forced his staff to flicker brightly.

Looking to the left of the trail, they saw the temple. Rising into darkness, layers of black stone, each about ten feet high, formed a pyramid. Before the pyramid was a tall, horned altar. As they went to the altar, Jodi and Rachael felt the strong presence of old, old death.

They watched the queen go close to the altar and kneel. They thought she was praying until they saw her fingers rubbing strange markings on the face of the stone.

"Those marks," Rachael began. "What are they?"

"Runes," Queen Sybra replied in a low voice, "ancient and well-nigh forgotten, even by me—and perhaps to the good, for it was a foul and harsh tongue. More light, please Waymond," she murmured. In the yellow glow upon the shiny black stone, Jodi clearly saw the marks:

When Sybra had read the inscription several times, she began to chant:

Drink deep the draught of death;
ever to dark be wed.
Night remembers all your failures,
but in death long peace shall be yours.
Thus, dark to dark be led,
there to sleep without breath.

As her voice pierced the empty stillness around the black pyramid, it seemed to stir the air. Jodi took courage and whispered, "That wasn't nearly as pretty as your other song."

"No," Queen Sybra stated flatly, "but that inscription tells what my ancestors believed during the Days of Darkness—before the coming of the Lord of Light. That is why our quest to recover the Lightning is so important: If we fail, Mankind again will sink into an age in which we gladly will 'Drink deep the draught of death.' "

Jodi shivered, feeling the utter coldness of the temple cavern. "I'm glad we know the Light," she whispered. Queen Sybra reached for Jodi's hand and held it lovingly.

They washed in a spring in which Sybra said the priests of old once cleansed themselves, then slept near the pyramid. Hours later, when Jodi awoke the first thing she did was call for Richard, having dreamed that he had been sacrificed on the ancient altar by black-robed priests. After Rachael had calmed her, they ate and soon resumed the journey—through a maze of low-roofed tunnels. In the dank air of the maze, Waymond's light again failed, and they were forced to go stooping forward, holding hands with one another as Queen Sybra led them.

Despite Sybra's unerring leadership, the total darkness brought claustrophobic confusion to Jodi and Rachael. The worst part came when Sybra took them to the edge of a chasm and told them to jump to the other side. As they leaped, they faintly heard water rushing in the space far below their feet.

When Jodi landed on the other side of the chasm, she wrapped her arms around herself to slow her trembling. "How much farther?" she asked weakly.

"Remember what happens in your dream!" Queen Sybra commanded, seizing one of Jodi's hands as she strode forward with a certainty that spoke of senses other than sight.

"Endless . . ." Jodi murmured dejectedly. "Endless . . . endless."

"Not quite," the queen whispered. She took Jodi's face between her cold, leathery hands and aimed it to the left. *"A-Abba seimt!"*

Jodi began to relax, for coming into their long tunnel of blackness was a light! She breathlessly watched the soft, white flaming light come toward them. And when Jodi clearly saw that the light was the King, she ran sobbing into his arms.

"Daughter, do you still doubt?" he asked mildly.

"No . . ." she snuffled, leaning against the warming radiance of his robe. "But I surely was afraid of the dark!"

"Fear is doubt," he said gently, wiping tears from her cheeks.

She felt ashamed. "But I didn't doubt *you;* I doubted myself . . . my courage," she explained, looking up into his comforting eyes.

"Those who learn that they cannot stand alone have only to trust me," the King said firmly, "for it is my desire that you become what you truly can become: a fearless Child of the Light." He kissed the crown of her head, and she reluctantly let him go so he could embrace Rachael and Sybra. Then, he stood before Waymond and asked, "Where is the other Kingsman?"

Waymond hung his head. "I've lost him, I'm afraid." Sadly, he held up the boy's armor and shield.

"He'd been saying the armor was making him itch," Rachael explained.

The King said nothing, and he seemed deep in thought for a moment. Then he led them on, illuminating the deep darkness before them. At one point, he held out his radiant arms so they could see to leap another chasm. This rift was wider than the one Sybra had had them jump, and, as they leaped, they could see white water swirling far, far below. Not long thereafter, they began to hear a faint, ringing sound.

"What's that noise?" Jodi asked, holding the King's hand tightly.

"Thorinsheld, the Swordsmith, is at work," the King replied.

"Did *he* make our swords?" Rachael guessed.

"Yes," the King answered, "and the blades made long ago for the Lords of the Swords—as well as your armor and shields." He led them on, ever deeper into the rock ribs of Eorthe. "I've come now to view the work the Swordsmith and Sea People have finished during the past year."

"Does that mean more Kingsmen are to be armed?" Jodi asked hopefully.

The King nodded.

"And will they help us fight the northern sorcerer?" Rachael inquired.

"For now, only your group, those with magician Eric, and . . ."

"Magician Eric?" Jodi interrupted, shying away from a nearby gorge.

The King helped her along the narrowing path. "As the next step in his service he has signed a Covenant of Apprenticeship with Master Acuerias. Even now he is helping Queen Dorcas, King Morgan, and their companions come here. In fact, Jodi and Rachael, soon you will have to go back to the entrance to meet them and lead them to Thorinsheld's workshop."

Jodi and Rachael were both thrilled and concerned. Silently, they marveled: *Eric a magician!* But return through the maze of passageways to lead Eric's group? . . . The ringing grew louder.

The tunnel ended at a rounded opening. From it a red glow and heat were issuing, mingled with strange odors. The place was very far underground, and Jodi felt sure the glow was from one of the rivers of fire in the skeleton of Eorthe.

They emerged from the tunnel's mouth and stood on a ledge at the top of a cathedral-like cavern. It was illuminated by fiery half-light. The rock- and stalagmite-covered floor fifty or so feet below spread out unevenly. The pale brown stalagmites glistened with frosty red highlights. Many soared to join stalactites growing from the ceiling. Heat and fumes—as well as the ringing of metal striking metal—filled the chamber.

The girls followed Waymond, Queen Sybra, and the King down a narrow trail that wound back and forth along the cliff face. When they reached the floor of the cavern, they were able to see the source of the hammering. At a great anvil of shining, silver-colored metal worked a creature such as neither Jodi nor Rachael ever had imagined. Almost twenty feet tall, he was extremely muscular. He appeared to be deep in concentration, and the carefully aimed blows of his enormous hammer made the ground and air vibrate with each *clang!* In one silver-gloved hand, the being held tongs. In the red glowing end of the tongs was a folded bar of metal, which, in comparison with the smith, was tiny. He was beating it together upon itself. With exact blows, he folded it again, then beat it flat upon the anvil. Nearby flowed a stream of molten fire, and into that fire the smith thrust the metal bar to reheat it.

Behind the smith was a pool of green water. Perched on rocks around the large pool was a circle of Sea People. Beside the Sea People were baskets of tightly woven seagrass, in which were what the girls assumed were chunks of raw, unworked *nathnor.* Seated away from the heat and flying sparks was Queen Eliadenor. The glow in the cavern glinted on her short, silver-blond hair and her gold cape.

She seemed entranced by the heavy, rhythmic blows of the smith's hammer and at first did not notice the King's arrival. When she did, she and the other Sea People quickly stood and bowed. Only then did the Swordsmith break his trance. He thrust the *nathnor* bar back into the fire, placed his hammer across the anvil, and bowed to the King—but he did not acknowledge the others. Quickly then, he turned back to the bar, which already was glowing red-orange. He pulled the bar from the fiery river, went to the anvil, bent the metal in half, and began beating the halves together to weld them.

"Fifteen times Thorinsheld folds and hammers each blade," Waymond explained to the girls. "Thus, each sword has more than 32,700 layers." He took a deep breath and shouted above the *clang! . . . clang!* of hammer on anvil. "That kind of patient workmanship, that metal, and the King's empowerment are what enable the swords of the Light to pierce anything!" He led them away from the shower of sparks. "Over there," he said, "is where the raw blades are sharpened and polished." He pointed to the circle of green-robed Sea People. They were arranged around the pool according to size; the larger workers sat by large, square whetstones, while the smaller ones sat by smaller, round whetstones. Seaweed-wrapped blades were stacked by each of the twenty or so workers, who dipped water from the pool onto the stones as they whirred the blades back and forth against them. While Jodi watched the Sea People at work, first Waymond, then Queen Sybra spoke seriously to Rachael. All Jodi caught was the word, ". . . tested."

Before Jodi could ask what Waymond and Sybra had said, the King came. He sat on a flattened stone between Jodi and Rachael; the girls sat nearby, facing him. "Let me tell you something of Eorthe's history," he began. "Long ago, in the First Age, this planet was created as an outpost of Light in the midst of endless Void. Its light was called the First Light, for it was the Father's Light: Perfection. His Light flowed in everything on the planet and coursed like liquid silver through the veins of it.

"But Ingloamin, who long had been jealous of my Father's work, corrupted the first people with fear. They thereafter befouled the rivers of light—with the blood of human sacrifice. The rivers burst forth in a vast explosion, and water forever was separated from fire. From the exploding rivers, bits of the First Light hardened. These bits of condensed light are *nathnor* nodules. Ocean currents washed the droplets into deep-sea canyons during the Days of Darkness. Now, Sea People risk their lives to dive for the precious, metallic remainder of that first, pure Light.

"Therefore, the metal of your swords, armor, and shields, like the metal of the great swords, is precious to the people of Eorthe. It is a tangible reminder that once Mankind lived *in* the Father's Light." His deep brown eyes became sad, and he closed them. "Once, there was no fear . . . no doubt, no longing, no wanting." He raised his head and looked for several seconds into Rachael's eyes, then Jodi's. "If you and all your companions are strictly obedient, a time again will come when the people of Eorthe can live completely in the Light." He smiled, laid a hand on each of their heads, and added, "Now, it is time for you to go back and guide the others here."

Jodi and Rachael stiffened. Reluctantly, they looked toward the trail that led up and out of the cavern. "Must we?" Jodi asked.

The King gave her a stern, fatherly look. "Jodi, sooner or later, in one way or another, you *must* learn once and for all time that my Light is always with you—as long as you ask for it." He looked at her until she nodded, then he added, "And do not stop at the Temple of Rainath. Unless you are protected by the Tava Jewel, that is a dangerous place."

Rachael led Jodi away from the King. He stood and watched them cross the uneven floor of the cavern, climb the trail, and pause at the mouth of the black tunnel. With a final wave, the King went to talk with queens Sybra and Eliadenor. As bravely as they could, Rachael and Jodi entered the yawning passage of darkness and began groping their way forward.

Chapter 7

Fears and Decisions

Richard had let go of Waymond's hand to take off his armor for a moment and enjoy a really good scratch. Then, he had asked himself, *"Why put it back on?"* Queen Sybra had said they were in a safe place—so he had laid down his chestplate and shield. Almost instantly, huge jaws swallowed him.

Headfirst in the stinking mouth of an unimaginably large beast, Richard madly kicked his legs. His face was jammed against a tongue that stank of rotted food, and slimy saliva almost drowned him. It's a wonder Richard did not die of fright then and there as the beast waddled down the side passage with him. Fortunately, the Bogloam was carrying its prey loosely because its young—which lay in a nest of slime far below—would not eat dead food.

But the boy's kicking legs pounded the Bogloam's wide nose once too often. Disgusted that prey should struggle so greatly, it tossed the boy into the air, intending to catch him by his other end.

Despite Richard's desperate condition, he literally kept his head. He had not been fool enough to cast away his sword with his armor, so when the Bogloam tossed him, he snatched out his blade. It flickered blue, and in its glow, he aimed. As he fell, he thrust the point into one of the beast's eyes. The Bogloam snapped shut its gaping mouth and grunted mightily in pain as the weight of the boy's body drove the sword deeper.

The beast bucked, bellowed, and jerked back. When it jerked backward, it dislodged the sword . . . and Richard. Half blinded, the Bogloam hissed at the boy. But Richard, having definitely located his courage, did not hesitate. Gripping the hilt with both hands, he held the sword up like a dagger, glaring into the face of his enemy. As the Bogloam rushed madly at him, Richard drove the blade up to its haft into the beast's forehead. Propelled by the falling body, the head slid forward, scooping Richard onto its broad nose. He rolled off as the creature twitched a few times and died.

For a long while, Richard stood in the darkness fighting panic and his frantic heartbeat; he became terrified by—and fascinated with—the thought that he almost had died. It was then, for the first time in his entire life, that he truly felt proud of himself.

Unfortunately, his pride soared and swelled out of control. He kicked the beast disdainfully, wishing the King and the Kingsmen were there to tell him how proud they were of him. He even wondered if he could cut off the Bogloam's head and take it home with him; the guys on his block would get sick with envy! He tried to jerk his sword free so he could whack off the monster's head, but the blade was stuck solidly in the skull of the brute. His feeling of elation vanished, and he kicked the sword handle, muttering, "Dumb old thing!" Quickly, though, he thought, *I've just killed a monster, so I* won't *let a piece of metal get the better of me!* Setting one foot on the Bogloam's snout, he jerked the sword this way and that, becoming angrier by the second. When the blade came free, he fell backward and landed hard on his seat.

Painfully, he stood, fighting back tears as again his emotions collapsed. Gradually, he became still. It then occurred to him that if the King actually had witnessed his "victory," instead of saying how proud he was of Richard he'd ask, "Where's the armor and shield I gave you?" And the Kingsmen really would say, "Gosh, how'd you *ever* get out of those caves?" And as for his friends back home, even if they *saw* the Bogloam's head, they never would believe that *he* had killed the monster. Crushed, he was left with one question: How would he get out of the caves?

Oh well, his old self said with certainty, *it should be easy. Just go back and turn right at the first main tunnel.* He set off, not realizing that the Bogloam had taken several turns while he was suffocating in its mouth. Within an hour, he was thoroughly lost in the Caves of Rainath.

Bewildered, hurt, and very thirsty, he sat down. For an hour, he hollered and screamed . . . then simply cried. When he was drained, and still no one had come to get him out of his mess, he fell into an uncomfortable sleep. He slept even as Jodi and Rachael slept by the rune-carved altar far away and worried about him.

When Richard awoke hours later, he jumped up and promptly bumped his head against a sharp rock. He struck the rock with one fist and cursed the darkness . . . then doubled up with pain from his fist. By then he was **mad.** He grew hotly resentful. He muttered, among other things, "No one *loves* me! They *left* me because they don't *care* about me! I hate them all!" On and on he ranted until he was exhausted and miserable.

In the silence that followed, Richard curled up on the cave floor, overwhelmed by a sense of failure.

Desperately, he prayed to anyone—even the Lord of Darkness—to come get him out. Almost immediately a voice found him in the darkness. Softly, but with great authority, it urged Richard to heroically end it all.

He snuffled, rising to look at his blue shining sword. How quick it would be, how easy, the Voice said, to fall on his sword point like warriors of old did when they were defeated. *"They made you fail, so show them!"* the Voice urged. *"Go on . . . the end won't hurt. I will come for you, and you will forever sleep without pain or remembering."* When Richard hesitated, the Voice eagerly added. *"Do it! Kill yourself now, while you have the courage! Besides,"* the Voice purred, *"who will miss you?"*

Richard, looking at his Kingsman's sword, was surprised by his own quick answer to the Voice's last question: *The King would miss me!* The dark voice fell silent as Richard's memories of the King rushed back. *He loved me and showed me how to love others!* Richard thought, straightening. *As a matter of fact, the King would love me no matter what I am or do!* But he knew his anger, resentment, and thoughts of death would hurt the King.

Richard smiled, feeling much calmer. He sighed, shuddering once, and said out loud, "I'm tired . . . I'm tired of messing things up and hurting myself." So, also aloud, he said a timid prayer, "King, I know I'm not worth much, but could you help me, please?" He waited breathlessly for the King to answer in some way. This time, Richard promised himself, he would obey.

But nothing immediately happened that Richard could see or hear. He wondered then why the evil voice always answered so quickly, so eagerly, whereas the King's voice came in unexpected ways. Doubts came to him. His disappointment was great, and his feeling of being totally alone overwhelmed him. Desperately, he shouted, "My King, *help me!*"

Even he, however, heard the self-pity and demandingness in his voice. Ashamed and knowing the King would not answer such a plea, he sat down to calm himself. With determination he forced away his thoughts of self-pity and despair. Then he prayed again: "My King, please help me."

He waited, staring up and down the black passageway. As he became more attuned to things outside himself, he heard the sound of water trickling. He stumbled toward the sound, using his sword as a light cane, and found a spring. Richard thrust the tip of his sword into the tunnel floor and bent to scoop water from the spring's pool with both hands. Quickly, he scrubbed the dried slime from his body and drank his fill from the pool—while thinking about the King's fountain in Espereim and how *clean* its water had made him feel.

As water dripped from his fingers and chin, Richard leaned close to look at his reflection in the pool. The dripping water sent ripples across the water, which shimmered with blue light from his sword. From the ripples sprang a spark. The spark darted toward the boy, who drew back. But the fleck of light lingered near his face. "You've come for me!" Richard whispered excitedly. When the spark darted off down the tunnel, he grabbed his sword and followed.

For a long while, Richard thought the spark was going to lead him back to Jodi and the others. But after going several miles, he realized that it was not. He stopped and asked, "Where are you taking me?" On impulse, he closed his eyes. Quickly, he saw a strange vision: A group of mounted riders was soaring through a nighttime sky toward a bright star. Richard did not recognize the riders, but he felt that they were going north.

The vision changed. Richard saw another group of people shooting along an underground river. He felt that they, too, were racing northward—as he himself was. "I'll be rescued there," he concluded. Quickly, he opened his eyes and followed the spark . . . not even imagining what his obedience to the King would lead him to do.

Hand-in-hand Jodi and Rachael re-entered the maze of black passageways, feeling their way forward with outstretched hands. They stopped and drew back at each obstacle, then groped their way around it. Soon, they were disoriented, and frequently they wondered if they were walking in circles. Constantly their fear grew, for they knew that pitfalls, pools, and chasms lay alongside and sometimes across the trail.

As her fear of the blackness grew, Jodi's dream of dying returned to her. Rachael felt her pulling back. "What's wrong?" she whispered.

"I'm afraid," Jodi admitted, trembling.

"We'll be all right," Rachael assured her. "The King said so."

"We're being tested, aren't we?" Jodi asked, fighting off the spinning dizziness of her dream-fall down the dark tunnel.

After a moment, Rachael answered, "It's important that we, especially you, do this errand right."

"Me?" Jodi asked. The dream faded. "Why me?"

"Oh, nothing much," Rachael teased. "Just that Waymond said maybe you'd find something special when we meet the others."

"You mean, about Eric?"

"Not . . . exactly," Rachael said, feeling their way forward.

Jodi's dizziness returned as she tried to walk into the blankness. She sighed. "I'm tired of being tested, especially when it's about something that absolutely terrifies me—*like this darkness!*"

Rachael stopped and gripped both of Jodi's hands. "I'm sure the King wants us to overcome all our fears, especially the deepest ones. Maybe he showed us the Swordsmith to teach us that . . . that *we* have to be heated, folded, and beaten out time after time to make us strong . . . and trusting."

"I don't care!" Jodi cried. "I just know I'm scared!"

They stood still, listening to the sighing of the air as it passed through the labyrinth. Bogloams, the Scourge of Scorius—anything, even the dark sorcerer himself, could be lurking nearby, they imagined. Jodi hung back more and more firmly, but Rachael was determined to continue.

"Come on!" she said emphatically. She tugged on Jodi's hand—but it slipped away as Jodi fell from the trail.

At that moment the world around Jodi began to spin. She saw only the black walls of a downward reaching tunnel into which she was falling. She began to scream, though she could not hear her voice, and she clawed at the spinning black walls. Yet down and down she fell. She looked toward the distant end of the tunnel and felt the last shred of hope that she could save herself leave her. "Oh, my King," she prayed, "I love you so much! Please come! Save me, and take my fear!"

The spinning stopped. She found herself holding Rachael's hands and crying.

"What happened?" Rachael asked.

"The light," Jodi murmured. "Where's the light?" She looked around frantically, afraid that the light had been part of the dream. To her very great relief, the light was real, and Jodi pointed to it, smiling as she said, "The light came and got me out of that . . . that nightmare. Come on. I'll be okay," she added quietly, "as long as I can see that light."

Rachael asked no further questions as she followed Jodi and the dot of light. It led them across chasms of untold depth and turned left and right up long, crooked tunnels. Surprisingly soon, they found themselves in the chamber of the Temple of Rainath. Jodi practically dragged Rachael across the chamber, hurrying to keep the spark in sight. In only a few more hours, the girls saw that their guide had stopped. They had come to the stone portal of Tophinole's mouth. From outside came dull thuds as the Obnars of Torang beat upon the unyielding rock with their knives, blindly still trying to carry out their master's orders.

As they flew on Win-dor's stallions, Eric and his companions became bitterly cold in the high, open sky. They did not begin to warm until the herd descended through the overcast. Then, dead grasslands seemed to rush up at them. In moments the thunder of the horses' hooves upon the slopes was loud and vibrating. Martin, for one, was awfully glad they were slowing, for now he could dry the tears streaming down his cheeks, take a deep breath, and try to stop shivering. By the time the ground had ceased to blur with speed, he saw that they had gone beyond a ghostly city of painted, terraced buildings and were curving up out of a valley at an easy pace.

"There, on that high ridge," Lord Baldwin called, "gleams a stone that may well be a way marker."

Win-dor led the herd toward the white slab. Atop the ridge, the stallions swirled around the stone and pranced to a halt.

"Magician Eric," Morgan said, leaping from his mount, "can you read the marker?" The young king and his companions, including Win-dor, leaned forward to squint at the strange code:

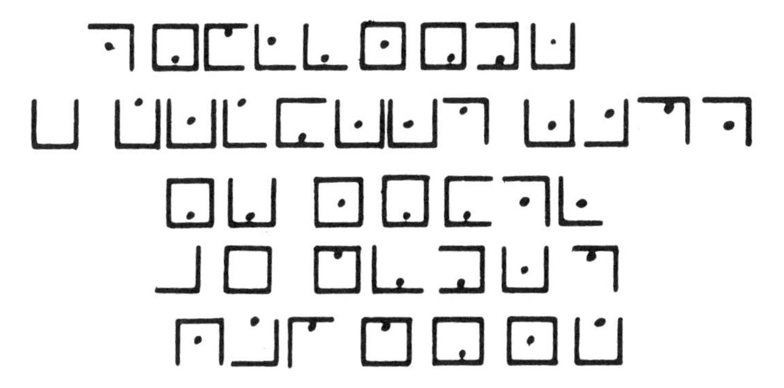

Morgan soon straightened and said, "It means nothing to me."

Eric, conscious that even the horses were looking expectantly at him, dismounted and went to study the marks. After a while, he blushed and said, "I'm afraid Acuerias hasn't taught me that language yet."

Martin, who was a bit envious of Eric's new status, went to have a look. His eyes widened. "Why . . . it's *my* code!" he exclaimed. Quickly, he unslung his pack and dug out his stubby pencil and a scrap of paper. On it, this is what he wrote:

1 A B C	2 D E F	3 G H I
4 J K L	5 M N O	6 P Q R
7 S T U	8 V W X	9 Y Z

Morgan and Eric looked over his shoulders as he began to translate the message.

"This mark: ·˥ ," Martin pointed, "goes with the bottom left corner of the code's key, and the position of the dot shows the letter to be the middle one: 'T'. Then, the square with the dot in the bottom position is an 'O'." Slowly he spelled, "T-O-P-H-I-N-O-L-E." He drew back, looking at what he had written. "That doesn't make sense," he said, looking up at Morgan and Eric.

"Oh, but it does," Queen Dorcas smiled. "It means Queen Sybra hoped to lead her companions to a nearby haven. Read on, Kingsman of the Code."

Martin nodded and did so. "   means two. Two d-e-g-r-e-e-s, degrees," he slowly pronounced, "east . . . of . . . north, fifteen . . . miles. W-a-y . . . Waymond!" He jumped up and stuffed the pencil and paper back into his pack.

Morgan sang out, "To Tophinole, and may the King's providence be with us!" Hastily, the three young men remounted.

Away thundered the herd, flying over the long slopes that had exhausted Jodi and her companions two nights earlier. Soon, the horses crossed the battle plain at the feet of the purple-red hills, and there the riders saw the many mounds of white ash where the Leohtians valiantly had slain the Wolvors. The horses then leaped up the hills and swooped down into the canyon leading to Tophinole.

Surprised, the gray Obnars of Torang turned in terror and flung their knives at the onrushing wave of horses. But the weapons merely glanced off the steel-hard muscles of the thundering stallions. Like clay statues, the demon-possessed warriors were shattered as the herd galloped over them. There was no cry, no sound save the horses' hooves clattering up the stone canyon. The herd skittered to a halt at the towering rock wall at the end.

Inside the cave, Jodi and Rachael were startled to hear the sounds of hoofbeats and human voices. "Should we open the door?" Jodi asked. "Do we know *how* to open it?"

Rachael laughed. "You should have been listening to Queen Sybra's instructions." She stepped back and faced the thick stone door. In a voice that surprised Jodi with its deep gutteral tones, Rachael commanded, *"Tus, Rukl p-uld!"*

The enormous door began to move. Gray light flooded into the cave's utter darkness. Jodi and Rachael peered out, then grabbed their sword hilts when they saw the awesome archer and his herd. But when the girls saw Eric, Jon, and Martin jump from their mounts and Mark Mansbridge grinning at them, they knew everything was all right. Jodi almost flew into Eric's arms while Rachael greeted the boys and went to look at the horses.

Jodi quickly saw that Eric had changed—in more than garments. No longer did she feel his warmth; now, he carried a staff and seemed distanced from her. "So you have become an apprentice?" she asked.

"I've become what I've dreamed of being ever since I first met Waymond," Eric softly replied.

Jodi looked down and murmured, "Congratulations." Quickly then, she kissed him on one cheek, turned, and went to hug Martin. For once, he actually was glad to see his sister. But before he could say anything to her, Jodi saw Morgan.

She stared at him—hardly aware that Queen Dorcas, her Jewel flaring brightly, and the men were dismounting. Morgan, steadily gazing at Jodi with the beginning of a smile, dismounted last, and Rachael had to nudge Jodi to get her attention away from the young king. Together then, the girls curtsied to the queen, who graciously introduced them to Morgan, Lord Baldwin, Asaph, Lucian, and finally to Win-dor.

"Greetings!" the archer boomed heartily, startling the girls. He bowed, smiling in a way that made Rachael think of sunlight breaking through clouds.

Win-dor leaned back, watching Rachael caress his tall stallion as she walked along the animal's side. The horse turned to study her, even as Win-dor did. "And would you like a ride, beautiful dark miss?" Win-dor inquired.

"Oh, yes!" Rachael said, her black eyes flashing. "I'd wish that more than almost anything!"

"We *flew* on these horses," Martin declared proudly.

Rachael looked enviously at him, then reached up to pat the archer's stallion. "In my country," she said, "we'd teach such fine horses to dance."

"To dance!" Win-dor boomed, staring down at her with a blazing look. "What an ignoble use for such . . ."

"No-no," Rachael interrupted. "Our horses *like* to dance; they dance for their own pleasure as well as for their riders' and ours."

"We need," Morgan said, looking at the girls, "to go on and meet . . ."

"I'll lead you," Jodi quickly said.

"Lead on then, Miss Jodi," Morgan smiled, his sea-green eyes flashing. He began walking beside her, but abruptly turned and called, "Thank you, Win-dor, and your herd. Without you, our way would have been harder by far."

"It yet will be!" Win-dor thundered. "To the hills, my friends!" he called to the horses. To King Morgan, Win-dor added, "We will await your summons!" In a whirl of mingling winds, the herd sprang upward, and in moments they had soared with ease out of sight above the cliffs.

Jodi led the way into Tophinole, and Rachael closed the door behind them. Again surrounded by darkness, Jodi became acutely aware of her responsibility. She led the group slowly and, at first, surely. However, thoughts of the handsome young king clouded her judgment. She stumbled into a cross tunnel and stopped. "Rachael?" she asked uncertainly.

"The light's going that way," her friend said from behind her.

Morgan took Jodi's hand and helped her from the side passage. His touch made her feel secure, and she did not want to let go of his hand. She did so only when she saw the dot of light and went ahead to follow it as it bore to their right, bobbing and weaving in the velvety blackness. Behind her, she heard the bump and scrape of the winged helmets of Baldwin and the warriors; that noise made her even more conscious of her responsibility as guide. Thereafter, she warned the others of low roofs, chasms, and pitfalls. And in that way they safely reached Thorinsheld's workshop.

Queens Sybra and Eliadenor met them at the foot of the trail and joyfully embraced Morgan, then Dorcas. While they talked quietly, Baldwin, Mark, and the two warriors drifted over to watch the intent smith at his work. Eric, Jon, and Martin, meanwhile, were shown around the cavern-workshop by Rachael, and Jodi looked for the King. Seeing her hopeful look, Queen Sybra soon went to her and said, "He has gone, child; but he left very specific instructions for us."

Sybra then called the group together and told them what the King had said. They listened carefully, despite the whirring of blades upon wet whetsones and the rhythmic blows of Thorinsheld's hammer.

"The King began his instructions by saying that the Darkness now has covered all Eorthe. Beasts and monsters, warriors twisted to do the sorcerer's will, and even armies of animals are ravaging the lands. Sor Titensor and his people are waging a desperate battle to hold Palátkwapi, called Red House, on Oraibi." She turned to Queen Dorcas and her brother and her voice became sorrowful: "Even the walls of Espereim are under siege. Corlis has fallen." She paused, clasping her hands and looking down into the blue light shinning from the Tava Jewel.

"We have had," she continued in a low tone, "no word from Master Slyne and his force, so I assume that Trogs or other beasts overcame them. We eleven are left," she said, looking at her listeners, "and that is a broken number since one Kingsman has been lost."

Eric and Jon shot looks at Jodi, who whispered, "A Bogloam . . . took him."

Queen Sybra held up her blue shining necklace. "However, the Three Jewels are joined! Also, to give us further hope, I understand that Win-dor has come. He and his herd will bear Morgan Evnstar, Queen Dorcas, the Duke of Corlis, magician-apprentice Eric, and Kingsmen Jon and Martin to Tavares, the dark kingdom. If you survive the Guard of Fearsors and Trogs, you are to attempt to enter Hidlothnath, the sorcerer's castle, which lies within the ring of the Volcanoes of Tava. The King said that if, once inside Castle Hidlothnath, you should confront the Scourge of Scorius, *only* Eric is to do battle with it. Against the Scourge, ordinary weapons will be useless—and, in fact, can be flung against you by the power of the demon. Thus was Scorius overthrown; the Scourge laughed as the defenders were destroyed by their own weapons."

Eric cringed, hoping no one was looking at him.

Queen Sybra turned to Lord Baldwin and his pair of

warriors. "You three servants of the King will accompany magician Waymond, Queen Eliadenor, Kingsmen Jodi and Rachael, and me. By subterranean passages, we will attempt to enter the sorcerer's lair—the Cave of Tava; it lies, as you may know, among the throats of fire that feed the volcanoes."

Baldwin frowned at Asaph and Lucian, then bowed to the queen. "Think me neither lazy nor cowardly, but will it not take us many weeks to work our way through the Caves of Rainath?"

"Our passage has been arranged by Queen Eliadenor. We will go up River Othnath." She frowned when Baldwin stiffened and set one hand on the hilt of Sulnspen.

He bowed again, hesitant to argue with the queen whose powers he always had feared. "But, Lady, we have heard tales about Othnath, about . . ."

"Yes," Queen Sybra snapped. "I know the perils. However, remember with whom you go!" As he uncomfortably resettled his thick chestplate, she added, "Furthermore, it is not *our* power upon which we depend."

Uneasily touching her sword, Jodi went to stand near the black-gowned queen. "Ma'am," she began hesitantly, "I'm sorry, but I don't understand what *we,*" she faltered, looking at Martin, Jon, and Rachael, "can do against Fearsors, Trogs, and the other things you said the sorcerer has."

Queen Sybra sighed and drew Jodi close. "You're tired and probably hungry and thirsty, too. When you have been comforted, perhaps you can pray more easily to the King; let him remind you why each of you has been called. And remember, if we succeed—and our chances are slim and by no means certain—you will be rewarded . . . though later you may view your reward more as a task than as a pleasure."

"You mean we'll earn more service," Jon said softly.

The queen nodded, even as Jodi said, "I just wish the King would come with us."

"Child," Sybra said impatiently, "*we* must enter the Darkness—in much the same manner the Leohtians enter evil beings." She stiffened. "And if anything happens to me, you, Jodi, must take my Jewel; if anything happens to Queen Eliadenor, Rachael must take her Jewel, even as Morgan will take his mother's."

"You mean, Rachael and I are to be like your apprentices?" Jodi asked with a glimmer of excitement in her eyes and voice.

"By the King's command," Queen Sybra nodded, smiling. "And remember: *trust* in him who alone has the strength to take us beyond *any* obstacle!"

Thus began the final portion of the quest to regain and release the Lightning in the Bottle.

Chapter 8

The Caves of Rainath

After hot baths and a meal provided by the Sea People and after hours of deep sleep, the Kingsmen gently were awakened by Queen Sybra. As they gathered their few belongings and rejoined the others in Thorinsheld's workshop, they wondered when they would again see a normal day and the sun shining. Their thoughts were cut short when the queen announced, "To the horses, those of you who will ride. The rest, follow Queen Eliadenor and her people. And may the King's strength be with each of us!"

After good-byes and embraces, the group divided. One half went up the trail toward the black mouth of the tunnel. The other half hastened downward toward the sound of a rushing river. As Eric climbed the trail behind Morgan, he softly asked, "By the way, what is the Scourge of Scorius?"

Morgan neither turned nor slowed. "You don't want to know," he said.

Queen Sybra and Queen Eliadenor led their group downward into tunnels that became colder and narrower, more damp and musty; in each lower level, it seemed that breathing became more difficult. Baldwin, Asaph, and Lucian were increasingly uncomfortable; battle open and honest was infinitely preferable to them than this downward journey, for it reminded them of their recent sleep in the Darkness. Jodi and Rachael, for their parts, simply felt cold and afraid. They held hands, silently following the yellow light of Waymond's staff tip, the blue glow of the Jewel of Tava, and the green radiance cast by the Jewel of Imnatride.

The group at last came to a wide flight of stone stairs. Before them was a river whose far side was hidden by darkness. The river was rushing northward with thunderous force past a small cove. At the cove's near edge stood Sea People, ready with stout oars of glistening white wood. In the comparatively calm water of the cove was a long boat. At least it looked like a boat, Jodi thought, realizing that actually it was some kind of long, open shell, its sides inlaid with designs in colored stone.

The boat was pulled to the lowest step, and the group boarded one by one. The Sea People then rowed the craft into the current, which seized it and shot it into roaring, spray-filled darkness. Jodi and Rachael lay down as the craft's speed became breathtaking.

As Richard had envisioned, Morgan Evnstar and those with him flew smoothly for hours toward a bright star. When they reached the fuming mountains, however, their tranquil amazement with flight was shattered by shrieking, giant birds that attacked with sword-size talons. "Wraths!" Morgan shouted as he and his companions began wielding their weapons in desperate battle. Cold silver moonlight gleamed from the Kingsmen's upthrusting shields and from the hard, gray feathers of the diving Wraths. And all the while, the herd of Win-dor sped from the sky toward the Mother of the Sky Mountains.

In a lull, Martin—seeking comfort—looked toward Queen Dorcas. With the blue-dark sky as background, her hair shone palest yellow as it streamed behind her above her billowing white cape and gown. Calmly, she gazed at Martin and smiled, holding up her Jewel. The boy grinned in return, then looked down and around at the horizon-to-horizon overcast. The clouds were rumpled as they flowed over mountain ranges, and their rounded tops were frosted gray by the moonlight. Then Martin saw the five volcanic cones piercing the overcast. Each cone was spewing a black-gray river of smoke, and deep within each was the glow of a great fire. Martin suddenly felt something behind him and reflexively swung his sword upward, driving off a Wrath streaking toward him. This ride, Martin thought, definitely was not like the riding lessons he'd had back home!

Eric's massive horse, meanwhile, ducked its head as ten gleaming, scythe-like talons whistled past it. Whirling around, Eric aimed his staff and, much to his own surprise, unleashed snaking green lightning. The blazing light overtook the Wrath as it swooped into a tight turn. The lightning rattled over the Wrath's hard feathers, then ignited them. With a burst of yellow flames that briefly lit the herd, the Wrath disappeared.

"Down, Westwin!" Win-dor cried to his mount. The stallion plunged toward the cones of Tava while the archer notched and let fly a long shaft from his mighty bow. The arrow flamed upward through the darkness and struck a diving Wrath squarely in the chest. It fell, spiraling and shrieking as black smoke trailed from it.

The descent from the cold heights was dizzying to Martin. He clung to the rippling mane of his horse. When the herd entered the overcast, and the cold, bitter mist of the Darkness began stinging his face, he closed his eyes. Flattening himself on his horse's back, he held his breath—until he became aware that the yellow light of the Jewel of Corlis was flaring around the herd. Martin then opened his eyes . . . and saw that they were below the overcast, flashing past mountainsides streaked with gray snowdrifts. Martin flinched when he heard the growing thunder of hooves as the herd touched down on a stony road . . . a road, Martin saw to his horror, that wound upward toward the volcanoes!

From the gloom ahead, their destination appeared: Hidlothnath, the Awful. As his horse galloped up the snaking road behind Mark Mansbridge and the Kingsmen, Eric stared at the sorcerer's dark, imposing castle. It was perched on a pinnacle where five ridges came together. Stretched web-like, the ridges connected the Volcanoes of Tava—with the castle in the center.

The herd sped around sharp curves, passed smoking fissures gaping on each side, and climbed steadily toward the ridge that led to the castle. When the road swung up and onto that ridge, Eric saw that it broadened as it neared the black, towering wall encircling Hidlothnath. The massive wall was pierced by an enormous, closed gate; to the left of the gate soared a black, spearhead tower. In the top of the tower, two red lights glowed unwinkingly. And below the tower, massed in front of the wall where the ridge broadened, Mark and the others saw the Castle Guard: southern cave Trogs and huge earth demons—Fearsors. The Trogs and Fearsors patiently were waiting.

When he saw the frightened expressions of Jon and Martin, Mark called to them, "Just remember: Keep your shields outermost; don't try to guide your horses; and keep your fingers and knuckles inside the edges of your swordguards so you won't lose part of a hand!"

He looked encouragingly at them . . . but they could not even nod.

Meanwhile, Richard, deep in the Caves of Rainath, followed the spark until he was so tired, hungry, and footsore that he was certain he could not take another step. The spark had been slowing as he did, but when he stopped, it began anxiously bobbing up and down. "Just a little farther," Richard heard a gentle voice urge, "then you can rest."

Richard struggled on, and almost immediately he saw a faint orange glow coming from a split in the left side of the tunnel. He crept to the split, peered around its edge . . . and saw a dark river flowing past a torchlit stone landing. At crumbling steps, with its bow rope tied to an iron ring, was a boat, rocking in the current. And on either side of the landing, guarding the boat, were two alligators of great girth, balefully staring up at the entrance. When Richard saw them, he shrank back and became absolutely motionless.

After a while—when no sound came from the creatures—Richard mustered his courage and peeked around the edge of the opening again. The squat beasts were still glaring at the entrance, their slitted yellow eyes gleaming coldly in the torchlight. Richard guessed that each creature was at least twenty feet long, though it was hard to tell since most of their tails trailed over the edge of the landing, into the swirling water. Their dark green, scaled backs glistened. The tips of their snaggly teeth protruded between their twisty lips. *Now what am I going to do!* Richard thought desperately.

The spark hovered in front of his face and softly said, "Let your sword kill them. Then, take the boat. It was placed here to aid the sorcerer's escape, so in it you will find food and drink. But you must hurry because the tide soon will turn."

Richard frowned. "Their hides sure look thick," he objected weakly.

"Let your sword slay them!" the spark insisted. "And hurry!"

Richard took a deep breath, wondering if the alligators could be any more terrible than the Bogloam he had slain. He looked down at his sword, which he had been using as a light cane, and at once the spark dove into the blade! It glowed brightly as Richard dashed through the opening and leaped down onto the flat stones of the landing—amazing himself in the process. Instantly, both alligators opened wide their pink-lined mouths and HISSED! at him. The sword then took over.

Fairly dragging Richard forward, the sword plunged itself into the open mouth of the guardian on the right. Richard jerked the blade free from the blood-spurting mouth as the beast writhed into the river and was swept away.

As the second reptile waddled forward, Richard backed to his left. The creature's long claws scraped on the stones as it stalked him, *hissing* slowly as though it were about to enjoy a much-looked-for meal. When he bumped into the rough wall at the landing's end, Richard flinched . . . and the sword lifted and fell, slicing into the alligator's snout. Richard felt strength surge into his arm as the beast twisted away, exposing its neck, so he slashed downward. As the beast died, its tail lashed around, knocking the boy against the wall.

Gasping, he dragged himself up and saw the spark dart out of his sword. "Get into the boat!" the diamond fleck of light told him. "Go quickly before the tide turns or others come."

He ran and untied the boat, climbed in, and sat in the center. There he found a pole, which he used to push the boat away from the landing. As the current took the craft, Richard was hard put to keep its bow aimed ahead. Once it was in the middle of the surging flow, however, the boat's course was swift and almost arrow straight.

Richard then had time to look around in the hull by the light of his sword. He found a metal box containing very strange-smelling food. He sniffed the food with disgust . . . but the spark clearly said, "Eat it." So, ignoring the smell and weird taste, he ate, wondering, *What "others" are waiting ahead?*

With speed that took Jodi's and Rachael's breath, their craft rushed northward. To maintain their strength, both girls frequently smelled the still-fresh leaves from the King's throne, which Jodi had kept in her pack. They began to worry—about Richard and about what might lie ahead—so, to keep their imaginations quiet and their hands busy, they went to queens Sybra and Eliadenor. They asked if they could help in any way; but, though the queens seemed pleased, they declined. Jodi persisted, asking again if she could do something. Queen Sybra replied, "The time has not yet come. Until it does, daughter of the King, harbor your strength."

Time passed in darkness, which was filled with spray, up and down jarring motion, and cold flight through the broad passage. Once, a huge gaping mouth rose from the water to lunge and snap at the boat as it shot past. "Bogloam," one of the Sea People noted. Jodi shuddered, wondering again about Richard's fate. The wide head vanished into the swirling black water, and the craft passed on into more hours of swift travel.

After going what seemed to Jodi and Rachael an awfully long way, the craft flew over a roaring waterfall. It landed with a burst of spray that drenched them all, and the Sea People had to row strongly to keep its course straight. Looking ahead, past the rowers, Jodi became aware of a dim red glow.

Without warning, the dark ceiling above them was replaced by a widespread, hazy red light. They saw that they had burst into an enormous, vaulted cavern. The river broadened. Jodi saw a wide landing to the left. As the Sea People steered for the landing, Rachael and Jodi felt a strong sense of anticipation: They sensed that the end of their mission was at hand.

Gazing upward, they saw shadowy bridges of jagged stone arched overhead here and there in the murky light. The highest bridges were almost invisible in swirling red haze. On the rough walls of the vast hall, vague shadows flickered, suggesting the presence of unseen, moving beasts. The girls saw that Lord Baldwin and the two warriors were watching the shadows intently. Baldwin drew Sulnspen and it flickered into a yellow glow.

Behind the landing, a wide stairway led upward, lit by tall, iron torches on stands. The torches cast wavering red-orange light over the stairs and crumbling railing. The railing periodically was interrupted by pedestals; on them stood statues of fearsome beasts in writhing postures.

Glancing across at other rivers flowing into the hall's harbor, Baldwin, Asaph, and Lucian stepped ashore, followed by the others. They had no more than set foot on the landing than Queen Sybra pointed. In the darkness at the head of the stairs, red eyes staring from thin slits had appeared. A glowing red tongue snaked out, lingered, and then withdrew. The creature advanced to the edge of the torchlight. A broad, scaled head—crowned by two, small, incurving horns—appeared around the glowing eyes.

"It's huge," Rachael breathed, drawing her sword.

"It's a Fearsor guard," Queen Sybra hissed, staring at the shape.

Unseen even by her, a thick black fog slid from an upper chamber and drifted down the towering, rough walls. The humans soon would learn that the fog was a being far more dangerous than all the Fearsor guards in the Cave of Tava—whose upper hall they were about to enter.

Chapter 9

The Battle of Castle Hidlothnath

Win-dor's herd wound past long, smoking fissures, steadily nearing the looming castle and the murmuring Guard before it. Morgan, the Kingsmen, and Mark Mansbridge gripped their shield straps and swords, preparing for the inevitable battle. Eric wondered, however, why the sorcerer had stationed his forces openly before the walls . . . then suddenly the ground rumbled, shook convulsively, and collapsed into an inferno!

Where the road had been, sheets of flame shot skyward. Win-dor's steeds soared through smoke, which boiled toward the overcast sky. They landed on the broad part of the ridge before the castle wall. The trap had failed, but the riders now were caught between the new cliffs and fire pits behind them and the castle wall ahead. Trogs and Fearsors filled the space between.

In the firelight, Martin and the others saw the sea of beefy shoulders and round heads of the Trogs. Short, grossly muscled, each was not over five feet tall but weighed perhaps four hundred pounds. They stared with ember eyes sunken in primitive faces, and their huge fists gripped war clubs of spiked iron. A command was bellowed. A drum began to beat with great, hollow thuds. The tide of beasts surged forward to drive the invaders into the gulf of flames, and their wide, dark mouths grunted a war cry: "Uh . . . uh . . . UH-GNAR! Uh . . . uh . . . *UH-GNAR!!*"

As his horses of the winds attacked, Win-dor cried, "To the gate!" The great horses drove into the massed Trogs, hooves flashing, their ears laid back, their eyes furious. Win-dor spotted the Trogs' leaders—larger beasts draped with fur and strapped with iron belts—and let fly several arrows. The Trog leaders and their skull-topped battle standards disappeared in balls of yellow flames. Fear rippled through the mass of cave beasts, but onward they came.

Brightly shining swords sang in the hands of Morgan, Mark Mansbridge, Jon, and Martin. Protected in the center, Queen Dorcas sat perfectly upright on her horse, surrounded by the aura of light from the Corlis Jewel. Martin was not so well protected; he felt clawed paws tear repeatedly at his armored legs. Reflexively, he swung downward, lopping off the grabbing paws of a Trog. The beast fell away, howling in pain, but was replaced by two others, clubs swinging. Martin barely fended off their blows with his shield before his horse reared to strike three Trogs that had leaped, grunting, for Martin's head.

Leaving a trail of bodies, the giant horses pressed their way forward—toward the ominous mouth in the wall where the gate stood closed. There, darkly, the Fearsors rose up, growling heavily. Twenty or more feet tall, the beasts flicked fiery tongues slowly in and out. Their eye slits—almost hidden under knobby brows—blinked over red gleaming eyes. Their scaled bodies reflected the red glow of the inferno, and their flaring nostrils drank in the sharp smell of sulphur exploding. They were looking forward to their task.

The small band of warriors was now in the center of the plain before the dark, overtowering castle. Surrounded by a sea of raging beasts, the group fought without pause. Strangely, Eric felt little fear as the creatures surged around him. He calmly leveled his staff and called upon the Father of Light as Acuerias had taught him. He was jolted as green lightning slashed out into the tide of howling faces, beefy bodies, and flailing weapons. The Trogs cowered from the force, but the press of those behind was unrelenting, so again and again Eric let the power flow through him and flash from his staff. The lightning sizzled green as an emerald's fire; a foot wide, the fire cleared a path thirty or so yards ahead.

Gradually, the group led by Win-dor forced its way closer to the castle wall. The Fearsors then began wading through the lesser Trogs, impatient to test their might against the archer. Win-dor saw their intention and urged Westwin toward the greatest of the Fearsors. He unleashed a flaming shaft at the monster . . . who brushed the arrow aside. Win-dor smiled and slung his bow on his back. Drawing his six-foot broadsword, he lifted it and thundered a war cry: *"Obi, Fearsor, oa-glimm A-Abba!"**

A pause broke the howls. Eyes turned; heads ducked. War clubs were stopped in mid-air as Westwin sprang toward the chief Fearsor—Gondouhl. Gondouhl hoisted his sword and unlimbered his chain mace.

The clash between Win-dor and Gondouhl echoed across the ridges and against the flanks of the volcanic cones. The other warriors watched spellbound as the two gigantic figures swung at each other. Wind rushed from the swords; sparks flew when they

*"Die, Fearsor, in the Light of the Father!"

struck. Gondouhl swung his mace, and as the spiked head whistled through the darkness, Win-dor ducked and thrust his sword upward into his enemy's throat. The fire behind the Fearsor's eye slits died as its body fell. At once the battle again erupted as Win-dor and his mount plunged toward another Fearsor.

After that, Martin hardly could tell what was happening. Confused by the howls of Trogs, the rumbling volcanic eruptions, and the slashing swords around him, he tried to stick close to Eric. More than once the older boy saved him from being struck down. But Eric—like Win-dor—could not be everywhere at once, and surely both Martin and Jon would have been killed had they not had the King's armor and shields.

Unfortunately, Mark Mansbridge was not so protected. A gang of Trogs made a determined attack against him, and war clubs smashed against his left side. He would have been dragged down and killed had not Win-dor's herd dauntlessly kept pressing toward the gate—which still lay a hundred yards ahead. When Eric saw Mark wounded, he sensed defeat closing in, for the tide of Trogs and Fearsors seemed endless.

At that moment, the sky within the ring of volcanoes was split by silver lightning much more potent than Eric's power. Down the silver bolts shrieked, and where they struck, entire squads of Trogs were blown to bits. The tide of Trogs ground to a halt. Even the Fearsors paused, their fiery tongues flicking in and out with uncertainty. All eyes turned northward. There, on a mountainside, stood a large figure, his staff outstretched. He was guarded by a semicircle of six Kingsmen, crouching, swords ready.

"Master Slyne has arrived!" Queen Dorcas sang out.

Again the silver lightning—quick as a blink, bright as mercury—tore through the ranks of beasts. Fearsors not struck down by Win-dor were exploded by the silver light bolts. The remaining Trogs began to flee in confusion. In another fifteen furious minutes, the battle had ended. The fires in the gulf shrank, though the surrounding volcanoes rumbled more loudly. From their mouths leaped sharp tongues of lava, which cast a red-yellow glow over the body-littered plain.

Unconcerned, Master Slyne strode downward along the northern ridge. The Kingsmen with him, led by Lieutenant Andros, warily trailed behind. Most of them limped on fur-wrapped feet—frostbitten feet, Eric surmised. Master Slyne, however, seemed as strong as before, for he carried his robe-wrapped bulk straight to the towering black gate. He raised his arms—even as the volcanoes belched geysers of fire—and thundered to the gate, *"Otho, nea glimm na-Abba!"* The iron bands and hinges of the gate burst apart as he spoke, and the foot-thick timbers cracked. Patiently then, Slyne aimed his long, black staff; silver lightning burst from the tip and blasted the gate inward.

With a cheer the Kingsmen and the riders rushed forward. But Win-dor halted the herd and explained, "Into this place my stallions may not go, for here dwell the winds of Glimmrainath, the Void." While Andros's Kingsmen helped the Duke of Corlis from his horse, the others dismounted—as Win-dor shouted, *"A-Abba conseroth seu!"* To Slyne he added, "Until you call!", then led his herd skyward with thundering hooves and rushing wind.

The King's other servants followed Master Slyne and Eric into the outer chambers of the castle, looking in every direction for an ambush or a trap. A few torches shed dim light that suggested more than it revealed. Shapes, archways, corridors, and moving shadows lurked all around. Slyne, undaunted, walked slowly to enable the Duke of Corlis—who was leaning against his sister—to keep up. All of them, including Mark, looked from side to side toward strange sounds echoing from dark openings. Finally, they entered a large hall in which the dim light gave them glimpses of thick pillars formed like snakes twisting upward. The pillars rose toward a vaguely visible ceiling.

"Where do we go now?" Eric asked Slyne, looking up at the magician's swart, stern face.

Slyne turned his stone-gray eyes upon Eric and said, "We must reach the Cave of Tava, which surely lies below us, without letting the sorcerer escape with the Lightning."

"Escape?" Eric asked, puzzled.

Before Slyne could answer, he stopped and became quite still. All the rest stood listening intently, looking into the deep shadows among the pillars. Ahead, from a second vast hall below a short flight of stairs, came the scrabbling sounds of many clawed feet—and the heavy tread of something huge.

"The Scourge of Scorius—which the King let me know *you* would deal with—is approaching," Master Slyne stated, sniffing the foul-smelling air. He cast a questioning gaze at Eric.

With sweating fingers, Eric gripped the handle of his staff and stared toward the dark hall ahead.

Richard rested in comparative comfort until his small boat shot out of the mouth of the river. The craft spun slowly in the swirling water of the harbor where five rivers joined. As his boat drifted toward the wide landing where Queen Sybra's group recently had been, Richard felt the flow of the tide beneath the boat begin to turn. Led by the spark, he jumped onto the eroded stone steps and watched as the boat was carried southward. He shivered, looking up into the hazy red glow of the hall. Beyond and above the landing soared the roughly hewn, bridge-crossed space. He then became aware of the sounds of a battle raging beyond the long flight of torchlit stairs. As the spark darted ahead to guide him, he numbly followed, awed by his surroundings.

The battle sounds grew louder and more fierce as Richard climbed the steps. He heard steel clashing against steel, inhuman roars echoing, and lightning crackling. The noises made him so afraid that he lay flat on the stairs, crawled upward, and peered over the top step. What he saw made him regret not having been swept southward by the tide!

A motley company of strange creatures was gathered in the center of a stone floor, which covered perhaps two acres. The tallest of the creatures was a scaley, horned, thick-bodied demon. Around it was a variety of beastly attackers: giant toads with shells on their backs and huge maces in their hands, strange apes wielding whips, serpents that stood tall on muscular legs to strike forward, and huge spiders waving swords.

The beasts all were facing inward, where Richard could catch glimpses of a besieged group of humans—queens Sybra and Eliadenor, Sea People and Kingsmen, warriors and Waymond. He saw that Asaph lay wounded on the dark glistening floor and that the others were hard pressed to keep the beasts at bay. Baldwin's Sulnspen blazed as yellow as Waymond's lightning. The magician and the warrior fought back to back, turning to meet attacks. Richard was about to flee when the spark darted before his ashen face.

He focused on it as it danced away. Too afraid to disobey, he crept after the diamond light. It flew to another stairway, then up two levels and across a bridge above the melee. Richard glanced down and instantly was sickened by the sight of bleeding weird bodies around the battling humans and Sea People. Then, he saw a gigantic shadow gathering itself out of the gloom high in the hall. Richard ran on, not daring to ask the spark their destination.

Behind and below him the lightning flared yellow, and a monstrous death cry made him practically leap into a narrow chamber at the head of a musty-smelling shaft. Following the spark, he trotted down tightly spiraling steps. Widely spaced torches lit the way as down and down he went, becoming dizzy. After a while, he was sure they were far below the level where the battle was raging. The air around him steadily grew hotter, and sweat trickled down his ribs and dripped from his forehead into his eyes. A glow came from below as they approached the end of the stairwell.

Hand on his sword hilt, he followed the spark from the stairs and ran through a rounded opening. Blinking, heart pounding, he breathed only when he was sure no guards were nearby. He saw that he was in a hall filled with a red glow and with many soaring columns, each of which cast its own thick shadow. Looking upward, he saw that the columns were carved stone giants with upraised arms and angry faces glowering down. When the spark hovered before Richard's eyes, then darted away into the hall, the boy summoned his courage and followed. Sneaking from pillar to pillar, from shadow to shadow, he pursued the spark until he was near a large, open space brightly lit by the red glow. The spark stopped.

Peering around the knees of one of the stone giant columns, Richard saw that in the middle of the brightly lit space was what he quickly assumed to be a throne: Rising about twenty feet on jagged black slabs, it was topped by a large, carved black wood chair, its back and right side toward Richard. Richard instantly began to imagine the tortures done before such a throne. Beyond it he could see the edges of a yawning chasm, from which writhed smoke and bright flames. At the brink of the chasm stood a shadowy, hulking shape whose eerie, green-silver eyes were staring at the top of the throne. Richard was terrified to think what sat there!

The spark buzzed insistently before his eyes. He wrenched himself from his thoughts and followed the spark alongside the throne to another long shadow. From his new vantage point he saw that two enormous bears lay on guard before the throne. The bears were listening to the many sounds coming from within the castle, rattling the chains around their necks as they moved. The spark buzzed again and began to lead Richard to another column.

In shadow black against the pillar-giant's shins, Richard rested until he had caught his breath. Then he peeked around the pillar. He saw that a black tripod of three, wrought iron snakes stood before the throne. Where the snakes' heads met was a black platter; on it was a dome that glowed white hot as though intense heat were under it. *The bottle!* Richard thought.

"The invaders in the upper river hall have slain the Fearsor, my liege," the hulking shadow by the chasm rumbled.

Richard trembled as the shadow's voice made the air vibrate. But the answering voice was even more terrifying . . . and Richard recognized it! When it spoke, the bears whimpered and the fires in the chasm rose. "Ørestheius will defeat them . . . but if they reach us, you must keep them separated until my departure!"

"What will you do with the bottle?" the shadow shape asked.

The voice from the throne replied in a low, hard tone: "I will take that cursed vial with me. If the Lightning is not released, our goal will be achieved—a cold, dead planet awaiting Lord Ingloamin Tenebrus's return from the Void."

"He *is* coming?"

"Even now he speeds toward us with Tenebrut and Amanitid, two of his three sons by Haglung." As the voice spoke, Richard shrank backward.

"What of your mother, Leilamar, and that failure—Obit?"

Vibrations from the Volcanoes of Tava grew stronger as the dark voice answered. "The cursed King of Light and his . . . his armored *urais* have defeated my mother and her armies on Oraibi and are pushing back Obit's armies on Eoramia. She and he should be here soon." The shadows around the top of the throne shifted sharply as the figure on it turned and growled, "And though Orestheius and the Scourge yet may devour the invaders, are the boats ready?"

"Yes, master," the shadow replied. "But why not fly on the Void winds?"

A deep snarl grew into the voice of the sorcerer atop the throne. "If I appeared outside the Darkness, I would be destroyed! *Fool!*"

Scrabbling claw sounds made Richard cringe. A humped, scaled beast with bulging eyes raced past the boy, going too fast to notice him. It groveled before the throne. "Master . . . master!" it panted. "The magician of the north and those with him have fought through the outer Guard!"

"Silence, bearer of ill tidings!" the sorcerer bellowed. At a signal from him, the shadow creature by the chasm sent jets of fire from its sleeves. The fire struck the messenger and reduced it to ashes within seconds. Richard was petrified; he just *knew* that at any moment the sorcerer would sense his presence and have him blasted, too!

The boy was about to collapse from fear when the spark darted close to his right ear. "Listen!" it whispered clearly. "When the time comes, you must run before the throne and take the bottle of the Lightning, even if you have to wrest it from the sorcerer himself. Do you understand?"

Richard numbly nodded, but questions as well as terror flooded through him. How would he know when? How would he avoid certain death? There was, however, no time to ask such questions, for at that instant chaos broke loose in the sorcerer's great hall.

But first . . .

Chapter 10

The Final Battle

Eric, side by side with Slyne, advanced into the middle of the second great hall of the castle—constantly looking ahead toward the rattle of many claws and the thud-thud of the much heavier tread. Close behind them came King Morgan holding the blue-shining Gafailnath upright. Next came Queen Dorcas with her wounded brother leaning against her. The Kingsmen came last, holding their shields and glimmering swords before themselves. Frequently, they squinted into the shadows cast by the giant serpent pillars surrounding them.

On either side of the hall, near its center, hung a chandelier formed of twisted iron ribbons. On the tips of the iron ribbons were cups of cut glass in which fire burned, casting a lurid glow. Into the far edge of that light crept the vanguard of the inner castle defenders, their axes, swords, and spiked clubs held ready. They appeared unwilling to face the magicians' power—until a bellowed command made them lurch forward.

As the swish-clang! of weapons erupted around him, Eric hung back. He glanced at the perverted creatures—upright lizards, green with gaping jaws and human arms wielding weapons; huge brown and orange apes with narrow-set eyes and stupid looks;

one-eyed, dark green and gray creatures like angry sloths. Eric felt sorry for them, seeing in their eyes and postures the pain of their existence. He was roused from his thoughts by the flaring of Master Slyne's silver lightning.

With sizzling sounds that echoed deeply into the castle, the lightning killed and blew backward creature after slithering or crawling creature. And behind Slyne, the swords of his companions met the storm of the other beasts' weapons like steel through thin wood. The humans saw that if they kept together with their shields facing the attackers, the beasts soon would all be slain.

Suddenly though, a great shadow arose and spread across the floor of the hall. The lesser beasts hastily moved out of the way. "The Scourge comes!" said Slyne.

Calming himself by praying hard, Eric raised his staff—as the Scourge of Scorius plodded into the pale light with a thunk-rasp! of heavy claws. Thirty or more feet tall and wide, the dark monster looked as if it could envelop the whole group with its thick wings. Its chest was broad and muscular, and its lumpy body ended in a whip-like tail. The tail lashed across the stone floor as the monster came forward. Eric looked up and stared at the beast's head where wide eye slits blinked at him, revealing green burning eyes above a squashed nose.

Morgan—perhaps thinking that Eric was frozen in terror—abruptly ran ahead, crying, "For House Evnstar!" Like a javelin thrower, he hurled Gafailnath at the Scourge. The blue blade flashed toward the monster, but from its eyes shot twin beams of sickly green light that reversed the sword's flight. Back it whistled and slammed into Morgan, knocking him backward with one edge of the sword tip embedded in his chestplate. Eric instantly aimed his staff.

Lightning flowed through him toward the monster with a roar and wisps of silver smoke. The Scourge met the blast with the twin streams of light from its eyes. While the lights clashed, it opened its wide mouth and hissed a foul wind. All the other evil creatures skittered for cover, pursued by the Kingsmen and Slyne's lightning.

Eric became almost unconscious of his surroundings as he sent lightning from his staff again and again. He did not even see Queen Dorcas work the sword out of Morgan's red-stained armor. The young king flinched as she undid and removed his chestplate, then stanched the flow of blood with one corner of her gown. Holding her radiant Jewel over his wound, she murmured, "Why? You were warned!"

Weakly he answered, "I . . . I thought it was up to me." He sank back, crying, "I was afraid I'd fail . . . as Father did . . . so I hurried to . . ."

His mother sighed, seeing that the light from her Jewel had not even closed her son's wound. She glanced at Eric and the Scourge, then bent over Morgan and whispered, "You have not yet failed." She bound his wound and slid Gafailnath into its scabbard. "But," she added to herself, "I have failed, for I cannot even protect my own child." She cried silently as she helped Morgan into a kneeling position, set to run.

Eric, meanwhile, was not aware of the battle going on between the others and the castle beasts. All he knew was the tremendous surge of power he felt pouring through his body and out his staff. The power was so great that—despite the fact that the Scourge was a Void creature not easily destroyed by light—the monster gradually began to weaken and be driven back.

After killing the other beasts, the humans warily regathered. In silence, they witnessed the conclusion of the battle between the young magician and the towering shape of darkness. Martin and the others squinted in the blinding glare of green and silver that flashed even into the darkest recesses of the hall. Then instinctively they covered their eyes when the lightning pierced the Scourge and caused an explosion of white light needles that burst in all directions. Smoke slowly cleared . . . and the watchers saw that the monster had been reduced to a smouldering, ragged hulk—lifeless. Eric sagged to the floor, exhausted.

Slyne knelt by the young man's side, smiling at him. "Good work, lad," the bulky magician murmured as he helped Eric stand. "Now we must hurry."

Master Slyne hastened to lead the group, and Eric numbly followed. Martin and Jon helped Mark Mansbridge, and behind them walked the other Kingsmen, carrying Morgan. Queen Dorcas walked beside her son, holding one of his hands.

Across dark rooms, through strangely shaped doorways, down long passages, and across bridges they cautiously went. They came at last onto a bridge above Waymond's besieged group. Though the attackers of the group below all were dead, a huge empty shadow was closing in around them. Lord Baldwin called up, "It's the thief who stole the bottle!" In front of Baldwin, Waymond was holding the shadow at bay with his lightning. But the creature's burning mist and foul hissing breath were beginning to weaken the brown-robed magician.

Slyne lifted his arms, letting the edges of his loose robe fall back, and shouted, *"Othoy, Orestheius, Garainath na-pere ma conseroth, vocci A-Abba!"** In pain and anger, the shadow—Orestheius—arose to fill the

*"Go below, Orestheius, you evil thing that kills hope and strength; thus says the Father!"

hall; quickly, it towered many levels above the junction of the rivers.

As Master Slyne held his arms over the scene, white glowing light came. It was a peaceful, soft light, which made the humans' spirits rise as it filled the rough dome. Orestheius hissed in agony. And, as the light came more strongly, the shadow creature began to writhe in the way Morgan had seen it do when it had been cornered by Gafailnath and Sulnspen in the shaft in Imnatride. It began to scream—three shrill, unharmonious wails at once; wincing, the humans covered their ears. Ever louder screamed the shadow as the light began to absorb it. Soon, Orestheius faded into the white radiance, trailing a whisper of despair.

Slyne dropped his arms, blinked, and shook his head once. Looking at one another, the humans breathed sighs of relief and began to smile. Slyne, however, hardly gave them time to relax. Beckoning to Eric, the older magician whirled and ran to a spiral staircase that led down through blackness to the hall of the river landing. There, they joined Waymond. While the three magicians ran in search of openings leading to the Cave of Tava, Jodi went to the Duke of Corlis and placed her healing hands upon his crushed ribs. Then she turned to Morgan, crying when she saw his pain. She started to touch him, but Queen Dorcas stopped her. "Not yet," she whispered pleadingly. Puzzled, Jodi obeyed.

She watched the three queens go to one another and clasp hands, even as Slyne called, "Make haste!" The group did so, and, with the Kingsmen carrying Asaph and Morgan, they joined Slyne. He showed the queens one way to go, then he, Waymond, and Eric went a second way. Down they all hurried, their footsteps ringing hollowly on the uneven steps leading to the cave below.

When Richard heard the fast-approaching footsteps, the spark told him, "Now!" He responded without thinking and burst from the shadows like a launched arrow. Slipping, he sprinted in front of the throne. The bears lunged forward until their chains jerked taut. Before the shadow creature by the chasm could react, Richard knocked the white-glowing dome off the top of the tripod. As it crashed to the floor, he grabbed the radiant crystal bottle from the platter. Ignoring the heat of it, he scrambled away.

"Burn him!" roared Jabez from atop his throne. But light from the bottle dazzled the shadow creature. It turned uncertainly, sending smoking streams of fire from its hollow sleeves . . . which missed.

The boy, clutching the bottle, ran smack into Master Slyne's broad chest as he led the other magicians through a doorway. Ribbons of flame from the shadow slave crackled toward them. Slyne pushed Richard behind him, lifted his staff, and—with a grunt—sent silver lightning into the shadowy servant. Backward the creature was hurled, wailing shrilly as it plunged into the fiery chasm.

From the other side of the hall came the three queens and those with them—as the sorcerer stood. Hooded and robed in billowing black fabric, he seemed to tower upward, raising his left hand and holding an open book in his right. The King's servants gathered before the dark throne, and the sorcerer pointed at them, thundering an incantation. At once, misty Darkness began spewing from the mouths of the glowering giant columns. The queens reached toward one another as the radiance from their Jewels deflected the Darkness, but the thickening mist swiftly collected above them; from the cloud slashed branching, black lightning.

Queen Sybra was struck squarely in her chest; she crumpled as the glistening black lightning again shot from the mist-cloud; it enveloped Queen Eliadenor in crackling sable tongues that left her lifeless. Slyne and Waymond instantly sent bolts of smoking silver and yellow light toward the sorcerer, and a lightning battle began to rage. In the confusion, Jodi and Rachael stood immobilized . . . until inner voices screamed, "Now! Your purpose is *now!*" They sprinted forward and sprawled by the fallen queens while Queen Dorcas crouched under the jagged flashes of light and rushed toward them. The two cave bears, meanwhile, snapped their chains and would have mauled the huddled Kingsmen if Eric had not slain the enraged beasts.

Squinting into the glare, Jodi took the Jewel of Tava from the golden chain around Queen Sybra's neck, and Rachael unhooked the green Jewel from Queen Eliadenor's chain. They reached toward Dorcas . . . and the three Jewels were touched! Green as the sea, yellow as the sun, and blue as the sky, three dancing domes of light rose and flashed roundly. And louder than the crash of lightning, Queen Dorcas shouted, *"Abba, oeuconserd, kaomimt ey!* Father, by your kindness, appear to us!"

From each of the people gathered before the evil throne arose a glow of quickly brightening light. From Martin, Andros, Baldwin—all of them, the light rushed forth, surrounding them, then leaping toward the lofty ceiling. Before Jabez could flee, down sped the light. The sorcerer directed his black lightning upward, into the light, but his effort was smothered. His black robes began spewing black smoke, then burst into flames as light flooded into his being. With a fading scream, Jabez, eldest son of Ingloamin, was gone!

Everyone but Slyne closed his eyes as the glaring light continued to stream downward. It now appeared to be a bright shining star with four points. The bottom point grew long and came to rest at the top of the black throne. Slowly, the fiery white star became the King . . . the Lord of Light! When the glare had withdrawn into him, the witnesses opened their eyes.

"A-Abba seimt!" Queen Dorcas cried, raising her arms toward the King. The Kingsmen and warriors sheathed their swords and knelt. The King lowered his arms and slowly descended the black throne. With each step, a layer of it turned to marble. When he reached the bottom, the King looked at each of his followers. His eyes rested on the stiffened bodies of Eliadenor and Sybra . . . and life once more quickened them. Smiling, Jodi and Rachael gave the queens their Jewels. Joyfully, they all gathered around the King.

"You have done well, my brothers and sisters—but you must not rest," the King said. "Miss Jodi, heal the wounded. Master Slyne, as soon as the handmaiden is done, I will lead all of you to the western entrance of the Cave of Tava. When you emerge, you must summon Win-dor. The archer's horses will speed you to Imnatride."

He and Queen Dorcas closely watched Jodi kneel and lay her hands on King Morgan's red-stained chest. Morgan placed his hands over Jodi's as he felt her warm power surge into him, healing his wound. Together, their hands began to glow, and the line between them disappeared into whiteness. Queen Dorcas briefly felt jealousy, and—though the moment passed and she smiled—she suddenly felt alone. Tearfully, she looked at the King, who nodded as though confirming her unspoken thought. Queen Dorcas bowed her head . . . then unclasped her hands, bent down, and kissed Jodi on one cheek. Jodi touched the spot of the kiss and smiled at the Queen. She then helped Morgan stand.

"King Morgan Evnstar," the King said, "I ask that if you arrive in Imnatride, you take the bottle from

Richard and climb Glimmothtyrn. If you reach the top, you must immediately release the Lightning. Then, Eorthe will be purged of the Darkness."

Morgan nodded, still clasping one of Jodi's hands in his own. "I will not fail this time," Morgan vowed.

"You have not yet failed," the King said softly. His eyes sparkled as he added, "But sometimes those who would be first finish last, and," he said with a glance at Richard, "those who would be last finish first."

Morgan grinned, embarrassed. But Richard—holding the precious bottle against his chest—stepped forward. "I heard the sorcerer say that someone named Ingloamin Tenebrus was coming from the Void—with others called Tenebrut, Amanitid, and Haglung."

The King put one arm around Richard's shoulders and looked sternly at Morgan. "If you hurry, and let nothing sway you, they will be turned back."

After a moment of silence, Jodi went to Asaph to heal him. The King then led the way across the immense hall to a cobwebbed door. Slyne tugged open the heavy door, and the group saw before them, illuminated by the light from the bottle Richard was carrying, a foul tunnel. As they entered the passage of blackness, they each bid farewell to the King. He stood in the tunnel mouth until they had gone, then faded into a silver cloud swiftly uprising.

When the cloud had gone, the castle fires flickered out. The caverns, passages, and halls of Castle Hidlothnath once more were cold and dark. As though searching for their master, the winds from the Void moaned and swept round the hall of Jabez. They fluttered and turned the pages of the sorcerer's book, which lay behind the dead throne. Unanswered, the lonely winds then faded. The only sound in the vast place for a time thereafter came from the rivers rushing far below the castle, deep within the rock ribs of Eorthe.

Chapter 11

Lightning Unleashed

When the group emerged from the tunnel, the Kingsmen saw that they were on a mountainside. Below stretched a long, narrow valley—entirely dark and smoke shrouded. Behind and above them, the dead and silent Volcanoes of Tava rose out of sight into the overcast sky. Ash drifted from the clouds, sprinkling the weary group.

"Oh me," Martin moaned. "I wish we could get some sleep and wake up to find the sky clear!"

"We can't sleep now," Lieutenant Andros said, watching Master Slyne, "no matter how tired we are."

From under his robe Slyne withdrew a long, curving animal horn bound in several places by embossed silver bands. Martin suddenly became alert. "The Horn of Meet!" he whispered excitedly to Eric.

The young magician nodded. "The same you once blew from the summit of Hopesmont."

Slyne set the silver mouthpiece to his lips, took a deep breath as the others covered their ears, and blew a loud, clear blast. The sound caromed off the looming peaks and echoed over the dark valley.

The group waited, listening. A wind arose and began to whisper over the barren landscape. The magician blew the Horn of Meet a second time.

From the west and high above, the warm wind swept upon the land. Along its way, it opened a yawning passage through the black overcast. "Win-dor comes," Slyne announced as a thunder of hoofbeats, constantly growing louder, hastened toward the watchers.

Slyne blew the Horn a third time to lead the horses of the winds to his location. Then, from the deep of night, they appeared—white, yellow-tan, roan, and gray forms galloping up the mountainside. Hides glistened, manes swirled, and long feathery tails flowed as Win-dor led his herd to a skittering stop at the base of the cliff below Master Slyne.

"Ho, light bringers!" the archer boomed. "Quickly now. The Lord of Darkness comes!"

They hurried down the rocks and helped one another mount. Slyne vaulted up last, and the herd began racing off the instant he was seated. Slyne was the only one of the group except Win-dor who was large enough to straddle his mount; Martin and Jon, for example, perched behind their steeds' shoulders. They wrapped their hands in the long flowing manes and crouched as the herd burst skyward. Rachael, perhaps more than anyone else, was thrilled by the surge of speed. She began to laugh, gayly excited that she now had the first of her two wishes: to ride one of the horses of the winds.

The archer rode upright, and a mighty wind rushed before him, tearing a passage through the blackness. Soon, the riders emerged above the clouds blanketing the land. Shivering, they looked down on the mountaintops poking through the overcast into silvering moonlight. Win-dor apprehensively scanned the sky and fitted an arrow to the string of his great bow.

The horses gradually soared into a vast canyon in the higher clouds. The sides of the vapor canyon towered thousands of feet above the riders and seemed to touch the cold white stars. The moon shone brightly within the hundreds-of-miles-wide rift between gray-black cloud walls. Ahead, outlined by the moon's light, billowing cloud towers rose like a magnificent city in the sky above Win-dor's dwarfed herd. The moon bathed the herd with a *nathnor*-like glow, which made the air seem even colder than it was.

The frigid wind streaming past the highly held horses' heads tore tears from Jodi's and Rachael's eyes. The tears froze on their reddened cheeks. To escape the wind, they flattened themselves against the backs of their steeds. Jodi turned her head and looked at Morgan, who smiled at her, wishing he could warm the maiden who had healed him.

Southward flew the horses of Win-dor—high winds whistling through the dark, cold heights. Mere specks the wind horses were against the gray, silver, and black sky. Unfortunately they were not invisible specks.

The archer signaled to Slyne, then pointed high and behind. The riders all looked back, blinking in the freezing wind. Across the down-slanting light of the moon came an enormous shadow: Ingloamin, Lord of Darkness, was returning! Descending, the Shadow sped on a course that obviously would intercept the wind herd's path.

"Faster, Westwin!" Win-dor urged. One by one, the horses surged forward. The southward wall of the cloud canyon slowly appeared in the distance ahead. But even Martin sensed that escape from the Shadow would not be so easy as disappearing into clouds.

On stormed Glimmrainath's Shadow, stabbing fingers of night ahead and trailing ebony clouds behind. High it spread, faster than any storm on Eorthe or Earth. Richard clutched the glimmering bottle against his chest, wondering if he should open it now, before the mighty Darkness swept over them. But the King had said Morgan was to unleash the Lightning, so Richard simply did his best to hold onto his stallion's mane and silence his doubts.

As the herd began to descend, the leading fingers of the Shadow grew behind them. Arms of Darkness embraced the moon's glow and smothered it while the body-cape of black filled the cloud canyon. And just as the black fingers came within reaching distance of the riders, the herd dove into the southward cloud wall. Morgan and Baldwin drew Gafailnath and Sulnspen, which glowed in the misty darkness on either side of the light from the bottle like beacons for the riders.

The race against the return of Ingloamin seemed to go on for an eternity, though actually it lasted only a few hours. As thick gray clouds sped past, time and distance seemed to Eric to vanish . . . but eventually he sensed that the herd was nearing Eorthe's surface. The air warmed, and he caught whiffs of sea air; the tangy, warmer air revived him, and he sat upright. He then heard the rhythmic sound of waves crashing.

The herd of Win-dor burst under the cloud cover and began skimming gray ocean swells. Straight toward tall headlands lay their course. "Alamantia!" Win-dor turned and called as his horses soared above the cliffs to streak inland. When the towers of Castle Imnatride came into view, the herd slowed . . . then twice circled Glimmothtyrn tower, descending. Seeing no enemies, they alighted and came to a halt in the outer courtyard with a thunderous clatter of hooves on stone.

Morgan sheathed Gafailnath and swung from his horse. "The bottle!" he yelled to Richard, who quickly dismounted and handed him the precious vial. Morgan then whirled and sprinted into the castle. Slyne, Queen Dorcas, and the others were close behind him. Jodi and Rachael came last, looking skyward because of the approach of a hurricane roar. When a black, misty wind burst down to whip their hair, they ran for shelter in the castle. As soon as they were inside, Baldwin, Lucian, and Asaph struggled to close the huge doors against the wind, then raced ahead of the girls up the stairs of Glimmothtyrn.

Morgan, with Slyne pounding heavily behind him, climbed without stopping. He took the steps of the right-turning spiral two at a time. The tower, meanwhile, shuddered as the black wind drove fiercely against it.

"The Lord of Darkness is upon us!" Slyne shouted, hurling his bulk up the steps after the young king.

Wordlessly, Morgan climbed, looking neither upward nor out the slits in the tower sides. Had he looked he would have seen black lightning slashing against the tower, probing it for weaknesses. There were none, and Morgan reached the top unharmed. With burning lungs, pounding pulse, and trembling fingers, he grasped the crystal stopper in the neck of the bottle. But then he hesitated.

He was swayed by a question that flashed through his mind: Would he, his family and friends, and all they had known, be destroyed with the Darkness?

"DO IT!" Master Slyne thundered, stamping the tower room floor with the butt of his heavy staff. At the instant he spoke, the black lightning and wind raging against the tower suddenly ceased. "Release Abba's Lightning!" Slyne commanded, glowering at Morgan.

Morgan jerked out the stopper and held the bottle high above his head. He closed his eyes and fell as the Lightning erupted.

In a spreading flash, the bolts of brilliant light leaped in all directions through the narrow windows at the top of the tower. The lightning bolts flashed into the dark clouds, setting off several series of explosions that rumbled into the distances. Far and wide sped the

Lightning—over the Alamantian Ocean, over Eoramia and neighboring Corlis, over Rud even to the Circle of Blizzards, over Oraibi even to the eastern ocean. It stormed around Eorthe to the western shore of Ispenth, then flashed back toward Alamantia.

Winds rushed in all directions with the Lightning, and swiftly spread the cleansing of Eorthe. The winds purged first the oceans, then the lands, of the thick gray clouds and black mists. The sudden onset of a brilliant dawn broke over nations and cities, plains and mountains. Gueroness was first among the lands to feel rain from the white clouds that formed after the winds' passing. As the gentle rain fell it cleaned the dust and every vestige of the Darkness from the sky. And everywhere, faithful peasants and nobles, merchants and soldiers, and even entire families began to awaken from their enthrallment.

But because of Morgan's hesitation, Ingloamin himself had not been destroyed. Thus, his power was not vanquished, and many creatures of evil managed to escape the Lightning storm. Men like Th'ral and Tzarmsh, hiding in their fortresses in Rud, and beings like Haglung and her sons—who had taken shelter inside the Seven Caves of Púpsovi in Oraibi—survived the renewal . . . though presumably Leilamar, the Shadow Guardian, did not, since no one ever saw her again.

When the shafts of Lightning returned to Alamantia, they darted into the top of Glimmothtyrn and returned to the crystal bottle. Amazed, Morgan replaced the stopper . . . wondering what harm his hesitation had done. Those who had gathered with him in the tower room also were staring in wonder at the bottle. When the light in it subsided, they went to the narrow windows and began to cheer when they saw that gentle rain had begun to fall. They also saw that trees and fields for miles around were springing into life. Shades of green spread in waves over Alamantia. Flowers ran rivers of many colors over the greening hills and pastures. Then the streams and River Iverwain began to sparkle, for the sun had appeared! Joyously, the King's company came down from Glimmothtyrn's crown.

In the castle and courtyards and in the streets and squares of the city, some of the rain-washed corpses were awakening. There were, however, many small, eroded mounds of ashes where other people had dissolved. Strangely, no one ever could remember the names of those who did not awaken.

A growing crowd—some yawning and stretching—met the rescuers in the outer courtyard of the castle. Many of the citizens began to rejoice and sing praises to the Father of Light, and others murmured with questions. When the crowd began to press toward Win-dor and his prancing mount, he called to Morgan, "I must return to my domain!"

"And I," Master Slyne said to the Wind Lord, "must resume my duties in the northlands—if one of your steeds will transport me."

Win-dor bowed to Slyne and beckoned to a white stallion, which the bulky magician mounted.

"And will you take me to Tolan to greet my people?" Queen Sybra asked him, clasping her Jewel.

Win-dor again bowed; smiling, he then pointed to a gray stallion. Before going to it, however, Queen Sybra went to the other two queens. They embraced, spoke quietly to one another, and kissed farewell. Finally, Sybra mounted. And while Win-dor and his herd soared skyward, Unthoriumgai, Father of Whales, was sighted forging up Iverwain, towing a *maralaman*. Seeing him, Queen Eliadenor and her Sea People bade good-bye and made their way toward the harbor to begin their return home.

That afternoon, King Morgan was crowned ruler of

Alamantia in a ceremony hastily arranged by Queen Dorcas and Lord Baldwin. Also, at Morgan's request, Jodi was ennobled. The smiling, shyly silent young woman became Gloralanin—"healing friend"—Princess of Alamantia. Then, Queen Dorcas and Morgan fashioned a wreath of fresh flowers and laid it on the tomb of Mervintide Evnstar. Alone, Morgan remained for some time beside the tomb; no one overheard his murmured words.

In the late afternoon, King Morgan, Queen Dorcas, and their group left the Castle of Imnatride to board the *maralaman* for the trip to Espereim. They passed slowly through cheering crowds lining the streets. Seeing the way the citizens hailed and bowed to her, Jodi became embarrassed. She asked Queen Dorcas why Morgan had made her a princess, but the queen only smiled.

On board the warship, Morgan called, "To Espereim!" The drum began to beat; oar blades splashed and pulled; and the great ship slowly left the dockside to enter the main flow of Iverwain. Morgan ran to the stern and stood halfway up the dragon's tail to call back to Lord Baldwin; he, with Lucian and Asaph, had been left in charge of Alamantia.

Morgan cupped both hands to his mouth. "I will return soon!" he shouted. "Guard well the Lightning in the Bottle!"

"With my life, my lord!" Baldwin's deep voice boomed.

The city below the mountaintop castle slowly diminished from view as the ship glided down green Iverwain. Soon, the galley was on the blue, swell-ridged ocean; a colorful sunset lay ahead. The sail was raised and set. And as the moon rose behind the ship, the Kingsmen wearily sought beds. They slept deeply as a fresh, clean wind pushed the *maralaman* swiftly over the waves toward Espereim.

Chapter 12

Return of the Kingsmen

In the days of peaceful sailing that followed, King Morgan seldom left Jodi's side. And, seeing that the couple was building a sphere of love around themselves, the others smilingly stayed at a distance. Rachael and Lieutenant Andros walked and often sat talking together, and Martin and Jon began to discuss going home.

"Do you think Eric really will stay here?" Jon asked one afternoon as he and Martin sat near the dragon's head bow.

Martin frowned. "Well . . . he *is* an apprentice magician, and he's been one hundred percent Kingsman since . . . since Crossingsend. Yes, he'll stay."

Jon fell silent, thinking how sad Eric's parents would be; how well he remembered his own sense of loss when his parents had died.

Richard, meanwhile, had little to say to anyone. He was not unfriendly, however, and he usually could be found near Waymond. He never once bragged about his exploits in the Caves of Rainath or in the Cave of Tava. And it seemed that his brattish personality had died. It was he, standing in the bow beside Waymond, who first sighted the coast of Eoramia. Waymond winked one brown eye at him and nodded. Richard cupped his hands around his mouth and sang out, *"Land ahead!"*

The ship's company crowded to the rails. The great cliffs of Eoramia drew nearer and nearer until the green hills and darker forests could be seen. Soon, even the harbor and the thundering, sparkling waterfall of River Limmwain were clearly in view. And, as the ship entered the harbor, King Morgan and the others saw—among the waiting crowd—a snowy-haired figure astride a burro. "Acuerias!" King Morgan called joyfully. The old man slowly waved one arm.

As the ship coasted to its anchorage, Eric noticed that only the Duke of Corlis did not seem happy. He was bent despondently over the rail. The young magician went to him.

"What's wrong, friend?" Eric inquired.

Mark sighed, rubbing one broad, scarred hand through his thick blond hair. "Ah, lad, if you but knew."

"Knew what?" Eric asked, leaning over the rail to watch longboats being put out to take them ashore.

"Well, you see, I am alone except for my sister. I've no family, and even my prize stallion, Warinmount, is lost to me," the Duke answered. "Now, all I have left ahead of me is to spend the rest of my life ruling Corlis. That's a rather boring prospect."

"Ruling a land is boring?" Eric stammered. "What would you rather do?"

Mark brightened and straightened, and his eyes took on a faraway look. "I'd truly like to venture into *your* world—Earth."

Eric blinked and drew back. "Why don't you ask the King?"

Mark focused on Eric and began to smile. He

clapped the brown-robed youth on his back. They went down together to board one of the waiting longboats for the brief trip to shore. Ahead, on the stone quay, stood Acuerias and thousands of Eoramians, waiting to welcome the returning heroes.

As soon as he could, Acuerias came to Morgan and greeted him and the others. Then, with his hands gripping the young king's arms, he nodded toward a group of anxious-looking men—warriors who had returned in disgrace from the Swamps of Armazil. Acuerias said, "My lord, on the way home, many of those given into my keeping were killed by the Darkness; those who were revived have become thoroughly disheartened. They now regret their cowardice, and I beg forgiveness for them." He bowed his snowy head.

Morgan said only, "By the Father's grace, the Light has renewed our world; I pray, therefore, that the past will be forgiven . . . and forgotten."

Acuerias, wondering at the humble tone in the youth's voice, repeated the news to the warriors behind him. The forgiven men—and their families—began to cheer. Their voices were added to the rejoicing that swept up the crowd-jammed road. The people were not merely happy; they were thrilled with the innocence of a new beginning.

The following day—when King Morgan, his group, and the joyous throng finally came through the gates of Castle Glimpalatyrn—a courtier pushed his way to Dorcas. "The King," he announced breathlessly, "awaits you and his other 'servants of the quest' in the castle garden!"

They hurried through crowd-filled halls and the throne room into the garden. There, in the slanting golden light of sunset, flowers bloomed brightly. Birds eagerly sang, and the splashing fountain made calming music. It was a truly rare, harmonious moment. And, as though to crown the moment, the King appeared from within the grapevine-covered arbor. Behind him hung purple, frosted-looking bunches of grapes, ripening now in abundance on the vigorously green vine.

"A-Abba seimt!" murmured Queen Dorcas as she and the others bowed.

He went first to Morgan, and the look he gave the youth was stern. "You hesitated before releasing the Lightning," he said.

Morgan's first impulse was to explain why he had hesitated, but he saw that the King plainly knew all that was within him. He fell to his knees and lowered his head. "Forgive me," he pleaded.

"Look at me," the King said softly. When Morgan raised his head, tears were in his eyes. But he saw that the King's look no longer was stern. The King said, "It is because of actions like yours—human moments of fear and hesitation—that the Tragic Course of Eorthe continues." Morgan felt crushed by the words, though the King's tone was not accusatory.

"Please," Morgan said, "I'm very sorry."

For Morgan's ears alone, the King said, "Know this: In the Fourth Age now beginning, you would have been a king like none other than L'Ced. Now, however, a Son of Light will be born to another House, and you eventually will serve him. Know also that whereas the Third Age was a time of choosing, the Fourth Age will be a time of winnowing and in-gathering. Your task henceforth, if you accept it, will be to assist me and eventually the Son of Light in gathering those who love the Light and in protecting them from the servants of Ingloamin who survived Eorthe's renewal because of your disobedience." With a loving—and forgiving—look, the King gazed down at Morgan.

Chastised, Morgan quietly said, "With your love to sustain us, I pray to be given wisdom to help make the age all you would have it be."

The King helped him stand, then turned to Queen Dorcas. "Sister, your faith has been like that of the Jewel I gave you—as true as sunlight. Do you have any requests?"

"No, my lord. My requests have been fulfilled already," she replied.

"Your brother, though," the King resumed with a smile toward Mark Mansbridge, "has a request, I believe."

Mark seemed embarrassed. "Well . . . I wish to return with the Kingsmen to learn more about Earth."

Queen Dorcas frowned slightly, holding her breath, while the King asked, "Will you maintain your faith there—and continue to serve me when called?"

"Yes, lord," Mark replied quickly. "I will not fail you."

The King's look became penetrating. "You will be tested many times, though not by me. However, the choice to go beyond the Great River is yours, alone among Eortheans." He clasped arms with the tall duke, then turned to Jodi. "Princess Gloralanin, you also soon will have a choice: As soon as Morgan has the opportunity, I believe he will ask for your hand in marriage."

Both young people were embarrassed, but they looked at each other and smiled.

"However, Jodi," the King continued, "you are but fourteen, a marriageable age in Eorthe but one at which decisions may not be permanent. So, I ask that you return to your own land for two years—unless the call comes again before then. During that time, think well about which world you would rather live in. If you decide to return to Eorthe, your power of healing once more will be with you."

"You mean, I can't. . ." Jodi stammered.

"No," the King said quietly. "Your world no longer accepts or understands that kind of power. Therefore, it will be withheld from you . . ."

Placing his hands on the apprentice magician's shoulders, he said, "My young servant, you will be a student of Master Slyne for a year—if you choose to stay."

Eric seemed confused. "But Acuerias . . ."

"Acuerias is going home with me, and there he will stay."

Eric looked sadly at the snowy-haired magician. "Does he have to?"

The King replied, "Ask him."

Acuerias nodded to Eric. "I am thoroughly tired, my student, and my final task has been completed. So, to you I leave my book and stone, and I entrust you—if you are willing—to the care of Master Slyne. But know this," he added with an upraised forefinger, "that immortality in the King's service is not something to be undertaken lightly!"

Eric looked down for a moment, then at the King. "I made up my mind years ago about who my master would be."

"It will mean leaving your mother and father, friends and school—all you've known and loved," the King cautioned.

"I love you more than all that," Eric said with quiet firmness.

The King smiled, laid one hand on Eric's head, and looked at Jon. "When you return, you, too, will have a decision to make. Two people may grieve for their son so much that they—if they heed the thought that will be clamoring in their hearts—will reach out to someone who desperately needs loving parents."

Jon looked swiftly to Eric, who smiled sadly but peacefully. Speechless, with bright eyes at the thought of having a permanent home and parents again, Jon nodded vigorously.

The King laughed and turned to Martin. "Martin, you and Rachael are promoted to the rank of Lieutenant Kingsmen. Your new duties will include helping me conduct the Ceremony of the Upraised Swords when we return to Reginald-Wharford Hall. You will go before me to welcome the Kingsmen and apprentices as they return from the various parts of Eorthe where they have been battling the forces of Darkness. You and *Captain* Andros will have much to do to help magician Waymond enlarge the hall—for we have grown in number since last year."

Rachael smiled at Andros to congratulate him on his promotion, then looked at Acuerias when the aged magician spoke to her. "Lieutenant Rachael, you will find your life has changed when you return home. Your family even now is enjoying my final act of what you call 'magic': the sweet waters of a spring, very near your home."

"No more walking to carry water!" Rachael cried, looking happily at Acuerias, then at Jodi. "And *baths. . .*" Tearfully, she kissed Acuerias.

"Now, Children of the Light," the King said, "drink once more from the fountain. Be refreshed. Then we must part company."

As the Kingsmen silently drank, the King sat beside Richard. Together, they watched the fountain's sparkling flow.

"Do you know," the King began, "that I will be with you always?"

"Yes, Sir," Richard quietly replied, looking at the King. "And, Sir, I'm really sorry . . ."

"Waymond has your armor and shield in his carpetbag," the King said, gazing deeply into Richard's black eyes. "And, by the way, the spark and I are very glad you had the courage to rescue the bottle."

Richard scooped another handful of the precious liquid into his mouth. He swallowed, looked back at the King, and said, "Thank you, Sir. And by the way, what was the spark—your Light?"

"He was of my father's spirit—immeasurably powerful but easily hurt if you ever refuse to let him lead you," the King replied. He and Richard gazed into each other's eyes for some time, then the King stood. He and Acuerias went into the vine-covered arbor.

The others gathered in a semicircle nearby and held hands. Quietly but distinctly Queen Dorcas sang *"Efil Espere"*:

(1) Lighting ever bright,
from blue sky you shone;
banishing Man's night,
we cling to you alone.

(2) Come into our lives,
help us make our mark
though our ears hear lies,
and all the world be dark.

(3) Clearlight shining bright,
help us to be brave;
help us do what's right,
for it's your love we crave.

(4) As we daily pray
love from the Father,
show us now the way:
love for one another.
Eternally!

Slowly, as she continued to hum the melody, her voice faded into the clear, evening air.

"Farewell for now, my family," the King said as both he and Acuerias began to radiate a white light that became brighter and brighter. *"A-Abba conseroth seu!* The Father's strength is yours!"

Acuerias lifted one hand as he and the King faded into a white brilliance. The others tearfully waved back, knowing they would miss the wise, kind old magician; but it satisfied them deeply to know that he was going to the King's home. Then, as the setting sun's light faded from the sky and garden, the white brilliance rose quickly. Higher and higher it soared until it seemed to become a bright star shining in the western sky. A nightingale sang; the breeze rustled the arbor leaves. Night had come—and it was a night without fear, the first in a long time.

In the morning, in the Hall of the Throne of Eoramia, the Duke of Corlis—dressed plainly in a blue cotton robe—said farewell to his sister. Meanwhile, King Morgan got Jodi's attention and slipped with her into the garden.

"Well, Princess Gloralanin," he began with a shyness she had not seen in him before, "as the King and my mother know, I planned to ask you to join me in *Omiglorimm,* which is, to us, the first stage before betrothal and marriage." Jodi held her breath, afraid he had changed his mind. To her relief, he knelt before her near the fountain. "Because I love you with all my heart," he resumed with gentle shyness, "and because I believe it is Abba's will, I wish you to be my wife, Queen of Alamantia. Thus, I beg your hand in marriage, subject of course to your and your parents' wishes."

Jodi took his hands in hers and bent to kiss his cheek. "I accept," she murmured with wildly beating heart. "And I promise to return within two years' time."

Morgan stood and held her close. "I hope I'm not rushing you . . ."

She stopped his words with a kiss, then whispered, "I think the King knew my greatest, most impossible wish and brought us together."

He nodded, pleased, and stood back slightly to look into her eyes. "You'll have many responsibilities as my queen," he warned.

Jodi laughed, thinking: *If only you knew how perfectly marvelous all this is!* But she said only, "I'll manage."

He laughed, and they walked hand in hand back into the castle.

That afternoon, the Kingsmen, Mark Mansbridge, Waymond, and Eric left. King Morgan and his mother stood in the garden with them as they slung their packs onto their shoulders. Queen Dorcas—who was carrying a small, leather bag—hugged Mark and talked quietly with him for a while. Then she went to embrace Jodi and said, "I shall look forward to the day when you join the Sisterhood of the Jewels—if that be the King's will." She then took a slim ring of gold from her leather bag and placed it into her son's hands.

Morgan took Jodi's left hand and slipped the ring onto her third finger. "Remember me," he whispered as he kissed her gently.

Tingling, Jodi managed to say, "I don't think I'll forget you, or you, my lady," she added to Queen Dorcas.

"That reminds me. . ." Dorcas said suddenly. She reached inside her leather bag and withdrew three golden chains like the one her Jewel hung upon. Two she placed around the necks of Rachael and Jodi. The third she gave to Mark. To the girls, she explained, "As you have gladly given to others, so gladly receive these gifts. They are signs of your service to the King—though no one else need ever see them."

Rachael looked at Mark, who was putting the third chain in his pack. Rachael asked, "And who . . ."

Queen Dorcas smiled faintly. "It is . . . in case."

Martin then impatiently asked Waymond, "Are you going to zap us through time to the Land of the King?"

Waymond tousled Martin's hair and said, "No." When the boy's expression clouded, Waymond added, "Eric will perform that chore."

Jodi lingered and hesitantly asked Morgan, "*You* won't forget *me,* will you?"

He came close to her and took her hands in his. "No

matter what glory I find, no matter how the kingdom demands my time, no matter what other maidens I meet, I shall *never* forget your healing touch of love." Slowly, they separated as Eric lifted his staff.

Queen Dorcas and Morgan raised their hands, but before they could even wave, the Kingsmen, Mark, and the two magicians disappeared . . . to the Land of the King!

The King, Lord of Light, came back to his Land when Reginald-Wharford Hall had been enlarged by the magicians. The Ceremony of the Upraised Swords was, to say the least, magnificent. More than two hundred apprentices walked down the banks of the Dain River under the outstretched swords of the Kingsmen. When the apprentices reached the leafy throne that spanned the river at the south end of the Hall, they knelt before the King and were fitted with armor, shields, and swords. Captain Andros and lieutenants Martin and Rachael helped buckle on the many swords that had arrived from Thorinsheld. Princess Gloralanin—Jodi—was seated on the King's left, and magician-apprentice Eric was seated on the King's right. Mark Mansbridge stood nearby, watching intently. And at the conclusion of the Ceremony, all the veterans of the late war, as well as the newly commissioned Kingsmen, gave the "servants of the quest" three rousing cheers for their parts in the recovery of the Lightning in the Bottle.

During the banquet that followed, the veterans—few older than Jodi and none taller than Eric—exchanged stories of the battles they had fought and won in the four corners of Eorthe. Martin and Jon entertained them with retelling after retelling of their journeys and of the final battle against Jabez. Richard, though, said little, and he did no bragging. He seemed content to once more have his armor and shield and to be near the King. Captain Andros and Rachael exchanged promises of friendship and made plans to meet again.

The next morning, sadly, was time for partings. As always, Jodi and the others found it very hard to leave the King. But he told them all, "You now are needed in Earth, to show by your actions what you have seen and learned here: how to be truly brave and how to boldly love your brothers and sisters of the world." One by one the Kingsmen passed him; many hugged him tearfully, and he held each of them until he or she was filled with warmth and security.

For Jodi, the departure was triply difficult. She was leaving her childhood sweetheart, Eric, as well as Morgan and the King.

"Don't cry, Jodi," the King said as she took her turn before him. "The Land always will be here—'just a step away yet more than a step beyond,' as Waymond likes to say. And you now *know,* beyond all doubt, that my Light goes with you!"

She hugged him, then let Martin and the others have their turns. Next, she embraced Eric and asked him, "In the future, if the call goes out, can you arrange to come for us?"

"I can't say," Eric hedged. "You will see me again, though. Some day, I'll appear—maybe like Waymond did, or maybe you'll just see me leading other children to the Land of the King for . . . for an adventure." He laughed, holding her hands, then became serious as Mark, Martin, and Jon joined her. "Please, tell my parents that I'll see them again . . . some day."

They waved to Rachael and Captain Andros and his Kingsmen as they went their separate ways. Then, three little children—newly commissioned Kingsmen—came to Martin. "Um, excuse me, Sir," the boy shyly began, "but you're to guide us home. We're from the same hometown."

Martin hitched up his sword belt and said, "You'll have to keep up."

"Yes, Sir!" the boy said eagerly.

"Good," Martin nodded. The boy grinned up at him as Martin put one hand on the boy's shoulder. Slowly, Martin led him and the two little girls down the river trail. "This river," Martin began with authority, "is the Dain, one of five that flow through the Land of the King from the Great River. Remember that so when the call comes again . . ." His voice faded and was lost under the purling of the silver-green river.

"Good-bye, Eric," Jodi said, kissing him before hurrying to catch her brother and his charges. Jon, Richard, and Mark Mansbridge silently shook the older boy's hand as they left him. They turned twice—each time farther down the grassy trail. Soon, only Waymond, Eric, and the King were left, standing beside the towering green walls of the Hall.

The journey into Earth passed quickly. The armor, shields, and swords of the Kingsmen disappeared into them, of course, when they crossed the Great River. When they arrived in their own town, Martin took his three young charges home to overjoyed parents. Then, Martin, Jodi, Richard, and Jon took Mark Mansbridge to a jeweler's shop. Because the jeweler had known Jodi and Martin all their lives, he believed their story that Mark was a royal foreign visitor. Therefore, he paid Mark a large sum of money for some of his jewels.

The young people next took the bewildered but eager Mark to a clothing store and to a barber shop. After that—looking like any other tall, ruggedly handsome person of Earth—he promised he would see them again. Finally, he waved and left to begin his adventures.

With great reluctance, Jodi led Martin, Richard, and Jon to Eric Vanover's home. When she told his parents that their son had entered the King's service permanently, she expected them to be angry, demanding, hysterical—or all three. But they took the news calmly . . . as though they already had guessed as much. His mother listened silently to Jodi tell about all that had happened to Eric, and she saw his father's eyes take on a proud, pleased light. When Jodi finished speaking, Mrs. Vanover sighed, looked at her husband, then looked toward Jon.

Clasping his hands in his lap and staring at them, Jon said, "Eric wanted you to know he'd see you again . . . some day."

Both Vanovers seemed amazed that the boy could speak. Mr. Vanover stammered, "I thought you couldn't . . ."

"The King healed me," Jon said, glancing at Richard.

The Vanovers stared at each of the grinning young people, then Mrs. Vanover said, "Please excuse us for a moment." She and her husband left the room, giving Jon a lingering look of sympathy . . . and affection.

When they returned, Mrs. Vanover went to Jon and took his hands. "Would you . . . that is, we'd like to invite you to stay here, to live with us. We'd have to get the state's approval and check with Mrs. Harkess, of course. But having you stay here would seem natural, somehow. You see, we have an empty room—a boy's room."

Jon was delighted beyond words. Jodi, feeling satisfied, decided it was time for Martin, Richard, and her to leave . . . so they did, and soon they were racing up Mulberry Street to burst into the ordinary white house of the Westphall family.

"Where *have* you been *this time!*" came their mother's voice almost immediately.

"Oh, you children have given us such a *fright!*" Richard's mother exclaimed as she and his father ran to him. They had, naturally, remained with the Westphalls until the children could be found. They anxiously examined Richard, making such a fuss that Jodi was surprised he stood it so calmly.

"Don't *ever* make us worry like this again!" Jodi and Martin's stepfather said sternly . . . then hugged them both.

When their mother had finished hugging and kissing them, she looked them over and saw Morgan's ring on Jodi's left hand; she asked, "Where did you get that gold ring? And what's it for?"

Before Jodi could answer, Richard's mother and father—who were the most bewildered of all—demanded of their son, "What *has* happened to you?" His mother added with a smile, "You're . . . you're so *different!*" She turned to Jodi as her smile became apologetic. "I'm sorry to have thought badly of you, Jodi; it seems you *did* take care of Richard after all . . . and quite well, too."

Jodi and Martin's stepfather laughed and said, "They all three have such fierce, grown-up looks that you'd think they were veterans come home from a war!" He and his wife and Richard's parents stared expectantly at the silent children.

"Well?" Jodi's mother finally asked. "Are you going to explain?"

Should we begin at the beginning? Jodi wondered, grinning at Martin and Richard.

That night—after Richard and his parents had gone home and Jodi and Martin's parents had gone to sleep—Jodi whispered loudly to Martin, who was across the hall, "Are you awake?"

"Of course," said Martin rather irritably—irritably because she had interrupted his memories of riding with Win-dor and casting out the Darkness and being with the King.

"Well, if *I* go to sleep, and *you* hear the call, will you wake me?"

"Yes," Martin whispered back, "if you'll do the same for me."

"I will," Jodi agreed, thankfully snuggling under *clean sheets* on *her own bed.* "Just listen for the call!"

As she closed her eyes, colorful memories came to her—of Morgan and Castle Imnatride and of the marvelous thrill she had felt when people had been healed through her and when she briefly had worn the Jewel of Tava. She tried to imagine what it would be like to reign as a queen, a Jeweled Sister. Then, as she slipped into sleep, she saw before her the comforting radiance of the King, Lord of Light. Knowing then that all would be well, she slept peacefully.

Glossary and (English) Pronunciations of Characters and Places

Acuerias: Ah-QUER-e-us, Master Solemnus Acuerias Trg: a King's magician.
Alamantia: Ala-MAN-sha: an island kingdom, "Guardian of the Light."
Allumeria: Al-loo-MARE-e-ah: a nation on the continent of Rud.
Andros: AN-dross, Constantine: a lieutenant of the Kingsmen, from Greece.
Armazil: Ar-ma-ZIL: a country in the southern part of the continent of Rud.
Asaph: A-saf: a warrior for House Evnstar.
Baldwin Evnstar: BALD-win EVEN-star: youngest brother of Mervintide; Lord of Ispenth.
Basmoth Bonasorte: BAZ-moth BONA-sort: Lord of House Bonasorte, ruler of the civilized tribes on the continent of Oraibi.
Bogloam: Bo-GLOW-um: huge, salamander-like creatures.
Branchus: BRANCH-us: ferryman of the Alamantian Crossing.
Byzarnium: Bi-ZAR-ne-um: capital of Gueroness; City of the Dead.
Corbansul: Cor-BAN-sul: the sword of Light of House Mansbridge.
Corlis: CORE-liss: a duchy of the kingdom of Eoramia.
Dorcas Evnstar: DOR-kus EVEN-star: Queen of Eoramia, mother of Morgan.
Eliadenor: L-e-ADD-in-or: Queen of the Sea People.
Eoramia: E-o-RAM-e-ah: a kingdom in western Eorthe; a continent.
Eorthe: E-OR-tha: the first world.
Eric Vanover: ERR-ic VAN-over: a lieutenant of the Kingsmen; later a magician.
Espereim: Es-PEAR-e-im: capital of Eoramia; name literally means, "Place with hope."
Falrn: FAL-run: a desolate nation on the continent of Rud.
Fearsors: FEAR-sores: giant earth demons; guardians of Jabez.
Gafailnath: Ga-FAIL-nath: sword given by the King to L'Ced, first Alamantian king; name means, "That which fails not."
Ghazi: GAH-zee: Lord of Tsur, a desert kingdom in Rud.
Glimmothtyrn: Glim-MOTH-turn: the central tower in the Castle of Imnatride; built to hold aloft the Lightning in the Bottle.
Glimpalatyrn: Glim-PALA-turn: Queen Dorcas's castle in Espereim.

Gueroness: Gare-un-ESS: southern continent and kingdom.
Haglung: HAG-lung: witch and childbearer for Ingloamin.
Hidlothnath: Hid-LOTH-nath: castle built by Ingloamin, later used by Jabez; name means, "Great wound stored by."
Imnatride: EM-na-treed: capital of Alamantia.
Ingloamin: In-GLOW-min: Lord of Darkness.
Ispenth: Is-PENTH: a fiefdom of Eoramia.
Iverwain: IVER-wayne: the great river of Alamantia.
Jabez: Jah-BEZ: eldest son of Ingloamin; name means, "He will cause pain."
Jodi Westphall: a Kingsman, later named Princess Gloralanin.
Leilamar: Lee-ILL-a-mar: childbearer for Ingloamin; Shadow Guardian.
Leohtians: Lee-OH-shuns: Light People, guardians of Queen Dorcas.
Lucian: LOO-she-un: a warrior for House Evnstar.
Mark Mansbridge: Duke of Corlis, younger brother of Queen Dorcas.
Martin Westphall: a Kingsman from Smithville, Texas.
Mayic: MAY-ick: the pole star.
Mervintide Evnstar: MER-vin-tide EVEN-star: Morgan's father, once king of Eoramia and Alamantia.
Michael: MI-kul: ferryman of the Great River Crossing at the Dain River.
Morgan Evnstar: MOR-gan EVEN-star: son of Mervintide; king of Alamantia.
Obit: O-bit: a sorcerer, servant of Jabez.
Omcrac: OM-crack: the Great Desert of Rud.
Oraibi: O-RAB-ee: the eastern continent of Eorthe.
Orestheius: O-RES-the-us: giant Void shadow; servant of Jabez.
Palátkwapi: Pa-LOCKED-wa-pie: the largest city (and only university) on the continent of Oraibi; called Red House.
Púpsovi: PUP!-so-vee: called Seven Caves; located on Oraibi, it is a large opening into the eastern Caves of Rainath.
Rachael Saenz: Ray-CHEL Sah-E-nez: a Kingsman from Zihuatanejo, Guerrero, Mexico.
Rainath, Caves of: RAY-nath: the subterranean passages that underlie Eorthe; name means, "Evil thing" because during the Days of Darkness evil penetrated to the core of Eorthe through the caves.
Richard Brogan: Jodi and Martin's suburban-dwelling cousin; a Kingsman.
Sarx: SARKS: youngest son of Ingloamin by Leilamar; necromancer-ruler of Gueroness; name means, "Flesh."

Scorius: SCORE-e-us: a land in northern Oraibi conquered by Jabez's army led by a Void being called the Scourge.
Slyne: SLINE, Archibald: a King's magician of the northlands.
Sulnspen: SULN-spin: a sword; the Flame of Ispenth.
Sybra: SIGH-bra: Queen of Walunlan, a kingdom on Rud; wife of murdered King Tyzar; escaped from Conqueror Go'drun; mother of Tzarn.
Talaman: TALL-a-man, Omanist: a general in service of Queen Dorcas.
Tava: TA-va: a group of volcanoes in Tavares, a small country on Rud; the cave of Ingloamin beneath the volcanoes; one of the Three Jewels.
Terserius: Ter-SARE-e-us: Acuerias's burro.
Thorinsheld: THOR-in-sheld: the Swordsmith, earth Guardian.
Thrumingold: THRUM-in-gold, Capt. Oli: a Leohtian in service of Queen Dorcas; captain of the castle guard.
To'bol: TOE-bole, Quismar: a lord of Smy'ra, a kingdom on Rud.
Tophinole: TOF-in-ole: an entrance to the Caves of Rainath.
Torang: Toe-RANG: capital of Armazil.
Triamedes: Try-a-ME-dees: a Sea People pilot.
Tschuma: Tus-CHEW-ma: Tsur name for the sun.
Tsur: Ta-SURE: a desert kingdom on Rud.
Tuwachu'a: TO-wat-CHEW-ah: the Serpent Guardian of the South (Rud).
Unthoriumgai: UN-thorry-UM-guy: Father of Whales; ocean Guardian.
Waymond: WAY-mond: a King's magician from Edessa.
Win-dor: WIN-dor: the archer; Wind Lord of the West.
Wolvors: WOOL-vorz: giant, demon-possessed wolves.

NOTE:

As explained by Dr. Archibald Slyne, visiting Professor Emeritus of Linguistics, University of Texas at Austin, the following terms are (rather arbitrarily) associated with their accompanying meanings:

Magic: ". . . the art which claims or is believed to produce effects by the assistance of supernatural beings . . . hence, seemingly requiring more than human power; startling in performance; producing effects which seem supernatural . . ." *(Webster's New Collegiate Dictionary).* In communicating with prospective Kingsmen, the King's magicians found that they could use almost no other term to describe the power available to them. In Eorthe, however, the term for their "magic" simply is *"glimmoth"*, meaning "lightning"—a word derived from the word for the Light (Abba's power).

Magician: a person (celibate) recruited and trained in an apprentice system for service to the King, Lord of Light.

Sorcerer: an evil supernatural being allied with Ingloamin.

Glossary of Ancient Eorthean Words

A

a- : the
abban(s) : rule(s), reign(s)
Abba : Father (God)
al : stop
ala : war
alanin(s) : friend(s)
alaman : fortress, defense
alo : spiritual guide, angel
aloe : a healing oil
áloivet : "songs of the spheres"
alton : stop! (imperative)

B

bre : many
brede : wheat
bredet : bread
bremins : grass
brenor : sand

C

c- : my, mine (+ noun)
ce : our
cemari : daughter
ci : me
co : all, every
cogi : know, mean
cogiim : head
cogon : hair
cogun : beard
comen : eat
comens : meat (to be eaten)
con : grow, growing, grown
confil : bread (other than wheat)
conserd : kindness
conseroth : strength
corseroth : meekness, humility
cor : give
corabba : eye
corban : gift
cosule : common, ordinary
coton : cotton

D

dac : eight
de : grain
dec : ten
deco : hundred
dic : nine
do : number (n.)
docogi : to count

E

e- : to
-em : animal ending for nouns
Eorthe : the (first) world
es- : with; yes
et : no, none, without

F

fail : fail, defeat
fil : fill, indwell
firl : a king

G

ga- : that (which)
gentis : people, tribe, clan
gi : real, fact
glim : white
glimm : light
glimmoth : lightning, magic (power)
glimmothin : magician
Glimmrainath : the Void
gloam : dark, darkness
gloaminoths : vultures
glom : black, night
glor : heal
glorimm : love
gloralanin : healing friend, doctor
gloror : a salve

H

hid- : great
hidlav : gate (as of a castle or city)
hidminoths : large blue and gray geese
hidtyrn : mountain
hir- : small; retiring (shy)
hirte : finger
hirti : toe

I

-i : (past tense ending)
-ib : (future tense ending); will (h.v.)
id : good
idd : better
idglimm : forever, eternity, "heaven"
im : place
imt : here (this place)
-in : person ending for nouns
in : person
iv : flow, flowing
iver : blood, water (flowing), life
iverim : heart
iverseimt : home
ivet : music
ivetweyid : harvest celebration (gen., any songfest)

K

aom : come
kaomimt : appear
koma : have, make (and possess)
komanathse : to think
komi : invented (lit., "made first")

L

lav : door, entryway
lavet : lock
los : plant (n.)
loth : wound (n.)

M

ma : and
mar : sea, woman, birth(place)
maralaman : warship (lit., "sea fortress")
mari : girl
marn : water (standing)
maron : blanket, robe
mi : but
min : leaf
minoth : wing
mongwi : chief, chieftain

N

n- : of
na- : kill (cause not to be)
nar : man
nart : boy
nath : not; stored by
nathid : bad
nathhid : small
nathnor : precious metal; "not of earth"
nathon : under; beneath
nathse : seems; appearance
nathsult : cold
ne : for
nega : what
nor : of earth
noth : air; the sky

O

-o- : in
oaonz : wilderness
ob : dead
obi : to die
obit : death
obtenot : stick, firewood
oe : by, beside
oen : near, nearby
oeuconserd : please; "by your kindness"
ole : cave
omen(s) : jaw(s)
om : one
omi : first
Omiglimm : the moon
omrai : line; path
on : on; cover
oncogiim : hat
ons : salt

onser : need
onsernoth : to breathe; breath
ont : against
onza : wild cross of "lion" and "jaguar"
onz : wild
or : earth
orcon : wood
orconim : forest
orodon : thank (you)
ot : above
oth : go
othe: gone
othi : send
otho : open, go in
othon : go! (imperative)
othre : return, go back
oy : below

P

pala : peace
pere : hope

Q

qua : four
quai : fourth
quarai : square
quaraiscukyx : the ancient alphabet; writing
quas : six
quat : seven
quin : five

R

rai- : thing, it
rainath : evil thing; "thing of nothingness"
rainathomens : poisonous locusts
ronin : bandits, outlaws

S

-s : (plural ending)
scu : iron
scukin : scribe
scuoncogiim : helmet
scusulkaom : steel
scusulkaomhirte : chisel, writing tool (called a "*scuk*")
scutu : shield
scututreo : "pine" tree
se : is
sei : was
ser (-er-) : spirit, soul
ses : are
si : am
som : two
soma : again
somakomi : teach, taught
somi : second
somrai : angle
speth : fast, speed
sri : lord, sir
su : be
suib : will be
sul : flame, the sun (when capitalized)
sulde : corn
sule : day, daytime
sulkaom : fire
sult : hot

T

t : this
tho : stay
te : those; hand
teglimmoth : sword
tenot : arm
ti : these; foot
tom : three
tomi : third
tomrai : triangle; triad
-ton : (imperative ending)
toph : ancient
treo : tree
treod : stump
tride : fear
tu : round; circle
tyrn : stone
tyrnomrai : highway
tyx : change; "changeling"

U

u- : your (+ noun)
un- : very

unot : more; more than
urai : coyote; dog
uraiun : wolf

V

vista : saw
vistai : seen
visti : see
vocci : say, says
vocciglorimm : hymn; song of praise (to Abba)
voccid : said
voci : voice
volor : fly (v.)

W

wain : carrying thing
wainem(s) : horse(s); burro(s)
wainet(s) : cart(s)
wey : journey
weybredet : twice baked wheat cake
weyid : harvest
weyon : trail, path
weyse : to walk

Y

y- : us, we, our
ya : he, him, his
yan : who, whom (masc.)
ye : they, them, theirs
yi : she, her, hers
yin : who, whom (fem.)
yo : I
yx : process or continuing action; - ing

Correct Pronunciation of Eorthean Vowels:
"*a*" is always pronounced as "ah"
"*e*" is always pronounced as "a"
"*i*" is always pronounced as "e"
"*o*" is always pronounced as "o"
"*u*" is always pronounced as "oo"
"*y*" is always pronounced as "i"

"*c*" is always pronounced as "k"
"*q*" is always pronounced as "k"

Notes on Eorthean Language:

The glossary is very incomplete; however, Dr. Archibald Slyne is attempting to compile a *Dictionary of Ancient Eorthean.* He, though, is familiar only with the northern dialect of the ancient tongue. Therefore, any Kingsman who has visited Eorthe and understands the principles of the ancient language is welcome to contribute Eorthean words or phrases to the dictionary by sending them to Dr. Slyne in care of Thomas Nelson Publishers.

Regarding the languages of Eorthe and Earth, Dr. Slyne has an explanation that is regarded in the academic community as fanciful at best; however, he repeats the following with the comment that "one can take it or leave it, depending on how one judges history!":

"In the early part of Eorthe's Third Age, two kingdoms became great trading nations: Edessa and Calazar. From the port of Battersea, traders began to range far and wide. They, however, found difficulty with the many dialects of the ancient Eorthean language—which is an 'additive' language and results in words such as *teglimmothminscututreo* (sword "pine") that are understood only in a limited area. Because of that difficulty the traders began promoting what came to be called the Common Tongue. Actually, that language was Edessan.

"When Eortheans learned 'legends of Earth' from the magicians, the great trading houses of Edessa became fascinated. Some men of the time were devoted to finding *nathnor*, but adventurers from Edessa became devoted to finding 'Earth.' It is said that at least one such traveler—whose House name may have been 'Bede'—crossed the Great River, made his way into Earth, and settled in the northern lands. Legend has it that he became a scholar/poet of renown. Legend further tells that this Edessan helped shape the language later called 'English.' Thus, we find many words in both the 'Common Tongue' of Eorthe and the 'English' of Earth, enabling Kingsmen and other travelers across the boundary to communicate."

In my own opinion as *glimmothinscukin* (magicians' scribe), ancient Eorthean and English may be compared in this way: both are pyramids. In English, the pyramid stands on its point (that being the meaning intended), and the bulk of the pyramid above the point is made up of many words. But in ancient Eorthean, the pyramid is upright; the capstone is a single word, and the bulk of the pyramid below is *meaning:* implications, nuances, and connotations. In ancient Eorthe, thinkers, therefore, could literally write a whole book in one sentence.

Common Ancient Eorthean Phrases

A-Abba conseroth seu: The King's strength is yours.

"Efil Espere": "To Fill with Hope" (a song title).

Garainath na-pere ma conseroth: That evil thing that kills hope and strength. (A curse phrase.)

Othre-nath, vocci A-Abba: Return not, says the Father. (An incantation to dispel evil.)

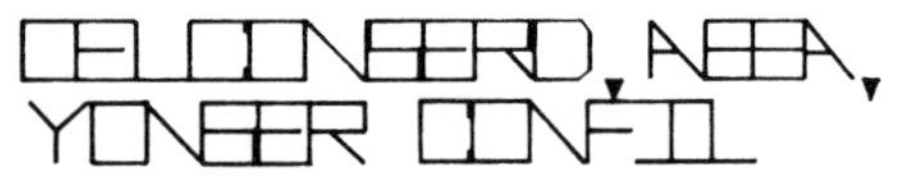

Oeuconserd, Abba, yonser confil: Please, Father, we need bread (food). (A prayer for sustenance.)

Corban A-Abba, visti neci: Gift of the Father, see for me. (An incantation to awaken the Corban Stone.)

A-Abba seimt: Literally means, "The Father is here!", but is understood to mean, "The Father is here (with us) in the person of the King!"

Ce-corban A-Abba!: Praise the Father! (literally, "Our gift [is to] the Father!").

Explanation of Eorthean Music

(Notes and Transcriptions by Mark Jaeger)

Music from Eorthe is mostly vocal and monophonic, somewhat chantlike, with occasional two part voicings and additional instrumental accompaniment. Built from the same overtone series as exists in our world, the basis for both systems remains the same. However, our system of tempered tuning has changed the original interval structure. The Eorthean intervals have remained constant with the overtone series. Therefore, certain pitches will sound out of tune to our ears. Eortheans also tend to improvise using intervals not present in our twelve-tone system, causing inaccuracy in transcription.

Four basic symbols on a two line staff are used in notation. The first is "Abba": ◆. It is the fundamental tone of their scale and can be found anywhere in the staff. "Alo" is the normal scale step found in their music: ◤ . "Sul" indicates that the pitch is raised a semi-tone from the normal scale step: ▲ . "Omiglimm" indicates the opposite: ▼

Only two rhythmic values exist in Eorthean music: short and long. Relative duration is left open to the performer. Long notes are indicated with a line extending from the top of the particular symbol used. For example: ◆‾‾‾ , ▲‾‾‾‾ . The length of the line loosely indicates the relative length of the pitch.

All Eorthean music uses the pentatonic scale as a basis. Notes are then raised or lowered using the "Sul" or "Omiglimm" symbols to reflect the *sercogi* or "deep meaning" of the song. The pentatonic scale used is shown below in Eorthean and Earthean notation:

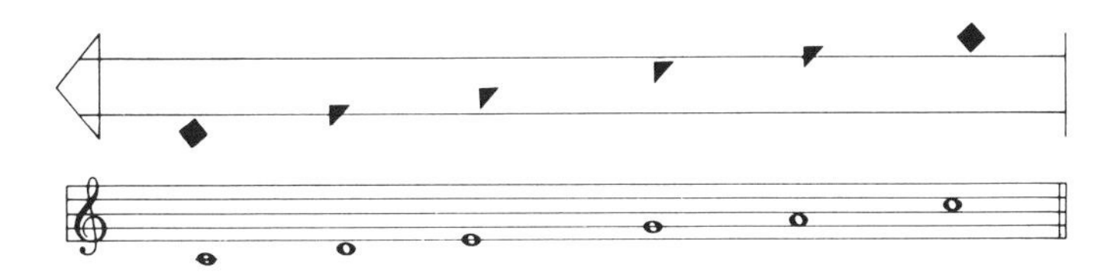

There is no chromatic scale in Eorthean music as of this writing, but if we were to write our own chromatic scale in their system it would look like this (in Eorthean and Earthean):

Because of the inaccuracy of the pitches and the free improvisation, it is difficult to be precise in transcription. After hearing several renditions of the songs in this book, I have attempted to write them in our notation and using our instruments, yet still maintaining the mystic, luminous quality that appears in so much of "the King's" music. The following is that attempt.

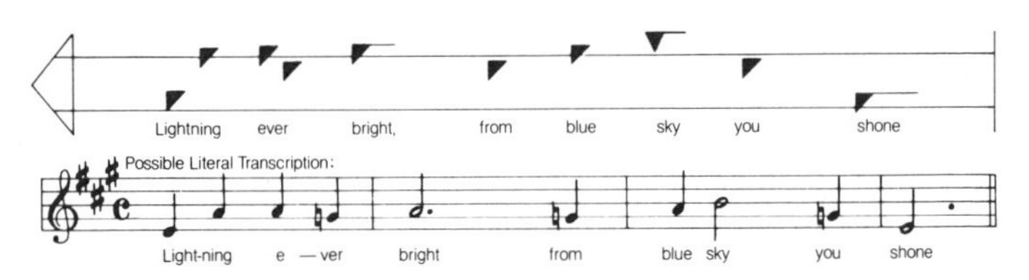
Lightning ever bright, from blue sky you shone
Possible Literal Transcription:
Light-ning e — ver bright from blue sky you shone

Earthean Music for Eorthean Songs

LAMENT OF THE CHILDREN WHO LOST THE LIGHT

♩ = 60
D/C D/B D/B♭ D/C (♭9) Asus
All chil-dren born to choose Think not what they can lose; Our
D/C D/B D/B♭ Dm7 Am7
fear to temp-ta-tion an o-pen door, we see on-ly our-selves and cry for
B♭/A D/C D/B D/B♭
more. Now wan-der-ing, we mourn what we have lost, And
B♭/A (Tacet)
ev-er through the night, we count the cost.

Actual transcription

EFIL ESPERE*

♩=80
A(9) 3
Em7 / G
Light-ning ev-er bright from blue sky you shone,
E7sus / F♯
E7sus / F
ban-ish-ing Man's night; we cling to you a-lone.
A(9) 3
Em7 / G
Come in-to our lives, help us make our mark, though our
E7sus / F♯
E7sus / F
ears hear lies and all the world be dark. Clear
A(9) 3
G
light shin-ing bright, help us to be brave;
F♯m7 / A
Fmaj7
A(9) 3
Em / A
help us to do what's right, for it's your love we crave.
(guitar inter-lude optional)
D(11)(9) / A
A(9)
G6 / A
As we dai-ly pray love from the Fa-ther,

(* EARTH VERSION)

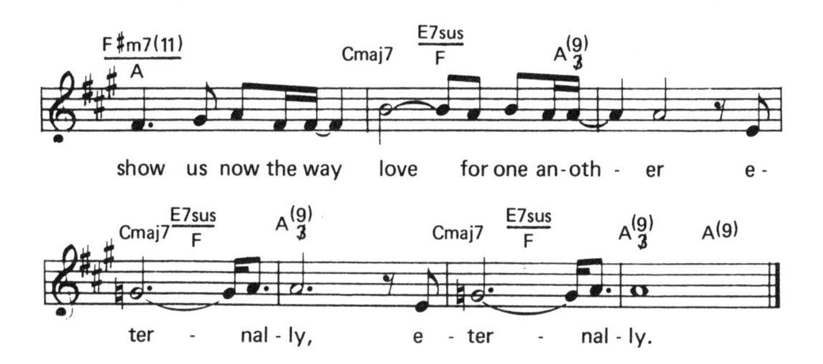
F♯m7(11)
A
Cmaj7
E7sus
F
show us now the way love for one an-oth - er e -
ter - nal - ly, e - ter - nal - ly.

MORGAN'S HUNTING SONG

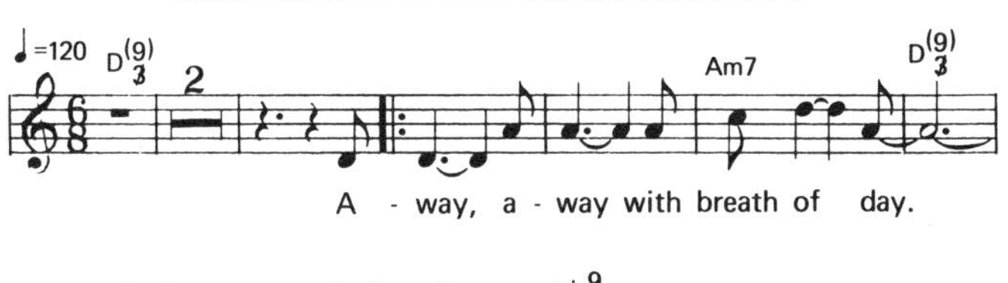
♩=120
Am7
A - way, a - way with breath of day.

Dm7
Am7
G
Soon comes sun, down dark runs. Feet feed hun-ger,

1. 2. 3.
4.
ev-er, ev-er. A -
ppp

2) Away, away
with moon's full sway.
Soon comes sun,
down dark runs.
Hands feed hunger,
ever, ever.

3) Away, away
with rain's light play.
Soon comes sun,
down dark runs.
Eyes feed hunger,
ever, ever.

4) Away, away
when fogs delay.
Soon comes sun,
down dark runs.
wits feed hunger,
ever, ever . . .
ever . . . ever!

CHANT OF THE TAVA TEMPLE INSCRIPTION*

Drink deep the draught of death Ev - er to dark be wed.
Night re - mem - bers all your fail - ures,
But in death long peace shall be yours.
Thus, dark to dark be led,
There to sleep with - out breath.

*Chant has no definite meter. All notes are of equal value, except the last note of each phrase, which is held to the performer's discretion (indicated with a whole note). A slight pause should occur at each bar line. The notes marked (x) are played by *hirscutus,* which are shaped somewhat like finger cymbals. They produce a bell-like sound and signify a release from the trials of life. The whole ceremony is accompanied by a large drum that beats a human heartbeat rythm. Just before the word "breath," it slows and stops.

SONG OF THE JEWELS OF POWERS BEGATTING
Lights down-ward stream - ing, blue, green,
yel - low, gleam - ing. from the Fa - ther's brow.
Him who said, "Be thou." Light at first
flood - ing through void un - lov - ing.
It found-ed E - or - the in liv - ing green,
flow-ing blue and yel - low keen.
Yel-low be-came south, sun, youth; green came in - to east, land,

truth; blue spread west to sky and death; black north quick for -
got light's breath. Then by the hand of Him who
came, three jew - els were wrought and by Him named:
Cor - lis, yel - low as sun's fire; Ta - va, blue as sky's de - sire; and

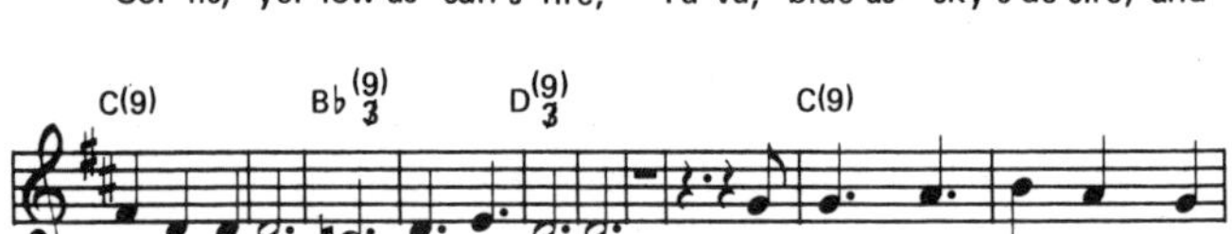
Im - na - tride, green as sea's fame. The con - quering Fa - ther passed

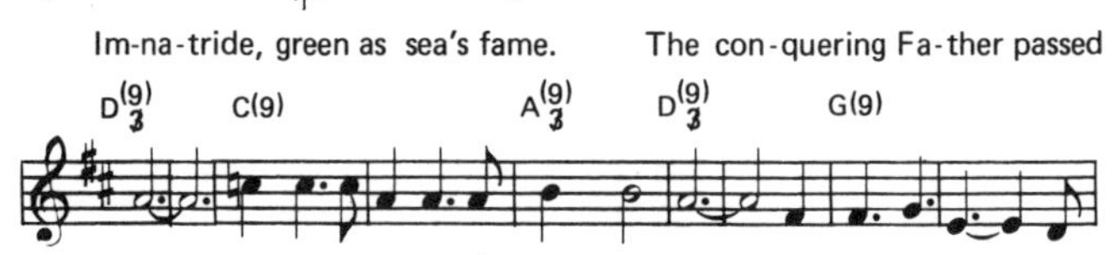
on, leav - ing E - or - the its bright new dawn; His light He left 'gainst

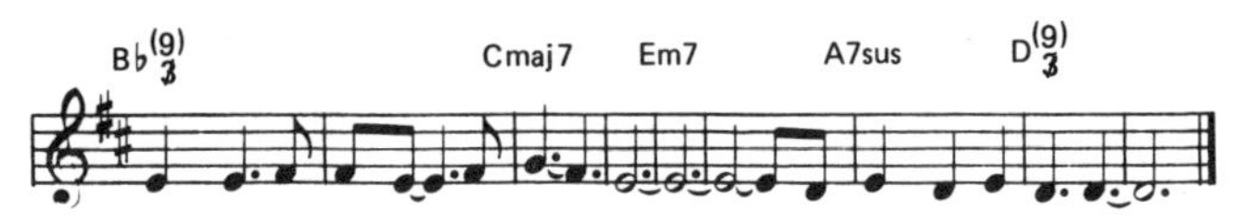
dark - ness at - tack - ing in three jew - els of pow - ers be - gat - ting.

Guitar Chords for Eorthean Music

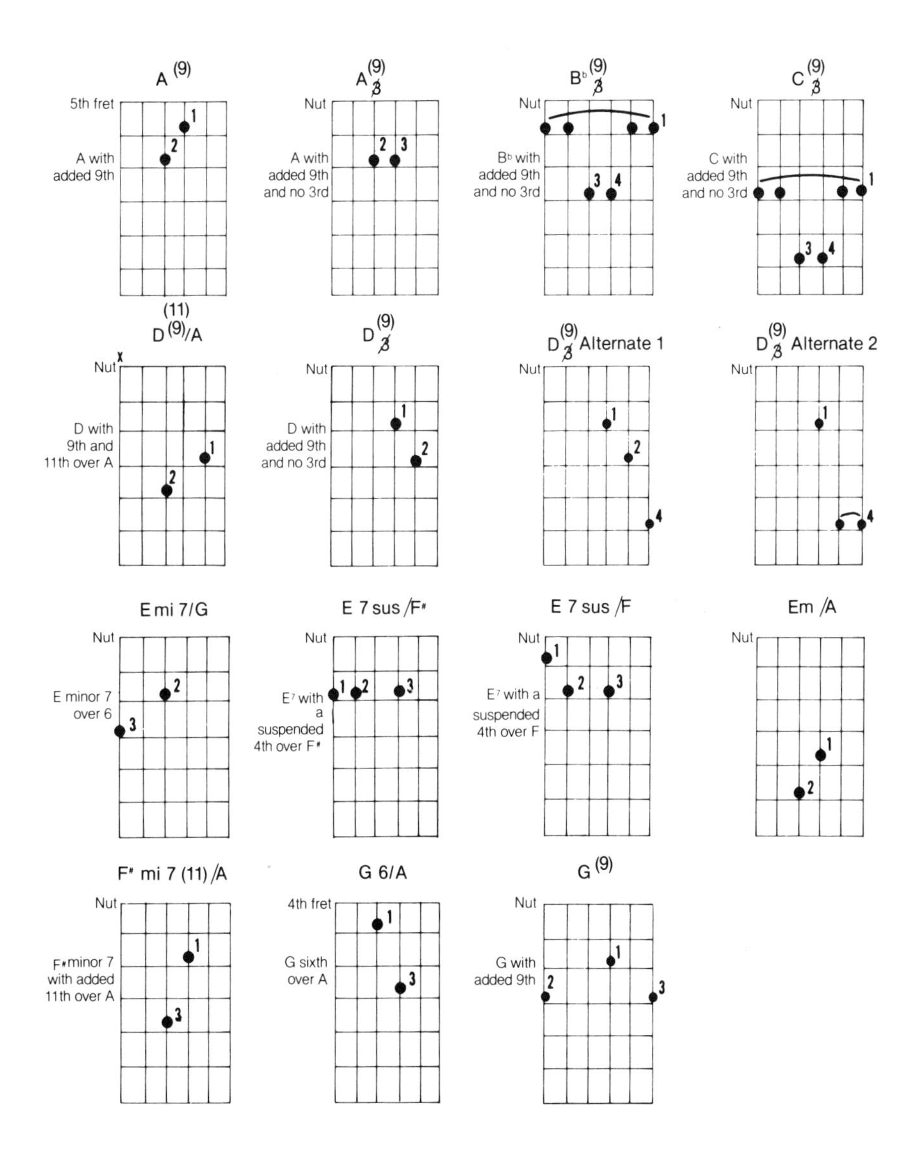

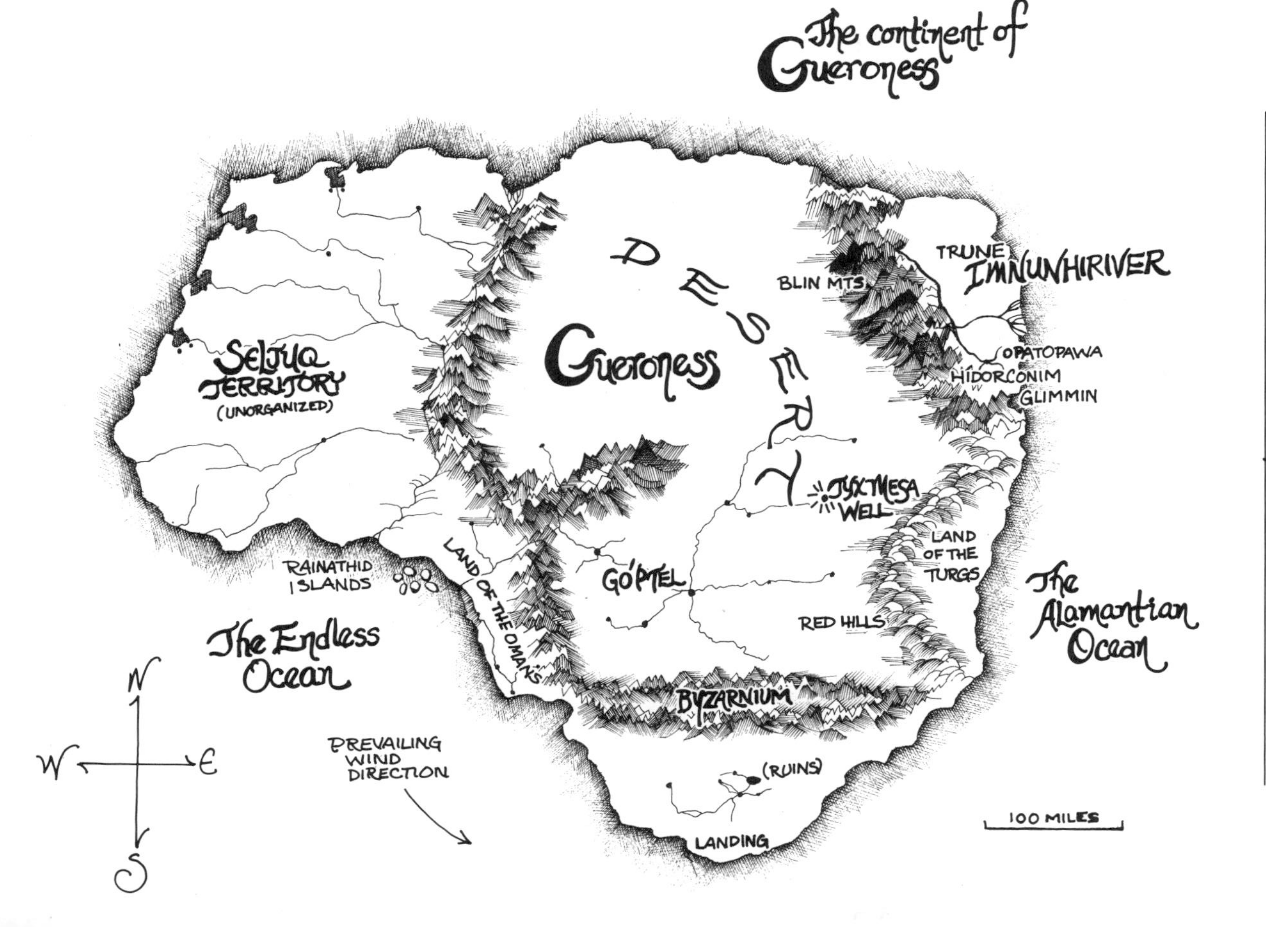

The continent of Gueroness
TRUNE
IMNUNHIRIVER
BLIN MTS
OPATOPAWA
HIDORCONIM
GLIMMIN
DESERT
Gueroness
SELJUQ TERRITORY
(UNORGANIZED)
TYXTMESA WELL
LAND OF THE TURGS
GO'PTEL
RED HILLS
RAINATHID ISLANDS
LAND OF THE OMAN'S
The Endless Ocean
The Alamantian Ocean
BYZARNIUM
PREVAILING WIND DIRECTION
(RUINS)
LANDING
100 MILES
N
W
E
S

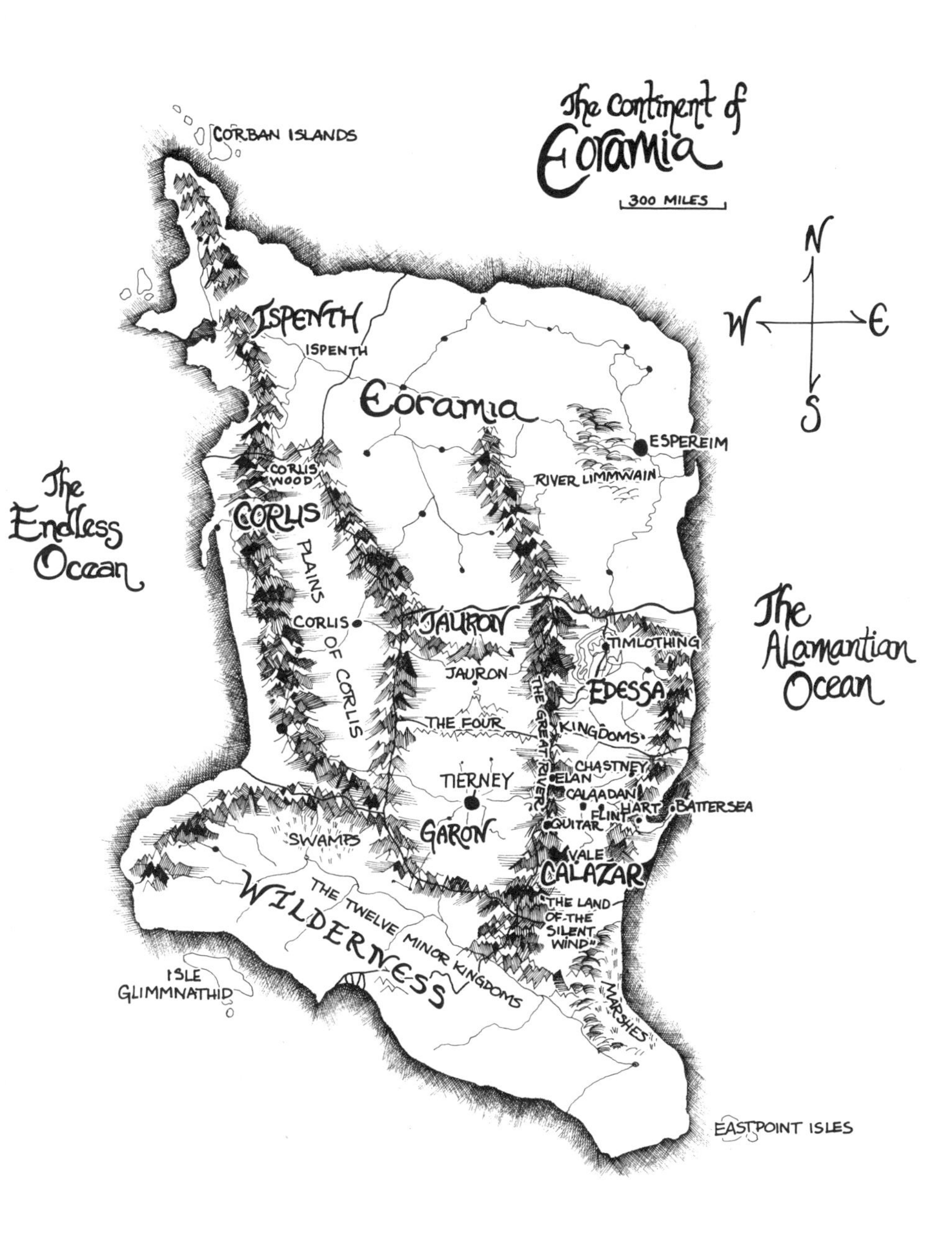

The continent of Eoramia
300 MILES
N
W
E
S
CORBAN ISLANDS
ISPENTH
ISPENTH
Eoramia
ESPEREIM
RIVER LIMMWAIN
The Endless Ocean
CORLIS WOOD
CORLIS
PLAINS OF CORLIS
CORLIS
JAURON
JAURON
The Alamantian Ocean
TIMLOTHING
EDESSA
THE GREAT RIVER
THE FOUR KINGDOMS
CHASTNEY
ELAN
TIERNEY
CALAADAN
HART
BATTERSEA
FLINT
QUITAR
GARON
SWAMPS
VALE
CALAZAR
WILDERNESS
THE TWELVE MINOR KINGDOMS
"THE LAND OF THE SILENT WIND"
ISLE GLIMMNATHID
MARSHES
EASTPOINT ISLES

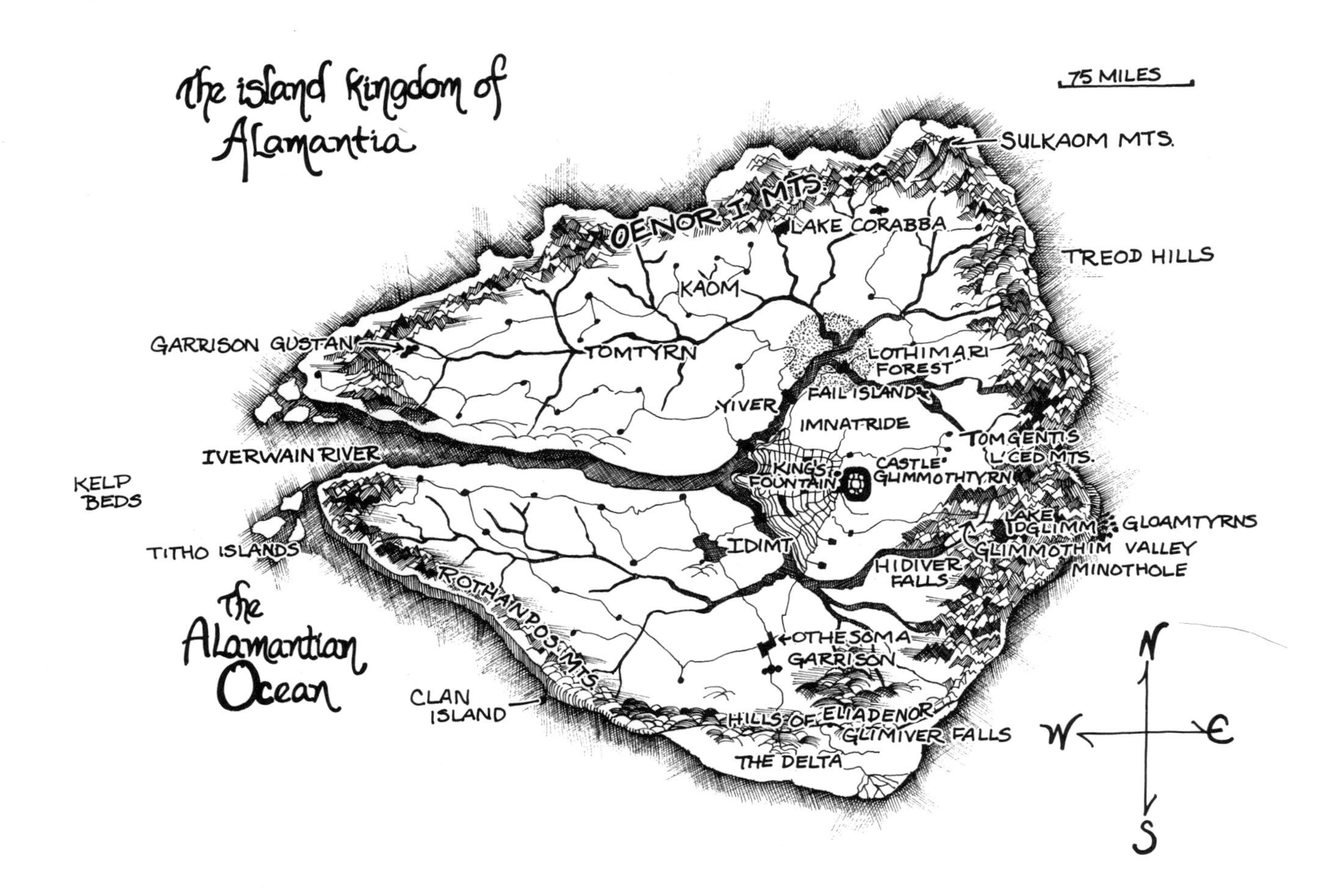
The island Kingdom of Alamantia
75 MILES
SULKAOM MTS.
OENOR I MTS.
LAKE CORABBA
TREOD HILLS
KAOM
GARRISON GUSTAN
TOMTYRN
LOTHIMARI FOREST
FAIL ISLAND
YIVER
IMNATRIDE
TOMGENTIS
L'CED MTS.
IVERWAIN RIVER
CASTLE GLIMMOTHTYRN
KING'S FOUNTAIN
KELP BEDS
LAKE IDGLIMM
GLOAMTYRNS
TITHO ISLANDS
IDIMT
GLIMMOTHIM VALLEY
HIDIVER FALLS
MINOTHOLE
ROTHANPOS MTS
The Alamantian Ocean
OTHESOMA GARRISON
N
CLAN ISLAND
HILLS OF ELIADENOR
GLIMIVER FALLS
W
E
THE DELTA
S

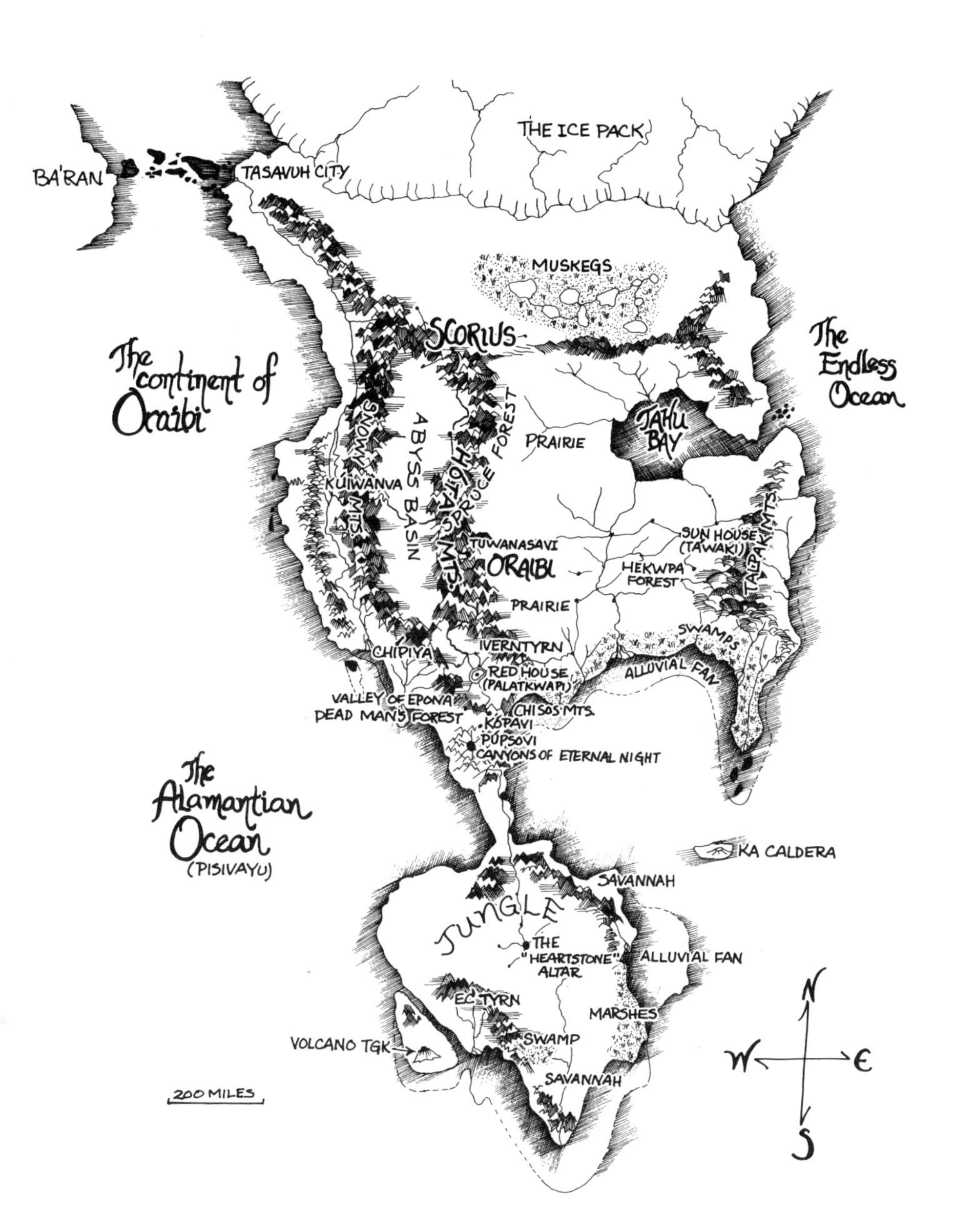
THE ICE PACK
BA'RAN
TASAVUH CITY
MUSKEGS
SCORIUS
The continent of Oraibi
The Endless Ocean
TAHU BAY
SNOWY MTS.
ABYSS BASIN
HOTAPSI MTS.
SPRUCE FOREST
PRAIRIE
KUIWANVA
TALPAK MTS.
SUN HOUSE
(TAWAKI)
TUWANASAVI
ORAIBI
HEKWPA
FOREST
PRAIRIE
SWAMPS
CHIPIYA
IVERNTYRN
ALLUVIAL FAN
RED HOUSE
(PALATKWAPI)
VALLEY OF EPONA
DEAD MAN'S FOREST
CHISOS MTS.
KOPAVI
PUPSOVI
CANYONS OF ETERNAL NIGHT
The Alamantian Ocean
(PISIVAYU)
KA CALDERA
SAVANNAH
JUNGLE
THE
"HEARTSTONE"
ALTAR
ALLUVIAL FAN
EC TYRN
MARSHES
VOLCANO TGK
SWAMP
SAVANNAH
200 MILES
N
W
E
S

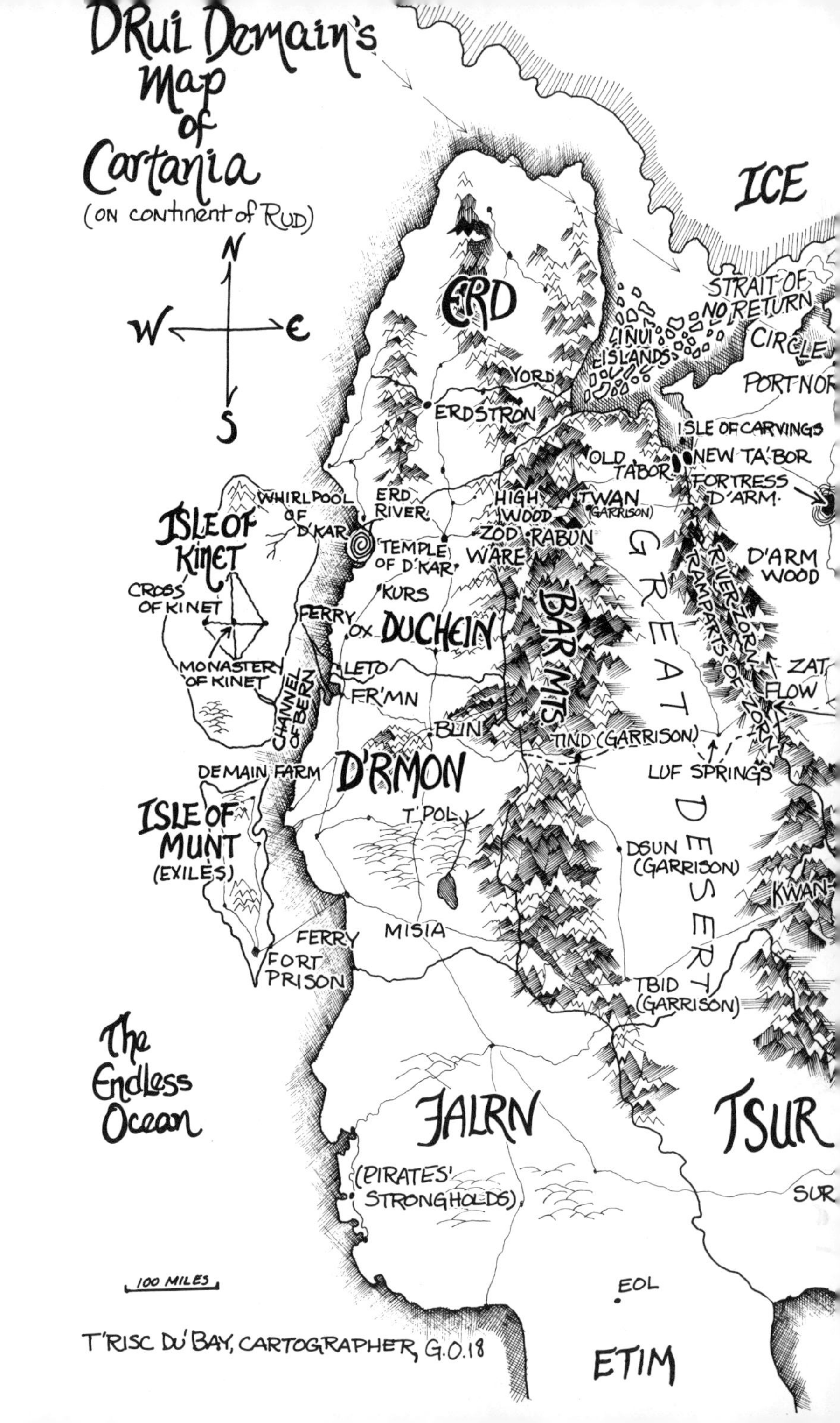
Drui Demain's Map of Cartania
(ON continent of RUD)
N
W
E
S
ICE
STRAIT OF NO RETURN
CIRCLE
PORT NOR
ERD
YORD
ERDSTRON
LINUI ISLANDS
ISLE OF CARVINGS
OLD TABOR
NEW TA'BOR
FORTRESS D'ARM
WHIRLPOOL OF D'KAR
ERD RIVER
HIGH WOOD
TWAN (GARRISON)
ISLE OF KINET
TEMPLE OF D'KAR
ZOD WARE
RABUN
D'ARM WOOD
CROSS OF KINET
KURS
RIVER ZORN
RAMPARTS OF ZORN
GREAT DESERT
FERRY
OX
DUCHEIN
BAR MTS.
MONASTERY OF KINET
LETO
ZAT FLOW
CHANNEL OF BERN
FR'MN
BUN
TIND (GARRISON)
LUF SPRINGS
DEMAIN FARM
D'RMON
ISLE OF MUNT (EXILES)
T'POL
DSUN (GARRISON)
KWAN
FERRY
MISIA
FORT PRISON
TBID (GARRISON)
The Endless Ocean
FALRN
TSUR
(PIRATES' STRONGHOLDS)
SUR
100 MILES
EOL
T'RISC DU'BAY, CARTOGRAPHER, G.O.18
ETIM

FIELD
ICE BERGS
OF BLIZZARDS
CAPE LONE
CAPE GRACE
BAY OF BLED
LANDBRIDGE TO CONTINENT OF ORAIBI 1008M ±
N'BTH
TIMIN
TGU
FLOW
RIVER MAIM
BA'RAN
(UNINHABITED)
DESERT OF THE SUN
K'BOR
RYB
WU
TZN
QAR
ARTAGE
TYRNE
ZIZT
DOE
SYM
RTI
PLAINS OF ARTAGE
TGU MTS.
WRM
RYE
RHODAN
ALLUMERIA
VALLEY OF MEGANON
LAKE L'OD
MEI
ZOD (GARRISON)
TRUNK ROAD
XAN
TZARMSH RUINS, PLATEAU, AND MT
EAD
SMOKING MOUNTAINS
GO'DRUN'S BRIDGE
CANYON DETH
TUNNEL OF GRAG
SADO
QIR
FOREST OF R'BOLT
DAWNS FORD
ZARMSH WOOD
R'BOLT MINES
ZARMSH
WALUNLAN
SMYRA
LAKE BOD
MOTHER OF THE SKY MOUNTAINS
PLAINS OF KIDRON
TOLAN
MT TAVA
TAVARES
K'BALL
SLOPES OF TAVA
YE RIVER
SULINET
TOPHINOLE
SULIN
(POST)
SID
(POST)
SWAMPS
TORANG
PIT OF COA
AA'DURK
RIVER K'WIN
LAKES OF YORE
(ARMAZIL)
(POST)
TEMPLE OF TAVA I
PORT FAR
(SW POST)
The Alamantian Ocean

ICE
ERD
INUI ISLANDS
DU CHEIN
ISLE OF KINET
FR'MN
D'RMON
ISLE OF MUNT
ALLUMERIA
ARTAGE
WALUNLAN
TOLAN
TSUR
SUR
FALRN
EOL
SULINET
ARMAZIL
ETIM (UNIHABITED)
RUD
The Endless Ocean
CORBAN ISLANDS
ISPENTH
EORAMIA
ESPEREIM
CORLIS
JAURON
EDESSA
GARON
CALAZAR
EORAMIA
THE TWELVE MINOR KINGDOMS
IMNATRIDE
Alamantia
SELJUG TERRITORY
IMNUNHIRIVER
GUERONESS
GUERONESS
BRANCHUS' LANDING
DAIN RIVER

FIELD
BA'RAN
TZARMSH
SMYRA
K'BALL
SCORIUS
TAHU BAY
ORAIBI
RED HOUSE
ORAIBI
KA CALDERA
HEARTSTONE
VOLCANO TGK
EC'TYRN
N
W
E
S
the Alamantian Ocean
EORTHE
LAND OF THE KING
CYLINDRICAL PROJECTION
HOPESMONT

The third book of *The Legends of Eorthe* is entitled *Sisters of the Light*. Ingloamin's eldest surviving son, Amanitid, has trained hundreds of followers and has led them to Earth! Their mission: to either destroy Earth or to so weaken the Kingsmen that no longer will the children's army be able to respond to the call of the King. Eric, now a magician in his own right, comes to Earth to call Jodi, Rachael, and Ula Marston (the Faithful), as well as Mark Mansbridge, to accompany him on an apparently hopeless mission. The five must attempt to recover and unite the three, almost mythical Jewels of Earth. But, as their mission unfolds, they learn that the quest for Earth's Jewels is by no means their only task. Theirs is the challenge of maturity and faithfulness . . . on Earth!